DESERT DREAMS

"This isn't good enough for you," Travis murmured into Sadira's hair. "You should have a bed of silk and satin, strewn with rose petals."

She laughed softly, her breath tickling his ear. "Have you forgotten, *Frangi?* I am desert-bred. The sand is my natural element. Where else but on the sand should I give myself to you?"

"We should at least have a tent over our heads."

"I prefer a canopy of stars—and the wind blowing across our bodies. Look up, my love. Look up and see the sky. For us, the stars shine bright this night. For us, the wind sings a song of love and happiness."

Travis tilted back his head and studied the stars. Brighter now than before, they resembled a million sparkling jewels flung across a sweep of black velvet. The desert wind caressed his face and ruffled his hair, and it did seem as if the wind were singing, sighing a sweet love song, whispering of joy and pleasure. He filled his hands with the silky wealth of Sadira's hair and marveled at its texture. He stroked the soft skin of her cheek, the softest thing he had ever touched.

She rested her head on his shoulder and leaned into him. "There is no one else in the world this night but us. We are the only ones who exist, Travis. . . ."

KATHARINE KINCAID
WINDSONG

NEW! Windsong

The cover blurb on this book is a tad melo-
dramatic, but this is an excellent story about
the clash of cultures between a bedouin
woman from Arabia and a Kentucky horse
breeder fallen on tough times circa 1877. The
reason they meet? Horses. Lots of intrigue
and excitement follow as Sadira, Keeper of
the Mares, struggles to honor her commit-
ments to her tribe, and follows her heart to
Travis Keene, the brave American whose code
of honor is altogether different. *Highly recommended.*

ZEBRA BOOKS
KENSINGTON PUBLISHING CORP.

ZEBRA BOOKS are published by

Kensington Publishing Corp.
850 Third Avenue
New York, NY 10022

Zebra and the Z logo Reg. U.S. Pat. & TM Off.

First Printing: December, 1994

Printed in the United States of America

For Jessica, Sarah, and Erin,
Who have ridden and loved Arabian horses
Like those written about in this book . . .
May your trails all lead to happiness.

Prologue

El Hamad, Arabia, 1877

So it had come to this: a desolate windswept plain redolent with the mingled odors of coffee, dust, horse, man, and the elusive but persistent scent of lavender . . . her people gathered behind her, not to protect, not to defend—but to hand her over to her enemies . . . another line in front of her, bristling with long Bedouin spears and the occasional carbine . . . a silence that hung thick and heavy as smoke but could not drown out the savage beating of her heart.

It had come to this—the moment she had somehow always known lay in wait for her. Mounted on a magnificent white war mare, his robes billowing in the wind, the sheik of the *Shammar* held tightly to the reins of her mare as he led her across the invisible line dividing friend from enemy, the familiar from the unknown, security from danger. He kicked his horse into a trot, and her horse obediently followed. The wind lifted the end of his *keffiya* and flung it back across his shoulder, so that it snapped almost in her face. Turning her head to avoid the whipping cloth, she managed to keep her body erect and her face impassive. No matter what happened, she would not show fear. No one watching would ever guess that she was terrified and

furious, resigned as well as indignant, and most of all—
grief stricken.

Never again would she know the embrace of the man
she had come to love above all others. Never again would
she feel his hands on her body and savor the sweetness of
his kiss beneath the desert stars. . . . Too late had these
treasures been revealed to her, and too soon had they been
snatched away! Tears pressed hot and heavy behind her
eyelids, but she refused to shed them. Pride had always
carried her through difficult moments, and pride did not
fail her now. It gave her the strength to conceal her feelings
and submit to her fate, though every bone, muscle, and
sinew screamed silently for escape.

But there was no escape—could never be any escape for
her. For this had she been born, to serve her people until
the end of her days. To hold herself apart from men and
look for happiness in doing her duty. Only by submission
and sacrifice could she earn the twin prizes of forgiveness
and redemption; this very day, she would finally redeem
herself.

Halfway back to the line of waiting horsemen, her ab-
ductor met several of his followers who had ridden out to
meet them. One of them—a fiery-eyed man with sun-dark-
ened skin—maneuvered closer to her. A sneer twisted his
features as he placed his palm flat against her breastbone
and shoved. She saw no point in resisting and let herself
fall. The stony earth rushed up to greet her; she landed
hard on her side with the breath knocked out of her. Her
mare's hooves flashed overhead, and an equine scream of
outrage rent the air. There was a brief scuffle, the drum-
ming of hoofbeats, a shout or two, and then . . . silence.

She lay still, counting each beat of her heart, each breath
that remained to her. She had never been so conscious of

the inner workings of her body, had never felt the blood pulsing so strongly through her veins. All her quivering senses leapt to life. Pebbles embedded in the hot sand dug into the palm of one hand. A wetness trickled between her breasts. The feathery tendrils of some hardy desert plant brushed her cheek—it was lavender, which in springtime bloomed with purple spikes and scented the entire desert. Even now, the smell of the crushed, dried leaves emitted the delicious odor, and she greedily inhaled it. To die breathing lavender might be a blessing, a way of making death more bearable. She had always loved lavender and perfumed her hair and garments with its essence.

But the end was not to be so easy. Strong hands seized her beneath her arms and dragged her upward. She struggled to gain her feet only to be pushed back down to her knees on the stones. Someone grabbed her hands and wrenched them behind her back. Another man lifted the thick, long fall of her hair and held it off to one side. A metallic scraping sound signaled the parting of scimitar from scabbard. She tensed and waited . . . then heard the last sound she would ever hear: the ominous whisper of a sword sweeping upward . . . up, up . . . and finally . . . *down!*

In that blink of an eye before it struck, memories came rushing back of the first time she had knelt awaiting the blow of a sword, a blow that never came . . . and of all that had happened since to bring her to this moment when death could no longer be avoided.

One

Empty Quarter, Arabian Peninsula, 1867

"Sadira! Come quickly, child! Thy father wishes to see thee."

Even before Alima rushed into view around the side of the black goat-hair tent, Sadira could sense the excitement in the usually placid, unperturbed first wife of her father, Emir Akbar el-Karim, the Great and Generous One, who had never before paid Sadira the slightest attention.

Sadira's own heart began to pound, but she quickly suppressed any outward show of emotion as she slid from the back of the old war mare she had been riding, scratched the horse's nose in affection, and deftly slipped off its halter. "Go, my pretty one," she whispered. "And may Allah watch over thee in thy coming labors."

Heavy with foal, the gray mare nosed her hand and finding nothing, lumbered away in the direction of the other horses of the emir's great herd. There was no need to hobble the animal; she would not wander far, and if she did, Sadira had only to call her by name, and the mare would come as fast as her advanced stage of gestation would allow.

Dreading the upcoming interview, Sadira turned back to the tent with a heart as heavy as the mare's belly. For thirteen years—all of her entire life—she had been waiting for this summons; now that it had finally come, she feared answering it. Her father doted on his many children; of all of them, she alone had not found favor. The emir never called her into his private quarters, gave her sweetmeats from his table or treasures obtained from his many raids against rival tribes of Bedouin, never so much as acknowledged her presence.

Were it not for Alima, not her mother but the woman who had mothered her since infancy when her own mother had died, Sadira would have starved long ago. Because of her father's attitude—and her own unusual coloring—she was outcast from the harem where her father's other female children spent most of their time in company with their pampered mothers. Now, with a small cry of triumph, Alima came around the side of the tent, took Sadira's arm, and boldly marched her into the women's quarters of her father's huge black tent.

"Sadira, my precious one, has been summoned before Akbar, the Sheik of Sheiks of all of the *Anazah*," Alima proudly announced as the lesser wives and children scattered out of her way.

For the first time in Sadira's memory, her father's second wife, Jaleel, the mother of his eldest son, spoke her name. "Sadira? Our beloved Akbar has summoned Sadira?"

Jaleel narrowed her kohl-lined eyes in speculation. She was very beautiful in a turquois silk caftan embroidered with crimson and gold threads, and she knew it. Her beads, bangles, and other jewelry all proclaimed that she was the emir's favorite wife. She had borne him his first son, his successor, while Alima was barren, but for all her beauty and high standing, Jaleel was neither pleasant, calm, nor happy. She kept the harem in a constant state of agitation with her jealousy and intrigues.

Alima paused in the act of shepherding Sadira into her private quarters. "Yes, he has summoned her at long last, Jaleel. Perhaps he has found Sadira a rich husband; she is almost of an age to marry. Or perhaps he simply wishes to right the wrong he has done her all these years, allowing thee and the others to treat her with contempt though she is his offspring the same as *thy* children."

Jaleel shrugged her elegant shoulders in haughty amusement and disdain. "Or perhaps he has finally decided to slit her throat as he ought to have done when she sprang forth from her mother's womb. Look at her! She is not one of us and never will be."

Jaleel tilted her nose in the air as if she detected a noxious odor, but Sadira did not think she smelled bad; she smelled like horses and camels, her only true friends in all the world. Kind, plain-faced Alima scowled at the beautiful, imperious Jaleel. "Thou art right that she is not one of us. She is *better* than we are. What thou scorn—her green eyes and that streak of golden hair down the center of her head—are the mark of the star after which she was named, which shown so brightly on the night she was born."

"Oh, I have many times heard your story of the mysterious, brightly shining star. Why is it so few others recall that star—or attach any great importance to it? Akbar has never accorded his respect to either the star *or* the child. Thou art the only one who insists that Sadira is special; the rest of us in the harem, and indeed in the whole tribe, know her for what she is and despise her for it."

"But what *am* I, Jaleel?" Sadira boldly interrupted. "Why do all of thee hate me so, when I have done no wrong to any of thee?"

Jaleel seemed shocked by her audacity in posing the question, but Sadira wanted an answer. She had wondered about it, secretly wept over it, and begged Alima to explain it to her. But Alima would not. Instead, she would only stroke Sadira's hair—the dark hair with the alien gold streak in it—comfort her, and assure her that one day her unique beauty and special gifts would be appreciated by her father and indeed, by all of the *Ruala,* the particular tribe of the *Anazah* to which Sadira belonged.

"Thou must trust in Allah to correct these wrongs," Alima had repeatedly insisted, and because Alima's name meant "wise," and her wisdom was esteemed by many, Sadira had respectfully swallowed her questions, along with her resentment and hurt . . . but now, she wanted an answer.

"Because . . . because . . . it is forbidden to speak of it!" Jaleel finally burst out. "If thou wishest to know the truth, thou must ask thy father. Now that he has at long last summoned thee, this will be thine opportunity."

"I *shall* ask him," Sadira said, though her palms grew clammy at the mere thought of it.

Emir Akbar el-Karim, her father, was not only a prince of the *Ruala* but the Sheik of Sheiks of all of the *Anazah,* the great horse-breeding tribe of the desert, which consisted of many smaller tribes and sub-tribes such as the *Ruala.* Neither Akbar's wives nor sons and daughters ever challenged him in any way. Nor did the lesser sheiks of the individual tribes, nor did their people. His word was law, his good will ardently sought, his opinion always consulted. He embodied every trait cherished by the Bedouin, and Sadira deeply admired him. She also feared him and longed for his approval. . . . Still, she would ask him the question that plagued her day and night: *Why am I an outcast in the tent of my own father?*

"Come," Alima urged. "Thou must bathe and change

thy garments. Thou more closely resemble the son of a
camel herder than the daughter of the great Akbar."

"If thou ask me, she resembles a heap of camel dung."
Jaleel flared her delicate nostrils. "And smells like one, too."

"No one asked thee," Alima flared amid the titters of
laughter that followed this statement.

Sadira glanced about self-consciously. Figures moved in
the shadowy corners of the partitioned tent—her father's
other wives, female children, and servants. Suddenly, she
realized how different from all of them she really was. Except for those times when the tribe was on the move, the
members of the harem spent their days lounging in luxury,
waited upon hand and foot by slaves and servants. Sadira
spent her days among the horses and camels, learning all
their ways and training them to respond to her commands.
She much preferred the life she had made for herself to
the one that had been denied her.

"Thou dost not seem to mind the odor of camel dung
when it makes a fire to warm thee during a cold night," she
coolly observed. "Even camel dung has its purpose." And
today I will discover *my* purpose, she silently added, and
then followed Alima into her private section of the tent.

A short time later, bathed, oiled, perfumed, and dressed
in a crimson caftan and *aba* of soft, gold wool, Sadira stood
on the threshold of her father's opulent quarters. Thick pat-
terned carpets and beautifully embroidered pillows in
jewel-like colors with gold tassels furnished this area. An
imposing figure in his lavish robes, her father lounged
among the pillows before a stone-ringed fire. He wore no
headcloth, and his traditional black braids and beard
gleamed in the yellow light.

Engaged in eating the evening repast of dates dipped in
melted butter and wrapped in bread, he did not at first

appear to notice Sadira, which gave her a moment to compose herself and furtively study him. Emir Akbar el-Karim was a fierce-looking man with intelligent black eyes, brows that met in the center of his forehead, and a nose like the beak of a hawk. Sadira had many times studied him at a distance, but his *keffiya* or headcloth partially concealed his strong, hawkish features. Up close, he was even more intimidating than at a distance.

Sadira shivered slightly and reminded herself that she was his daughter, and he had sent for her. Surely he meant her no harm. After a long moment during which the only sound was the sputter of a nearby oil lamp and her father's concentrated enjoyment of his meal, expressed by frequent sighs and belches, Akbar glanced up and saw her standing there. His eyes widened in surprise—or perhaps displeasure.

"Father, thou sent for me," Sadira dared to inform him.

The black eyes slowly looked her up and down. "So I did, Sadira," he responded in a deep, hostile growl. A slave rushed forward to offer him a bowl of camel's milk, but Akbar impatiently waved it away and sat up. "Come closer so I may better look at thee."

Sadira's knees wobbled as she obeyed. The slave retreated until she and her father were quite alone. The carpet beneath her new sandals was so soft and plush that for a moment, she feared she might sink into it and disappear from sight—no great tragedy at this moment! Akbar regarded her silently for several moments, and overcome with nervousness, she let her gaze drop to the intricate pattern of interlocking rings and flowers underfoot. The colors of the carpet were rich and incredibly brilliant—and the smells! Her father's quarters exuded the enticing odors of frankincense, musk, and coffee, mixed with other delightful spices and a distinctive, unmistakably masculine aroma.

"Thou hast become a beauty like thy mother," Akbar said at long last. His deep voice betrayed both pain and pleasure.

Sadira's head snapped up. She met her father's intent gaze. "I should like to learn more about my mother. No one will tell me anything, except that she died on the night I was born."

Akbar scowled—a most fiercesome sight!—then sighed. "And so thou shalt learn more, for such knowledge is necessary for thee to understand the path I have chosen for thee."

Sadira drew a deep breath. Now, she would finally learn the truth of her mysterious past! And discover what the future held.

"Thy mother's name was Bashiyra, which means joy," Akbar began. "I loved her the best of all my wives, but she brought me no joy, only sorrow."

"Why is that, Father?"

A look of great sadness flickered across her father's face. His black-eyed gaze pierced her soul. "Before thou wert born, a golden-haired, green-eyed *frangi,* an Englishman, visited the tribe seeking to purchase several of our most valuable mares. I sent him away disappointed, for I did not trust him—and with good reason, I later learned. Nine months after his departure, Bashiyra gave birth to thee. From the moment I first laid eyes on thy streak of gold hair and thy grass-green eyes, I knew thou had been sired by the *frangi,* not by myself."

Sadira gasped, then clapped her hands over her mouth.

"Yes, my daughter. Thou canst see now that thou art *not* my daughter. My beloved Bashiyra betrayed me, and I was forced to slay her as she lay weeping with shame upon her pillows. In my great anger, I would have slain thee also,

but Alima threw her own body across thine and begged me
to spare thee. She proclaimed Bashiyra's innocence and at-
tributed thy unusual coloring to the 'mark of the star,'
which we call Sadira. It was shining brightly on that terrible
night. . . . No one—myself included—believed her story,
but her tears moved me to pity, and I permitted thee to
live. I also forbade everyone, on pain of death, to mention
Bashiyra's name again or to discuss the incident, for I refused to become an object of ridicule within my own
camp."

"Then . . . then that is why I am outcast from the
harem," Sadira managed to whisper.

"Yes." Akbar nodded. "I could not compel my other
wives or children to accept thee as an equal. Nor did I
myself look upon thee with favor. Thou art the image of
thy mother—possessed of her same grace and beauty—except for the gold streak in thy hair and the color of thine
eyes. Only Alima could see past all this; because she is
barren, she took thee to her heart and gave thee all the
love she would have given to the children of her own body."

Tears welled in Sadira's eyes. "I love Alima also—now,
more than ever."

"She is a kind, wise woman," Akbar agreed. "Which is
why I never divorced her though it is my right since she
can bear me no heirs."

Sadira slowly sank to her knees, overwhelmed by the
shame of her birth and heritage. In the eyes of her people,
she was unclean—defiled. No wonder they treated her with
such contempt! She was the daughter of a *frangi,* a foreigner, and a woman who had betrayed her husband.
Among the women of the *Ruala* and indeed of all the Bedouin, no worse crime than adultery existed—unless it was
losing one's virginity before marriage, or refusing to marry

the man chosen for her by her father, brothers, uncle, or whatever man had authority over her.

"Forgive me the stain of my mother's shame!" Sadira wailed from the depths of her heart. "I am unworthy to be called thy daughter, but perhaps I can still serve thee in the capacity of a slave! If not that, then punish me now, great Akbar! Take my life in recompense!"

Sadira groveled at her father's feet and tore off the fine silk veil that covered her head. She pushed aside the thick dark hair that fell almost to her waist. Fully expecting to feel the bite of a sword against her neck, she waited passively, without fear or terror. Death would be better than to live in such dishonor—*knowing* who she was and how she had come to be. There was no way to erase the stain of her mother's betrayal, no way to atone for the ignominious sin. As everyone knew, the sins of the father—or in this case, the mother—fell upon the heads of their children. Her mother's shame was her own and would haunt her until the day she died.

"Get up, Sadira. Rise and listen to me," Akbar said. "Thy reaction does thee honor. 'Tis proof that indeed thou art marked by the star, as Alima always claimed. Thy debt can yet be canceled, thy stain wiped away. Rise and I will tell thee how."

Trembling and grief stricken, having no wish to live with her shame, Sadira rose and wiped the tears from her cheeks. Her pride lay shattered and broken. Her heart was torn and bleeding. Never had she imagined she could be so worthless!

Akbar reached out a strong brown hand and caught a tear that trembled on the tips of her lashes. "Thy face is thy mother's," he said softly. "But thine eyes art all thine own. They are not the eyes of the Englishman. Thine art clear and guileless, while his were shadowed with the knowledge of his sins."

Sadira gnawed her lower lip until she tasted blood. She could not bear to endure her father's—no, *not* her father's!—close regard.

"Sadira, daughter of the star, I have been watching thee all these years as thou hast been maturing in my camp." Akbar leaned back on his cushions. "To my great delight, I have observed that thou possess the *Ruala* love of horses and the gift of communicating with them that Allah has granted to only a few."

Dumbfounded, Sadira stared at him. Akbar had been observing her all these years when she had thought he never noticed? He had known that she lived among the horses and camels, only rarely entering the harem? That she often dressed as a youth and rode his most precious war mares across the desert?

As if he divined her thoughts, he nodded. "Yea, Sadira, I know all about thee. Thou hast not breathed that I was unaware of it. Only Allah knows thee better. . . . And what I know is that thou art kind and generous of heart. Thou art gentle and loving with all of Allah's creatures—most especially with the splendid, sacred animals Muhammad called 'The Drinkers of the Wind.' My war mares will come to thee on the merest whisper; they trust thee as they trust not even me, their master. They welcome thee among them as if thou wert one of them, and that, Sadira, is an honor given to very few. . . . In my lifetime, I have seen but one other person who possessed such a gift—and he was a slave. Because of his gift, his master freed him and accorded him the same respect and affection he would a brother. Can I do less with a young woman I call my daughter?"

Sadira could not find breath to answer. She sensed that no response was needed; Akbar was speaking to himself as much as to her.

"Nay, Sadira," he continued with a sigh. "I must restore thee to a place of honor. From this day forward, thou wilt be called Sadira Atiya—*Atiya* signifying that thou art a gift to the *Ruala* of the *Anazah*—and we must cherish thee as such. No horse will be sold or bestowed as a gift unless thou personally approves of it. No mare will be bred unless thou sanctions the union. No foal will be weaned until thou declarest the hour of its readiness. . . . Thou wilt be known as Keeper of the Mares, and the destiny and wealth of thy people will depend upon the wisdom of thy decisions."

Again, Sadira fell to her knees. "Father, I am unworthy of such an honor and responsibility!"

"Ah, but thou *wilt* be worthy, Sadira, for this honor demands its own sacrifice. There is a price to be paid for this chance thou wilt have to redeem thy mother's honor and good name."

"What is the price, Father? Simply tell me what it is, and I will gladly pay it!"

Gazing at her long and hard, Akbar solemnly stroked his beard. "First, thou must learn English so thou wilt be able to judge for thyself whether or not the foreigners who come here to buy our horses are worthy of owning them. They will never suspect thee—a mere female—of knowing their language. I shall use our same interpreters, but thou wilt sit among us and observe them when they think thou canst not understand what they are saying. In this way, thou wilt discover if they are pure of heart or devious and deceitful."

"Yes, Father. I will learn English! But who will teach me?"

Akbar grinned. "The very next *frangi* who comes desiring to buy a horse. That will be the price—to teach thee

English. If he teaches thee well, so thou canst speak as well as he, I may perhaps give him *two* horses, though not our best."

Sadira could not suppress a smile; not for nothing was the great Akbar known for being a shrewd leader and brilliant tactician!

"Thou must learn to read and write English, as well as Arabic, and to do sums. I will obtain books, such as those cherished by foreigners, for thee to study. The *Ruala* must not have an ignorant woman as Keeper of the Mares," Akbar warned, sobering. " 'Tis not normal for a female to be educated, but it has come to me in a dream that thou must be entrusted with this knowledge."

"I will do my best and with Allah's help, succeed." Sadira envisioned herself spending hour upon hour, day upon day, studying and learning, poring over scrolls and counting beads, and a new worry intruded. "Will I still be permitted to ride and train the horses?"

"Of course!" Akbar negligently waved a beringed hand. "Thy gift must not be wasted. Indeed, it is *because* of the horses that thou must learn all this. The best must not be sold, no more than we would permit them to be stolen by our ancient enemies, the *Shammar.* However, I see no harm in enriching ourselves by selling off the slightly inferior. We need the guns that foolish foreigners are willing to exchange for our horses."

Sadira frowned. She did not approve of allowing any *frangi* to buy their precious mares and only reluctantly would she part with a stallion. Strangers and foreigners were unworthy to possess even a flawed descendant of Muhammad's "Drinkers of the Wind." But she knew better than to argue. Aside from horses and camels, a Bedouin counted his gun—be it musket, rifle, or pistol—as his most precious possession. He might not know how to use it, but he revered and honored it, taking a plain-barreled English weapon and having it adorned in gold or silver to suit his own taste.

No, she must not argue with her father, but she would certainly take great care in selecting buyers and require enormous recompense.

"Look here, Sadira . . . a gift for the new Keeper of the Mares!" Akbar directed her attention to one side of the tent. The flap was suddenly drawn back to reveal a beautiful, dainty, flame-colored young mare: Sherifa, the Noble One, as she was called. Ears pricked, nostrils flared, Sherifa gazed curiously into the tent. Whinnying her recognition when she spotted Sadira, she attempted to pull free from the slave who held her halter.

Awe-stricken, Sadira could not immediately react. The two-year-old filly was the pick of her father's herd, a baby Sadira herself had secretly begun to train. Sherifa's legs were solid-colored, but a white blaze—like a bolt of lightning—shot down the center of her face, and her large dark eyes were both trusting and intelligent. Gold brushed her mane and tail, and her coat was a rich, russet red, like a glowing flame. She pranced in place on small, delicate hooves—all grace and beauty, every motion elegant, hinting of speed and stamina. Sherifa was the pride of the *Ruala*—a gift beyond price.

"Father, I do not deserve her."

"She is thine, Daughter, a symbol of my forgiveness and favor. Look there now, on the other side."

Sadira turned her head. Unseen hands opened another flap to reveal a fine riding camel—also a baby. "Lulu!" Sadira cried, clapping her hands. At the sound of her name, Lulu, whose name meant Pearl, lifted her finely shaped head and blinked her long-lashed brown eyes. Upon seeing Sadira, she gave a great bawl of happiness and struggled to break free of the two slaves who held her, one on either side.

"Take her out before she wreaks havoc in my quarters." Akbar's order could scarcely be heard over Lulu's whine.

Sadira raised her hand. "Lulu, be still!"

The young she-camel uttered a mournful sound and ceased struggling.

"So thou hast been working on this one, too!" Akbar's tone held pride and amazement. "Teach her well, Sadira Atiya, and she will serve thee gladly all the days of her life."

"I will, Father. Oh, I will!" Sadira knelt at her father's feet and kissed his sandals in joy and gratitude. "Thou could have given me no finer gifts than Lulu and Sherifa— unless it is thy forgiveness for my mother's sin. I know not how I can ever repay thee for all thou hast given me this day, but I will study and learn English! I will master sums . . . I will . . ."

"Sadira Atiya . . ." Akbar's hand touched her shoulder. "Temper thy joy, Daughter. I have not told thee the full price yet. There is more besides learning English. Henceforward, thou wilt also be called *'Adra'*. Sadira Atiya *'Adra'* wilt be thy full name. Dost thou understand the significance of that?"

Sadira rose to a kneeling position at her father's feet. *"Adra* means . . . virgin."

Akbar nodded. "The Keeper of the Mares is always a virgin, a holy woman who presides over all the ceremonies and rituals involving the war mares. 'Tis she who sends the men of the tribe to battle or *'jihad,'* holy war. During those times, the Keeper of the Mares rides a maiden mare, one who has never been bred. That mare will be Sherifa. And thou, Sadira, wilt be *adra,* virgin. Thou wilt *never* marry, but must content thyself serving thy people as the ceremonial maiden for the rest of thy life."

Sadira could scarcely comprehend what he was saying. Among the Bedouin, marriage was the natural state of all women. Even the ugliest, the sick, and maimed, eventually married. They became third or fourth wives and did all the work for the pretty, healthy ones—the favorites.

"For the rest of my life?" she timidly inquired. "I may not marry at all?"

Akbar slowly shook his head. "This, too, I have been ordered in my dreams, Sadira. Thou wilt never marry. Thy virginity must be preserved forever, and thou must swear an oath, on pain of death, that thou wilt honor thy sacred position and covet no man for as long as thou live. In this way—and this way only—canst thou atone for thy mother's sin and erase the stain upon her bloodline. . . . Art thou ready to swear that oath?"

Sadira said nothing for a moment. Sometimes in the loneliness of the desert night, lying upon her back gazing up at the stars, she had dreamed of being loved and cherished by a husband—had dared to study who among the young men of the tribe was the best horseman, the youth she might one day wish to wed. There was one who had caught her eye: Hamid, whose name meant praiseworthy. He was a serious, good-looking young man who gave every indication that he would, indeed, live up to his name.

Now, she would never have Hamid, or any other man for a husband. She would live alone until the end of her days. . . . She would never bear children. Her heart ached with the pang of loss, but then she remembered something: at least, she would have her beloved horses! And her camels. She had always been different, but no longer would she be outcast. This was her destiny—and her chance to redeem her mother's blood. She must bend to the will of Allah.

"I am ready, Father."

Akbar smiled and offered his hand to help her rise. "Then stand and repeat thine oath. . . . I, Sadira Atiya Adra, on pain of death, solemnly swear before Allah that . . ."

Sadira repeated the words as he said them. She managed to keep her voice calm and clear, without a tremor in it. She must be brave and strong and courageous. She must never count the cost of her sacrifice. She would never miss what she was giving up. Sherifa and Lulu would be her family, the horses her life. Praise be to Allah. . . . Praise be to Allah.

Two

"Travis, darling, you've won! Your horse has won!" A pair of slender arms wound around Travis's neck, and he caught an almost nauseating whiff of some cloying scent before Elizabeth drew back to beam up at him. "Think of all that lovely money you just made and how much fun we're going to have spending it!"

The remark struck Travis as presumptuous, and he stepped back from the lovely blonde in her narrow-waisted sky-blue gown, dripping lace, and flowered hat, and pulled her arms from around his neck. "Spending my money already, Elizabeth? I should think you could at least wait until after the wedding."

Instead of being chagrined, she laughed. "Why are you scowling so, Travis? You should be delighted! Your horse has won!"

Undeterred by his lack of enthusiasm, Elizabeth began chattering to the crowd around them. It seemed as if every person in attendance at the races today wanted to shake Travis's hand or clap him on the back in congratulations. Swallowing his irritation, Travis endured the well-wishing with as much grace as he could muster. His horse had, after all, won the day's main event. Never mind that the time was far slower than he had anticipated, and Emperor's Ransom had looked winded when he came down the home-stretch; he had still won, and Travis ought to be happy. . . . But he wasn't, and it was hard to pretend otherwise.

He had to grit his teeth all through the victory ceremonies—extra-long due to the Centennial celebration—and then fight his and Elizabeth's way through the crush of people in order to get to the paddock beneath the tall trees for which Saratoga Springs was renowned. Established in 1864, the track had a fine one-mile course and a grandstand with reception rooms, saloons, and a colonnade running the entire length of the building. But the paddock with its lush trees was what symbolized Saratoga Springs for Travis. Beneath the trees was a vast lawn where the horses were saddled; every stable had outdoor stalls and an exercise area within its own cluster of trees.

Here gathered everyone who was anyone in the fast-growing world of Thoroughbred racing—horses, grooms, trainers, owners—and the avid onlookers hoping to size up the horses and predict the winners. Before they had even reached Greenbriar's stabling area, Travis lost patience altogether with his dawdling fiancée who was too busy conversing with her friends to worry about Ransom's well-being and whether or not the big colt was being cooled out precisely according to Travis's instructions.

"Elizabeth, if you don't hurry along, I'll leave you to find your own way!" Impatiently grabbing her arm, Travis attempted to steer her around yet another group of well-wishers.

Jostled by a fat man in a bright red suit, Elizabeth had to grab her hat to keep from losing it. "Travis!" She skidded to a halt and glared at him. "Whatever is the matter with you? Instead of rejoicing in your victory, you're behaving like a bear with a thorn in its paw. You're barely civil, and I've had just about enough of it."

"The time was too slow," he growled by way of explanation. "And Ransom was heaving. He hasn't enough stamina. Hell, he damn near collapsed on the homestretch. Willy had to take the bat to him, and then he only won by a nose."

"What difference does it make so long as he won!" Two flags of color stained Elizabeth's usually alabaster cheeks, and she fanned herself furiously with the program of the day's races. "Really, Travis. Must you demand perfection in everything? Greenbriar horses—*your* horses—are already among the finest to come out of the bluegrass country since the end of the war. Why do you always have to find something wrong and quibble about insignificant things?"

"I hardly think it insignificant that my horse barely completed the race. If he hadn't had such poor competition today, he never would have won. *None* of them had any stamina; the whole damn lot were stumbling and weaving like a bunch of old women staggering down to the finish line."

"You exaggerate terribly, Travis Colin Keene. And you're rude and inconsiderate. I don't know why I put up with you." Elizabeth folded her arms, tapped her dainty slippered foot, and glanced away from him. "I shall not budge another step until you apologize."

Travis felt more like strangling her than apologizing, but he paused a moment to consider whether or not she had a point. Sighing to himself, he decided she did. He *was* being rude and inconsiderate—a perfect ass, actually. He reminded himself that he was lucky to have won Miss Elizabeth Marie Covington. Elizabeth was widely accounted the most beautiful girl in all of Lexington, maybe even in Kentucky—maybe even in the world. She had silvery blond hair, enormous blue eyes, a creamy complexion, and a figure full of lush curves that never failed to make him think of endless nights of exquisite marital ecstasy. They were engaged to be married. People said they made the perfect couple—he being tall, dark, and supposedly handsome, and she being small, blond, and breathtakingly beautiful. Their children should be stunning.

The only problem was that Elizabeth seemed to arouse his anger as much as his desire. Since they had so much in common, Travis could not understand it. Fox Hall, her family's farm, was a respected Thoroughbred breeding operation rivaling Greenbriar. He and Elizabeth came from the same world, relished breathing the same rarified Kentucky air, and understood the same truths—or so he had managed to convince himself prior to proposing to her.

"All right, Elizabeth. You've made your point. I apologize." He bowed low at the waist and tried to sound contrite. "Can you possibly forgive me, impossible boor that I am?"

"Well," she sniffed. "I suppose I can try."

He had hoped to make her smile, but her eyes softened only slightly, and he felt a new surge of annoyance. "I'm just concerned about my horse, that's all. As a horsewoman yourself, you should understand," he couldn't resist pointing out. "Is it necessary for you to bestow an hour of your time on every person you meet between the grandstand and the paddock?"

Pouting in a manner he found childish and unappealing, Elizabeth countered his question with another question. "Is it necessary for you to be so grumpy even when you're a winner? There's no such thing as perfection in a horse, Travis.

You should know that by now and learn to enjoy what you've achieved instead of always finding fault and wanting more."

"I'm not always finding fault, Elizabeth. I know I've got good horses. It's just that they would be better still if I could breed my English mares to a stallion from the undiluted bloodstock of the Darley Arabian. Now, *there* was a horse with stamina *and* speed."

Trying hard to be less boorish, he offered her his arm, and she grudgingly took it. "Oh, the Darley Arabian! I weary of hearing about him—an overrated nag by some accounts."

Travis chomped down hard and struggled to restrain his temper. "Elizabeth, if you think he was overrated, you haven't heard *enough* about him. Why, he's improved generations of Thoroughbreds both in England and America. Had you ever seen the great Lexington, one of his descendants, you'd know why I'm so obsessed with the idea of obtaining the Darley's bloodlines."

They began to stroll together through the paddock, headed toward the Greenbriar stabling area at a snail's pace it seemed to Travis, but he was determined to cease complaining.

"Did *you* ever see the great Lexington?" Elizabeth queried.

"Yes, I did. As a matter of fact, he was my childhood hero—the reason I'm a horse breeder now." Travis's mood lightened as he thought about the distant past and that magical moment in 1854, when he had been privileged to witness Lexington defeat Lecomte at New Orleans. "I was only ten years old, and it was the first race I ever attended. I'll never forget it. His spirit . . . his great heart. He gave all he had pounding down the homestretch. I was standing right at the finish line with my father, and the thrill of seeing that magnificent animal straining toward the wire . . . hearing the thunder of his hooves . . . haunts me still. Sometimes, I dream of it. I wake up in the night with my heart pounding like it did then. Young as I was, I knew I was observing something rare and glorious, something you see only once in a lifetime, if you're lucky. I've been trying to recapture that moment ever since. Twenty-two years later, I'm still trying to recapture it."

With a short ironic laugh at his own folly, Travis stopped walking and turned Elizabeth to face him. "That's what I'm trying to produce, Elizabeth—that pure perfection. That excellence. That grace, beauty, and power. Isn't that what *you* want, too? Isn't it why we breed horses, your family and mine? Isn't it why we race them—and stay in this crazy business through thick and thin, good times and bad, when any sane person would quit in disgust or invest their capital in something that makes more sense?"

Elizabeth's answer was suddenly very important to him. Travis wanted his future wife to share his dream, his obsession, his very life and breath. They were going to be married, and he still didn't know how she felt about his life's ambition. Never mind that her father was a Kentucky breeder; Travis wanted to hear from her own lips that Elizabeth shared his passion, that she didn't merely accept it as a way of life . . . and that she wasn't in it only for the money, the social status, or the excitement of racing. Plenty of people did it for these reasons. They had no real love for the horses themselves. He didn't want his wife to be one of those soulless people, as he had always thought of them.

Elizabeth's blue eyes held a measure of exasperation. "Well, of course, Travis. I feel exactly as you do, but I'm not a . . . a *fool* over horses, as you are. I'm not head over heels. You go too far. You demand too much. You're winning, but you're still not satisfied."

"Because it's *not* enough." Travis gripped Elizabeth's arms more tightly. "Winning is secondary. It's . . . it's the pursuit of excellence that stirs my blood. It's the creation of something swift, superb, and beautiful. All through the war, when I was getting shot at—when I took that ball in the knee that almost made me a cripple—all I could think about, the thing that kept me going, was that one day I would go home to Greenbriar and start breeding the best, the fastest, the bravest, most courageous horses to run on a racetrack anywhere in the world, England included. That's what gave me life and hope, Elizabeth. It's what kept me alive when I came close to despair. Can you understand? I wanted to live long enough to produce another Lexington. I came home to find both my parents dead and Greenbriar in shambles, but my dream sustained me and brought me through that terrible period. It's been the driving force of my entire life. . . ."

He stopped because Elizabeth was glaring at him again, as if she were hardly listening. "Travis, the War Between the States has been over for a long time now. Your knee is all better. You only have a little limp, a barely noticeable stiffness. Why must you make a big thing of it . . . ? And why must you romanticize the breeding of horses? It's a business, not a . . . a reason for living. There's more to life than hanging over a stall door waiting for a stubborn mare to drop her foal, or scraping mud and manure from your boots every day of your life, or studying bloodlines until the wee hours of the morning, then getting up at five for the morning workouts. . . . Honestly, Travis, you're going to have to change your way of life once we're married.

You'll have to leave these tedious details to others. You and I will have more important things to do with our time."

"More important things!" Travis could not have been more astounded—or dismayed—if she had accused him of being a devil worshipper or suggested that he doff his clothing and run naked through the paddock. "What do you envision me doing all day—decorating tea parties?"

She smiled winsomely, as charming as ever, but chilling his heart at the same time. "You do decorate them rather well, darling. And I *will* expect you to make the obligatory husbandly appearance at my little gatherings when we're in residence at Greenbriar. After all, I intend for us to be the leaders of the entire bluegrass social scene. Greenbriar will become the center for culture, tradition, and entertainment, even as Fox Hall was during my mother's day."

When he didn't immediately say anything, but only stood gaping at her in amazement, she added, "But I thought that's why you asked me to marry you—so I could bring a woman's touch to your cold, lonely mansion and make you a social success, instead of a gloomy old recluse who reeks of horses day and night."

"I thought we were getting married because . . . because . . ."

"Because we're in love, Travis?" She burst out laughing. "Well, I appreciate the sentiment, my dear, but I sincerely doubt that love has much to do with it. Just as there's more to life than horses, there's more to it than silly romantic attach . . ."

"Then hang the romantic attachments! I still don't want you redesigning my entire life!" Travis bellowed. "I thought you felt the same way about horses that I do! You know what I am, what I aspire to be. I thought you understood that, at least."

"Oh, I do, Travis, darling. Didn't I just say I did? Horses are money, and I *do* love money. Hence, I love horses. And as today as amply proven, you have the best horses of anybody. Therefore, it's clear I must love you, too. . . . Dear, dear, we're getting rather too emotional here, aren't we?"

She laughed as if she'd made a clever joke, but Travis could find nothing humorous in her attitude. He loved a good joke as much as anyone, but *this* was no joking matter. They were discussing their lives together, their future happiness.

"But that's what I've been trying to tell you, Elizabeth; I'm afraid I don't have the best horses," Travis gritted between clenched teeth. "Indeed, I have been seriously considering a trip to the east to purchase some new bloodstock to strengthen my breeding program. I was going to tell you about it tonight."

"To the east?" Elizabeth's blue eyes glinted in the afternoon sunlight dappling her face through the treetops. "What do you mean—to the east?"

"To Arabia—the land that produced the Darley Arabian." *"Arabia!"*

Travis could tell from her expression that Elizabeth was less than thrilled by the idea, and he had botched the job of telling her about it. Before he could smooth things over somehow, his head groom, Jem, a tall lanky black man, came hurrying toward him. "Mr. Keene, suh, did you forgit that Lady Emily is runnin' in the next heat?"

Travis stopped in his tracks. In the excitement of Ransom's major victory—and the irritation of his argument with Elizabeth—he *had* forgotten that the promising young filly was running her first race this afternoon, a minor race but an important one for launching her career.

"Elizabeth, we've got to get back to the stands." He spun on his heel and started back in the opposite direction.

"Travis! You can't possibly go to Arabia!" Elizabeth almost tripped over the hem of her gown as she hurried to keep up with him. "It's too far away! And what about our wedding—what about our plans?"

"We can marry first, if you like. Indeed, I was going to suggest it." Travis took her hand and literally dragged her through the throng of people blocking their return to the grandstand. "Then you can come with me. Instead of charming half of Lexington, people who already think you're wonderful, you can work your wiles on the Bedouin—see if you can convince them to part with a stallion to rival the Darley Arabian."

"But I don't want to go to Arabia!" Elizabeth huffed and puffed, red-faced.

"Why in hell not? Bear in mind that I'll be looking for a horse who will advance not only my fortune, but yours, Elizabeth. This is our future we're talking about. Since you love money so much, I should think you'd want to help me search for a stallion to improve our fortunes. You'd want to make certain I get the best horse possible. While we're there, we'll also buy a few mares. If the idea is so distasteful to you, just think of them as our little moneymakers."

"Travis—no!" Elizabeth wailed. Her eyes had gotten huge, and she seemed in danger of falling down in a fit of apoplexy.

Travis knew he was being unreasonable, but suddenly, he didn't care any longer. Something perverse and wicked inside him made him drag her along even faster.

"Well, we're going, and that's that. . . . Hurry up, my love. The race is almost ready to start."

They didn't speak for several moments as he maneuvered

Elizabeth through the crowd, across the Back Yard, as the area behind the grandstand was called, through the colonnade, up a flight of steps, and out onto a balcony overlooking the racetrack. The race was about to begin, and Travis strained to catch a glimpse of Lady Emily and his colors—green, white, and black—in the lineup.

"Travis Keene, you listen to me!"

Heads turned at Elizabeth's unladylike tone, but she did not appear to notice or care what people might be thinking. Hands on hips, she planted herself in front of him. "I refuse to go to Arabia—and you can't go either! It will take a year or more to search the desert—I assume it's all desert—and find the sort of horses you want and then to get them safely home. Besides, it must be a terrible place—hot and dirty and dusty. . . . Why, the very idea makes my stomach hurt."

"Can't, Elizabeth? What do you mean—*can't?* I can and I will. You can come with me, as my dear devoted wife, or you can stay here by yourself. I'd prefer you come with me, but either way, I'm going. A year isn't much time out of our lives if the trip will serve to improve our breeding program and enable us to produce more and better winners."

The crack of a pistol sounded the start of the race, but Elizabeth snatched Travis's arm and stood on tiptoe to keep his attention focused on her instead of on the scene going on behind her. "You expect me to sit home twiddling my thumbs while you're gone from the country for a year or more?" she demanded. "You honestly believe I'd be willing to do that?"

"I was hoping you'd *want* to come, Elizabeth. I've decided I'm going, and if you refuse to accompany me, that's precisely what you'll have to do—sit home twiddling your thumbs all by yourself."

"Like hell I will, Travis Keene! This is what I think of *that* idea!" She seized the engagement ring on her left hand—an heirloom diamond that had been in his family for several generations—and wrenched it off her finger. Then, with a haughty toss of her head, she flung it as far as she could over the railing.

As if in a dream, Travis saw it fall through the air. In the next instant, it was gone—churned into the dust by the hooves of twenty horses, Lady Emily among them—pounding past. Travis didn't know whether to laugh or cry. It was all so bizarre and unbelievable. His lips twitched in indecision—until he looked into Elizabeth's furious white face as she lifted her chin and shot him a look of pure venom.

"Goodbye, Travis. It's quite obvious we do not suit each other," she announced in a shaky voice. "I can't think what I ever saw in you. Or you in me. You are insane over your precious horses, and I refuse to compete for your affections with four-legged beasts whose only value is in how fast they can run."

You're right, Elizabeth. You can't compete, Travis thought, but didn't say. He felt a deep stab of shame that he should feel as he did—and that he should have disappointed her and demanded so much from her. But then he remembered Lady Emily and Emperor's Ransom nuzzling his hand for sugar in the early mornings before their workouts.

He recalled the sun shining brightly on their glistening coats and how their beauty never failed to bring a lump to his throat when he saw them galloping or bucking in the paddocks. He pictured the mares nosing their new foals and proudly trotting beside them through the long green grasses of summer. . . . He had always imagined his wife treasuring these moments with him, but now he saw that Elizabeth would never—could never—be that woman. It wasn't her fault; it was his. He had misjudged her from the start and expected things she was incapable of giving.

"I'm sorry, Elizabeth," he apologized, not even regretting the loss of the heirloom ring. He doubted he would ever find a woman to whom he wanted to give the ring anyway. He was totally unsuited to marriage and should have known it would never work out between them.

Elizabeth whirled in a flounce of sky-blue skirt and marched away from him. The crowd roared, and Travis's attention was drawn back to the race. Lady Emily was running neck and neck with a big bay. As he watched, the filly slowly began to pull ahead. He cursed under his breath because he hadn't been watching the time. He leaned forward, studying her form, and noticed the patch of wetness across her sleek, seal-brown shoulders. . . . Damn! She shouldn't be sweating that hard. She hadn't gone but half a mile.

The filly held the lead to the three-quarter post. With only a quarter mile to the finish line, she began to falter. The big bay drew abreast of her. Travis leaned over the railing, exhorting her onward. He could see the rise and fall of the whip on her gleaming flank as the jockey urged her forward. He hated it when the jockeys went for the whip and only permitted it if the horse was being deliberately lazy and not giving its best. This was clearly not the case in this instance. Lady Emily's nostrils were flared, showing blood-red. Her sides heaved. *Not enough stamina. Not enough heart.*

She lost the rhythm and seemed to stop trying altogether. Four horses thundered past her. Travis smacked the railing with the flat of his palm. Lady Emily was the best youngster he had, and she hadn't even placed. As with Elizabeth, the fault was his, not hers. He hadn't bred the best to the best. Her dam had been exceptional, but her sire—for all he was much touted—left much to be desired. The best was over in Arabia, running free somewhere on the desert. Toughened by the desert heat. Hardened by the harsh terrain. Tempered by centuries of selective breeding designed to create an animal surpassing all others in courage, speed, and endurance.

If he could only find some lost descendant of the Darley Arabian and bring him home to breed to his mares . . . mares such as Lady Emily who lacked only one elusive ingredient—the will to win that he had witnessed in Lexington all those years ago. There was nothing to hold him here. Elizabeth had made her position quite clear. Their relationship was over; the marriage would never take place—thank God. Why shouldn't he go search the desert for horses to fulfill his dream?

Love was a foolish illusion anyway. A man should never put his trust in it, never dare to hope that he would one day meet someone whose heart beat in unison with his heart. If Elizabeth could not understand the demons that drove him, how could any other woman? She had been right about one thing; his heart belonged to the horses, not to a social-climbing little twit who wanted to turn his entire life inside out and upside down.

His only regret was that he had unintentionally hurt her. He would never forgive himself for that. He thought of her hurling his ring over the railing, and he shook his head in self-disgust. . . . Then he allowed himself a small grin. Despite the pain, there had been humor in the moment. He doubted he would ever forget it. The grin blossomed into a bitter laugh that rocked his shoulders, then died abruptly.

Ah, well. . . . What was over was over. Time to get on

with life. Tomorrow he would make arrangements for an extended journey to Arabia to locate the Bedouin tribe who had bred the Darley Arabian.

Three

Aleppo, Syria, 1877

A cacophony of sound assaulted Travis's ears—camels bawling, horses whinnying, donkeys braying, merchants hawking their wares. . . . Overpowering odors filled his nostrils—exotic spices, coffee, garbage, animal and human waste, and unwashed bodies. His eyes feasted on strange sights—men in long robes, their heads swathed in turbans or headcloths bound with heavy cords, boys in short tunics waving sticks to keep their livestock in line, tents flapping in the wind, camels protesting as they were being loaded for some trek into the desert. . . .

He was finally here—in Aleppo, having first arrived at Alexandretta or Scanderoon, as it was also called, a hundred miles to the west on the seacoast, and then having made the journey overland to this ancient city from which caravans had been setting out to cross the desert on trade routes for thousands of years. Travis doubted the city had changed much since the days when the spice caravans first began transporting frankincense, myrrh, gold, pearls, ivory, silks, cinnamon, tortoise shell, lapis lazuli, grain, and wool.

He imagined that earlier visitors had noted the same distinguishing features of the town bordered by trees and gardens. The same towers and minarets, and lofty citadel set on a high elevation overlooking the city must have impressed them. The citadel of Aleppo in particular commanded attention; it was a circular mound half a mile across at the top, three hundred feet high, encased in smooth stone. A broad, sixty-foot-deep ditch had been cut into the rock around it, and walls of red sandstone crowned its summit. The walls contained a staircase and covered walkway built by *Khosroes,* the King of Persia, during the sixth century.

At the lower elevations, the terrain was marshy, the streets mostly swampy at this time of year—the beginning of winter—the surrounding land surprisingly green. The trip from Alexandretta had taken four days and cost 400 *piastres;* now that he was here, overwhelmed by the bustle and strangeness of the marketplace, he had to decide what to do next, where to go, how to make arrangements for his journey into the desert to find the Bedouin and his dream horse.

Having no idea where he would spend the night, he hoped to locate someone who spoke English and could direct him to suitable lodgings. In Alexandretta, a British army officer had warned him that there were no public inns, but he would probably be welcomed at the British Consulate. W.S. Skene, the consul general, reportedly appreciated the Arabian horse, had cultivated friendships among the desert sheiks, and had already made arrangements for a number of horses to be exported from the country, mostly to England.

Travis hoped that being American would not be held against him. He knew he wasn't the first Kentucky breeder to want to bring Arabian horses into America. In 1855, a gentleman bearing Travis's own name—Keene Richards—had journeyed to Arabia, purchased several horses, and transported them home to the bluegrass country. Unfortunately, the progeny of those horses had been scattered during the war years, and no one was quite sure what had happened to them.

Straining to decipher a few words of English in the babble of voices, both human and animal, Travis wandered the marketplace. Suddenly, he heard what he was seeking.

"Anne, dear, don't you think that's an outrageous price to pay for onions?" The question came from an aristocratic-looking gentleman accompanied by a plain-faced but pleasant-looking female garbed in practical, Western-style dress.

"Who knows what is outrageous or not in this country, Wilfred?" The lady directed a turbaned merchant to gather up a dozen or more strings of onions. "Tell him we shall need more than this," she instructed a native youth standing next to her. "We'll purchase all he can provide."

Travis boldly approached the obviously English couple. "Excuse me, but I could not help overhearing your conversation. I'm Travis Colin Keene, an American and new to this country. And you are . . . ?"

"Wilfred Blunt, sir." The gentleman extended his hand in a friendly but somewhat reserved manner. "And this is my wife, Lady Anne."

"Forgive me for intruding, but I'm wondering if you could direct me to the British Consul. I've only just arrived and find myself desperately in need of . . ."

"But of course!" Lady Anne exclaimed. "We'd be delighted to help a fellow traveler. We were just returning there ourselves, weren't we, Wilfred? You can accompany us. Our translator will see to the safe delivery of our purchases, won't you, young man?" She smiled at the youth, and he happily nodded, as smitten by her gracious manner as Travis himself.

"Thank you. I would appreciate it."

Wilfred Blunt did not seem as enthusiastic as his wife to be of assistance, but the dapper gentleman nonetheless took his wife's arm and proceeded to lead the way. They made polite conversation on the journey through the crowded streets and finally arrived at a solid-looking building set on stone arches that spanned a river. A few willows and mulberry trees framed the cloistral-looking abode that overlooked some pleasant gardens.

"Here we are," Lady Anne bubbled. "Just in time for tea. You're probably famished. Come along, and we'll take refreshment while we're waiting for Mr. Skene to return. I believe he had lengthy business to attend to in the city today, did he not, Wilfred?"

"Yes, my dear. He said this morning not to expect his return until late in the day."

"Never fear. We shall manage quite well without him." Lady Anne preceded Travis through the front door of the building. "Follow me, Mr. Keene."

"Call me Travis, please," Travis insisted.

"Certainly. And you must call me Lady Anne. We westerners must stick together in this very Eastern land, mustn't we? Let's go into the salon; we can be comfortable there."

She led the way to a large airy room with windows that opened onto a balcony. The soothing sound of running water could be heard from below. Impressed, Travis stepped into the chamber where a combination of western-style furniture and eastern opulence greeted him. He hated to walk across the jewel-like colors of the thick Persian carpet underfoot. Several large tasseled pillows lay scattered about on the floor, and he speculated as to their purpose; would they sit on the floor or on the long narrow sofa? Lady Anne led him to the sofa.

"Make yourself at home, Mr. Keene—Travis. I will inform Halim that we are returned and ready for tea. Or would you prefer coffee? Coffee is more Arabic, but we English do cling to our tea, even in coffee-drinking countries."

"I'll have whatever you're having." Travis smiled at her gentle enthusiasm.

It was difficult not to like Lady Anne immensely, even on so short an acquaintance. She was not a pretty woman, but she exuded a zest for life that made her seem vivid and memorable. He had no doubt she was enjoying her visit to the east. Wilfred, on the other hand, struck Travis as a typically reserved Englishman, less apt to embrace new things but still game for adventure. Both were dressed in sturdy, somber-hued clothing of no particular grace or style, but they looked ready and able to deal with anything that came their way.

As Lady Anne departed, Wilfred seated himself at the opposite end of the horsehair-covered sofa. "So what brings you to the east, sir?"

Travis debated how much to tell him, then decided he had nothing to gain by being secretive. "Horses. I came here to buy horses from the Bedouin—the best they've got."

The simple statement had an amazing effect on Wilfred Blunt. He leaned forward. Sudden excitement lit his face, and his reserve melted like butter on a hot day. "Why, that's why we are here, Mr. Keene! We're hoping to obtain horses from the same bloodline as the Darley Arabian."

"The Darley Arabian?" Travis could barely conceal his own surprise—and dismay. How many others had come for the same reason—and how many horses of that coveted bloodline still existed?

"Oh, surely you've heard of him," Wilfred continued. "He was a dark bay stallion of fifteen hands with a white blaze and two white stockings. Fellow named Thomas Darley bought him in 1704 and exported him to England during the reign of Queen Ann. His brother, then commission agent here at Aleppo, had procured him from wandering Bedouins somewhere near Palmyra. Bought the horse with an English musket, then the brothers sent him onto John Brewster Darley at Aldby Park in York. None of the Darleys really knew what they had at the time—till they started to breed him. Why, the rest is history. . . . Horse's name was Manicka, and he was four years old when they got him. He was out of the *Mu'ni qua* bloodline, from the *Ras el Fedawi* family."

The depth of the other man's knowledge shocked Travis. No one but a true horse enthusiast would have bothered to accumulate such details. "You are well-informed, Wilfred. Do you plan to use the horses you purchase to improve your own bloodstock? Do you breed Thoroughbreds for racing?"

"No, sir! We plan to breed Arabians only—not mix them up with other breeds. They're grand horses in their own right. No need to dilute their bloodlines. Hope to establish them back home in England—at least get a few out of this country and start our own breeding program. . . . What about you, sir? What are you planning to do with 'em?"

"I breed race horses," Travis informed him. "And also race them. I hope to improve the stamina and endurance of my Thoroughbreds with a fresh infusion of Arabian blood."

"Ah, you intend to do for your own horses what the Darley Arabian did for so many English-bred—and American—horses. I don't blame you. If you look at our classic races—the Derby, Oaks, and St. Leger, for example—you'll see that ninety-five percent of our winners are descendants of the Darley Arabian."

"I'm well aware of that. It's precisely why I'm here. Studying the success of the Darley's descendants convinced me I could not possibly go wrong mixing his strain with the bloodlines I have."

"Ah, but does your jockey club approve?" Wilfred Blunt leaned back and crossed one leg over the other. "Are they underwriting your endeavors, I hope? This is already proving to be an expensive expedition, more so than we had anticipated."

"Sadly no," Travis admitted. "But then I never approached them with the idea. I prefer to pursue this folly— if it turns out to be folly—on my own."

"Quite understandable. If you succeed, the glory's all yours. If you fail, no one but you—and your heirs—will ever know."

"Fortunately, I have no heirs and don't anticipate producing any in the foreseeable future."

"Tut, tut, sir. . . . You sound bitter. What you need is a good wife like my Anne. She's the granddaughter of Lord Byron, you know. Excellent bloodlines."

"No, I didn't know." Travis could not suppress a smile. "Did you choose her on the basis of her bloodlines?"

Wilfred Blunt had the good grace to laugh. "No, sir! I'd have picked her were she the daughter of the lowliest groom in our stable."

"Then you're a lucky man, Wilfred. It appears you've made a good match."

"Oh, we have our disagreements from time to time. Happens to the best of us, but I wouldn't trade my Lady Anne for any other female in England."

"Well, I am relieved to hear that!" Lady Anne entered

the room with a dark-eyed Arabian servant bearing a heavy-laden tray that he set down atop a small square table in front of them. "Halim will serve tea now, while I hear what you two have found to discuss so eagerly."

She perched between the two men on the sofa. While the servant poured fragrant, steamy tea and served tiny pastries saturated with honey, Travis became better acquainted with the Blunts. They invited him to join them on their journey into the valley of the Euphrates where they hoped to locate the Bedouin tribes from whom they might purchase horses. Travis seriously considered it, then politely declined. He did not want to compete with them for the same horses and was relieved to hear that he could travel in another direction and still be reasonably certain of locating one or more of the horse-breeding tribes.

"They are called the *Anazah,*" Lady Anne explained over her second cup of tea. "Many smaller tribes make up this main one, and within the smaller tribes are many sub-tribes. Mr. Skene has been teaching us all about them. Having lived here thirty years, he has a wealth of experience and is most willing to share it."

"Which is the one you most hope to find?" Travis asked.

"Oh, I should think the *Ruala,* though all of them are rumored to possess excellent horses. Mr. Skene has been trying to prepare us for the rigors of the journey and the cultural differences we will encounter."

"I should like to hear what you've learned."

They spent the next hour discussing how the Bedouin tribes lived and the fact that they were mostly Muslims devoted to their religion. Islamic teachings mightily influenced the Bedouin character. Foreigners were thus advised to avoid discussions of religion or tribal politics. The people of the desert could be generous and friendly or hostile and suspicious, depending on how they were approached.

"Mr. Skene says it's best to leave your arms behind or at least keep them out of sight, and to place yourself completely in their hands. They will then feel obliged to protect you, and by the code of the desert will do you no harm. However, if you act as if you suspect them of thievery or deceitfulness, more than likely you will encounter the very behavior you most dread." Lady Anne smiled at Travis. "I intend to treat them as if I trust them totally."

Travis exchanged glances with Wilfred over Lady Anne's bent head as she finished her tea. Wilfred obviously did not share his wife's sanguine views and meant to take precautions behind her back. Travis decided he would not flaunt his pistol but he would wear it at all times and keep his Winchester rifle handy. His baggage was currently in the keeping of the *bashi* or caravan leader with whom he had traveled from the coast. Tomorrow, he would return to the busy marketplace and tell the man where to send it— assuming he would be invited to stay at the consulate.

Lady Anne appeared to guess his thoughts. "Mr. Skene will, of course, insist that you reside here for however long you are in Aleppo. There's no where else to go in any case. Foreigners are not welcome in the places where the natives stay."

"I would be delighted to stay here. Perhaps your Mr. Skene can also recommend a guide and assist me in arranging for my own journey into the desert."

"You *should* come with us." Lady Anne scolded. "The country out there is enormous. The pasture lands of the *Anazah* occupy the entire area between the Euphrates and Damascus, reaching from Aleppo as far south as Jebel Shammar—which reminds me. Whatever direction you decide to go, you must take care to avoid the *Shammar* lands. The *Shammar* and the *Anazah* are bitter enemies, you know."

Travis didn't know. Much as he had tried to educate himself before leaving America, he had been unable to discover much about this part of the world. It was a land of mystery that western historians tended to ignore. "Where are the *Shammar* lands? I'll certainly avoid them."

"Between the Tigris and the Euphrates," Wilfred answered for his wife. "But are you certain we cannot convince you to accompany us?"

Travis shook his head. "No, I appreciate your offer, but if what you say is true—the Bedouin don't like to part with their horses—we ought not to travel together or they will consider us one group. We'll be arguing over who gets which horses. And we may disagree."

"True." Lady Anne sighed. "Well, we must exchange addresses before either of us leaves here, so that we can relate our adventures once we get home again."

"Quite right," Wilfred agreed. "As soon as we arrive at Crabbet Park in England, I shall post you a letter detailing our success or lack of it. You must do the same when you arrive at Greenbriar."

"I will," Travis promised.

A short time later, the illusive Mr. Skene appeared. In his sixties, he seemed a quietly determined man who took pains not to stand out in his surroundings or to alienate the local inhabitants. Introductions were made, invitations issued, and Travis enjoyed an interesting meal with his newfound friends. He could hardly wait until the next day. Mr. Skene was departing again on business, the Blunts had their own plans, and he would be free to return to the marketplace and begin making arrangements for his journey into the desert. He decided to set out for the interior where the tribes were said to graze their animals during the winter months, the only time of year when the barren country could support the herds. Perhaps he would be lucky enough to find the *Ruala*. Mr. Skene told him where to go in the marketplace to procure a guide and advised him on what he ought to purchase for the journey. He highly recommended onions as a staple; consumed between flat rounds of Syrian bread, onions made a meal in itself.

Excited about his prospects, Travis could hardly sleep that night. He fell asleep dreaming of fleet-footed horses galloping across long, broad stretches of sand.

In the archway of a mosque the next morning, Travis hefted the bag of *beshliks* or Syrian coins he had just received from a money changer. He disliked walking around with such conspicuous wealth, but unlike those around him had no flowing robes in which to conceal it. Everytime his jacket flopped open, his pistol was also on display. Add to that his height and western clothing, and he drew a fair amount of interest. Eyes narrowed and lips curled, which did not bode well for his success at bargaining for supplies or procuring a guide.

He suspected the money changer had already cheated him, and he wished he had taken Mr. Skene's advice and invited Halim to accompany him today as translator. The Blunts had been studying Arabic and were willing to forego Halim's services for the day, but Travis hadn't wanted to inconvenience them; they had been there first, after all, and were planning to start their journey within a week—a time span he hoped to match if possible.

Concealing his bag of coins beneath his jacket, he

headed for that part of the sprawling city marketplace where Mr. Skene had assured him he could find an English-speaking guide. Men in long, flowing robes frequently jostled him; they marched about as if they owned the city and found his presence an abomination. Travis wondered if his pistol provoked this hostility, and he began to wish he had not tucked it into his waistband that morning before leaving the consulate.

He finally reached a section of the marketplace where one could purchase flasks of oil, strings of onions, and the flat Arab loaves of bread Mr. Skene had recommended. He paused to look over his list, which also included salt, pepper, a frying pan, coffee, sugar, a pot for making the coffee, and perhaps some dates, honey, olives, and goat cheese. Then there was the important matter of transportation. Mr. Skene had recommended camels over horses or mules, because they could travel farther on less water and carry more supplies. Travis hadn't yet decided, but he suspected he would feel more comfortable riding a horse than a camel. Mules might be a good compromise. Next to an onion seller stood a likely looking mule, and he strolled closer to inspect it.

"Dost thou wish to purchase excellent mule, *Frangi?*" The onion seller, a man with a thin face and slightly slanted eyes, peered out from beneath a filthy turban.

"How much?" Pleased to have found someone who spoke English, Travis debated whether or not he ought to buy half the man's stock and have him hold it for a few days. The onion seller named an absurdly high price— much higher than Mr. Skene had told him he would have to pay for a mule. Travis shook his head. "Too much. I will look further."

He started to walk away, but the onion seller grabbed

his sleeve. "Do not cheat a poor onion seller, *Frangi*. I have two wives and eight children to support. That is a fair price for a fine mule."

"I think you might be trying to cheat me. The price is much too high for a miserable animal whose ribs are showing. You ought to feed him better. He looks hungry."

"As Allah is my witness, I do not starve my mule—nor do I cheat anyone, even though they be infidels!" The onion seller switched to Arabic and began to berate Travis, pointing and gesticulating as if Travis had done him a great injury.

Travis suddenly found himself the center of a hostile crowd of dirty, rag-tag vendors and onlookers. With a sinking feeling, he realized he had wandered into a rough dark area of the marketplace away from the usual hustle and bustle. Three young men jostled him deliberately. He hugged the bulky bag of *beshliks* close to his chest, and one of the men noticed the movement, as well as the bulge of the pistol beneath his jacket. A dagger suddenly appeared in the man's hand. Alarmed, Travis reached for his pistol, but had no chance to grab it before someone kneed him in the back.

Another man punched him in the belly. Grasping hands tugged at *his* hands. Two youths jumped on his shoulders, and Travis dropped the bag of coins. As the coins spilled out onto the cobblestones, everyone scrambled for them. In the confusion, Travis landed a punch on the jaw of one of his attackers. He flailed and kicked and shoved, giving better than he got. But there were too many of them.

Something hard and thick struck him repeatedly about the head and shoulders. Travis slipped to his knees. Cursing and swearing, he sought to rise, but bodies swarmed over him. Unseen hands searched his clothing. Lightning and pain exploded in his brain, and red stars danced before his eyes. With a deep groan of protest, he succumbed to a wave of blackness.

"Master, wake up! Thou must come away from here at once!"

Travis heard the summons as if from a great distance. His head was pounding. His body ached. He felt sick to his stomach. With great effort, he roused himself enough to focus on the face of the small wizened man bending over him. The eyes gazing down at him were alight with sympathy—the only human quality in a visage that resembled a monkey's rather than a man's. Could a wrinkle-faced monkey speak English?

"Master, thou must hurry before someone else comes along to harm thee further. This part of the marketplace is no place for a *frangi*. Come . . . come. I will take thee someplace safe."

The little man began tugging on Travis's arm. Travis forced himself to sit up. The throbbing in his temples increased, and now he felt dizzy. But the small, scrawny man in the long dusty robe and striped turban—the man with the face of a monkey—relentlessly maneuvered him to his feet.

"Lean on me, Master. I will take thee to my tent and give thee coffee. Then thou will feel better."

The last thing Travis wanted was coffee, but he did need time to collect himself and get his bearings. He hoped the man's tent wasn't too far away, or he might collapse before he got there. He had to hold his ribs with one hand—had probably broken a rib or two in the scuffle. He had also lost his coins and his pistol. He could replace the coins, but the loss of the pistol was devastating. Pistols might be hard to come by, and clearly, he would need one.

"The British Consulate. How far away is it?"

"Oh, long way, Master. Too far to walk yet. Thou must rest first in the tent of Fadoul."

"Fadoul? That's you, I take it."

Fadoul grinned, revealing a missing front tooth. "Yes, Master. I am Fadoul. My name means honest, and I am worthy of it."

"All right, Fadoul. Take me to your tent." As he leaned on the little man, Travis was surprised by the wiry strength in Fadoul's thin body.

Fadoul led him through the maze of the marketplace and the narrow streets to a low-ceilinged black tent set up on the fringes of the city. Travis doubted it could be any closer than the consulate, but he was too eager to sink down on a pile of pillows strewn across the faded carpet to argue.

"Rest now, Master. I will prepare coffee," Fadoul urged, and Travis gratefully complied.

Sprawled on the pillows in a state of semiconsciousness, he barely noticed Fadoul bustling about the tent, tending a tiny fire in a ring of stones, or preparing coffee. But when Fadoul held a miniature brass cup of the steaming beverage beneath Travis's nose, Travis awoke in an instant. Taking the cup in trembling hands, he lifted it to his lips and tasted the burning-hot, aromatic brew. It gave him new life. Wordlessly, he drained the cup until it was empty, then held it out to be refilled. Fadoul poured more coffee from a skinny pot with an ornate, long-necked spout and an intricately carved wooden handle.

Sitting cross-legged in front of Travis, Fadoul regarded him owlishly. "Master, what were thou doing in that part of the bazaar? Hast thou no servants to make thy purchases for thee?"

"I was searching for an English-speaking guide to lead me into the desert to find horses to purchase from the Bedouin."

The coffee had revived Travis. He had no broken bones, he had discovered, but he would probably be stiff and sore for days. He glanced around the small cramped tent; the furnishings were old and shabby, but every item had been placed with care and was reasonably clean. The tent offered modest but adequate comforts, and Travis half expected a veiled female to emerge from some dark corner; surely the overall neatness of the little dwelling could be accounted to the touch of a woman.

"Master," Fadoul solemnly announced, still holding the coffeepot in his slender brown hands. "Thou need search no more, for thou hast found what thou needs. Thou seest him here before thee."

"You? You are a guide?"

Fadoul looked affronted. "I speak English, and I know the desert like I know my own tent. What more dost thou need?"

What more indeed? The man had rescued Travis from the street and brought him to a place of shelter, but Travis was still wary. "Tell me about yourself."

Fadoul set down the coffeepot and spread his hands in front of him. "What is there to tell, Master? I have done much in my life—not all of it praiseworthy. I have been a merchant, a scribe, an advisor to a man of great wealth and influence . . ."

Travis studied Fadoul more closely. "An advisor?"

Fadoul grinned and shrugged. "Perhaps not a true advisor since my advice was rarely taken. But I did work for a rich man until the day he died. Sadly, I had little respect for his son, so I left my position and since then have made my own way by my wits and persistence. I manage to eat morning and night, and for the rest . . ." He waved a hand dismissively. "My needs are simple."

"You have no family? No wife or children?"

Fadoul shook his head. "Allah has not seen fit to bless or burden me with such treasures, Master. I was married once, but the girl ran off with a goat herder. It was no great loss. All she ever did was complain. 'Fadoul, I want some silver bangles.' 'Fadoul, I need a new pot in which to cook your dinner.' 'Fadoul, I want more kohl to line my eyes and make them beautiful.' . . . The kohl did not help much, for she was ugly as a vulture, Master. Allah forgive me but I was glad to be rid of her."

Travis bit back laughter and clutched his aching side. He decided he liked Fadoul. "What were your duties with the rich man for whom you worked?"

"I bought and sold for him, Master. And I can do the same thing for thee. I can make all the arrangements for thy journey into the desert. Thou wilt need camels and supplies—plus gifts to give the tribes over whose land we shall trespass."

"Gifts—or bribes?"

"Think of it as a tax, Master. Thou must pay to use the grazing lands and the wells or water holes of others. Thou cannot simply take what thou hast need of."

"I see. I had not heard of the practice, but I'm not surprised by it."

" 'Twas I who arranged these things for my former master," Fadoul said proudly. "I also negotiated the trades he made with the desert tribes."

"Then you do know the tribes."

"Oh, yes, Master! I am particularly acquainted with the *Anazah*."

Travis could scarcely believe his good fortune. "You would know where to look to find the *Ruala?*"

"At this time of year, they will be grazing their herds on the winter pasture lands. Those lands cover a broad area, Master, but yes, I am certain I can find the tribe. However, it would be better if we did not travel alone. We must form a caravan—or join one going in the same direction. There is safety in numbers, Master. One never knows when one will meet thieves or assassins. We must take precautions to avoid another attack such as happened today. Thou wilt have to don robes and wear the *keffiya,* so it is not so obvious that thou art a *frangi.* 'Tis good thy hair is black, but thy blue eyes wilt still be a problem. Also, thou art taller than the average Bedouin. . . . Still, we will do the best we can to conceal thy true identity."

"Are foreigners hated so much then?"

"Not hated, Master, but not welcome either. A man never comes to a strange land to give, but to take. He comes because he wants something he cannot find in his own country. We allow this because foreigners usually have money to spend for what they want. But they do not worship Allah, and they trample upon our beliefs and customs while they are here. Therefore, we do not always love them—except for thee, Master. I believe I can learn to love thee."

"Why me?"

Fadoul straightened his thin shoulders and managed to project an air of dignity and pride, despite his monkeylike face. "I did not plan to find thee lying in the street today; it must have been my fate, my destiny . . . the will of Allah. I knew as soon as I saw thee that thou wert the reason

I came that way—a way I do not normally travel. I am in need of employment, and thou art in need of an English-speaking guide to lead thee into the desert to find the *Ruala*. Can it be mere coincidence that we found each other, Master? I think not."

Travis did not believe in predestination, but decided not to debate the point with someone who did. It was certainly a strange coincidence that he and Fadoul had stumbled across each other. "How much time will you need to prepare for this journey?"

Fadoul's thin face lit up with a smile. "If I am indeed hired, Master, I can be ready to depart in little more than seven days."

"You are hired, Fadoul, and we will leave in one week. Let's have another cup of coffee to seal our bargain and then you must show me the way back to the consulate. You'll need funds to begin purchasing our supplies."

"I am delighted to serve thee, Master." Grinning from ear to ear, Fadoul hastened to prepare another pot of coffee.

Four

Cold, wet, rainy weather, accompanied by thick mud delayed Travis's departure, so that it was more like a month
than a week before Travis bade farewell to the Blunts and
Mr. Skene and set out with Fadoul to find the Bedouin
tribe known as the *Ruala*. Fadoul had arranged for them
to travel with a caravan of a dozen men taking a herd of
camels across the desert. Travis did not particularly like
the fierce look or chilly attitude of their travel companions,
but when he mentioned this to Fadoul, the little servant
again assured him that it was better to make the journey
in a group rather than alone.

Fadoul had procured two camels—one of which he rode,
seated in a *mohaffa,* a wooden box or pannier about five
feet high that was fitted with curtains and a mattress for
comfort and protection from the sun. A second pannier
filled with supplies balanced the load on the other side of
the camel's single hump. He had wanted Travis to ride the
second camel in a similar contraption, but Travis insisted
he would be more comfortable on a horse or a mule. Fadoul
had thus bought an old sway-backed donkey.

"Soon, thou wilt have a better mount, Master. Be patient,
and all things will come to thee," he assured a skeptical
Travis.

Of the dozen men they were accompanying, four were

riding attractive mares in the Bedouin manner, without bit
or bridle, using only decorative halters and controlling them
solely with their legs while seated in saddles made of thick
pads of cotton to which stirrups were attached. One of the
mares aroused Travis's envy—and interest in purchasing.
However, when Fadoul raised the issue, the young man an-
grily jerked his head, then galloped off to join his friends,
most of whom were riding camels in ornate saddles especially made to fit over the humps of the beasts. Brightly
colored-tasseled camel bridles and long sticks to tap the
camels on the shoulder completed the riding tack.

As they rode through the Syrian Gates, the mountain
pass of Aleppo, the sky was a brilliant blue, the sunshine
like golden honey pouring down upon them, and Travis
was able to quell his misgivings. Beneath their flowing
robes and headcloths, his companions were hardly more
than boys. They indulged in typical boyish teasing and
laughter as they herded about thirty head of camel, grunting and bawling, through the rocky pass.

Once through the pass, they encountered a marshy area,
and Travis was amused to see a score of kingfishers sitting
on telegraph wires strung across the marsh. Other travelers
shared the road, most of them riding camels, mules, or donkeys. Here and there were horses, but none of exceptional
quality—other than the one ridden by the youth who
seemed to be the leader or *bashi* of their own caravan. The
day passed without incident, and they spent the night at a
place called Beylan, sleeping in a *khan,* a row of empty
rooms on the upper floor of a building regularly used by
passing caravans.

Fadoul waited on Travis hand and foot. Irritated by his
obsequiousness, Travis scolded him for it, and Fadoul
frowned in affront. " 'Tis my duty to serve thee, Master,

and it tells the others that thou art an important man. Dost thou not see how Gamalat is treated?"

"Gamalat?"

Fadoul pointed to the young man Travis had already marked as the leader of the caravan. "That one. His name means Beautiful One, though his face has been ruined by that scar near his mouth. It appears to be a fresh one and gives him a twisted look whenever he smiles. Anyway, thou canst tell by the way the others treat him that he is the favorite son of the leader of his tribe. Mark how the others show him great respect and serve his needs."

At the moment, the scar-faced young man was reclining on a pile of pillows heaped on a colorful carpet, and eating a meal prepared by one of his friends. Travis met the young man's intense, black-eyed gaze and again felt a stab of wariness. He instinctively did not trust Gamalat; cool hostility lurked in his eyes, and the scar only added to his appearance of ferocity. They were traveling in the same caravan, but Gamalat had made no effort to be friendly. Suddenly, Travis was glad of the new pistol Mr. Skene had found for him—a pistol he kept hidden in his waistband concealed beneath the long flowing robe Fadoul had insisted he don for the journey.

Travis didn't mind wearing the robe, a kind of woolen tunic over his trousers and shirt, for the winter days—and especially the nights—were cool. He hadn't yet donned the *keffiya* to cover his head, but he would when they reached the open country, away from the heavily traveled main road. Gamalat arrogantly fingered one of seven black braids into which his long hair was plaited, and exchanged an assessing glance with Travis. Travis gave him a polite nod but Gamalat gazed past him as if he hadn't seen it.

"Young Gamalat isn't exactly thrilled we came along on the journey, is he?" Travis commented to Fadoul.

"He is simply a young man filled with self-importance, Master, and the need to prove himself before his comrades. He does not wish to appear too eager to please thee—a *frangi*. In time, he will warm to thee. The longer thou ride a donkey while he rides a horse, the more firmly established his superiority will become in the eyes of his friends."

"I think he's offended that I tried to buy his horse."

"He does not know thee, Master. As I have told thee before, thou must be patient. Had he sold thee the horse, what would he himself ride? Most of his camels are pack animals, not riding beasts, and a long journey lies ahead of him. Do not lose heart. Establishing a relationship with a Bedouin takes time, but once thou hast won him, he may sell thee—or even *give* thee—his horse out of friendship. Allah commands his followers to be kind and generous, and a man can ensure his redemption and enhance his reputation at the same time by the giving of valuable gifts."

"I'd certainly take it if he gave it to me, Fadoul, but it's not that great of a horse anyway. It does have a few flaws. For one thing, its front legs are bowed. It simply looks good compared to my poor donkey."

"The donkey was the best I could find in so short a time, Master. I am sorry if thou art displeased with it. I beg thee to forgive me."

"I am *not* displeased, Fadoul. So far, you're doing a magnificent job. Now if you can just locate the *Ruala*, I'll be delighted."

"Five or six days' journey, Master. Then we can leave Gamalat and the others, and pitch our tents among the

Ruala. Their horses will probably be much better than Gamalat's."

"I hope so, Fadoul. Now put out that smoky oil lamp, and let's get some sleep."

Three days later found them making camp on the fringes of a broad windswept plain that was nothing like Travis had expected of the desert. Juniper, aloe, tamarisk, and various species of cacti dotted the area. The plain was green with salt grass, sweet-smelling purple flowers, and seedlings that the camels, horses, and donkey eagerly attacked each night. They were making reasonably good time—traveling fifteen to twenty miles a day by Travis's reckoning, and encountering no difficulties. Rain pools and water holes were easy to find.

He had spotted small fleet-footed gazelle, a hedgehog or two, a fox, and a tall stately oryx that the young men had chased and killed. Since everyone had plenty of food, Travis could not see the sense of killing merely for the sport of it, and he refused to eat any of the meat, though Fadoul relished every bite of the small charred portion deposited outside their tent that evening. Travis supposed that the gift of meat was a gesture of friendship, but he was still disappointed that Gamalat seemed to be avoiding him and would engage in little or no conversation.

The wind tugged at his tent that night and made a forlorn, whining sound. Shivering, Travis wrapped himself in a rug to ward off the cold. It seemed ridiculous that he and Fadoul should each have their own tents, instead of sharing the warmth that might be generated by two bodies occupying space in a small enclosure, but Fadoul had been adamant. The master must have his own quarters—better than the servant's. Travis's tent was slightly larger than Fadoul's and had nicer carpets and pillows, a fancier coffeepot, and a few other amenities, but Travis would gladly have sacrificed all of them for the comfort of another human being's presence.

He hardly slept and only fell into a deep slumber just before dawn. A welcome warmth finally encased him, and he did not awaken until he heard a shout outside the tent. He opened his eyes to discover sunlight bathing one wall of the tent. It had grown very still and quiet. The usual morning sounds of men stirring, camels bawling, and his donkey braying were missing. Swept with uneasiness, Travis rose, unfastened the flap of his tent, and stepped outside.

A terrible sight greeted him. All twelve men of the caravan stood in a semicircle around his tent. In the center stood Gamalat, scowling fiercely, and at his feet cowered Fadoul—completely naked. The scrawny little man wore not a stitch of clothing and more than ever resembled a monkey—a very frightened monkey. Gamalat prodded him with his boot, and Fadoul cried out.

"Master! Gamalat has commanded we strip down to our bare flesh. He means to steal everything we own and leave us here to die on the desert. If we do not do as he commands, he will kill us outright."

Travis cursed himself for being so foolish as to step outside his tent without pistol or rifle. All twelve men were armed, several with rifles or muskets, some with gleaming, curved scimitars, and others with long lances made of bamboo. These were Bedouin lances, fifteen to eighteen feet long, with steel heads on them, and decorated with black and gray feathers. Fadoul had told them they were good for killing wolves.

"Is this Bedouin hospitality?" he demanded, remembering what the Blunts had told him about the desert code of honor. "Ask him that, Fadoul. We have put ourselves under Gamalat's protection. Allah would not approve of his robbing or killing us."

"Master, he says that since we are seeking the *Ruala* and he is a *Shammar,* the rules of the desert do not apply. The *Shammar* and the *Ruala* are ancient enemies. Therefore, we are his enemies, and by rights, he *ought* to kill us."

"Nonsense! I have yet to meet a *Ruala,* so I can hardly be considered their friend. However, I *have* met the *Shammar* and shared this journey with them. Has Gamalat no honor? Would Allah approve of his treachery?"

"Master, I have already presented these arguments, and Gamalat refuses to listen. I am truly sorry, Master. I did not recognize the name of his tribe as being *Shammar,* or I never would have joined his caravan to find the *Ruala* who are *Anazah.* I deserve to die for the grave error of leading thee into this ambush. But *thou* dost not deserve to die. Do as he says and remove thy clothing, Master. Perhaps someone will find us, and we shall live after all."

"We shall freeze to death. This may be the desert but we shall freeze—or starve. Tell him I refuse."

"Master, thou must do it!" Fadoul pleaded as Gamalat poked him in the ribs with a rifle.

Travis gauged his chances of dashing back inside his tent to retrieve his pistol or rifle and decided he would never make it. His best chance was still his mouth.

"Master, do it now or they will kill me!" Fadoul sobbed, groveling at Gamalat's feet.

Travis fingered the front of his shirt, as if he meant to comply, but instead of disrobing, began to walk slowly toward Gamalat. Show no fear, he silently counseled himself. Maybe you can bluff your way out of this yet.

Gamalat shouted at him and waved his rifle.

"Master, stop where thou art!"

Like hell I will, Travis thought. I'll be damned if I'll die naked, shivering, and blubbering in fear. If I'm going to die, I'm going to die like a man—fighting for my life.

"Master, stop!"

Travis began to run. He took a deep breath, filled his lungs with air, and let out a great yell. Screaming like a mad man, he charged the line of waiting men.

Relieved to be away from the ever-present demands of her people, Sadira urged Sherifa into a full gallop and let her fly across the desert. The mare sensed her need to be free and alone beneath the bright blue bowl of the sky; joyously she extended herself and carried Sadira far away from the *Ruala* campsite—so far that the tents and herds disappeared from sight, and only a faintly shimmering dust cloud marked their location.

Lately, there was always something to occupy Sadira's time—a horse that needed special care, a translation to be made for her father, decisions to be rendered regarding the breeding of this or that mare. Sadira relished the acceptance and respect she had finally found among her people, but sometimes their demands depleted her, and she needed to escape.

Busy and fulfilling on the one hand, her life was bleak and empty on the other. At night, for instance, she slept in her own small tent pitched in the midst of the mares, and if she awoke shivering with cold or anxious because of a bad dream, there was no one to hold and comfort her, no one upon whom she could depend to meet *her* needs. The members of the tribe revered and praised her, gave her gifts, consulted her on matters both great and small—but still maintained their distance, now for entirely different reasons from what they had when she was a child. They held her in awe, not in friendship, and in the midst of her people, Sadira suffered from loneliness.

She was the Keeper of the Mares, the ceremonial maiden who brought the *Ruala* good luck and success in all of their endeavors so that their herds were the envy of the desert, but she lived apart from them . . . and could find solace and peace only in the wide open spaces. The vast limitless sky and endless horizon soothed her in some odd way. Alone at last, she did not feel so alone. She and her mare were one entity, one being—galloping across the desert sharing a bond and a comradery too deep for words.

Only Sherifa understood Sadira's unfulfilled yearnings. Sometimes in the night, the mare would stand outside Sadira's tent, pawing and neighing, begging to be allowed to run with a stallion beneath the desert moon. On such nights, Sadira would invite the mare to come inside the tent, and she would stroke her and feed her sweetmeats, and they would console each other. Among the females of the *Ruala*—horse and human—only Sadira and Sherifa were doomed to separateness. Their wombs would forever be empty, their desires suppressed. They would never know the hot sweet flood of passion or the perfect unity of love everlasting.

These wild gallops across the desert were their compensation for never being allowed to take a mate, and on this particular golden afternoon, the desert revealed its treasures with uncharacteristic generosity. The air was brisk and sweet, the green produced by the winter rains a benediction for the eyes, the blue of the sky almost blinding. The wind plucked at Sadira's headcloth, and she tore it off—the better to feel the wind ruffling her long hair so that it streamed behind her like a banner. As she usually did when she rode out alone, she had donned a robe and *keffiya,* so that if she chanced upon strangers, they would think her a young man.

Today, the flatness of the plain revealed no other living presence save her own and Sherifa's—until she spotted a human shape lying stretched out flat upon the ground.

Reining in sharply, she trotted over to investigate. The shape was a man—naked, bruised, bloodied, and beaten, lying on his stomach as if embracing the earth. Eyes closed, face partially buried in the grass, he appeared to be dead. Then Sadira detected the slightest of movements, and she slid from Sherifa's back and hurried over to him.

The man was tall and well-muscled, much larger than the average Bedouin. His black hair was short rather than plaited into braids, and his skin was exceptionally white— that portion of it that remained unbruised or unbloodied. The winter sunlight had stained his buttocks a rosy red, and she blushed to see his nudity so blatantly displayed. Hesitating a moment before turning him over, Sadira wondered if she ought not to ride back to camp and send some- one else out to help him . . . but she was a long way from camp, and the man needed immediate assistance. He had apparently been robbed and left for dead—a not uncommon tragedy on the desert where the tribes constantly warred with each other and the Turkish government.

Without a swift horse or camel and the safety of num- bers, travelers were easy prey for the ungodly. She herself could only risk her solitary rides because she rode a horse no one could catch. Whatever the stranger's circumstances, she could not leave him there to broil beneath the sun or freeze when night came; even in winter, the desert could kill a man, especially a weakened one.

Swept with pity and curiosity, she touched the man's

broad shoulder and felt the warmth of his flesh. A little
shiver ran through her at the brazenness of the act; she had
never touched *any* man, let alone a naked stranger.

The stranger groaned and stirred, then lifted his head.
Blood matted his hair and obscured his features. One eye
was badly swollen. Whether he was handsome or not, she
could not tell; his face was too badly battered. He could
open only one eye, but she saw at once that it was a blue
eye—a *frangi!* With his short hair and blue eyes, he *must*
be a *frangi.*

His lips moved, but no sound came out. On his second
attempt, he mumbled in English, "Help me . . . please . . .
help me."

Sadira knelt and rolled him onto his back. Quickly, she
draped her headcloth, which she still clutched in one hand,
over the lower half of his body. Welts and bruises covered
him—as well as blood. Someone had bashed his left temple
with a heavy object, and blood still oozed from the lacera-
tion, glistening bright red and matting his hair. She tore a
piece of cloth from the hem of her robe and bound it
around his head.

"W . . . water," he mumbled. "Have you any water?"

She did not stop to consider that she ought not to let
him know she understood English. She simply rose and
went to Sherifa to get the water skin tied to her saddle.
Unstoppering it, she hurried back, again knelt down, slid
her arm beneath the man's head, and held the skin to his
lips. Grasping the water skin, he took several long swal-
lows, then lay back panting. Eyes closed, he lay still as if
gathering strength, then reopened the one blue eye and
stared at her. "Fadoul. . . . Where is Fadoul?"

She surmised he meant some other member of his party.
She gazed over the plain, only then discovering that another

man—a smaller, skinnier fellow—lay some distance away. He, too, was naked, and she began removing her *aba* as she rose and hurried toward him. Stick-thin arms and legs, protruding ribs, and shriveled genitals caught her eye before she flung her cloak over this second victim.

This man was uncommonly ugly and most definitely *not* a *frangi*. His wispy gray hair had been plaited, and his skin was darker, plus he had the slightly slanted eyes and flattened nose of another desert tribe she thought she recognized—the Fellaheen. His small wrinkled features, nut-brown in color, gave him a wizened aspect.

After retrieving the water skin and offering him water, which dribbled out of his slack mouth and down his chin, she took stock of his injuries. He had a large hard lump on the back of his head, but had not been beaten so severely as the *frangi*. Still, he was an old man and appeared close to death. His face was ashen, his lips bluish. Gently, she laid his head back down on the ground and returned to the *frangi*.

"Fadoul . . . did you find Fadoul?" The *frangi* was trying to get up. He seemed not to notice that he was naked and her headcloth offered little in the way of concealment.

She decided he must be told his friend was dying. Akbar would not approve of her speaking English to a *frangi*, but pretending ignorance was foolish in view of the situation.

"I found him a short distance away. He has not regained consciousness. I am not certain he will."

"We've . . . got to help him." The *frangi* achieved a sitting position and lifted both hands to his head. "I'm so dizzy. Last thing I remember is being cracked in the head with a rifle butt."

"Whoever attacked thee probably thought they killed thee. I am amazed thou art still alive."

His one good eye squinted at her. "*I* am amazed to find an English-speaking female in the middle of the desert. Your story should be most interesting. Unfortunately, it'll have to wait, because I'm not up to it at the moment . . . and we've got to help Fadoul."

"Better tie that headcloth securely about thy waist. Here is a cord." She handed him an *agal,* the ropelike tassel that normally kept her *keffiya* securely on her head. It was an extra-long one that should easily reach around his waist.

The *frangi* glanced down at himself and uttered an exclamation. "The bastards! They even stole my clothing! I knew I never should have trusted them—they were hostile right from the start."

As he fumbled with headcloth and cord, she debated whether or not to assist him. Now that he was awake, she feared touching him again. His masculinity unnerved her. He was all hard muscle, flat plains, curly chest hair, wide shoulders, and a narrow waist, his big body enticingly different from hers. She mentally scolded herself for noticing these things, but she could not help it, and despite her misgivings found that she *had* to assist him. He could not manage without her.

"I could use a little boost here." He reached for her hand, his gaze scanning the blush burning on her cheeks—a phenomenon she was helpless to subdue. "Look, I'm hardly in a position to be a threat to you. Beautiful as you are . . ." He squinted his good eye again. "And you *are* beautiful, I'm incapable of ravishment at the moment."

She blushed even harder. His directness both offended and excited her; she had already observed that *frangis* were generally blunt-spoken, but this one seemed more so than most.

Wordlessly, she took his hand and helped him rise. He

leaned on her shoulder, panted a moment, then determinedly limped over to Fadoul. "Did you give him water?"

"I offered it, but he would not drink."

The *frangi* eased down onto his knees, leaned over his friend, and gently peeled back an eyelid. "If I ever catch the bastards who did this to him, I'll flay them alive," he growled with chilling menace. "He begged for mercy, and they laughed at him. They wanted everything we had and that was that."

"And didst thou beg for mercy also?" she astonished herself by asking. She could not imagine this man begging for anything and was not surprised when he cut her a scathing glance.

"No, I took on the lot of them, but I was outnumbered."

"How many were there?"

"A dozen or so. I managed to break a few noses," he informed her with ill-concealed satisfaction, ". . . before they clouted me over the head. I wish I had killed a few, but I foolishly left my pistol and rifle out of reach."

"Perhaps it was just as well thou didst not have a weapon. Hadst thou shot someone, they surely would have killed thee."

"Perhaps, but it would have been worth it. . . . Fadoul!" he earnestly implored. "Fadoul, can you hear me?"

The old man did not move. His chest barely rose and fell, and as Sadira watched, a shudder wracked his thin frame. The *frangi* gently slapped the old man's face. "Come on, Fadoul . . . wake up. Don't die on me now." He picked up the clawlike brown hand and rubbed it between his hands. "Come on, old fellow."

"I will summon my horse. We can put Fadoul up on her and take him back to the camp of my people." Sadira raised her hand and wiggled her fingers in the silent signal she had taught the mare, and Sherifa trotted over to her and halted in a spray of sand and gravel.

The *frangi's* good eye widened as he spotted the mare. "That's a fine-looking animal," he murmured distractedly.

Sadira only nodded. She had grown accustomed to hearing compliments about Sherifa. As if the mare knew she was being admired, she tossed her head and set the crimson and gold tassels of her halter to jingling. The blue beads entwined among the tassels clacked faintly.

"Sherifa, kneel . . ." The mare obediently buckled at the knees and went down. "We can lay thy friend across the saddle. He is a small man. I can probably lift him by myself if thou art too weak to help. I will take thy servant to the camp and send others back to get thee. 'Tis not far. Thou wilt not have to wait long, but I will leave the water skin with thee anyway."

"No . . . wait a minute." The *frangi* bent down and put his ear to the old man's lips. He straightened, frowning. "I think he's stopped breathing." He placed his palm flat on his friend's chest. "I don't feel his heart beat."

He suddenly grasped the old man by his thin, bony shoulders. "Fadoul! Damn it, man, don't die! You have to fight, do you hear me? Don't give in! Fight, damn you! Fight!"

He began to shake the old man, startling Sherifa who scrambled to her feet and blew alarm through distended nostrils. "Stop it!" Sadira cried. "If he has indeed departed from this life, let him make the journey in peace."

The *frangi* ceased shaking the fragile lifeless body and gently lowered it to the ground. "He's dead," he said in a dull voice. "The bastards killed him." Shakily, he rose, and his face contorted. *"The bastards killed him!* May God strike them dead for their wickedness and greed!"

To curse someone was a terrible thing, and Sadira stared at the *frangi* in surprise. Her people would not have counted the life of a skinny old man so valuable. It must have been Fadoul's fate to die today; it must have been the will of Allah. On the desert, death was a constant companion, ever ready to claim the old and weak. One grew to expect it.

"This Fadoul was thy friend?"

"I barely knew the man! But he didn't deserve to die at the hands of those scoundrels. I should have protected him. Should have shot and killed the leader of the caravan before he had a chance to harm Fadoul or myself."

"I do not understand." Sadira could not comprehend the *frangi's* anger and grief. "Who was Fadoul to thee?"

"My servant! My guide. We weren't yet the best of friends, but given the chance, we might have been."

Sadira wrestled with confusion. Masters rarely showed grief over the loss of a servant or slave—unless it was a particularly valuable one. Fadoul was old and nearly useless, well past his prime. He would not have brought much in a slave market, and few people would wish to hire him as a servant. Besides, it was the duty of the servant to protect the master. As a guide, Fadoul had failed his master by leading him into danger. The *frangi* ought to have been upset about *that;* he had lost all his worldly goods and very nearly his life because of his servant's ineptness.

"His death is the will of Allah," Sadira patiently repeated. "It was his time to die. I am sorry for thy loss, but there is no use grieving over him. . . . Come, I will take thee to my father's camp." She plucked her *aba* from the dead man's body and handed it to the *frangi.* "Here . . . wrap thyself in this. Then my mare will carry us both."

"He must be buried." The *frangi* carelessly flung the

cloak about his massive shoulders. "I will bury him first, before I go anywhere."

"Didst thou think I meant for the jackals to have him? My father will send others to see to the task. Thou art not fit to do it. If thou canst, get up on my mare. Here, I will have her kneel for thee. . . ."

"That's not necessary." The *frangi* grabbed hold of Sherifa's halter and made as if to mount her. He managed to get one foot in the stirrup, but lacked the strength to swing his leg over the mare's back.

Sadira had to give him a boost—which meant she had to touch him. And she could not forget that he was naked beneath the thin soft wool of her *aba*. Her heart pounded so loudly she feared he might hear it, and as soon as she could, she removed her hands from his body. She was about to swing up behind him, when he clutched her shoulder and stopped her. "In front. Ride in front of me."

He was white-faced and gritting his teeth in pain. She did not argue, but easily swung up and settled herself in the narrow space at the front of the saddle, between his sturdy thighs. This was a contact she had not anticipated, and she stiffened in shock and embarrassment. He pulled her back against him, and the arm that slid around her waist did not belong to a weak and injured man; it was firm and strong. Yet she could feel him trembling slightly against her back. Perhaps it was only the support of her body he sought to steady himself.

"Forgive me for being so gruff," he murmured as she signaled Sherifa to head in the direction of the camp. "I am glad you came along when you did. Thank you for helping me."

"I only did my duty." She attempted to sit up straighter,

for her body and his were pressed together much too intimately.

"I would not have lasted long alone out here. You saved my life. What are you doing here? Where do you come from? You look English or American, but you have an accent and speak with thees and thous, so you can't be a Westerner."

"Thou art right. I am no *frangi*. I am Bedouin. I belong to the *Ruala,* a tribe of the *Anazah,* and we go wherever we wish on the desert. 'Tis our home."

She could feel him stiffen. "Your tribe is the one I came to the desert to find."

"Then thou hast found it. My father is Emir Akbar el-Karim, the Sheik of Sheiks of the *Ruala.* I am taking thee to him."

"But you don't look like a Bedouin! Your eyes are green, and you have a streak of blond in your hair. I thought all Bedouin were dark. And I never dreamed that Bedouin women were taught English."

He ought never to have had the opportunity to notice her unusual coloring or to have discovered that she spoke English. She did not intend to explain how or why she looked as she did or had learned the language. It was none of his business. Besides, some tribes of Bedouin had lighter coloring; if he stayed in the desert long enough, he would probably meet them one day.

"Thou dost not look like a *frangi,*" she countered. "Except for thy blue eyes. Why hast thou come here?"

"To buy horses. Starting with yours. What I've seen of her so far, with only one eye, I like. She's exactly what I came here to purchase."

"Then thou wilt be disappointed. Sherifa is not for sale, *Frangi.*"

"My name is Travis. Travis Colin Keene. What's yours?"

"Sadira."

"Sadira . . ." He said it softly with a peculiar emphasis that caused a stirring in the pit of her belly. She had never heard her name spoken that way before. "A beautiful name for a beautiful woman."

A hot flush crept up her neck. She did not understand her physical responses to this man—an *injured* man, a *frangi*—and she was greatly dismayed by them. She could think of no reply.

"Are you married, Sadira? No, you're too young. But perhaps you're engaged. Or would you say betrothed? Promised . . . already committed to some lucky young man. Yes, you're probably engaged. A girl who looks like you couldn't possibly be unattached. Men must be swarming around you like bees to honey. Beautiful women always have lots of admirers—lots of hearts they can break."

From his odd rambling, Sadira thought he must be feverish. His comments bordered on being offensive, and she sought to change the subject. "Where didst thou find Fadoul?"

"In a bazaar. But I did not find him; he found me. Almost the same way you did—flat on my ass. Except I still had my clothes. So beware of aiding strangers, my beautiful Sadira. Poor Fadoul paid a terrible price for rescuing me from thieves in a bazaar in Aleppo. Who knows what price *you* might have to pay for saving my neck out here in the desert?"

Sadira did not want him to think she had any personal reasons for rescuing him. "Allah smiles upon those who aid men in need, and my people always offer hospitality to strangers." She forebore to add that when a Bedouin saved a person's life he or she became responsible for him.

"Allah . . . the Muslim god. An interfering fellow, isn't he? If he willed Fadoul's death today, he must have willed that you and I should meet. What do you suppose good old Allah has in mind for us?"

Sadira could not decide if the *frangi* meant to blaspheme or was merely teasing in some mysterious *frangi* fashion. No one she knew would speak so disrespectfully of Allah. His fever must be doing the talking. She could be sure of only one thing: Allah did not intend for her to sell Sherifa to this man—nor did He want her to become too friendly with him. The *frangi* was an unbeliever, an infidel—*and* a virile man.

"Allah has nothing in mind for us, *Frangi*. I will take thee to my father. His servants will tend thine injuries. When thou art better thou wilt return to Aleppo—and eventually to thine own people."

"Not without a few good horses like the one we're riding." His tone had a hard edge. "I came here for horses, and I'm not leaving without them. Tell that to your Allah. . . . No, don't. I'm sorry. Being robbed and beaten twice in the short time since I arrived in your country has made me grouchy. I don't mean to vent my anger on you, who's shown me nothing but kindness. But if I ever run across the men who killed Fadoul . . ."

She knew what he was thinking. She expected nothing less of him than to want revenge; men always wanted revenge. It was their reason for living. Bedouin males spent half their lives avenging real and imagined insults. One of her duties was to send them off to righteous battle with a prayer and a flourish. She sighed, hoping her father would not decide to make this man's fight his own. It all depended upon who was responsible. If *Shammar* had done it, her father would view the attack as an excuse for all-out war.

It could just as well have been *Anazah*. They, too, had tiny splinter groups who disobeyed Muslim precepts and raided, robbed, and murdered the unwary. This poor *frangi* had encountered the worst of her people before he had discovered the best. She wanted to change his opinion of the Bedouin, especially the *Ruala* . . . but that did not mean she would sell valuable horses to him. No matter how masculine or charming he proved to be, or how many apologies he offered, he could not have Sherifa—or any other horse of true quality.

Five

Travis felt terrible, muddle-headed and aching, but he was nonetheless acutely aware of the young woman who sat in front of him on the lovely chestnut mare. He had to brace himself against her in the saddle to keep from toppling over—and he could not help noticing her slender, curvaceous body. Combined with her stunning face, hair, and eyes, her lush figure seemed too good to be true. Even clad in a shapeless brown robe with a simple black, tan, and white border, she was incredibly beautiful—or else his one-eyed vision could not be trusted.

She resembled some exquisite apparition, unreal and improbable, but she *felt* real, all feminine hills, valleys, and softness. Her unique scent contributed to her allure; it was tantalizingly familiar, yet eastern and mysterious—an elusive musk that teased his senses with its suggestion of innocence and sensuality. He was certain he knew the scent, but he could not place it.

As for the girl herself, he could not help wondering who she really was and why she wouldn't answer his questions. He doubted she was actually Bedouin—and *Ruala,* no less! Disoriented and in pain, he could not solve the riddle of her identity . . . nor could he forgive himself for Fadoul's death. It was all his fault; he ought not to have been so careless about his pistol and rifle. He should have seen what was coming and taken precautions. Instead, he had allowed himself to be caught unawares. That was what rankled the most: he had suspected treachery and done nothing to avert it . . . and poor Fadoul had suffered the consequences.

His beautiful, mysterious rescuer did not appear too upset over the death of the old man—but then she had not known him and had perhaps grown accustomed to treachery upon the desert. Considering his experiences so far, he dare not trust even *her*. He had nothing left to steal, but he wouldn't put it past some wily old Bedouin to hold him up for ransom.

You've got yourself in a fine mess, Travis. No weapons, food, money . . . clothing. How in hell are you going to buy horses from these people when you're now dependent upon them for your very survival?

Swept with a new wave of dizziness, Travis clung to the slim figure in front of him and concentrated upon remaining upright. The young woman did not complain, but her sudden rigidity seeped through his consciousness. She did not like his touching her; closeness made her uncomfortable. Well, he couldn't help it. He either had to hang on to her or fall off the horse. Her scent filled his head like a breath of life-giving air. Lavender! That was what she smelled like—lavender, only this was not a dusty dead lavender he remembered from his boyhood, when his mother had tucked sweet-smelling, lacy little sacks among her linens; this was a fresh, delicate, but heady thing that made his head spin.

He wondered that he could smell it at all when his nose hurt so badly. It was probably broken. How did one fix a broken nose? Or didn't one? If his face was ruined, he wouldn't have to worry about women throwing themselves at his feet anymore—especially Elizabeth. Not that she had ever thrown herself at his feet. Not that it mattered to him if he ever saw her again. He had a sudden sense of freedom and was abruptly glad to be alive and breathing. He had been sure he was going to be killed . . . but he hadn't been. Through some miracle, he still lived. He couldn't think about the rest. Somehow it would all work out.

He must have dozed slumped against Sadira, for he dreamed that she was calling him. *"Frangi . . . Frangi,* wake up."

He could not remember where he was, until she began thumping his leg with a small clenched fist. "Yes," he mumbled. "Yes, I'm awake."

He tried to open his eyes, but one was too swollen, the other too gritty. He unclamped his hands from around her waist and wiped the gritty eye—squinting to see better. Ahead of them on the flat plain stood—thousands?—of long, low-to-the-ground black tents. Surrounding the tents, spread out in every direction were—hundreds of thousands?—of animals. No, there couldn't be that many, but there were more than he had ever seen gathered together in one place. Creating a great volume of noise and confusion, horses, camels, sheep, and goats milled about huge glassy pools of water shining yellow in the sunlight.

Travis blinked in astonishment. Certain he must be hallucinating, he gaped at the huge encampment. A large, earth-colored camel came loping up to them, bawling a welcome. At least, it sounded like a welcome. Travis shook his head to clear it. The mare slowed to a walk, and the camel lowered its head and sniffed at Travis.

"Greetings, Lulu, my friend." The young woman— Sadira—reached out to caress the creature between its long-lashed eyes and to pat its neck. The length of the camel's eyelashes surprised Travis, but then he had never been nose to nose with one before. Fadoul had taken care of the camels, and Travis had paid them little heed—until now. This one could not be ignored. The camel—Lulu—sniffed at him again, then without warning, butted him in the chest with her head.

Travis lost his already precarious balance and tumbled backward. As he hit the ground with a thud, he heard Sadira scolding the creature. "Lulu, that is no way to behave! Oh, thou art a naughty girl!" She lapsed into Arabic and continued to berate the beast.

The fall jarred every bone in Travis's already aching body. Clutching the cloak around himself to preserve his modesty, he rolled onto his side and confronted the camel's feet only a handspan from his head. Those feet could do real damage; if the animal kicked him, the blow would finish him off. He wasted no time struggling to his feet. As soon as he was upright, the camel repeated her performance, butting him and knocking him over, then making a gurgling sound deep in her throat. Adding insult to injury, she spewed something green and slimy down the front of him.

"Lulu, be gone!" Sadira made a gesture of dismissal, and the camel whined and turned away—looking woebegone and chagrined. Had someone told Travis that camels could express sorrow and apology, he would not have believed it, but this one had shown an entire array of emotions, including, if he wasn't mistaken, contempt and jealousy. She obviously hated him and loved Sadira. And was devastated to be banished from the presence of her mistress.

"Art thou hurt?" Sadira turned Sherifa on her haunches to face him.

"Not worse than I was already. What's a few more bruises? As for this green stuff, it's charming—adds the finishing touch to my already fashionable wardrobe. Don't you agree?"

His sarcasm earned a faint smile from Sadira. Travis wasn't prepared for the horse's reaction, however. As he wiped away the green slime with the edge of Sadira's cloak, Sherifa opened her mouth and executed the closest thing to a horse laugh he had ever seen. "Damn it, I think your mare's enjoying this!"

Sadira's lips twitched with suppressed laughter. "Thou art probably right. Neither Lulu nor Sherifa care much for strangers. I am sorry, *Frangi*. Please forgive their bad manners."

"My name is Travis," Travis reminded her. "I dislike being called *Frangi.*"

"Travis. That is a strange name. I have not heard it before. What is its meaning?"

"I don't know its meaning. Must all names have meaning?"

"Our names do."

"Just call me Travis."

"As thou wish, Travis. . . ." Looking past him, her eyes lit with recognition and welcome. "Ah, here is someone with a mule thou may use for the rest of the ride to my father's tent. This is Hamid, and he will help thee mount while I ride ahead and inform my father of thy arrival."

She conversed in Arabic with a man coming toward them leading a mule, and the man scowled at Travis, but nodded, as if approving Sadira's plan with great reluctance. No sooner had she finished speaking with the fellow she had introduced as Hamid when she pivoted her splendid mare as if she meant to leave him and ride away immediately.

"Wait!" Travis cried. "I can't speak Arabic. Don't go off and abandon me to a man who doesn't speak English."

But Sadira had already set her mare into a rocking canter. Without a backward glance, she disappeared into the maze of tents and animals. Travis sighed and grimly studied the growing crowd of people spilling out of their homes to gawk at him. The men wore typical desert garb—long flowing robes or loose tunics over voluminous trousers, with headcloths or turbans on their heads. Their feet were either bare or strapped into sturdy sandals; only a few wore leather boots.

The women were not clad much differently; they, too, wore concealing robes and headcloths or veils. Many had their faces covered by a type of cloth with eye holes that Travis already knew was called a *burqa*. Some of the bare-faced women drew their veils across their faces as they saw him looking at them. He felt indecently exposed among these modestly dressed people and clutched Sadira's cloak more tightly about him.

The man called Hamid motioned to his mule and assisted Travis in climbing aboard. The mule had no saddle and like Bedouin horses, only a plain rope halter. Travis expected Hamid to continue leading the mule, but instead, the wiry young man leapt up behind Travis and kicked the mule into a trot. Travis had ridden bareback before, but was in no condition to endure a bumpy ride at the moment. He nearly fell off. Only Hamid's strong, surprisingly muscular arms about his waist kept him upright on the mule's ridged and bony back.

By the time they arrived at a long tent strung out across the plain and conveniently located in a choice spot near a water hole, Travis was fighting nausea and the urge to be sick to his stomach. He attempted to dismount gracefully, with some degree of finesse, but only succeeded in falling flat on his face. When he tried to rise, he found that his strength had finally deserted him. His stomach churned, and he fought the urge to vomit.

By sheer dint of willpower, he managed to grab hold of the mule's foreleg and pull himself upward. The animal sidled away from him. Unable to hang on, Travis sprawled once more on the rocky ground. This time, he struck his head on a rock as big as a man's fist. Sparks danced before his eyes, and a roaring began in his ears. Deciding that it was futile and undignified to keep resisting oblivion, he actually welcomed the blackness that descended like a curtain on a scene from a very bad play.

"He has come to buy horses, Father, that is all I know," Sadira explained to Akbar in his private quarters.

Her father lounged on a pile of cushions and thoughtfully stroked his silver-streaked beard as he leaned over a tray of sweetmeats. At his side knelt Alima, her plain round face aglow with the pleasure of serving her beloved husband and having him all to herself for a few precious moments. Sadira had found the two together sharing conversation and laughter, which pleased her immensely. More and more as he grew older, Akbar turned to Alima for companionship, bypassing his younger, more beautiful wives. A warm affection shimmered between the two that no amount of kohl or perfume worn by the haughty Jaleel could threaten. Akbar preferred the company of his barren wife to that of the woman who had borne him his son and successor.

Jaleel would probably have appealed to her son to intercede with Akbar to show her more favor—but Nuri had departed on a long journey. Fulfilling the dream of every true Muslim, he was making a pilgrimage to Mecca. No one knew when or even *if* he would return. Such journeys were fraught with danger and hardship, yet Nuri had ignored his father's advice that he ought to delay at least until one of his two wives had conceived a suitable heir. Nuri chafed at Akbar's rule and often disagreed with him. The young man believed that Akbar should step aside and relinquish the reins of power, but Akbar was still strong and healthy. Despite his advancing years, he possessed a younger man's ambition and zest for life. Nuri, unfortunately, was immature, impetuous, and lacking in wisdom.

Sadira could only hope that the religious aspects of the pilgrimage would make Nuri a better man. In the meantime, Akbar had Alima to console him for the loss of his beloved son's company. Only Alima could banish the emir's occasional brooding silences—and the love between Akbar and his barren first wife never failed to warm Sadira's heart and make her long for something similar in her own life.

"So he has come to buy horses," Akbar repeated after a long pause. "And he already knows that thou canst speak English."

"Yes, Father. I could not keep it a secret when he needed help so badly."

"Praise be to Allah." Akbar sighed. "Perhaps it is just as well, because thou wilt have to act as translator while he is here. I had to send Rashid to Sherif Awad who had need of his services. I did not want to let him go, but I could not refuse the request. Sherif Awad is my friend."

"Of course, Father. I understand. I will be happy to serve as translator. It will give me more time to judge the *frangi's* character. I know of one or two old horses we might allow him to purchase—but only if he is worthy."

"Tell me who thou art considering."

"Farasat for one . . ."

Akbar grinned. "A good choice. Farasat is blind in one eye and lame more often than not. . . . What irony that her name is Farasat, which means she of the keen eye! She has also failed to conceive for the last two years." Delighted with her choice, Akbar burst out laughing, and Alima echoed the laugh with a small, discreet smile. When Akbar was happy, *she* was happy.

"Yes, I suppose we might sell him Farasat," Akbar chortled. "But only if he is worthy."

Sadira instantly sobered. "For all her faults, Farasat is a sweet-tempered creature with excellent bloodlines. She may yet conceive, and her foal would be most valuable. The *frangi* will be fortunate indeed if I consent to part with her."

"Yes, yes, Sadira. We all know of thy great reluctance to part with horses. . . . That is why thou art Keeper of the Mares. No other maiden would care so much for even the blind and the lame." Akbar turned to Alima and squeezed her hand. "Feed me another sweetmeat, my dove. I need strength to deal with this interloper who probably wishes to steal all I own."

"He has lost all *he* owns, Father," Sadira reminded him. "He and his servant lay naked beneath the sun."

"Naked! And thou witnessed him unclothed?"

"I . . . I looked the other way as I was covering him."

"Thou hast better have done so," Akbar growled, all levity gone. "A woman is forbidden to look upon any man's nakedness save her husband's. Thou art and always will be a virgin. As Keeper of the Mares, thou must remain pure of heart."

"I was extremely careful, Father. I gave the *frangi* my headcloth and his servant my cloak. When the servant died, the *frangi* took the cloak as well."

"Then thou hast nothing to fear regarding thy behavior. It was proper. I am not displeased with thy conduct, Daughter. Yet I do worry when thou art riding alone—as this incident demonstrates, there is good reason for worry."

Anxious to keep Akbar from forbidding her the one great pleasure of her life, Sadira hastened to reassure him that she was perfectly safe. "I have been riding out alone for years, Father, and no harm has come to me. If someone did seek to harm me, Sherifa would easily carry me to safety. Our gallops in the desert are one reason she is so fit and fast. If I am forbidden to do this, she will lose her speed, and it will not be there when I most need it."

Sadira was about to offer further arguments when Hamid appeared in the entranceway to her father's quarters. *"As salám ' alaikum!"* Hamid greeted Akbar. *Peace be with thee, my friend.*

Hamid's intense dark eyes found Sadira, and in them, she read his thwarted longing. After all these years—even after marriage and several children—Hamid still coveted her.

"Alaikum as salám!" The same to thee. "Hast thou brought the *frangi?"*

"Yes, but he is unconscious. What shall I do with him?"

Akbar's silver-shot brows drew together as he considered the problem. "He was attacked and injured upon our lands—lands I supposedly control. Therefore he is my responsibility. Bring him into my quarters and I myself—and my wives—will care for him until he recovers. Instead of the customary three days of hospitality, he may remain here as long as he wishes. It is the least I can do to repay him for my failure to keep him safe upon my lands."

Hamid respectfully bowed. "Yes, Akbar. I guessed that would be thine answer, oh Great and Generous One. I myself am of the opinion he ought to be tossed to the jackals. He is only a *frangi* after all, my lord, not a believer."

"Young men sometimes forget the teachings of Muhammad," Akbar scolded. "My son Nuri would think as thou dost—he is only this or that, not *Ruala,* and therefore unworthy of our concern. But I say to thee, he is our responsibility, our brother, and it is our duty to minister to him."

"Yes, my lord." After another quick bow, Hamid left the tent and returned several moments later in company with another man. Between them they carried the inert figure of the *frangi.*

Alima quickly scrambled to her feet and prepared a place on the cushions for him. "Put him here," she directed. "Sadira, go and fetch a water skin, a basin, and some cloths. We will bathe him first, then wrap him in a fresh robe."

Akbar watched with interest. "Thou wilt bathe him? Should not Hamid or a servant see to that?"

"One cannot entrust servants with so important a task. If thou art worried, my dearest husband, thou canst sit and watch. Thy presence alone will be sufficient to protect our honor. Sadira can avert her eyes when it becomes necessary, and thou canst bathe certain parts thyself, if thou insists. It cannot be wrong for us to look upon him when he is unconscious, and thou art here."

"True," Akbar conceded, settling back on the cushions. "I *will* watch, but I will not do the task myself. That is going too far. . . . He is very tall, is he not?"

And well formed, Sadira thought as she went to fetch the required items. Thinking of how well Alima and her father got along together and resolved their differences by discussing them, she smiled to herself. Alima was not afraid to stand up to Akbar, but she also knew when to practice diplomacy. From the way they spoke to each other, one might almost think they were equals. . . . Was such a thing possible between men and women? With Rashid gone, she was going to have to do a great deal of talking to the tall, well-formed *frangi,* and she did not know how to go about it. Usually, she just listened or translated; rarely did she carry on an actual conversation, such as she had already been doing with the stranger.

By the time she returned with all that was needed to bathe the *frangi,* Alima and Akbar were alone with him in the tent. Alima had the *frangi* nearly clean already. Impatient to begin, she had dipped a corner of her robe in a cup of water and begun washing his face.

"His eyes are blue," she noted, nodding to Sadira. "Quite a lovely color—like the winter sky."

Sadira set down her cloths, water skin, basin, and a flask of ointment used to treat wounds. She knelt down beside Alima. "He has not yet awakened? I do not understand it. He was conscious enough to sit a horse for the ride to camp."

"Perhaps it was stubbornness that kept him going so long." Alima wiped away the last vestiges of blood and grime from the man's features to reveal a degree of handsomeness that even bruises and swelling could not hide. "When he knew he had arrived where he would soon receive help, his strength gave out. . . . See here? He has a stubborn jaw. And these lines on either side of his mouth indicate great determination."

Akbar chuckled. "What wouldst thou say if thou wert cleaning *my* face, Alima? What character traits wouldst thou mark?"

"Well, my lord, I would say that thou art fierce in anger and loyalty, gentle in love, and generous even to thine enemies." Alima gave Akbar a radiant smile. "It is all there in thy face, if one knows where to look for it."

Gazing down at the *frangi* and studying his face for more clues to his character, Sadira felt a strange flutter in her lower abdomen. She could not tell much from the *frangi*'s one good eye—except that he had long dark lashes any woman would envy. His brow and nose hinted of nobility—no matter that his nose was swollen and might be broken. His upper lip was also puffy, the entire side of his face enlarged, and she wondered just how handsome he had been before his beating. No amount of battering could hide the fact that his face had an arresting quality; she could scarcely bring herself to glance away from it.

Alima was slowly working her way down the *frangi*'s body. "Oil, Sadira. We will be needing oil. Thou knowest where to find it in my quarters, dost thou not?"

"Yes, Alima." Sadira rose and went to fetch the oil. By the time she returned this time, Alima was working on the lower legs of the *frangi*. She had finished washing everything between neck and knee and draped several robes across the *frangi*'s body. Undoubtedly, her speed was a deliberate effort to prevent Sadira from seeing more than Akbar deemed proper.

"Good, good," Alima murmured, taking the oil. "Now we shall need coffee. Plenty of steaming hot coffee to restore his strength."

"I will summon old Samir," Sadira offered. "No other servant in camp can make coffee as well as he can."

"I could use some coffee, too." Akbar's hawkish face wore a petulant look. "Alima, let Sadira finish. I am growing lonesome for thy company."

"Yes, my love."

Alima glanced up from her work with a weary smile for Akbar. It was not overly warm in the tent, but perspiration had beaded along her upper lip. Sadira thought the older woman looked tired; her skin was rather sallow, and a pinched look hovered about her mouth. A little prickle of alarm raced down Sadira's back. Lately, Alima was always weary. The simplest tasks seemed to drain her strength these days, while in the past, she had always been indefatigable.

"Rest, Alima," she urged. "As soon as I have summoned Samir, I will bathe the feet of the *frangi* and get him into a robe."

"Samir can help thee." Alima dabbed at her damp face with the edge of her veil. "I am not so young anymore, it seems; caring for the *frangi* has quite exhausted me."

"Thou must not allow thyself to become exhausted," Akbar scolded, patting the pillows beside him. "Come and take thine ease, my dove. Samir and Sadira can complete the task of bathing and caring for the *frangi*. Samir!" Akbar shouted. "I know thou art within hearing distance, thou miserable old scorpion! Come at once and do thy duty!"

A small cringing figure scurried into the chamber; it was indeed Samir who must have been spying upon them from behind a curtain all this time. "Yes, Master! Yes, Master!" He threw himself on the rug at Akbar's feet. "Tell me what thou wouldst have me do, and I will gladly do it."

"Help Sadira get the *frangi* into a clean robe and then prepare coffee. I want the man alert enough to answer my questions, so be sure and make the coffee strong and hearty."

"Do I not always make the coffee hearty, Master?" Samir whined. "It will be strong enough to wake a dead man."

"If it is not, thou wilt be a dead man," Akbar snapped. "Or at least as bad off as *he* is."

While Alima reclined on the cushions near Akbar, Samir helped Sadira lift the *frangi* and settle a robe over his head. He efficiently tugged it into place, then turned his attention to the preparation of the coffee. Sadira knelt and picked up the *frangi*'s foot in both hands. His flesh was warm and firm, his soles hard and slightly callused. It occurred to her that his toes were as masculine as the rest of him. She began to wash his foot very carefully, dragging the cloth Alima had been using between each of the *frangi*'s toes. When she had finished, she realized she had no towel to dry him. It seemed the most natural thing in the world to take a length of her heavy hair and wipe away the glistening droplets. Bedouin women sometimes dried their babies thusly, and no one counted it strange or improper.

She glanced up suddenly to find one slitted blue eye intently watching her. "You do me an honor I do not deserve," the *frangi* said in a low, quiet voice. "Your hair is too beautiful to be used to dry my ugly feet."

She drew back with a jerk, stunned by the ferocity of her feelings as the blood rushed to her cheeks, and her heart hammered erratically.

"Ah, the *frangi* has awakened," Akbar boomed. "What did he say, Daughter?"

Sadira gulped a lungful of air and struggled to find her voice. "He said . . . he said that I do him an honor he does not deserve."

She did not want to repeat the rest of what he had said— nor did she believe it. Her hair with its alien gold streak was *not* beautiful. His feet, on the other hand, *were*. Touching and handling him so intimately had given her a guilty pleasure, and she nervously released his foot as shame and embarrassment poured through her.

"He is right. Now that he has recovered consciousness, there is no need for thee to continue thy ministrations. Move back and veil thyself, Daughter. 'Tis time I ask this *frangi* some questions."

"Yes, Father."

Sadira hurried to obey. After she had hidden her hair beneath a veil and drawn its lower half across her face, she could still feel the *frangi*'s one good eye on her. His gaze seared her skin through the layer of fabric concealing her features. She had the unnerving sensation that she had been naked before *him* and not the other way around. Merciful Allah! What was wrong with her? One look from this man, and all sorts of dangerous, forbidden images rose in her mind. Many men had looked at her and she at them, but *never* had she felt like this before!

"Now, *Frangi*," her father said. "Tell me who did this to thee. . . . Sadira, translate."

With a shaky voice, she complied.

Six

Travis answered the questions he was asked with as little detail as possible. Hurting as much as he did, he found it difficult to concentrate on anything or anyone but Sadira. She alone eased his pain and gave him something to focus upon—she was so beautiful! Her eyes above the rim of her veil were as green as Kentucky bluegrass and shone with a brilliancy that reminded him of emeralds. They held secrets he could not fathom, sorrow he could not understand.

She possessed the same grace and suppleness as a blade of grass rippling in the wind, but her posture proclaimed a deep sadness—as if she stood apart from her surroundings and did not actually belong to them. Travis examined the tent, its luxurious furnishings, the presence of its other occupants—especially noting the authority of the older man, her father, with his hawkish face and eagle eyes—but all he really wanted to do was watch Sadira and ponder the mystery of her unhappiness. It compounded the mystery of who she was and how she had come to know English. He wanted to make her smile, to laugh, to abandon her tense reserve. She was so serious! Too serious. For one so young and lovely, she seemed to be carrying the weight of the world upon her slender shoulders.

"Dost thou remember nothing more, *Frangi*—I mean, Travis?" she probed in her petal-smooth voice.

He tried to think of what else he could tell her besides what he had already explained, but the effort only increased the acute throbbing in his head. "That's it. There's nothing more."

Sadira's father said something, his tone excited and angry. Travis wished he understood more Arabic. He had been trying to learn, but had not mastered more than a few simple words and phrases. "What is he saying?" he asked Sadira.

"My father thinks that the thieves and murderers must have been *Shammar* trespassing upon our lands. If they were *Ruala*—from our tribe—they would already have come here and found us. They would not have attacked and robbed thee, then fled. They would especially not have done so without my father's permission, which they know he would never have given. Thou hast said they were driving a herd of camels and journeying to meet with their kinfolk. There must have been some other detail thou canst recall—some distinctive thing that set them apart."

Travis wracked his brain and did recall something else. "Their leader had a fresh scar cutting across his mouth. It had ruined his smile. Not that he smiled much. Fadoul remarked upon the irony that he was called Gamalat, meaning Beautiful One, for the scar had rendered him no longer beautiful."

"Gamalat. . . . A common enough name. There are many among the Bedouin known as Gamalat, but none bearing such a scar. At least, none that I know."

Sadira's hawk-faced father erupted into a tirade which gave Travis the opportunity to lie still, momentarily close his eyes, and try to recoup his waning strength. The servant bent over him, offering fragrant coffee. When the man held the cup to his lips and lifted his head so he could drink, he gratefully gulped it down. He wished it were Sadira cradling his head against her soft bosom and assisting him. After he had drained the cup, he felt a little better—strong enough to again request a translation.

"My father vows to avenge the insult done to thee and to him. Tomorrow, he will ride out with his men to find this Gamalat, slay him, and recover all thou hast lost and more."

A jolt of alarm and protest shattered Travis's budding sense of well-being. He wanted Gamalat punished, but sudden visions of the bloodbath that might befall anyone unfortunate enough to be found by the sheik, scar or no scar, gave him pause. "Tell your father he must wait until I am strong enough to ride with him. This is *my* battle, not his. I won't stand for another man doing my fighting for me. I claim the right to settle my own disputes. Wouldn't he feel the same were he in my place?"

Sadira's eyes held a spark of admiration, but she was also frowning, as if she both approved and disapproved of his sentiments. She spoke at length with her father, and they conversed heatedly for several moments before she turned back to Travis.

"Akbar wishes thee to know that he relishes this opportunity to conduct a raid against a rival tribe who insulted not only thee but him, since they attacked thee upon *his* lands. It is a matter of honor that he protect and defend all travelers through *Ruala* territory, and honor means more to him than life itself. However, if thou art certain that thou wilt be recovered enough to ride within a few days' time, he will wait until thou canst accompany him. If not, he will go tomorrow, while the trail is still fresh."

"It will still be fresh three or four days from now. They are herding camels, and some are riding horses, and the animals will have to stop and graze. They won't be going fast because they think I'm dead or soon will be."

Sadira's look of admiration increased. "Thou art right. Besides, if they *are Shammar,* we can easily guess which direction and route they will be traveling. We know where the *Shammar* can usually be found at this time of year, just as they know where we normally encamp."

"Then it's settled." Travis lowered his throbbing head to the cushions again. "Give me a little time, and I'll be ready to go after those bastards. No one will be able to stop me."

"I will tell my father thou wilt need at least a week. That will perhaps give the robbers the opportunity to escape altogether."

"A week!" Travis searched her veiled face and saw that she hoped there would *be* no retribution. No bloodbath. Her father wanted it but she did not.

She met his gaze defiantly. "When my father finds them, there will be death and the shedding of blood. I have seen enough violence. I do not need to see more."

"Why should you have to see anything? You can stay here and avoid the whole confrontation."

She shook her head. "No, I cannot. I will have to accompany thee and exhort the men to victory. It is my duty."

Her duty? She did not elaborate, and Travis was suddenly too weary to pursue the matter. As he had already discovered, she would not volunteer a single shred of information, and he could hardly keep his eyes open. Another woman's voice intruded. It belonged to the female seated on the cushions beside Sadira's father. Could she be Sadira's mother? No green eyes or blond hair there. . . . He heard Akbar himself speaking, but no longer cared what anyone was saying.

He had to sleep—to rest and recover. There would be

time enough later to sort it all out. He needed time to make his peace with the idea of actually riding out with the intention of killing Gamalat. He had killed during the war, but this was different, a personal matter. He had never sought vengeance against another human being. . . . But then he had never before been beaten, robbed, stripped naked, and left to die either. He had never witnessed another man's death from such senseless abuse. He owed it to Fadoul to punish his murderers in this lawless land where governmental authorities were too far away to be of any use . . . and despite what Sadira thought, he meant to pay that debt. *His* honor demanded it.

Sadira avoided her father's tent for the next two days. She knew that Travis needed rest, food, and sleep, and that Samir and Alima would take good care of him. Her presence was unnecessary. She need not endure his disturbing company until he recovered enough to require a translator. She herself desired the opportunity to sort through the emotions he aroused in her and to erect a defense against them. She could not remember being so intensely and physically aware of a man—not even Hamid, whose hungry gaze followed her wherever she went. She supposed it was because she felt no answering hunger for Hamid, but the *frangi* was a different matter entirely.

Travis made her acutely conscious of her femininity. For the first time in her life, she wondered how she appeared to others. Found herself dreamily combing out her hair, considering what garments she might wear to enhance rather than conceal her womanhood, and taking more care with her daily ablutions. The burgeoning water pools made cleanliness easier than at any other time of year, and she could indulge in washing and scenting herself as she rarely could at other seasons.

Yet she did all this with the guilty knowledge that she ought not to be thinking about such things, much less worrying about them. Travis was forbidden to her—as much or more so than any man of her tribe and people. Aside from his long-lashed blue eyes and well-proportioned body, he could scarcely be accounted attractive, not with his bruises and swollen features . . . so why did she find him so? Why did she awaken on a cold night all flushed and feverish, knowing she had been dreaming of him but unable to remember those dreams?

She consoled herself with the thought that if she were going to be tempted and tormented, it was better to harbor such feelings for a man who would eventually be leaving the *Ruala* than to feel them for someone such as Hamid whom she would have to face everyday for the rest of her life. On the morning of the third day after she had found Travis on the open desert, she forced herself to return to her father's tent. Courtesy dictated that she at least inquire after Travis's well-being and see if he needed anything not already being provided. To her surprise, her father's quarters were empty, and neither Akbar nor Travis was anywhere in sight.

She quickly passed through to Alima's chamber and discovered her dear friend, pale and dreary-eyed, lying upon her cushions. "Alima, what is it? What is wrong with thee?"

Alima hastily sat up. " 'Tis nothing, my dearest child. I but thought to rest a moment. I fear that something I ate did not agree with me, and my body is protesting."

"Are thou positive that is all it is—indigestion? Thou dost not look well. Art thou in pain?"

Alima waved a hand dismissively. "No, no . . . do not

concern thyself. I am perfectly fine. 'Tis only that I have been spending so much time lately with thy beloved father. He keeps later hours than those to which I am accustomed, leaving me much fatigued. But it is a fatigue I welcome," she added with a wan smile.

"But where is my father? And where is the *frangi?*"

"Thy father has gone out riding. I presumed the *frangi* was still sleeping on his cushions."

"He is not in the tent, Alima. I must go and search for him. Who knows what trouble he will get into, unable to understand our language or explain himself to others? Samir never should have left him alone. Where is that worthless servant anyway?"

Alima shrugged. "Thou knowest Samir. He disappears whenever possible. If anyone is to blame, I am. I should have watched over the *frangi* better. He is getting stronger each day, but he is still not ready to explore the camp or remain on his feet for long."

"Do not worry, Alima. I will find him. Stay here and rest." Sadira pushed her friend back down onto the cushions. "I will also speak to my father about keeping thee up so late."

"Thou must not!" Alima protested. "I treasure every moment I spend with thy father. Besides, as I told thee, this ailment is a minor one—nothing serious. I promise I shall soon be well again."

"I hope so, dear Alima. I could not bear it if anything happened to thee."

Sadira gently kissed Alima's cheek, then headed back through the tent the way she had come. After a lengthy search and questioning several onlookers, she found Travis where she least expected him to be—among the horses, making friends with Sherifa. He had managed to walk out on the windswept plain away from the tents and stood in the center of the grazing herd of mares. Scratching Sherifa beneath her blowing red mane, he seemed oblivious to all else—until he saw her.

He grinned widely, like a little boy caught stealing dates, and she was taken aback by the change in him. The swelling of his face had receded, and both eyes were open. His temple was still bandaged, but a healthy color had returned to his features, and he was every bit as handsome as she had feared. In the golden morning sunlight, his black hair gleamed like the wing of one of the many species of birds who flocked over the desert when it bloomed.

"I had to see if your mare was really as fine as I thought she was when first I saw her," he greeted her. The breeze flattened his white robe against his body, outlining the lithe physique she had been trying so hard to forget.

"And is she?" Sadira coolly inquired, only then remembering that she ought to have worn her veil this morning and drawn it discreetly across her face. Once again, she was bareheaded before him, her hair streaming loose in the gentle zephyr blowing off the desert. If he saw her, Akbar would be displeased.

He nodded. "She's even better than I thought. You *must* let me buy her."

"I have told thee before; she is not for sale. Thou couldst not afford to purchase her anyway. What would thou use for coin or barter, since all thou hast was stolen?"

"I left a portion of my money in Aleppo with the British Consul. And I can obtain more from home though it will take a while before it arrives. I don't care. I will do whatever is necessary. Your mare is exquisite. Name your price, and I'll find a way to meet it."

Sherifa pranced away from him and stretched her neck

to nuzzle Sadira's hand with her silken nose. Sadira stroked the mare's neck, pleased that her old friend had not been seduced by the caresses of a *frangi*. "I would not sell her for all the money thou possess—nor indeed for all the coins on earth. Her worth to me and to the *Ruala* is beyond calculation. She is our ceremonial mare, even as I am the ceremonial maiden of our tribe, the one who cares for the mares and performs rituals before battle. Neither of us can be bought, sold, married, bred, or given away. We belong to our people, the *Ruala*."

"So that accounts for why you behave so differently from the other women—and are treated differently, too." Travis's dark brows slanted downward. "But lifelong chastity is rather a big sacrifice they're expecting you to make, isn't it? You honestly mean you can *never* marry and the mare can never be bred?"

Sadira ceased looking at him; his blue eyes could see too deeply. Idly, she smoothed Sherifa's forelock to still the slight trembling of her hands. "In many tribes, the position is temporary. *Any* maiden or maiden mare can serve in a ceremonial capacity for a short time—but I have sworn to maintain the position for life. That is my destiny, the will of Allah. Sherifa and I will be maidens until the day we die."

"I've never heard of such a thing!"

"Thou hast heard of it now." She smiled, relieved to have proclaimed her unavailability. Maybe now she could relax in his presence, and he would stop looking at her with such intensity in those blue, blue eyes.

"But . . . that's barbaric! A mare as fine as this one *should* be bred, and a woman like you . . ." He paused.

Unwittingly, she lifted her eyes to meet his glance. Fleecy white clouds sailing overhead momentarily obscured the sun—patterning his handsome face in sunlight and shadow. For a moment, neither spoke. The heat of his gaze consumed her, and she had the sensation of fire flashing down her spine.

"*You* should have a husband," he continued softly, his tone deep and husky. "Otherwise, it's a terrible waste, a sacrifice with no reason or logic."

Another long moment slid by before she could find breath to answer. When she inhaled, the air smelled unbearably sweet and fresh. "To my people—and to me—my sacrifice is reasonable. Few would even consider it a sacrifice. After all, I do not need a husband. I . . . I have the love of my people. And Sherifa. And Lulu . . . and all the rest of the horses and camels. As the Keeper of the Mares, I am beloved by all."

"But not loved by a lover—a very different kind of love, Sadira. Much more satisfying than mere admiration. Surely, you would like to experience it one day."

She shook her head to break the spell of his mesmerizing gaze. "No, I have all I want and need in my life. . . . But thou must see why I cannot sell thee Sherifa. She is my sister. We share the same fate, the same duty. We can never be parted."

He leaned toward her. "I'd consider taking you both. Any man would." Then he seemed to realize what he was saying, and he straightened and moved back a step. "What I mean is. . . . Oh, forget it. I'm not trying to insult or offend you. It's only that your customs are so strange and perplexing. I'm afraid I don't understand."

She could have enlightened him, but she did not want to explain about her mother and how she was atoning for her mother's sin. "Our ways are different from thine, *Frangi*. Thou canst never understand them, so there is no use trying to explain."

"I'm not as stupid as you seem to think. And I'm certainly willing to listen. There are many things I'd like to ask you—so much I'd like to know."

"Perhaps another time," she hedged, noticing that Farasat was among the horses milling about them, vying for attention. "Ah, here is a mare I might consider selling to thee."

She pointed to Farasat whose dusty gray coat made a poor comparison with Sherifa's gleaming red. Farasat sorely needed grooming, but at least today, she wasn't limping. Travis's eyes sought the mare, providing Sadira a welcome respite from his attention. He watched the horse for several moments, and Sadira went up to her and smoothed down her tangled mane. Pleased by the attention, Farasat shoved her nose into Sadira's stomach and whinnied with pleasure as she scratched along her withers.

"What is the mare's name?" Travis finally asked.

"Farasat. It means she of the keen eye."

"A bit of a misnomer, isn't it? Since she's blind on her right side."

His observation startled Sadira who had not expected him to be so observant, especially since Farasat had long ago learned to compensate for her affliction. Only an expert would notice anything wrong with her; the average person would see nothing.

"The defect does not seem to bother her." Sadira tried to keep the defensiveness out of her voice. "Her conformation is excellent. Notice the beauty of her head. She has the typically dished forehead of her line, and she is very intelligent."

Travis approached the mare, placed a hand on her nose, and gently pried open her mouth. He peered at her teeth. "About ten years old, isn't she? How many foals has she dropped?"

"Only two," Sadira reluctantly admitted. "But they were fine babies. Swift and strong."

"So she's not an easy breeder, or she would have had more than two by now. . . . She also favors her left foreleg. My guess is she's chronically lame."

Sadira could feel her cheeks flaming. He had discovered everything that was wrong with the mare—and in a mere matter of moments! Seeing her expression, Travis started to laugh. "Oh, you'll have to do better than that if you want to sell me a horse I can't use! What do you have in a stud colt? Until I saw Sherifa, I was more interested in buying a stallion than a mare. Has Farasat dropped any stud colts?"

"Yes," she said stiffly, much chagrined. "But he is not among these mares. I will have to take thee farther out into the desert to find him and his little band. We keep him separate, allowing him access only to those mares we wish for him to service."

"I would like to see him."

"When thou art well enough to sit a horse again, I will take thee to see him—or my father will. But he is not for sale. And he is not as valuable a horse as Farasat. She is a mare, after all, and I doubt her breeding days are completely over."

"Why do you count the mares more important than the stallions?" Travis rubbed the foreheads of two other mares crowding close to be noticed.

"Because they *are* more important. They possess more stamina, more courage, more heart. They are the ones who give life to others. The horses we ride to war are always mares, because their loyalty is unquestioned. They are not distracted by the mating instinct, as stallions are. When there is a need for quiet, they will be quiet, while a stallion will betray his master's presence by nickering when he scents a ripe mare. Our mares are carefully bred to retain the qualities we treasure; they are all descendants of the five mares Muhammad used to establish the breed."

"Muhammad founded the breed? An interesting tale. I should like to hear more about these five mares. Will you tell me while we return to the tent? Much as I hate to admit it, I feel the sudden need to sit down."

She noticed that he had grown paler in the last few moments, and he was limping as they turned away from the horses and began to walk back toward the encampment. This was his first foray out of the tent, and he had probably overtaxed himself. She thought about taking his arm to steady him but decided against it; there must be no more touching, no more physical contact between them, especially now when he was so much better and stronger, his masculinity almost shouting its presence.

She welcomed the distraction of telling him the legends surrounding the five distinct bloodlines of desert horses. " 'Tis said that Muhammad wished to breed horses that would not falter during the rigor of his many campaigns. He therefore penned up a hundred mares within sight of a sparkling stream and kept them from water for four days. At the end of that time, he freed them, and they all began to run toward the water. When they had nearly reached it, he had his bugler sound the call for battle. Five obeyed and charged back to their masters, while the rest galloped on toward the stream. These five were known ever after as the 'Prophet's Mares' and they founded the five leading families whose bloodlines we maintain to this day."

"Amazing! You can trace all of your horses back to those five animals?"

"We can recite the genealogy of each horse, yes. And

each possesses the characteristics of its line—whether
Kehilan, Seglawi, Abeyan, Hamdani, or *Hadban."*

"Wait a minute," Travis protested. "You're going too fast.
Which line, for example, produced Sherifa?"

"She is a *Seglawi,* characterized by great delicacy and
grace. She prances when she walks and will often kick out
in joy when she gallops."

"And she is directly descended from one of Muhammad's mares." Travis shook his head in apparent wonder.

"Yes. However, thou shouldst know that some tribes have
a slightly different version of the story. They claim it was
King Sulaiman bin Daud who actually possessed the five
original mares. King Solomon, son of David, thy people
would call him. Anyway, one day King Sulaiman was so
busy contemplating his beautiful horses that he missed the
hour of prayer. To atone for this grievous sin, he ordered
his horses to be slaughtered. Five mares escaped and fled
into the desert, where the Bedouin captured them. One
mare was in foal who gave birth to a colt who fathered
five different bloodlines from the mares. The names of the
bloodlines came from the Bedouin. They bestowed them
on the basis of certain characteristics."

"Another incredible tale. Which one do *you* believe?"

She lowered her lashes to shield the effect he had upon
her whenever he looked at her. Even his sidelong glances
were like swords piercing her heart. His every gesture and
movement enthralled her. Her whole body tingled. Struggle
though she might, she could not smother the fire his nearness ignited.

"I do not concern myself with such matters. To me, it
makes no difference which tale is true. I love each and
every horse, no matter what its lineage. Each line has its
own strengths, its own unique value. Among all of them,

Sherifa shines. She embodies the best of each—possessing grace, beauty, stamina, and speed. But I prize her most for her loyalty. Like Muhammad's mares, she will always put duty before her own needs."

"And is that what *you* are doing—putting duty ahead of *your* own needs?"

Again, she could not resist making eye contact, which she had been trying so hard to avoid. "I have no needs, save the earnest wish to serve my people. I told you; I am sacrificing nothing."

But she knew as she said it that she was lying. This man could test her commitment in a way no man ever had. Another disquieting thought occurred to her: Was this what had happened to her mother? Had she gazed upon the face of her Englishman and felt the same inexplicable leaping of the senses—the same burning flood of want and desire for things she could never have?

It made no difference that she barely knew Travis; she recognized the threat he presented.

"You are very fortunate, Sadira." Travis's blue eyes darkened. "If indeed you have all you want and yearn for nothing more. I myself am full of yearnings. They are what brought me here. I have journeyed far, risked much, and endured a great deal to gain what I came here to find—and I'm not about to leave empty-handed. I'm not content to let others rule or manipulate my life. I'm willing to fight for what I want—horse *or* woman."

He did not elaborate as to *which* horse or woman, but the implication was there; she did not need to ask. In answer to the unspoken challenge, she walked faster, making no allowances for his weakness or his limp. She would return him to her father's tent and then go about her own business, avoiding him as much as possible, except for those occasions when her skills as translator were required . . . and she would *not* sell him Sherifa. Nor would she respond to the fiery invitation in his eyes or the smoldering temptation in her own heart and body. She would die before she committed the same sin as her mother and betrayed the trust and love of her people.

"Sadira . . . wait a moment."

She paused long enough for him to catch up to her. "Wilt thou teach me thy language?" he inquired, using *her* phrasing, not his own clipped and dried manner of speaking.

"Art thou mocking me?" she demanded.

He grinned, revealing a deep indentation in his chin she had somehow not yet noticed. "I would never do that. I find your thees and thous charming."

"But thou dost not speak like that. Yet I was taught I was speaking correctly. 'Tis the nearest translation to what I would say in my own language."

"Undoubtedly, you are correct. It's very biblical to speak as you do, and the Bible *was* written in this part of the world."

"I know of thy Bible. 'Twas the book I used the most when I was first learning English. I learned to read and write from it."

"You can write, too?"

"Of course."

"Then you must teach me to speak, read, and write Arabic. In return I will polish your English to make it more closely resemble what Americans and Englishmen would say. 'You' instead of 'thee' or 'thou,' are instead of 'art,' 'have' instead of 'hast' . . ."

"There is no need for thee—*you*—to speak Arabic," Sadira quickly interrupted. "Not while thou hast—*you have*—me to translate. And thou wilt not—*you will not*—be here long enough to learn anyway."

"You don't know that for certain. I'll be here long enough to punish Gamalat *and* to buy horses. Who knows how long it will take me to change your mind about Sherifa?"

It would take him forever to change her mind about Sherifa—and just about as long to learn Arabic.

"No," she said, walking faster. "I have little time for the task." *And little inclination to spend any more time than necessary alone with thee—you.* "Thou wilt—*you will*—have to find someone else to teach thee—*you.*"

"What are you afraid of, Sadira?"

This time, she was sure he was mocking her. She did not answer, but only hurried away, leaving him to limp back to the tent at his own slow pace.

Seven

"And what do you call this?" Travis held up a small brass tray used to carry coffee cups from one place to another. Samir gave him a bored look and muttered something unintelligible.

"Could you repeat that?"

Samir shrugged as if he did not understand what was being asked.

"What do you call it?" Travis shouted in exasperation, thrusting the tray under the servant's slightly hooked nose.

Samir gave a long drawn sigh and spat out a few syllables that made no more sense than the first time he had said the word. Travis grimly repeated the incomprehensible sounds. He was determined to learn Arabic so he could understand what was going on around him without the necessity of Sadira's presence—since *she* refused to teach him and only made herself available to serve as translator during the evening meal when he conversed with her father. During the entire remainder of the day, she left him to his own devices, which was akin to abandoning a blind man on a busy street. He could barely function, and he hated being at such a disadvantage.

During the early part of his journey, Fadoul had taught him a little Arabic. He didn't know how little until he tried surviving on his own, without the assistance of someone who spoke English. Now he had the reluctant Samir. Unfortunately, the scrawny servant preferred tucking himself deep into his robes and sleeping in some forgotten corner to teaching an impatient *frangi* his language. Akbar himself was more helpful, but the emir spent his daytime hours receiving visitors, settling disputes among his people, and going God-alone-knew-where on his horse or camel. Travis wasn't permitted to accompany him; he was supposed to be resting. Only at night did Sadira's father shower hospitality upon Travis, urging him to eat more than he could comfortably hold and engaging him in long-winded, often one-sided conversations.

Sadira appeared in the evenings to translate, but Travis had no time alone with her, and she took little part in the discussions between himself and Akbar. He had learned no more about her than he had discovered that day among the horses—that she was the Keeper of the Mares, a position that required she never marry, and that the mighty Akbar was her father. Travis still didn't know who her mother was, why she alone of all the shy, reclusive women spoke English, or why she had green eyes and a streak of blond in her silky dark hair. . . . Curiosity was eating him alive. He wanted to know everything about her, regardless of the fact that she obviously intended to have nothing to do with him. Still, he craved the knowledge—another reason for learning Arabic.

"All right, Samir. . . . What's this?" Travis pointed to the rug underfoot.

Samir responded, and Travis attempted to commit the word to memory. Then Samir ran his fingers across the design in the rug, apparently pointing out colors, and Travis realized that the word he had thought was "rug" might in fact be the word for "crimson." Discouraged, he sat back on his heels.

"That's enough, Samir. We're getting nowhere. Go on . . . get out. Go find someplace to hole up and sleep, which is all you really want to do anyway."

Samir had no trouble understanding that he was dismissed. With a grin that revealed a wide gap where a front tooth was missing, Samir bowed to Travis and hurried away, quickly losing himself in the maze of the emir's many-partitioned tent. Travis lounged on a fat green pillow—the exact color of Sadira's remarkable eyes—and gazed moodily into space. It had been five days since Fadoul's death, and he was nearly himself again, eager to do something besides "rest" and fantasize making love to a female who wasn't interested. If the issue of going after Fadoul's murderers wasn't mentioned tonight, he would bring it up himself. The little bouts of sudden weakness he continued to experience, the headaches and stiffness, weren't enough to justify another day confined to the tent. He had to do something or go mad from boredom.

Sprawling atop the heap of cushions, he briefly closed his eyes and conjured Sadira's beautiful image. A virgin. What a ridiculous waste! She had a face that belonged in madonnalike paintings but a body that belonged only in bed. *His* bed. She was enough to drive a man wild with passion—and apparently, one or two other men felt the same way, though they took pains to conceal it. Hamid, for instance. Twice, the young man had stopped by at night to see Akbar, but his eyes had jealously sought Sadira. Travis knew lust when he saw it; Hamid lusted after the tribe's precious Keeper of the Mares. . . . How and why had Sadira ever consented to accept that position of dubious honor? And why for life? And why condemn Sherifa to the same bleak, barren existence?

He had to find a way to convince Sadira that the mare, at least, deserved better. She could be the foundation piece of a whole new dynasty of horses in America. In his mind's eye, Travis could picture the flame-colored equine galloping through the lush green grasses of his Kentucky paddocks. But then the picture dissolved, and once again, he found himself conjuring an elegant human profile, a face with a tender pink mouth, high cheekbones, wide-set, long-lashed green eyes . . . accompanied by a slender but womanly body just begging to be initiated into the heady delights of the flesh.

He imagined Sadira's breasts naked in his hands, exposed to his searching lips . . . the kisses he would lavish upon them! The gentleness with which he would awaken her ardor. He *knew* she was capable of profound and honest passion. . . . Unlike Elizabeth, she would give herself freely, without calculating every move or wringing every possible advantage from the situation. There was nothing coy or flirtatious about Sadira. She may think she never hungered or thirsted, but he knew better; she was a cauldron of steamy emotion. She would be a fireball in his arms. He could unleash the passion that simmered beneath that cool, collected surface—though what he would do with it once he got it, he didn't know, he wryly conceded. He certainly couldn't marry the girl! And if the emir ever discovered that his daughter had been compromised, he'd have Travis's head on a platter. Travis would never get his horses—might never see Kentucky again!

Abruptly, he opened his eyes, only to discover the object of his heated imaginings standing nearby, quietly watching him. He bolted upright. Plowing his fingers through his

hair, he nearly dislodged the bandage still wound around
his temple like a turban.

"I am sorry. Did I wake you?" Sadira asked in her velvet
voice. "I tried to be quiet."

He noticed right away that she had said "you" not
"thee"; perhaps she had been practicing all by herself. She
glided closer, her enticing shape undulating beneath the
neck-to-toes garment she wore—this one a pale, faded yellow with embroidered sleeves, yoke, and hem. A light veil
skimmed her long dark hair, partially concealing the unique
golden stripe, and Travis was struck anew by how beautiful—how exotic—she was . . . and how very sensual. If
ever a woman was made to delight a man's senses, Sadira
was. Travis could not envision a more comely, desirable
female, and he suspected that if he got the chance to know
her better, he would like her every bit as much as he wanted
to make love to her.

"I wasn't sleeping," he answered truthfully, fighting a
wave of dizziness from having risen too rapidly. "Did you
want something?" Since she had taken great care not to be
alone with him in the tent during the past several days, he
assumed she had some purpose for her unexpected visit.

"Yes, Akbar sent me. We have selected the mare thou
wilt—you will—ride tomorrow when we leave to find the
men who beat and robbed you. He wants you to come and
examine her—to make certain you and she will get on well
together."

Tomorrow. They were leaving tomorrow. "Whatever you
select will be fine with me. I trust your judgment."

She arched a delicate black eyebrow. "What if I told you
I had selected Farasat?" A hint of teasing laced her tone.

"You wouldn't do that."

"How can you be so certain?"

"Because it would stain your father's honor—and your own, as Keeper of the Mares, to have me mounted on an inferior horse."

She almost smiled, then seemed to think better of it. "Her name is Najila."

"Which means . . ." he prompted.

"She of the wide, brilliant eyes. She is *Kehilan,* of the line of horses so named because their eyes appear to be lined with kohl, after the fashion of the Berbers—and our own fashion, too."

"Do you line your eyes with kohl?"

In the semigloom of the tent, her eyes were enormous and luminescent as she shook her head. "I am not wearing kohl at this moment."

"But you also have wide, brilliant eyes," he said. "Perhaps you, too, should have been called Najila."

A smile continued to hover about her lips. "My name was chosen because of a star that shone brightly on the night I was born. We call the star Sadira. My unusual coloring—my green eyes and the gold in my hair—are the result of being marked by that star, which is why I was chosen to be Keeper of the Mares."

In a pig's eye you got your coloring from a star, Travis thought. "Your mother doesn't have green eyes?" he probed, eager to unravel another thread to her past.

The humor left her face, and he knew before she spoke that she would evade the question. "My mother died soon after I was born. I never got to see her."

"But you must know if she had green eyes and blond hair. . . ."

"I know very little about her. Come. We must go and meet Akbar. He is waiting for us out on the plain with Najila." She whirled away from him and padded soundlessly across the emir's colorful rug, and Travis had no choice but to follow.

Either her mother had green-eyes and blond hair or her father did, Travis silently speculated. But her father was Akbar. Travis couldn't detect the resemblance, except in the proud, graceful way they both moved. Sadira's face had none of the hawkishness or fierceness of Akbar's. Neither did she possess his eagle-eye. Perhaps Akbar had learned how to intimidate people after he had become Sheik of Sheiks. Travis had gleaned some of his history from their nightly conversations, but he suddenly realized he had not learned much. Akbar had a way of saying little but cloaking it in such flowery language that it seemed like a lot.

Travis, on the other hand, had told his host all about Kentucky and Greenbriar and the horses he wanted to breed and race. He saw then that he had been a fool to reveal so much, while learning so little. And he resolved not to make the same mistake with Sadira. She already knew more about him than he did about her—but he would soon remedy that. . . . He wondered who would know and could be persuaded to tell him.

Alima. The plain-faced older woman, the one he had thought might be Sadira's mother. She obviously doted upon Akbar and Sadira. Yes, he thought, he would go to Alima. Maybe *she* could teach him Arabic. She seemed kind and gentle—and she had understood when he asked her name one afternoon in the tent, when the two of them were alone with Samir. He resolved to waylay her that very day, before they left in search of the robbers.

Sadira watched with indrawn breath as Travis examined Najila. He ran his hands over the mare's body, lingering long on her legs and feet, seeking to discover heat or swelling, anything to indicate unsoundness or other problems that might hamper them on their journey. He found nothing, of course, and at last he turned to her and Akbar and grinned broadly.

"She's a magnificent animal—not as good as Sherifa, mind you, but I won't be ashamed to be seen riding her." Having made that outrageous statement, he continued his meticulous examination.

Sadira found no shame in riding any of their animals, and when she translated for her father, she omitted that part of Travis's comment. It greatly irritated her; at the same time, she was pleased that Najila had met his approval. She had taken great care to select a mare without any defects. This one also had an unusual color—a golden coat with black points like a bay. Her lower legs, mane, and tail, and of course, her eyes were black. Najila's great dark eyes did indeed seem outlined with kohl, and she was as fast as she was beautiful.

"He is no fool when it comes to horses, is he?" Akbar murmured beside her.

"No, Father, he is not."

"Thou wilt never persuade him to buy Farasat," her father opined. "Not after he has seen Najila and Sherifa. Just wait until he lays eyes on Tahani."

Tahani was her father's war mare—a striking, large-boned creature the color of ebony. She was Sherifa's equal in every way, except she lacked Sherifa's grace and delicacy. Her looks were further marred by the shortness of her tail. The bottom half had been cut off by the *Shammar* who had once succeeded at capturing her. Akbar had raided and destroyed several *Shammar* encampments in retaliation, vowing to continue his vendetta until his favorite mare was returned. The *Shammar* had then returned her—minus the long flowing tail that had once swept the ground and been Akbar's pride and joy. For some mysterious reason, it had never grown back to its former glory.

"He has already refused Farasat," Sadira admitted. "But he wants to see Farasat's son."

"Bachir? He is interested in Bachir? Then that proves he is a fool, does it not? Who would want a stallion with so many fine mares from which to choose?"

"I have told him he cannot have our mares; it's Sherifa he desires. And no doubt he will want Najila and Tahani, too, once he has seen her."

"Thou might consider selling him Bachir. A stallion will be easy enough to replace. Or he can take his pick of the colts we will sell anyway in the border towns. Does he not realize that only the mares are truly worth keeping?"

"We had some discussion of that point. . . . Hush now, here he comes." Sadira composed her face into a pleasant mask that revealed none of her emotions—she hoped! "I am glad you find Najila acceptable," she said to Travis, remembering not to say thee as he came up to her and Akbar.

"Is she for sale?" Travis cocked his head in question. Today, he struck Sadira as being devastatingly handsome. Except for a few lingering bruises—and the slight limp— one would never know he had been severely beaten. He radiated vigor and good health, along with a challenging masculinity that was almost overwhelming. The width of his shoulders strained the seams of his blue and white robe, and he towered above Akbar and every other Bedouin male. When he gazed at her so assessingly, she found it difficult to concentrate upon his question.

"No, she is not for sale, but you may use her while you

are among us. For that period of time, she will belong to you. I trained her myself, so I know she is reliable."

Travis's blue eyes gleamed in the afternoon sunlight. "So it's Farasat or nothing, is that it?"

Sadira met his gaze with a steady one of her own and was proud of herself; no one could possibly know how fast her heart was beating. "Our horses are our wealth, our sustenance, our identity. You should realize that by now and not keep hoping that we will part with them easily."

"What art thou saying?" Akbar testily demanded.

Sadira paused to translate. When she had done so, Akbar said, "Tell him that when we return from our journey, we will take him to see Bachir."

Sadira did not really want to part with Bachir either, and she gave her father a warning glance, which he pointedly ignored. "Tell him," Akbar ordered. "If he likes Bachir, thou must give the matter thy serious consideration, Sadira. We owe him this for failing to protect him upon our lands. Also, we can use the money to purchase rifles to protect ourselves from the endless aggression of the *Shammar.* Did he not say he could replace his money in Aleppo—that he could send for more money from his own people?"

"Yes, Father," she meekly agreed, though she was not at all happy about the situation. She told Travis what her father had said, and Travis made a short, stiff bow to Akbar.

"I look forward to seeing this Bachir." His deep, smooth voice sent a shiver down Sadira's spine.

"Wilt thou—you—be ready to ride in the m-morning?" she stammered foolishly. "We will be leaving at dawn. However, if you do not yet feel up to it . . ."

"I will be ready," Travis cut her short. "You need not worry. I won't hold you back or be a burden."

"Perhaps you should ride in a *mohaffa* instead of on horseback. I could lend you Lulu. That way you can sleep when the need overcomes you."

Travis shuddered and frowned. "No, I'd much prefer Najila to Lulu, thank you. Your camel and I did not get along well on our first acquaintance. Besides, I'm not accustomed to riding camels."

Akbar again demanded to know what they were discussing, and Sadira quickly told him. Then Akbar surprised her by making another suggestion. "Lulu can carry Alima. I should like to have Alima accompany us on this trip."

"Alima!" Sadira gasped. "But, Father, this is a war party. Why should Alima come along? 'Tis not customary for any other woman besides myself to ride with thee and the men on raids or war parties."

"She will come because I desire her company." Her father lifted his chin in a haughty gesture that brooked no argument. "We may be gone for a long period of time, and I have no wish to be parted from her."

Sadira could appreciate his romantic sentiments but did not think he was being very practical—or solicitous of Alima. "But, Father, she has not been feeling well lately. Surely, thou hast noticed."

"She claims it is only indigestion, Daughter, but I suspect it could possibly be another malady—the need to see new places and experience new things. She spends too much time in the tent, subject to Jaleel's jealous ravings. Accompanying us on the journey would free my dear one from that heavy burden and invigorate her health. And she could provide good company for thee, as well. Yes, the more I think on the advantages, the more determined I am that she escape the harem for a short time and come with us. New places, new things, new sights to see . . . they would all be good for her."

"And what of the danger, Father? Hast thou thought of the dangers involved?"

"If I can keep *thee* safe, I can keep *her* safe, Sadira. We will put her on Lulu, the swiftest of our camels. No harm will come to her. . . ."

"But Father . . ."

"Enough. 'Tis decided. And I will go myself now to tell her to prepare. We will keep her quite comfortable, I assure thee. We must keep the *frangi* comfortable, too, so if we must carry the extra baggage anyway, we might as well bring along the one person who ensures *my* comfort."

"All right, Father. If thou insist."

"I do insist." Akbar gave her a brief nod then stalked away without a backward glance.

"Trouble?" Travis had been standing there quietly watching while she argued with her father. "Some disagreement?"

" 'Tis not your affair," she curtly informed him.

"Perhaps not, but since it's obviously upset you, I'd like to know about it."

She tossed back her hair and straightened. "Why?"

"Because I care about you, Sadira. It makes me unhappy to see you unhappy."

She blinked away the sudden mist that obscured her vision. No one in her lifetime had expressed any great concern for her feelings—not even Alima. Bedouin women expected their feelings to count for little or nothing in the grand scheme of things; only the feelings of *men* were considered important. As much as Alima cared for Akbar and he for her, Alima would never express a desire to do anything but what Akbar wanted—no matter what her personal wishes. She could be dying, and she would still make the effort to please the emir. That was her role in life—to put Akbar's feelings ahead of her own.

"My happiness is not important, *Frangi*. Rather, I find happiness in doing my duty. So long as I fulfill my duty, I will always be content."

"Nonsense! There's far more to life and happiness than mere duty, Sadira. You also have a responsibility to yourself. You have needs and desires of your own to consider . . . and it's *right* that you should consider them. Now, what's made you so upset? Tell me. Maybe I can help."

Sadira stared at him. No one had *ever* wanted to help her—to make her happy—to deal with her problems. Alima had offered compassion and sympathy, but never a resolution to her many problems. Sadira did not know how to respond to Travis's offer; it shocked, dismayed, and excited her. Unable to think of something to say, she simply stared.

"You've built quite a wall around yourself, haven't you, girl?" he drawled in a faintly mocking tone. "You've been taught you can't let anyone get close to you. In fact, you've damn near convinced yourself you haven't got any feelings—but they're still there, aren't they, Sadira? Anger, passion, desire . . . all the troubling emotions. There are the tender ones, too—the need to be loved and to love someone. To have something uniquely your own. What about children? Don't you ever want children?"

To *that* question, she had an answer. "The horses are my children."

"Are they? I understand about loving horses, but even I don't consider them my children. You can't cuddle a horse, feel the same pride in it, rejoice in its accomplishments in quite the same way. A horse isn't human. It will never understand you as another human can. . . ."

"Sherifa understands me!"

"Perhaps she does, but answer me this, Sadira. Do you honestly believe that Sherifa doesn't want a mate—and has no wish to reproduce? I rather doubt that. You and she are living unnatural lives and denying yourselves unnecessarily. You don't have to limit yourself, you know. You can have it all. Closeness and warmth with another human being, not just with animals. But first you have to open up a bit. . . . You have to take the risk."

"Have *you* taken the risk?" she exploded. "Do *you* have a wife and family? If so, where are they? Why are they not here with thee—you? You preach to me about the wrongness of my being alone, my being unmarried, but where is the woman you love who also loves you? I do not see her. Are we so different then? I am alone because I *must* be, in order to better serve my people. . . . I have *chosen* to be alone, but why are *you* alone?"

She could see she had set him back on his heels. Cut straight to the quick. His handsome face flushed. His eyes darkened. When he spoke, it was through gritted teeth. "I haven't found the right woman—but it's not for lack of trying. God knows I've tried. I've taken the risk and been hurt in the process. You refuse to even try. You've cut yourself off from *all* human warmth and caring. You want nothing to do with it. What kind of woman are you, Sadira—to let yourself be controlled by others, to deny your most basic instincts? Your people have no right to forbid you to share your life with a man and to bear his children."

"Are you not listening? They did not forbid me! I agreed to it. I could have refused."

"Then why didn't you? Why in God's name—or Allah's—did you ever agree to such a foolish thing? It makes no sense."

"It does to me. That is all that matters. Why are we discussing this anyway? Why are you so angry? I see no need for shouting and arguing."

"Because . . . because I don't know the hell why! It just makes me furious. I look at you—a woman fashioned for love, ripe for passion—and I am enraged at the waste. I look at Sherifa, and I am further enraged. If we took her out onto the desert to meet Farasat's son, would she want to stay with him? Have you ever given *her* the choice? Does she know what she's missing? Do you?"

"Why must you plague me with these unanswerable questions?" Unable to bear the intensity of his blue-eyed gaze, she turned her back to him. To her surprise, he gently placed his hands on her shoulders and turned her back around to face him.

"Let's do it then, Sadira. When we come back from this trip, you promised to show me the stallion. Let's take Sherifa with us and give her the choice—to stay with Bachir or return to the camp with us."

She would not look at him. His eyes were too knowing, his mouth too sensual—and he was entirely too sure of himself. "I cannot do that. She is the ceremonial mare. She must be kept pure and untouched."

"If you truly love her, you'll do what's best for her. You'll let her decide for herself. You'll turn her out with the stallion and let her make up her own mind."

"The moment I call her, she will come running to me. She will remember her duty," Sadira staunchly defended.

"Will she? I'll make you a bargain. If she returns to you, I'll never say another word about it. I'll quit trying to get you to sell her to me. But if she wants to stay with the stallion, if she doesn't come when you call—within a reasonable period of time, of course—then you must agree to sell her to me. She won't be fit to be the ceremonial mare any longer. . . . She'll have disgraced herself. This can be another test like Muhammad's. What did Muhammad do with the mares that ran to the water instead of heeding the call to battle?"

"He . . . he destroyed them—or got rid of them somehow. I . . . I am not really sure."

"Well, if she loses, if she doesn't come when you call, I'll make you a grand offer for her—an offer you'll have to accept. You won't want her anyway, not if she's unworthy, will you?"

Sadira's heart thudded in her ears. She could scarcely draw breath. The *frangi* had tricked her. Talked her into doing something she did not want to do. Persuaded her to test her beloved Sherifa. Made it impossible for her to refuse. No Bedouin refused a challenge to prove the worth of his—or her—horses. Especially not the *Ruala;* their fame, fortune, and reputation derived from the loyalty and perfection of their horses. . . . Perhaps Travis was also testing *her.* Wondering if she, too, would remain true to her vows, her training, and to the beliefs of her people. Well, she would. She stepped back from him, lifted her head, and stared him straight in the eye.

"All right, *Frangi.* When we return from this journey, assuming we survive this confrontation with the men who almost killed you, we will take Sherifa out to meet Bachir, Farasat's son. We will test her loyalty. And when she proves herself, I will hear no more of your disturbing questions. You will promise to hold your tongue, and select the horses you wish to buy only from those I present to you—those such as Farasat."

"I'll buy Farasat if Sherifa spurns the stallion in favor of you. No matter if she has two broken legs and is blind in *both* eyes."

"She would still be valuable," Sadira stubbornly insisted. "And you would be fortunate to get her."

"Ah, Sadira. . . . That attitude is why I believe it such a waste if you never marry. Once you give your heart to a man, you will defend him to your dying breath. He could be a monster—and ugly as sin—and still you would stand by him."

She relished the opportunity to have the last word and pose her own disturbing question to crumble his arrogance all at the same time. "Is love to be measured only by the perfection of the beloved? If you believe that, *Frangi,* then I can well understand why no woman has accompanied you here to my country. You demand too much in a woman—do you demand as much in yourself? Or can you only love someone if she is perfect? No one is perfect, *Frangi.* You must learn to love the flaws as well as the perfection of the beloved, or your love will never last."

The slight narrowing of his eyes and flaring of his nostrils told her she had hit the mark. Apparently, he *did* demand the impossible in his women, just as he demanded it in his horses. He wanted only the best and would consider nothing less. She understood that drive and determination in him; she herself possessed a healthy measure of it—yet she knew that even the weak, lame, blind, and less-than-perfect could also be lovable. She had once found a bird with a broken wing and rather than abandon it to certain death, had fashioned a cage for it and taken it into her tent. It had delighted her for a long, long time with its peerless singing. Had it been perfect, she never would have experienced the wonder of its song.

"Come, Travis," she whispered. "We must go and prepare for tomorrow's journey."

Eight

As they rode out of camp the following morning, Travis could not help admiring the quality of the horses and camels selected for the expedition. Approximately thirty men made up the war party; most were mounted on splendid prancing mares whose tails streamed behind them on the wind. Others had chosen to ride sturdy but graceful young camels and to tie their war mares to the backs of their saddles. Only one camel—Lulu—wore a *mohaffa*, the weird-looking curtained contraption used mainly by women, but Sadira was the only woman accompanying them, and she was riding Sherifa. Travis surmised that Sadira expected him to tire quickly and had brought it along despite his protests that he preferred to make the journey on horseback.

Kneeing Najila closer to Sherifa, he could not conceal his displeasure at her lack of confidence in him. "Do you think I cannot keep up?" He nodded toward the swaying conveyance balanced precariously atop Lulu, who was doggedly following Sherifa.

Sadira's long-lashed eyes were as green as emeralds as she gazed at him from the depths of her headcloth, a portion of which concealed her mouth and nose. Dressed in flowing desert robes and *keffiya*, she looked like a young man, except she had more grace than any man, and her

eyes gave her away. Only from a distance did she resemble
a youth; up close, her femininity could not be mistaken.
She saw where he was looking, and amusement curved her
lips—lips that reminded him of a tender young rose.

"You believe I brought Lulu along for you? No, *Frangi,*
she carries Alima, at my father's orders. He did not want
to leave her behind. . . . A remarkable thing, is it not? That
he should be so attached to his first wife after all these
years? He cannot bear to be parted from her, even for a
short time. I doubt we will be gone more than a week or
two, but I could not persuade him to leave Alima at camp."

Travis's annoyance abruptly fled, and he sat back in the
saddle with a grin. "That *is* remarkable, especially considering that your father has younger wives he might choose
instead. How do you account for his preference for Alima?"

Sadira's delicate shoulders lifted in a slight shrug. "He
has grown to love her, and she loves him. They are like
two halves of a single coin, incomplete without the other.
It was not always this way, but has become so only in
recent years. Now, they must be together all of the time."

He could not resist pricking her. "See what you're missing? Wouldn't *you* like to feel that way about some lucky
man?"

"If I were someone's wife, I would not be here," she
answered smoothly, giving no indication that the question
ruffled her. "I would be languishing in a stuffy tent, arguing
with my husband's mother or other wives, disciplining children, and counting the days until the return of my lord and
master. I am here because I am the Keeper of the Mares,
and I must bless the men before they engage in battle.
There are some compensations for being who I am—my
freedom, for one thing—and I see no harm in enjoying it."

"But I thought you didn't like death and bloodshed. Yet you don't mind riding off to battle?"

She slanted him an exasperated glance. "Yes, of course I mind. I would rather this journey had some other purpose, but since it is going to happen whether I am here or not, I would rather be here, a part of it, than awaiting word at camp of who was killed and who survived long after the affair had ended. It is exciting to be a part of this."

She waved a delicate hand to encompass the colorful group of Bedouin riding across the desert on their gaily decorated horses and camels. Travis realized she was right; it *was* exciting to be among them. They made a romantic picture in their flowing robes and headdresses, mounted on their beautiful animals. Tassels and beads swayed from the halters of their mounts, mares and camels alike. Tossing their elegant heads and snorting with impatience, the mares pranced along like princesses, while the camels glided across the sand in haughty majesty. Pride and ferocity radiated from the band, and it was not just the weapons they carried—guns, spears, swords, and scimitars—that made them so ferocious; each man rode his war mare as if the act symbolized the very essence of his manhood. It was who he was and what he did that gave his life purpose and meaning.

Travis thought he understood the *Ruala* better, just by having seen them ride out on this journey for vengeance. Sadira's father, Akbar, seemed another person altogether. Gone was the gracious, curious, philosophical host, and in his place was the determined warrior. Akbar sat his black mare with an ease borne of countless hours in the saddle. His back was ramrod straight, his mouth a grim determined line, and his eyes glowed with an unholy light. He struck awe and a grudging admiration in Travis's heart, along with a distinct disquiet. For the first time, he understood that Akbar truly did relish the thought of punishing his enemies. To him, war was meat and drink, not an ugly task to be gotten over quickly and put behind him.

"Why do I have the feeling that if I had not come along to provide an excuse for this war party, your people would have found some other perfectly good reason?" he muttered.

"There are always excuses," Sadira agreed. "Though my father has maintained a fragile peace for a long time now. There have always been raids—and always will be—but he has avoided all-out war. Sometimes, the *Shammar* and the *Anazah* come together for the sake of trade and commerce. At such times, they bury their differences in order to advance their fortunes. Peace ensues for a welcome period . . . but then some small segment of one or the other of the two tribes does something wrong and must be punished for it. Then it is back to raiding. I think it a kind of game men play to prove their manhood, and I am thankful to Allah it does not flare out of control. The men steal each other's horses and camels, and occasionally someone is killed, but the violence rarely touches the women and children. The main encampments are usually left alone. Neither side wishes to fight to the death—to the complete annihilation of one side or the other. Both my father and the Sheik of the *Shammar* have thus far been able to avoid this. One could not call them peace-loving, but as they have grown older, even the raids have decreased in number and violence."

"What will happen when we find the men who killed Fadoul? We outnumber them more than two to one; I myself want to deal with Gamalat. As the wronged party, it is my right. But what will your father do to the rest?"

Sadira's beautiful eyes clouded. "I think he will beat

them, strip them naked, and steal their camels—as a warning, if nothing else. He will do to them what they did to you. Probably only one life will be taken in exchange for your servant's. If you do not slay this Gamalat, he will."

Travis considered this for a moment. He still found the idea of killing outside the context of war strange and alien, but he would do it nonetheless. Akbar had given him a rifle as well as a pistol; they were already loaded. When the time came, he would remember poor Fadoul's brutal, senseless death and do what had to be done. He would punish this Gamalat.

"You had better remind your father that Gamalat is mine. He showed Fadoul no mercy; I will show him none."

Sadira regarded him sadly. "Men are not much different the world over, are they? *Frangi* or Bedouin, they must have their vengeance. I am sorry your servant died, but I wish his death had not led to this."

"Would a man live long in your country if he were afraid to punish those who seek to harm him?"

"No," she admitted. "He would not. . . . 'Tis the same in your land?"

"In my land, we have laws to protect people—and we have officials to enforce those laws. The system works well, though there are still places where the law does not reach. In those places, violence occurs much more frequently, and a man must know how to use a gun."

"I wish there were places where violence did not exist at all." She sighed wistfully. "Would it not be wonderful if people could live in peace and prosperity, breeding and training their animals, increasing their herds, without threat of war and bloodshed?"

Travis thought of the tranquility of Greenbriar. War had once torn his country apart, but now, for the most part, it was safe and secure. He had the luxury of spending all his time breeding and training his horses. He wondered what Sadira would think of Kentucky, with its lush green farms, neat fences, flowering trees, and air of gentility. He would love to show it to her sometime and witness her reaction. . . . Cad that he was, he would love even more taking her up the stairs of his house to the master bedroom and introducing her to the comforts of the big walnut bed with its silken quilts and fluffy pillows. She might like it so much, she would decide to stay.

"My home is a place of peace," he began, then he happened to glance over his shoulder to discover the surly Hamid riding close behind them and scowling at him.

Hamid spoke a few short clipped sentences that Travis could not decipher except for the mention of Akbar's name.

"Please excuse me," Sadira apologized. "My father wishes to speak with me."

With nearly invisible signals even to Travis's trained eye, she asked Sherifa for a canter and wheeled away, Hamid jealously following. Travis watched her departure with mingled irritation and admiration. Sadira's flawless horsemanship continued to amaze him, and among all of the outstanding mares in the war party, Sherifa still stood out as being exceptional. Both mistress and mare moved with such fluid grace and elegance that Travis could not help coveting them for his own. . . . As examples of their species, they were perfection, and much as Travis hated to admit it, he wanted both of them. He might be able to win Sherifa by fair means or foul—but he wondered how in hell he could convince Sadira that everything in which she believed was wrong, and she ought to toss it all away and become his lover—maybe even his wife.

His wife. God have mercy, he must be sunstruck! He

must be crazy. She would never fit into his world in Kentucky. They shared a love of horses, true, but that was all they shared. He did not even know yet if she was capable of passion; he only suspected it. As for mutual interests and background, he needed a woman like Elizabeth—well, not like her—but someone with a similar heritage, from Kentucky, at least, not a female of another culture and language altogether different from his. And he wanted a family—children to fill the big empty house. He had no idea how Sadira felt about children; he himself had only just discovered this latent desire to reproduce. His near brush with death had reminded him he was not immortal, and there were no heirs to Greenbriar—no one to appreciate the legacy he had worked so hard to build.

Whatever had put the notion of marrying her into his head in the first place? The big walnut bed. He had been picturing her in his bed, her dark hair spread out across the pillows, her sweet pliant body waiting to welcome him, her green eyes warmly caressing him. He cursed himself for being a fool. Sadira was not for him, and he damn well knew it. Fastening his eyes on the distant horizon, he resolved not to think about her at all for the remainder of the day and indeed for the whole rest of the trip, if he could help it. The trouble was he doubted if he could help it.

The first part of the journey proceeded uneventfully, and Sadira did not know whether to be grateful for the lack of danger and discomfort or not. The weather was bright, sunny, and cool, water plentiful, and fresh food available in the form of game. It was the best time of year for travel on the desert. Blooming vegetation delighted the eye, providing plentiful grazing for the horses and camels. Sadira thought she ought to have been enjoying it more, but Travis's presence proved a constant distraction. She found she could not relax, not even at night, especially at night, for Akbar, Alima, she herself, and Travis spent the long desert evenings together—sometimes around a blazing campfire, at other times crammed into Akbar's small but comfortable traveling tent.

If the wind blew cold, they sheltered inside the tent, drinking innumerable cups of coffee prepared by Samir; if it was still and fair, they lounged outside beneath the stars, which were coldly brilliant and beautiful, much brighter than they appeared over the encampment where a layer of dust always hung between sky and land.

They were following a *wadi* or ancient riverbed, long since gone dry even in the rainy season. Akbar believed it to be the most likely route for Gamalat's party to have taken, and they knew they were going in the right direction because they found signs of his passage at frequent intervals along the way. Camel dung, stripped greenery, rings of fire stones, and other evidence told them he had passed through not long ahead of them. He seemed in no hurry, and they did not hurry either, though they were making better time than he had.

In the manner of all desert travel, time hung suspended, providing ample opportunity to think, converse, and trade ideas, including disturbing ones. Travis constantly challenged Sadira's well-ordered little world. During their evening conversations, he asked questions, exchanged opinions, and delighted her father and Alima with his agile mind. Alima cast off her air of sickness and eagerly joined the discussions in a manner she never would have dared in normal circumstances. After the first night, she ceased wearing a veil in front of Travis—something women did only when a guest was considered a good friend of the family. She took special pleasure in teaching him Arabic words and laughed like a delighted child when he returned the favor by teaching her English.

While Akbar and Alima found the *frangi* highly entertaining, Sadira became more and more wary of him. Almost every comment he made held a deeper meaning that completely escaped her father and Alima; but then only *she* knew how he felt about her position as Keeper of the Mares and ceremonial virgin. Travis was careful not to provoke a major disagreement, but when he explored Muslim beliefs regarding "the will of Allah," Sadira knew he did so only because he doubted that Allah meant for her to remain forever virginal.

When he probed the history of the tribe, only she realized that he was trying to discover if every Keeper of the Mares before her had "wasted her life" in that capacity. It did not help that she had to translate every other word he spoke—and that when Alima or Akbar could not explain an obscure phrase in Arabic, Akbar expected *her* to take over and spend as much time as necessary helping him to master the intricacies of the language. For the first several days of the journey, she managed to avoid Travis during the day, but thereafter had to ride alongside him, guiding and correcting him in his amazingly determined attempts to become proficient in such a short time.

While his clumsy Arabic left much to be desired, his horsemanship delighted her. It gave her pleasure to watch him ride Najila. Tall and straight in the saddle, he easily held his own among the best of the Bedouin riders. Most foreigners tended to be heavy-handed and impatient, but Travis demonstrated a gentle persuasiveness that encouraged Najila to become more responsive and give her best.

When the mare did as he asked, Travis always rewarded her with a quick pat on the neck or a kind word, and when they stopped to make camp, he always saw to the mare's needs before his own, the mark of a responsible and caring horseman.

Sadira simultaneously dreaded—and guiltily enjoyed—spending so many hours in his company, but only one person seemed to understand or appreciate her odd dilemma: Hamid. Hamid made certain she was never completely alone with Travis. By day, he trailed several paces behind her, and at night, pitched his tent as close to Akbar's—and hers—as he could get. Because there was little privacy in Akbar's small tent, Travis had been given his own tiny tent, about the same size as her own, and Hamid usually managed to insert *his* shelter somewhere in the void between them.

Even so, she was uncomfortably aware of Travis's every move, breath, and gesture. She wanted the journey to end, yet at the same time wished it could last forever. She hoped they never found the *Shammar,* but she knew they would—eventually. They were slowly gaining on Gamalat, as proven by the freshness of the camel dung marking the trail through the *wadi.* At first, the dung had been nearly a week old; now it was only several days' old. Gamalat was taking his time, letting his camels grow fat on the fresh salt grass that grew in clumps on the otherwise rocky, sandy ground. Hardly pushing the beasts at all, he was observing the tried and true Bedouin method of letting them feed and travel at their own leisurely pace.

On the morning of the fifth day of their journey, Sadira awoke to deep gloom and a sensation of freezing. The mild winter was nearly over, but today a bitter cold wind was tearing at her tent. She stepped outside to discover the

fierce buffet of blowing, stinging sand. Sherifa mournfully
gazed at her from the comparative shelter made by Lulu's
big body, and Lulu wore the patient, long-suffering expression that camels adopted only when forced to endure the
severest weather. Sherifa whinnied a complaint and nosed
her hand, then turned her haunches to the wind and lowered
her head, pawing and neighing in distress.

"I know, my friend, a storm is coming. Perhaps rain,
sleet, or snow. Perhaps only wind and sand. Either way, it
will not be a pleasant day for travel."

Sadira hurried to her father's tent, struggled to open the
closed flap, and finally managed to crawl inside. She found
Akbar and Alima cuddled together for warmth, Alima half
dozing in her husband's embrace. Akbar impatiently waved
her away.

"See to the *frangi*. Tell him to stay inside his tent. We
go nowhere today."

"I did not think we would. I will tell him."

She crawled back outside, again wrestling with the tent
flap before she could get it to close. In that brief space of
time, the wind had picked up, and blowing sand had made
it difficult to see. She headed for Travis's tent, but could
not find it. It was not standing where it usually did. Neither
did Hamid's tent occupy its normal spot between her tent
and Travis's. Both were missing, and she realized that they
must have already taken down their tents in anticipation of
departure.

Then she saw Hamid's mare, tail turned toward the wind,
standing with her head inside a tent erected close to a
kneeling pack camel, already hunkered down to withstand
the storm. Hamid must have moved his tent to take advantage of the camel's lee. A wise move. Hamid himself was

probably snug and safe inside his shelter, where he would sleep until the storm had spent itself.

Most of the camels were kneeling, rumps to the wind, and the horses had gathered in groups, finding what shelter they could amid the blowing debris. . . . Where was Travis? Sadira wondered as she made her way to Lulu, moved her closer to her own tent, and made her kneel to block the worst of the wind and sand. Slipping inside the shelter, Sadira grabbed a headcloth, exited again, and tied the cloth over Lulu's head to protect her eyes. Such a precaution was not really necessary, as Lulu's long lashes were more than adequate, but Sadira knew that her friend would appreciate her efforts to make her more comfortable, and she would remain absolutely still, shielding the tent, until the storm had passed.

Unfortunately, there was little Sadira could do for Sherifa. At the encampment, the tents were big enough to shelter the mares when storms raged over the desert. These were too small. Sherifa whinnied plaintively as Sadira patted her neck and led her close to Lulu, encouraging her to stand as close as she could get to the camel's body. The barrier was minimal but better than nothing. The two animals together helped shield each other and protected the tent from the icy, stinging blast.

Now all Sadira had to do was find Travis and make certain he was safe. Her hair whipped about like some maddened wild creature, and she could barely see a hand's length in front of her. It had grown quite dark. The wind make a demonic sound as it swept across the plain. She groped about helplessly, hoping she might find his tent in another location. Surely, when he saw how bad it was getting, he had realized he must erect it again.

A pair of hands suddenly encircled her waist. Her first

impulse was to struggle, but she half turned instead and recognized Travis's blue eyes peering at her over the fold of a *keffiya*. He pointed toward her tent, and she needed no further invitation. She nodded, and they fought the wind to reach the shelter. A moment later, they were safely inside. After securely closing the flap, she sank down on a sand-covered cushion and coughed to clear her throat. Travis was coughing, too. He unwound his *keffiya* and wiped his mouth with the end of it, recovering much sooner than she did. She had been bareheaded, exposed to the worst of it, and could scarcely catch her breath. She coughed and coughed, unable to stop. He seized the water skin propped in a corner, unstoppered it, and held the container to her lips.

She took a long, grateful swallow. The water cleared and soothed her throat, making it easier to breathe. Still unable to speak, she handed the skin to him. He drank also, then set down the skin and sighed deeply. Blinking away the grit, she wondered if she looked as awful as he did. Sand covered his hair, eyelashes, eyebrows, eyelids, and nose. Only his mouth remained relatively clean. Gloom and shadow filled the tent's interior, but she could still see him clearly. He lifted his *keffiya,* brushed it off, then shook it out. That done, he took the end of the cloth and gently began wiping her eyes, nose, and mouth.

It was a practical act, meant only to remove the sand and grime, but the intimacy of it reverberated clear down to her toes. He leaned forward, blue eyes intent, black hair dusted with sand so that it appeared almost blond. His touch was efficient, careful, and oh-so-gentle. When he had removed the worst of the grit, he wet the cloth from the water skin and proceeded to wash her face. She did not scold him for the waste—did not tell him that during a sandstorm, one conserved water in case the storm should last several days. She did not say a word. Nor did he.

When he had finished washing her face, he carelessly ran the cloth over his own smudged features, removing *some* of the grime but not all, then tossed it aside. Almost reverently, he picked up a length of her tangled hair. Holding it up, he gazed at her, and a question lit his blue eyes. She knew what he wanted and fumbled among the pillows behind her, finally producing an ivory-handled brush of camel's hair that had been a gift from her father many years before. Travis moved closer, turned her around, and drew her back between his knees. She shivered from nervousness and an odd expectancy; with great care, he began to brush her tangled hair.

It took a long time to work out the tangles, and he used his fingers as much as the brush. Sometimes it hurt, but she did not complain. She could not say a word; it was as if a spell had fallen over her. As the tangles worked free, the brushing felt wonderful. His behavior was perfectly reasonable, completely understandable. She would have no difficulty explaining it if someone barged into the tent searching for the two of them. But no one came, and the longer he brushed and massaged her scalp, the less innocent the act became. She leaned back against him as the languorous brush strokes continued—long and slow, starting at her scalp and ending at her waist where the hair curled about her hips.

All the sand *must* be gone by now. She picked up a pillow and shook the sand from it, brushed sand from the colorful rug upon which they sat. She pretended she did not notice he was still brushing her hair. Then he stopped and pulled her backward into the circle of his arms. His lips found the hollow where her neck met her shoulder, and he kissed her there, nibbled lightly, and kissed her again. Outside, the wind roared and tugged at the tent. Inside, they were snug and alone, and the feel of his lips on her skin ignited a bonfire within her.

He wrapped his arms around her, squeezing the breath from her body, then buried his nose in her fresh-brushed hair. She knew she should pull away and end this foolishness, but her body would not obey. . . . What would be the harm if he simply held her? If she let him steal one kiss . . . one stirring caress to savor and remember all the rest of her life when she had only the knowledge of her virtue to warm her on the coldest nights?

She moaned softly and leaned back against him, feeling his strength surround her, his warmth enfold her. All the hurt and rejection she had ever known seemed to melt away as his hand came up to cup her cheek. She turned to meet him. He gazed long into her eyes, then inclined his head and kissed each eyelid, then her nose, her cheeks, and finally her mouth. She gasped when his lips met hers. The impact was stunning. Something hot and sweet flowered inside her, leaving her breathless and tingling. She could no more have moved away—or done anything else to stop him—than she could have commanded the storm to suddenly abate.

Hunger and need, coupled with his gentleness, held her captive in his arms as he thoroughly, tenderly kissed her. His tongue entered her mouth and entwined with her tongue, deepening the kiss. It was an intimacy she had never expected or imagined. She had never realized that men and women did things like this together. Or felt like this. The revelation rocked her. Of course, she knew what mating was—and how a stallion took a mare, but until now, she had never dreamed that a kiss could foreshadow the

entire process. Travis told her with his mouth what he
wanted to do with the rest of his body. His kiss tantalized
her with the promise of pleasure beyond her imaginings—
and a oneness and security she had longed for all her life.

His kiss left her weak and wobbly, with no strength to
do anything but let him kiss her—and to shyly kiss him
back. She was uncertain what she was supposed to do, but
she tasted and enjoyed him as if he were some foreign
delicacy being offered for her delight. He tasted of sand
and grit and *man*—man most of all, and she loved the taste
of him. He broke the contact only long enough to find a
more comfortable position for them. Quickly tossing some
pillows together, he leaned her back against them and
stretched out on his side next to her, possessively draping
one arm around her waist and one leg across her lower
body.

Reminded of the impropriety of their behavior, she
surged upward in alarm, but he gently pushed her back
down. Pressing his lips to her ear so she could hear him
over the whine of the wind, he whispered, "Relax, sweetheart. I won't hurt you, I promise. I only want to be near
you."

Some small part of her reminded her that this was
wrong—dreadfully wrong! But another part insisted that it
was more wrong to deny herself this brief pleasure. She
was a woman, after all, and she needed to be held and
cherished. As long as she retained control of her emotions,
she could allow herself the comfort of a few stolen kisses
and caresses. For this tiny space of time while the storm
raged outside, she could pretend she was an ordinary
maiden in love with a handsome man, and they could hold
each other close, whisper endearments, kiss and cuddle.

It would go no further than that. She would not permit

it to go any further. As if he could read her thoughts, Travis stroked her hair back from her face and gazed down into her eyes. "You are so very beautiful, Sadira," he murmured, his face close to hers. "And I would like nothing better than to make passionate love to you, right here and now. I could easily allow myself to be carried away . . . but I won't. Not unless you want me to. Not until you want it as much as I do. I am no green boy who cannot control himself. And I would never harm you or cause you pain."

"I cannot . . ." she began, suddenly miserable, because she did want him to make passionate love to her. She wanted him to hold and kiss her . . . and more. She wanted to go wherever the kissing led, and she wanted *him* to take her.

He lay a finger across her protesting lips. "Hush, now . . . I know you can't. You're the Keeper of the Mares, the ceremonial virgin. You have a duty to your people."

She nodded. He understood—or did he? His tone held a mocking note, a trace of sarcasm. "I . . . I am sorry," she whispered. "Were I to . . . to give myself to a man, I should not mind if it were thee—*you,* Travis. You . . . you make me feel things I have never felt before. You awaken needs in me. You make me forget who I am and even *where* I am."

His teeth flashed in the darkness. Then his mouth found her ear again. "I'm flattered. Any man would be pleased to think he had such an effect upon such a beautiful woman. Too bad we aren't right for each other, Sadira, because I'm totally convinced that we could have something really special together—the sort of thing most people only dream about having."

"What is that?" Frowning, not understanding what he was saying, she pushed him away so she could see his face.

He spoke slowly and carefully, almost nose to nose with her, enunciating each word so she could understand over the roar of the storm. "The grand passion . . . the love of all time. The all-consuming fire. . . . The love that lasts forever. Didn't you feel it when we kissed? I swear the earth moved, and the ground shook."

"The storm . . ." she hesitantly suggested. "The wind singing its song over the desert."

"It wasn't the storm or the wind. Tell me what *you* felt. Why you didn't push me away and refuse to kiss me. Tell me why you won't stop me even now, if I decide to kiss you again."

She was helpless to explain her behavior. The mere thought of his kisses made her heart beat faster, caused her flesh to heat, made her breath catch in her throat. "I . . . I do not know."

"Well, *I* know, my little green-eyed innocent. We have it, you and I . . ."

"Have what?"

"That spark. That little ember that could blaze into a raging inferno."

"I do not think . . ."

"You don't need to think. Just feel. I'll prove it to you."

He leaned over her, gathered her into his arms, and again lowered his mouth to hers. They kissed, and she *did* feel it—for the second time. The spark leaping to life. The ember catching fire. Flames licking at the dry tinder of her heart . . . destroying her resolve. Weakening her resistance. She was burning . . . burning . . . dissolving into smoke in his arms.

No, she thought, 'tis not like fire at all. Rather, 'tis like the desert wind . . . the storm . . . blowing everything away. So I cannot remember duty, honor, responsibility. I know not who I am, nor do I care. I know only what I want: to love this man and to let him love me.

Nine

Travis knew the precise moment when Sadira stopped fighting their mutual attraction. Her hands crept around his neck, she arched against him, and he sensed that he could have everything she had to give . . . if he wanted it badly enough. And oh, he wanted it! But was he willing to pay the price, to accept the consequences—to have her hate him later? That was the question.

He had not lived this long without learning how to give a woman pleasure, how to make her enjoy lovemaking as much as he did, and how to soften any regrets that might surface later, after the deed was done. But with Sadira, it was all different. She was an innocent, a virgin. As yet, she knew nothing about the nature of passion—how it could sweep away rational thought and cause one to behave in a manner at odds with what one had always believed.

He could take her now, could seduce her easily . . . but if he did, she would never forgive him or herself. She would see her surrender as a betrayal of her people. Offering to marry her wouldn't make it right. All the arguments in the world would not ease her guilt. She would hate him for destroying her life and eroding her self-esteem. For making her a traitor. He couldn't do it. Somehow she had wormed her way into his heart—into his conscience—and he could do nothing that would harm her or make her miserable.

Reluctantly, he pulled away. She opened her eyes; they held a dazed look. Her mouth trembled, like a crushed rose exposed to an onslaught of heavy rain. Tears brimmed and spilled over, then trickled down her cheeks. He ached with loss and feelings of tenderness he had never felt for any woman. He kissed her forehead and her cheeks. Her tears were salty-tasting and accusing. Now she had some idea what she was missing, but he took no satisfaction in the knowledge. He had meant to teach her passion but only succeeded in teaching her pain.

"I wish I were free!" she murmured fiercely. "Then it would not matter if we continued where this is leading. I would be hurting no one but myself."

So she did realize that this was leading *somewhere;* that much he had taught her.

"If you were free, I would not stop." He kissed the tip of her nose. "I only did so because I don't want to complicate your life. I could ask you to come away with me when I leave here, Sadira, but I don't know if you would be willing to go . . . and I'm not sure I can bear finding out for certain."

Her response was instant. "I could never leave my people!" Her hand rose to entwine in his hair, and ruefully, she smiled and shook her head. "Not even for thee, Travis, the first man who has ever truly tempted me to stray from my vows."

"Then I'm glad I haven't asked." He forced a grin to his lips and fought down a sense of bleak despair. "Guess we'll have to avoid being alone like this in the future, sweetheart, for you tempt me too much. Perhaps I should leave now, and we can forget this ever happened between us."

Her arms flew around his shoulders to imprison him. "But thou canst not go now, Travis! Not while the storm is raging. When it begins to die down, thou—you—may leave, and we will invent some excuse for where you sheltered. We can raise your tent nearby, and you can say you were there inside the whole time. . . . For now, let us just enjoy being with each other. If we cannot love, we can at least talk. Tell me about yourself, dear one. I hunger to know you better; that cannot be wrong, can it? Were we men sharing a tent together during a storm, what else would we do but talk?"

He almost laughed. "We might sleep side by side, ignoring each other."

She shook her head. "I could never sleep with you beside me. You make me feel too alive. Too vibrant, as if I have been sleeping all this time and have only now awakened."

"All right then. Let's talk. What do you want to know? My life has had its share of exciting moments, but there have also been some dull ones."

"Everything. . . . I wish to know everything—the exciting along with the dull."

So he told her—all the things he ought to have shared with Elizabeth but never really had. He told her about his boyhood and his first view of the great racehorse, Lexington, and what it had meant to him. He shared his fears, hopes, and dreams of the war years. He described Greenbriar and his life there—told her about each horse, its habits, it strengths and weaknesses, and what he hoped to accomplish with it. He related his family history and much of the history of Kentucky and the world of Thoroughbred breeding and racing. He even told her about Elizabeth.

"This Elizabeth. She is very beautiful?" There was a slight tremor in Sadira's voice, suggesting she might be jealous.

Smiling to himself, Travis nodded. He was not above

arousing her jealousy if it would further his case with her. "I thought so when I asked her to marry me. She's considered by many to be a great beauty, but I don't think she can compare with you, sweetheart. Looking back, I can see I was blinded by her outward appearance, her breeding, and her family background. I never actually looked past those things to see who she was and find out how she felt about things. I thought we had everything in common and discovered we had nothing. She cared more about social position than she did about horses—or me."

"You need a special kind of woman, *Frangi.*" Sadira's fingers played with his hair. The sexual tension still shimmered between them, but for the moment, friendship held sway. Travis felt he could tell Sadira anything, and he had never trusted a woman like that.

"Yes, Travis, you need a woman who understands what you are trying to do, shares your dreams, and is willing to make the sacrifices to achieve them."

"I doubt such a woman exists—unless perhaps it's *you,* Sadira. If you weren't the Keeper of the Mares, you could be that woman. You feel the same way I do about horses. You have the same affinity for them, the same desire to protect and produce perfection, you . . ."

"Yes, but I *am* the Keeper of the Mares, so there is no sense discussing it, is there? More than that, I live in a different world than you do—a world of blowing sand, of camels, sheep, and goats, of black tents and Persian carpets. We are so very different, Travis. I worship Allah, while you pay homage to a God who is a stranger to me."

"They are probably one and the same," Travis snorted. "Known by other names is all. These are superficial differences, Sadira. We could overcome them."

"No, dear one, we could not. I am bound to my people

with ties that can never be broken. I owe them my loyalty, my love, and my allegiance. I must never betray their trust in me. I could not live with myself were I to disappoint my people."

Travis cupped her face in one hand and gazed deeply into her eyes. The gloom had deepened, and he could barely see her, but the wind had died down to a muffled roar, and he had no difficulty hearing her. "Why, Sadira? Why must you sacrifice your whole life for the sake of your people? It isn't fair, and I don't understand. What hold do they have over you? If you left, they could find a new ceremonial maiden and Keeper of the Mares."

"No . . . no," she murmured. "I owe them this. 'Tis my duty and destiny. . . . 'Tis the will of Allah."

Travis knew when a stone wall confronted him. He encountered it each time they discussed this subject. She would not be swayed. Nothing could move her. Defeat and disappointment twisted in his gut. A bitter taste came into his mouth. "Tell me about *you* now." He sighed. "So far I've done all the talking. I want to understand how you feel. I want to be able to look at life the way you do."

She smiled. "There is little to tell. You already know the important parts—and what you do not know is unimportant."

"Tell me about your mother. Explain where you got your green eyes and that streak of blond in your hair."

Her smile vanished. She lowered her eyes, her hands dropped to her sides, and she stiffened in withdrawal. Even before she spoke, he sensed the lie she was preparing to tell him. Spreading a falsehood did not come easily to her, but for some reason, she could *not* speak the truth about this matter.

"I have already told you. My mother died soon after I was born, and my coloring is the mark of the star after which I was named. 'Tis proof I am chosen by Allah to be Keeper of the Mares."

"It's proof that somewhere in your background, you've got a *frangi* or two hidden away," Travis disputed. Irritation roughened his voice. He wanted no pretenses between them, nothing hidden or veiled. That was how he had gotten into trouble with Elizabeth. Neither of them had been truthful with each other.

"What is so horrible that you can't face it, Sadira? Is it such a terrible disgrace to have the blood of some other race running in your veins?"

When she did not answer, but only lay there silently, Travis understood that it *was* a disgrace. As much as the Bedouin prized the purity of the bloodlines of their horses, he ought to have guessed as much. Even more would they prize the purity of their own bloodlines. It was a wonder they had let Sadira live when she was born. Considering the innate ferocity of the desert tribes, he would not have been surprised to learn that they abandoned babies who displeased them. He seemed to remember hearing that in this part of the world, people were still stoned for certain offenses. Is that what had happened to her mother? Could that be why Sadira ascribed her coloring to the influence of a star, of all things?

He longed to discover the truth, but the misery in Sadira's face kept him from prying. She was not going to tell him anyway. After all he had just shared with her, she did not intend to reveal her own secrets. Disappointment and resentment welled up in him; he was doing it again! Opening his heart to a woman, only to have her coldly trample it and laugh in his face. Except Sadira wasn't laughing; she seemed about to weep, and he had to harden his heart just to keep from weeping right along with her.

"Hey, forget I mentioned it," he chided. "It's none of my damn business. You can keep your secrets, and from now on, I'll keep mine."

He sat up, feeling as if his guts had been wrenched and torn out. He had laid himself bare to her—and for what? They had no future; she wouldn't even reveal her past. What he felt for her must be lust, pure and simple. Nothing more. Nothing nearly so dangerous and threatening as love. She was a beautiful woman, and he wanted what he couldn't have. Her virginity challenged him; that was all. And if he weren't such a damn fool, he would just take it and be done with it. Issues of morality had rarely bothered him in the past; why should they bother him now? Kentucky was a long, long way from the eastern desert. When he left here, he would never see or hear from her again. If ever he was going to be a rogue and a scoundrel, now was the perfect opportunity.

"Travis . . ." Her soft fingers touched his arm. "Do not hate me. I could not bear it if you hated me."

He jerked around to face her. Her eyes were enormous in the deep gloom. Pain and sorrow shadowed them. In the face of her obvious unhappiness, all his hurt and resentment suddenly drained away, leaving him weak and shaking, afraid that he was truly in love this time and couldn't do a thing about it. He would not be able to forget Sadira as easily as he had Elizabeth. Elizabeth had only shattered his pride, but Sadira had cut much deeper, finding the core of him and stirring emotions he had never realized he possessed.

"I don't hate you," he muttered. "The last thing I feel for you is hate."

"I am glad," she whispered. " 'Tis a comfort to me to know that. Now lie down beside me and rest, Travis. Sleep. I will wake you when the storm has passed."

She had sensed his need before he himself was aware of it. He *was* tired. His body and his mind ached. His knee—where he had taken a ball during the war and been hurt again when he was beaten—throbbed like the very devil. Why he should feel so exhausted he didn't know, since he hadn't done anything . . . but exhaustion claimed him now, as surely as if he had engaged in hard physical labor instead of conversation.

He lay down beside the woman who managed to sooth and torment him at the same time—the woman who exhausted him emotionally and physically. He did not think he would be able to sleep, but no sooner had his head touched the gritty pillow when he slid into oblivion and lost himself in dreams of Sadira whose smile taunted and teased him all the while he slept.

The storm lasted a full day and a night, ending well before dawn, which gave Sadira and Travis ample time to set up Travis's tent a discreet distance away from her own. Sadira did not look at him the whole time they worked—retrieving the tent from a pack of supplies buried in sand, choosing a spot to erect it, and then quickly and quietly doing so and furnishing it with the usual rug and pillows.

In the dark, Travis was clumsy, but Sadira had done this so often she needed no starlight to see by, which was fortunate for there was little to be had. The stars were shining, but only dimly, through a haze of lingering dust. She thought he would simply go inside when they were finished, but he grabbed her hand a moment and held it tightly. Fearing her own feelings more than his, she refused to look at him or be drawn into an embrace, but she could not escape him altogether.

He lifted her clenched fingers and kissed them, wordlessly reminding her of the kisses they had shared together in her tent—of the brief intimacy they had known there—of the emotions they had experienced. Forbidden things that must never be repeated. Reluctantly, she pulled away and hurried back to her own tent to await the morning. When dawn came, she intended to ask her father if he would mind if she sold Najila to Travis upon their return to the encampment. If she sold Travis a good mare, perhaps he would leave sooner. Once he had what he had come for, there would be no reason for him to stay. . . . Of course, there was always the possibility that he would not be satisfied even with Najila. But he would have to be, for she would give him nothing else. Not Sherifa, not Bachir . . . and most especially not herself.

Najila was an excellent mare, her bloodlines impeccable, exactly what Travis needed. Her foals would provide the strength and stamina Travis sought to improve his own horses. Sadira would never consider selling the mare to anyone else—but she knew Travis would appreciate and care for her as well as any Bedouin. She did not like to think about the bloodline being diluted—would have preferred that Travis maintain the purity of Najila's line. But in order to do that, she would have to sell him more horses, and breeding desert horses for their own sake was not what *he* intended anyway.

Travis would have to be satisfied with what she was willing to give him—and then only if he agreed to leave the *Ruala* as soon as possible. The sooner he was gone, the better. Once he had returned to his own country, the easier it would be for her to forget him . . . to cease thinking about his kisses and imagining what it would be like to marry and bear children, live with a man she loved, and enjoy all the womanly things she had sworn to forego forever. She could not picture the place called Kentucky, but she could easily imagine herself as Travis's wife—his woman, confidante, and lover.

She and Travis would share a special intimacy forged of friendship, and like Akbar and Alima, prefer each other's company to anyone else's . . . or so she believed. Since it could never be, she must arrange for his departure as quickly as possible. As soon as they had completed their mission and returned to the main camp, she would let him have Najila, and maybe then he would leave.

The sun rose in a reddish haze, and Sadira went swiftly to her father's tent. However, there was no time to raise the matter of Najila, because several of the men had gotten there first. They stood outside with Akbar, debating whether or not they ought to leave the *wadi* and cut across the desert to waylay the robbers at a certain well. Now that the watering holes were clogged with sand and covered over, they thought the band might head for the nearest well, and this would be the opportunity they had been awaiting. While Sadira visited with Alima, Hamid appeared and joined the argument, pointing out that the band might possibly bypass the well and press on to rejoin their tribe at a distant oasis.

Finally, Akbar ended the discussion with a curt order. "We will leave the *wadi* and set out for the well. 'Tis likely we will get there first, for we are not herding camels who must stop along the way to graze. The well will be a good place to mount an ambush."

He selected five men to remain behind to guard Alima, Lulu, and the rest of the camels. "We should be gone only a night or two," he assured Alima. "Thou wilt be safe with the guards I have chosen to watch over thee. Have no fear, my dove."

Pale and wan in the morning light, Alima mustered a warm smile. "I fear nothing, Akbar, knowing I have thy love. May Allah watch over thee."

After that, everyone hurriedly broke their fast with the foodstuffs they had in their supplies, horses were groomed and fed, tents taken down, and everything made ready for the long, hard ride to the well.

Sadira saw Travis only long enough to explain the change in plan, and then her own preparations occupied her time. At noon, beneath the dusky red ball of the sun, the party set out at a fast trot overland across the desert. Where the rocky uneven landscape allowed, they urged their mounts into a gallop, giving little thought to sparing them now that their goal was near. The mares had been bred and trained for moments such as this—to go all day without stopping, to cross barren rough terrain without faltering, to obey their masters with eagerness and joy.

Sadira was therefore much surprised when Travis cantered close to her and grabbed hold of Sherifa's halter to get her attention. "Your father is driving the horses too hard!" he shouted. "They will all collapse. If we get there at all, we'll have to walk back."

Indignation contorted his handsome face, and she had to bite down on a smile. "Is Najila winded? Is she stumbling?" she shouted back at him.

"No, but if we continue at this pace, she soon will be!"

"No, she will not, *Frangi*. Do not worry so. She is no weak-kneed, fainthearted creature bred in Kentucky. She is a desert horse raised by the *Ruala*. She can gallop all day and not tire. Reserve your opinion until you see what our horses can do. Do you see that pile of rocks in the distance?"

Travis nodded. "It's probably farther than it looks. Surely, your father means to stop and rest before we get there."

Sadira laughed. "He means to get there as quickly as possible. Enjoy the ride, Travis. And then you must tell me if *your* horses can compare to ours."

Travis gave her a doubtful look and spoke not another word until they were passing the pile of rocks. Then he threw back his head and shouted, "I cannot believe it! We must have covered miles already—but not one of your mares looks ready to drop. They've scarcely raised a sweat."

"Believe it, *Frangi*. That is why we prize them so. There are no horses like these in all the world."

Travis's face was exultant. "You won't hear an argument from me! I never would have accepted it on anyone's claim had I not seen the proof with my own eyes. No wonder you strive so hard to maintain the purity of their bloodlines. I can understand it now. These horses are magnificent! Beauty, speed, *and* stamina . . ."

She wondered then if she ought not to sell him a stud colt, too, now that he saw the value of the breed. Perhaps he would use them not only to strengthen the bloodlines of his own horses, but also to establish a line of purebred desert horses in his own country. . . . But no, she reminded herself, desert horses belonged in the desert—galloping free—carrying the Bedouin to war, not languishing in fenced pastures, serving no true purpose except to race every now and then.

Still, she took pleasure in Travis's pleasure and his admiration for the animals she loved so much. It was a joy to witness *his* joy and to share in his discovery of what her beloved horses could do. On across the desert they galloped, free as the wind itself, their robes and headcloths billowing out behind them. The wind swept the desert air clean and removed every last trace of the lingering dust from the sandstorm. By nightfall, they reached the well. Like most wells, it was little more than a stone cairn marked by a low stone wall built centuries ago by the Romans or some other conquerors passing through the lonely landscape.

A single goat herder claimed ownership of the well, and Akbar willingly paid the fee for water usage and sent the goat herder away with promises of a fat bonus if he did not interfere with their possession of it for a day or two. The herder gathered his complaining flock and disappeared behind a slight rise in the gently undulating land. Then the party settled in for the night, wrapping themselves in their robes and huddling beside the wall.

Sadira avoided Travis and stayed close to her father, while Hamid made it his business to claim a space between her and Travis. Everyone shared a simple meal of dates and cold rice, and the men conversed in low tones as they made coffee over a tiny, camel dung fire. Several times, Sadira glanced up to discover Travis's eyes upon her, but she did not go to him, and he did not approach her. She concluded that he had finally realized that any further contact between them could only be unbearably painful. From now on, they must confine their conversations to impersonal topics—and speak to each other only when absolutely necessary. To do any more would only invite pain and disaster.

Sadira at last sought the comfort of sleep; she knew she must rise extra early in the morning to enact the ritual that preceded battle, and the long hours on horseback had sapped her energies. Her own emotions had robbed her of strength. Leaning her head against the stone wall, she closed her eyes, but all she could see in her mind's eye was Travis's image. Travis gazing warmly down at her as she lay on her pillows, his blue eyes filled with yearning and gentleness. Travis slanting her a roguish grin as he sought to convince her to sell Sherifa. Travis enthusiastically describing the place he called home in far-off Kentucky. Travis whispering that he loved her and wanted her above all other women . . . except that Travis had never said that. She had only *wanted* him to say it.

Stop it, Sadira! You are betraying your people by thinking such dangerous thoughts. What you long for can never be. Remember your mother. Would you bring the same shame upon your people that she did? Only your shame would be worse. Your mother was only Akbar's wife, not the Keeper of the Mares. Not the ceremonial virgin. You are chosen of Allah to be what you are. Were you not chosen, you would not be able to speak English now. You would never have met Travis. Never have spoken with him. Never had reason to discuss his dreams or decide if he may have a horse. You would probably be Hamid's wife—the mother of his children. Your destiny is already decided; it was decided long ago. Do not fight it; be at peace, Sadira . . . be at peace.

But Sadira could find no peace as she huddled beside the wall, wishing for sleep. Travis had had such an effect upon her that even in her thoughts she was speaking as he spoke—not totally perhaps, but her thee's and thou's had almost disappeared, and she was starting to think in English. Long before morning, she rose and walked alone out onto the desert. The whole party, including the sentry, was asleep—and so was Travis. There, beneath the brilliant stars, she wept and prayed, trying to understand why she should be so tormented. She prayed for strength to resist temptation, then wondered if her own mother had done the same. Akbar loved Alima, not Jaleel or the other wives he had known. Perhaps he had never really loved Bashiyra, and Bashiyra knew it. Perhaps that was why she had sought love in the arms of another man—a *frangi.*

It was love—not simply lust—that had tempted her mother. Sadira was now certain of it. Lust might have played a part, but not the most important part. More important still was the yearning to be close to someone—so close that nothing could come between. It was the desire to be *first* with someone, first and only. Sadira could understand and forgive her mother for that. She knew what it was to be lonely all of her life. She had been alone until she met Travis. Only Travis wanted to know what she was thinking and to share his innermost thoughts with her. Only Travis seemed to care if she was happy and fulfilled. Only he understood how she felt about the horses, for he felt the same way. . . . It was cruel of fate to have brought them together and tantalized them with dreams that could never be fulfilled! So cruel of fate to thrust them apart again.

Yet part they must. She could see no other alternative, and she wept for what she had never had and never *would* have. Then she resolutely dried her tears, returned to the wall, and cuddled against its hard unyielding surface. Still unable to sleep, she watched dawn streak the sky with ribbons of purple, blue, and rose.

Ten

"Travis, wake up! Gamalat and his men are coming."

Sadira's hand on Travis's shoulder instantly shattered his dreams. He sprang to his feet and stood there a moment, swaying, trying to get his bearings. All along the wall, men were hunkered down—rifles, pistols, and sabers at the ready. The horses were nowhere to be seen. Sadira seized the edge of his sleeve and tugged on it. "Get down, or someone might see thee. Make no noise. They should be here shortly."

Reaching for his rifle, Travis crouched beside her. "Why didn't you wake me sooner? Why did you let me sleep so long?"

He squinted at the sun; it must have been a couple of hours past dawn already. For the first time since he had arrived among the *Ruala,* he had not heard the *muezzin's* morning call to prayer, which summoned everyone to give praise to Allah beginning at dawn and then again at noon, midafternoon, and in the evening.

"There was no need to wake you," Sadira explained. "You do not pray as a Muslim, and nothing else was happening—except for the battle ceremony, which would also be of little interest to you. We held it out on the plain, and it did not last long. Akbar then sent out scouts who discovered the robbers not far from here. They must have traveled all last night in their eagerness to reach the well. My father was right. The camels need to wash the dust of the storm from their throats, and the water pools have all been contaminated or disappeared entirely."

"Where are the horses?" Travis scanned the barren landscape for some sign of the animals. His concern spiraled for Najila. She did not belong to him, but he felt as if she did. Yesterday, she had proven her worth, and he now considered that if he could not have Sherifa, he would rejoice if Akbar consented to sell him Najila—and several of the other mares who at first glance had not caught his eye. Even the less attractive ones had managed to maintain the grueling pace.

"Hidden. Hamid took them away from here, to a place where they cannot be easily seen. He has hobbled Sherifa, so she will not come racing back to me. The others will stay with her; they accept her as leader—and Tahani, too."

"Tahani?"

"My father's black mare."

Tahani. The fine black mare with the shortened tail. Travis coveted her, too, but doubted he could persuade Akbar to part with her. He checked his rifle and experimentally aimed it at a patch of camel thorn. None of what was happening seemed real to him; the entire scene was dream-like, as if he had not yet fully awakened. Behind the stone barrier, Akbar's men were crouched down, waiting. Akbar himself held his rifle, and two pistols lay on the ground beside him within easy reach. . . . Did the sheik mean to kill all the robbers? Travis wondered. Slaughtering them from the shelter of the wall would be ridiculously easy.

"Please remind your father that I claim the right to deal with Gamalat. Is he certain that the approaching men are the ones we seek?"

"They are driving thirty head of camel, as you said. The scouts counted the camels, and they numbered exactly that. However, there were more men than you claimed. Not a dozen, but nearly two dozen—and most are riding horses."

"Two dozen! There weren't that many. There were only twelve, led by a young man with a scar. I told your father that. Maybe these aren't the same ones. Tell Akbar we can't attack them without first making certain they're the same men who attacked me."

"They are *Shammar,* Travis. The scouts had no doubt of that. They are carrying the banners and pennants of the *Shammar.* So it makes no difference if they are the same men as the robbers or not. My father will attack them."

"Damn! The men who robbed and beat me and killed Fadoul had no banners or pennants. Your father's making a big mistake. I'll tell him myself. We can't attack innocent men—*Shammar* or not. I refuse to be a part of this."

Travis threw down his rifle and started to rise, but Sadira again grabbed his sleeve to stop him. "Travis, wait! Maybe others have joined them. There are thirty camels—that is proof enough!"

"No, damn it, it isn't! I can't accept this, Sadira, and I wonder that you can. I don't care who the hell is out there—friend or enemy. If they aren't the men we're looking for, we have no right to attack them!"

Travis was dimly aware of figures along the wall motioning him to be quiet—telling him to get down. He didn't care. He was furious. He had gone along with this because he did not believe in allowing lawlessness to rule the land, and permitting robbers and murderers to go unpunished. But he had never envisioned attacking a group of men simply because they belonged to another tribe. How could Akbar behave so civilly in his own tent, drinking coffee and discussing the world's problems, then turn around and level his guns on a party of innocent camel herders just because they were *Shammar?* Akbar had probably been using him— looking for any excuse to attack his enemies and steal their herds. He was no better than Gamalat!

"Akbar!" he shouted, and three Bedouin, Hamid among them, leapt to their feet and attempted to pull him down behind the wall.

As he lost his balance and fell backward, Sadira screamed. "Allah protect us! They are coming!"

Travis's shoulder slammed against the wall, his head struck stone, and sparks danced before his eyes. At the same moment, the world erupted into smoke, fire, and concussion. Stunned, he lay there a moment and sought to recover his wits. All around him, men were screaming, shouting, and firing over the top of the wall. He struggled to his feet, and a ball whizzed past his left ear . . . Sadira! His first rational thought was that she was in danger and might be killed. He must forget about stopping the battle; it was too late anyway. All he could do now was protect Sadira.

"Sadira!" He did not at first spot her. She had been right there beside him but had suddenly disappeared. In their robes and headcloths, the *Ruala* all looked alike. He could not distinguish one man—or woman—from another. Then a slender body hurtled into his arms.

"Travis, watch out or thou wilt be shot!"

Again, he lost his footing and went down, this time with Sadira sprawled on top of him.

This isn't the way it's supposed to be, you donkey, a little voice in his head drawled sarcastically. You're supposed to save the beautiful damsel in distress, not the other way around. He rolled over, seeking to put his own body between Sadira and the gunfire, only then remembering Gamalat and his rifle. If Gamalat was indeed out there—shooting at Sadira and the rest of the *Ruala* with Travis's own Winchester—he had to stop him.

The morality of the battle suddenly ceased to matter. Men were trying to kill them; he had to kill the bastards first. A cry of outrage burst from his throat, and he scrambled to his feet, found the rifle Akbar had lent him, and took his place behind the wall.

"Keep your head down!" he barked at Sadira. Peering into the swirling dust, he spotted men on camelback and horseback milling about and firing their guns at the wall. It was all the incentive he needed. He leveled his carbine and started blasting away at them.

During the war years, he had learned to be an excellent marksman, and his skill did not fail him now. It all came back to him. Bodies fell, and riderless camels and horses galloped back and forth in terror and confusion. One dragged its fallen rider by an ankle trapped in a stirrup. Travis no longer debated the rightness or wrongness of the battle; he was too busy. He discovered that no one else behind the wall could load and fire as quickly as he could. It was up to him to win this conflict. A gun exploded nearby, and a howl of pain pierced his eardrums, but he could not take time to assess the mishap. A wildness took hold of him. Nothing mattered anymore except causing the figures out on the plain to topple.

He did not know how many fell because of him; horses, camels, and men were all going down, and he exulted in it. He had forgotten he could feel like this or behave this way. . . . There was something incredibly primitive and exhilarating about killing in the heat of battle. His victims did not have faces, personalities, or families—they were nonentities, mere targets he was trying to hit . . . and hit them, he did. Or thought he did. In the smoke and dust, it was difficult to tell for certain.

As quickly as it had begun, it ended. The attackers wheeled their horses and fled, leaving behind a dreadful carnage. The desert lay strewn with bodies—human and animal. Silence descended, a deep silence broken only by the sound of a pitiful whinny. On the other side of the wall from Travis, a horse tried to rise on shattered front legs. The animal's cry of anguish wrenched Travis's soul. Nothing in his lifetime had prepared him for that sound of utter misery and despair. It was eerily human and made the hairs rise on the back of his neck.

He shuddered, and the trance was broken. Dear God, what had he done? What havoc had he wrought with his own two hands? Slowly, he got up. The horse's cry drew him, but before he could respond to it, Akbar himself strode out onto the plain, leveled a pistol at the dying animal, and shot it between the eyes. The sharp retort made Travis's skin jump. The horse collapsed, twitched once or twice, then lay still beneath the puff of smoke drifting across its body.

Travis's gorge rose. He could hardly keep from vomiting. Fighting a wave of dizziness, he had to grab onto the wall to keep from falling. The men of the *Ruala* began to rise and climb over the barrier. They walked among the fallen, examining this one, turning that one, coldly snatching up anything of value. Travis could not bear to watch. He staggered in the opposite direction—and almost knocked over Sadira.

Straightening her shoulders, she gazed out over the battlefield as if it barely interested her. As if she had seen such things before and knew she would see them again.

Her pale face was an ivory mask, devoid of expression. Only her eyes betrayed her true feelings. In them, Travis beheld the tragedy of all mankind . . . the grief, the sorrow, the regret. He remembered that she had not wanted this. She had delayed their departure as long as possible in hopes of avoiding it.

Shame poured over him in a scalding-hot wave. He had taken part in the slaughter and reveled in it. For a few brief moments, he had acted as a man possessed and committed unspeakable acts. He had actually relished slaying men and animals for the sheer excitement of watching them fall. . . . How could he have done it? *How?* This was a side of himself he had never acknowledged until today. Somehow he had been able to rationalize, if not glorify, similar actions during the war, but now he had to face the truth. Nothing—*nothing*—justified what had just occurred.

Sadira's gaze met his, and he wished with all his heart that he could take back the last few moments and relive them, that he could undo what he had done. Behind him, someone shouted. Welcoming the interruption, Travis turned to see Akbar motioning the *Ruala* to gather near.

"What happens now?" he muttered, dry-mouthed and still reeling from the shock of it all.

Sadira's tone, like her face, revealed nothing. She might have been a carved wooden statue for all the emotion she revealed, and he marveled at her ironclad control. It must have taken years for her to master the art of submerging and concealing her true feelings—feelings she had let him glimpse only moments before.

"Some will be sent out to capture the horses and camels running loose on the desert. Others will stay here to ransack and bury the dead. You must go and see if your Gamalat is among them."

My Gamalat, Travis thought. It's because of *me* this happened; I permitted it. In my heart I wanted revenge for the death of Fadoul and my own humiliation at Gamalat's hands. Well, now I've got it. And has it helped any? Will it bring Fadoul back from the dead? Has it restored all I thought I had lost?

He dreaded searching through the bodies—hunting for Gamalat's scarred face among them, but it needed to be done. *He* needed to look into the faces of the fallen men; he doubted he would find forgiveness in them, but he had to see them up close. He never wanted to forget them. Only by remembering, by imprinting them forever in his mind, could he be certain that he would never surrender to this madness again. Never again would he lift a gun, if he could help it, because once he had it in his hands, he knew he could not trust himself not to use it.

Sixteen men lay dead or dying upon the plain. One man ended his own life by taking out his dagger and plunging it into his chest. Gut-shot, he must have realized that death would claim him anyway, and he might as well avoid needless suffering. It did not take long for Travis to locate Gamalat's body; someone else found him first and called Akbar to come and see. Travis recognized the disfiguring scar on the mouth of the dead man, even before Sadira translated Akbar's inquiry: "Is this the man who led the band who beat and robbed thee?"

"He is the one," Travis affirmed. "There's the scar I told you about."

Sadira did not bother to translate this, but merely nodded. In death, Gamalat appeared harmless and faintly surprised. He lay on his back, his face turned toward the sun, eyes and mouth partially open. Groaning as if he himself were injured, Akbar sank to his knees beside the body. Gently, Sadira's father closed Gamalat's eyes and mouth. Around him, his men gathered, their attention focused on their sheik as Akbar performed other small acts of respect and apparent grief.

Travis did not understand what was happening. Was this yet another curious custom of the Bedouin that defied logical explanation? "What is it?" he asked Sadira. "What's going on? Does your father recognize this man? He acts as if he knows him."

"Yes," Sadira answered, her eyes filled with a great sadness. "He knows him well. *This* Gamalat is the son of the Sheik of Sheiks of the *Shammar.* We all know him but did not realize it was he from your description; the scar is a new one we have never seen before."

"So what is the problem? He's still the man responsible for the death of Fadoul."

Before Sadira could reply, Akbar rose to his feet and gave a series of orders that sent the men around him scurrying to obey. Most followed Hamid who set off at a brisk pace across the plain behind the battle site. Several of the remaining withdrew their swords or daggers and began to move among the bodies of the dead and dying. Travis did not guess their intent until one of the *Ruala* knelt beside a moaning man and swiftly drew the blade of his dagger across the fellow's throat.

"Good God!" he exploded, turning to see the same grisly scene being repeated elsewhere. "Tell them to stop!" he demanded, grabbing Sadira's sleeve.

Sadira sadly shook her head. "It must be done, *Frangi.* That is where the others have gone—to get the horses and go after those who fled. We must kill them all now. We have no choice."

"What do you mean, you have no choice? Of course, you have a choice. Akbar—wait!" Travis hurried after Sadira's father. The sheik paid him no heed but continued walking calmly and resolutely in the direction of the men who had gone to get the horses. "Sadira, tell your father to stop! I demand an explanation. *Why* must he kill them all? We've more than made up for what Gamalat and his party did to me and Fadoul."

"You do not understand, Travis." Sadira caught up with him and held up her hand. "Listen a moment, and I will explain."

"There's no excuse for cold-blooded murder!"

A man's scream—and then a gurgle—rent the air. Travis whirled about, searching for others whose deaths he might prevent, but it was too late. Not a single survivor remained alive on the plain; the *Ruala* had slain all the injured, every last man who had been unable to flee with their comrades.

"They all must die if we are to live, Travis. Not one must escape to tell the tale of what happened here today." Sadira gently touched his sleeve, her green eyes dark and troubled. "Your Gamalat was no petty thief but the heir to the entire sheikdom of the *Shammar.* He is the beloved only son of Hajem Pasha who rules the *Shammar* and its people, just as my father rules the *Anazah.*"

"Gamalat was also a thief! Can you excuse his crime simply because of his father's exalted position? What kind of twisted justice is that?"

"The ways of the desert people are still a mystery to you, Travis. Had we known who he was, my father would have gone to *his* father and demanded restitution for Gamalat's misdeeds. And Hajem Pasha would have punished his son as he saw fit and returned your goods, then negotiated with Akbar to reach a settlement regarding the death of Fadoul. You would have been paid in coin for the loss of your servant and furnished with horses and camels in retribution for your own suffering. All would have been handled without bloodshed . . . but now it is too late. We have killed Hajem Pasha's only son; he will neither forgive nor forget. His honor will demand that the *Shammar* slay the *Anazah,* most particularly the *Ruala,* wherever they find them, and the *Anazah* in turn will slay the *Shammar.* There will be no end to the bloodshed. It will go on until the river *wadis* run red with blood, and the desert sands are drenched with it. Not a single well or watering place will be safe. All will become places of death and ambush. . . . You see why my father must go after the survivors.

"We cannot give life back to Gamalat." She nodded toward the dead man still lying some distance away from them. "But we can—and *must*—prevent the survivors of this battle from returning to Hajem Pasha and identifying *us.* If we can stop that from happening, Gamalat's father will draw the same conclusions we did. Assuming he eventually learns of his son's death, he will think it an isolated instance involving petty thieves and bandits. He will not go to war over it; all he will do is kill a few thieves and then let the matter rest."

"My God!" was all Travis could manage.

Over a slight rise, Akbar and his men suddenly came galloping—robes billowing, *keffiyas* streaming behind them on the wind. The horses were wild-eyed, their hooves barely skimming the ground, their tails flared out like colored banners. No longer did Travis find it an exciting, romantic sight. Death rode along with Akbar; before the day was over, more men would die, more blood would be shed. The stone had been cast into the pond, and the ripples it caused would go on forever, creating an ever-widening circle of violence and revenge.

"What about the goat herder who guards this well?" he suddenly remembered. "He will know the truth of the matter."

A single tear trickled down Sadira's cheek. "My father has probably already dealt with him."

No sooner had she finished speaking when they both heard the bleating of frightened goats. Over the same rise, a flock of black and white goats appeared, leaping and jumping on nimble feet as they scattered and ran. No one followed. The goat herder did not appear to gather them together and keep them from running in all directions.

"Your father's nothing but a murderer. A calculating, cold-blooded murderer."

"My father must think first of the safety of his people," Sadira defended, but more tears welled in her green eyes and trickled down her cheeks. "I do not expect thee to understand. Thou art a *frangi,* after all. Our ways are beyond thee."

"How *can* I understand? Any way you look at it, it's still murder! You don't approve of it either—or else why are you weeping?"

She turned on him with a cry of anguish and indignation. " 'Tis not my place to approve or disapprove! I am only the Keeper of the Mares, not the sheik of my people. My father must do what must be done to protect the lives of those entrusted to his care. He dare not show weakness, or none of us will be safe on our grazing lands or at our watering holes. If his own son, Nuri, my half-brother, should meet death on his pilgrimage to Mecca, my father will try to determine the how and why of it, and then he will punish those responsible for his son's death. Like Hajem Pasha, his honor will demand it."

"His honor!" Travis scoffed. "You people use honor as an excuse for everything—murder, revenge, ridiculous sacrifices . . ."

" 'Tis a man's greatest possession!" Sadira flared, eyes blazing. "And a woman's, too. Without honor, a person is nothing. Muhammad taught us to also value honor, loyalty, generosity, and courage. Without these—especially honor—men cannot live on the desert. 'Tis too harsh a place."

"What happens when honor conflicts with kindness, mercy, and compassion? Or maybe love. What happens when honor demands one thing, and love another? Which will you choose, Sadira? . . . No, don't tell me. I already know. You yourself will always choose honor. You may weep and mourn and suffer greatly, but you'll choose honor over everything else. In the name of honor, you can justify anything—even killing an innocent goat herder, just because he witnessed something you didn't want him to see."

Sadira wrung her hands together. "Thou art twisting everything around, Travis! We were speaking of honor and . . . and responsibility. And how my father must do what is necessary to protect his people. Why do you bring love into it? 'Tis a forbidden feeling! What we feel for each other has nothing to do with this! 'Tis separate and apart."

"No, it isn't, Sadira. It's all bound up together. Can't you see that? You're so blinded by false notions of honor and duty that you can't begin to admit you might be wrong about things—and your father is also wrong. Terribly wrong. We could have handled this whole matter some other way, without murdering innocent people and perpetuating an endless cycle of violence."

Travis reached for Sadira's shoulders, preventing her from turning away. "Don't you ever question what you've always believed? Isn't it about time you did? You have a heart and a brain of your own; why not use them? Why not trust your own instincts?"

Her eyes were huge. Brimming with tears and confusion, she gazed at him from the depths of her *keffiya*. "It would be wrong to challenge my father, Travis. 'Tis wrong to question all I have ever learned and believed."

He removed his hands from her shoulders and stepped back from her. "Then I guess you'll have to continue defending your father when he kills helpless people, won't you? You'll have to keep denying yourself the right to be a woman, with a woman's normal needs and desires. But at least you won't have to worry about me bothering you any longer—or tempting you to stray from the path of righteousness and honor. I've seen enough, Sadira. It's sickened me. I covet your horses, but I'm not willing to sell my soul for them. I'll buy my horses elsewhere. As soon as possible, I'm returning to Aleppo. I'll need a guide to take me back, of course. Tell your father he can have my share of Gamalat's booty in exchange for providing that guide."

Sadira did not run to him, fling herself weeping into his arms, and try to change his mind, as he had hoped. Instead, she merely stood there—wounded but unmoved. "Thou may have Najila," she whispered. "I give her to thee. She is thine now, *Frangi*. Thou dost not have to pay for her."

"Ah, but I've already paid for her," Travis ground out. "In ways you would not understand. I came here and met you, and . . . and . . ." He couldn't quite admit it, couldn't tell her he had fallen in love, not now, when his love had turned to ashes. "Coming here was a big mistake—one I'll be paying for the rest of my life."

There. He had said that much. Implied what he felt and what he wanted her to feel. Still, she remained unmoved.

"It should not have happened, *Frangi*. I am sorry I have hurt thee. May Allah forgive me."

"I'm sorry, too."

They remained there a moment, studying each other, but there was nothing more to say. She would soon forget him, he thought. How easily she slipped back into saying thee and thou again! It happened whenever she grew excited—or upset—or they argued. Just as easily would she forget she had ever met him. . . . Pivoting on his heel, Travis strode quickly away.

Eleven

Not until late that night did Akbar and his men finally return, trotting their exhausted horses back to the well for a drink. There, Sadira had assembled all the loose animals she could find, and Travis had managed to bury all the dead *Shammar*, including Gamalat, beneath a thin layer of sand right where they had fallen. Her father rode straight to her and greeted her with a curt nod.

"I should not have left thee here alone with the *frangi*," he said, reining in Tahani and dismounting. "Forgive me, Daughter, but other matters occupied my attention. I trust all is well?" Akbar glanced in Travis's direction, grunting in approval when he saw that the distant-robed figure had made a small fire of camel dung and was hunkered down in front of it, paying neither of them the slightest heed.

"Thou need not worry where I am concerned, Father. By now, thou shouldst know that." Sadira gave her father a weary smile. "Didst thou find all of them?"

Akbar sighed and passed a hand across his eyes. "No, Daughter, we did not. Five we caught and killed, but at least two others escaped. We lost their tracks when they fled across a place of flint and shale. The hard stony ground stretches a great distance, and to search it thoroughly could take days. 'Twill be too late, I fear, by the time we catch up to them. . . . I must think of some other way out of this predicament. Within several days, Hajem Pasha will hear what has happened, I am certain. I will pray on the matter, and perhaps some inspiration will occur to me."

Sadira threw her arms around her father in a quick embrace, then as quickly drew back again. She and Akbar had never been affectionate; between them stood the specter of her mother's betrayal. Akbar never encouraged little gestures of affection with anyone except Alima. Yet he rarely took Alima to his bed, Sadira knew. The haughty Jaleel and his youngest wife, Jahara, met his physical needs, while Alima supplied companionship and whatever else was needed.

"I, too, will pray very hard that a solution will come to thee, Father. Allah will not permit his desert children to go to war; he will show us a way to avert such a tragedy."

"I hope so, Daughter. Call Sherifa now and tell the *frangi* to prepare to ride."

"We will not stay here tonight? But thou must be tired, Father."

Akbar shook his head, his features nearly invisible in the shadow of his headcloth. The stars were bright, and a half moon had risen, bathing the plain in a silvery light, but the light did not reach his face. "I cannot sleep where the stench of my enemies invades my dreams."

"There will be no stench, Father—and probably no jackals either, at least not tonight. Dost thou not see that Travis—the *frangi*—has covered all the bodies with sand?"

Akbar glanced around. "I noticed, but I can still smell them. Alive or dead, the *Shammar* stink. Anyway, I prefer to return to Alima as soon as possible. 'Tis good thou hast gathered the animals. We will take them and leave this place. It offends my eyes as well as my nose. We will not drink from this well again. Hereafter, it shall be known as the well of sorrow."

Sadira interpreted her father's comment to mean that he was no happier about what had occurred here than she her-self—or Travis. But Akbar had not been able to avoid it. She wished Travis could understand. She had rejected his love but still wanted his respect. Now she did not even have that. He despised the Bedouin and could not wait to leave them. He refused to see the truth, yet accused *her* of being blind.

"Father, I have given Najila to the *frangi* who now wishes to depart from us," she blurted out. "He has re-quested a guide to take him back to northern Syria—to the city of Aleppo, from whence he came."

"He wishes to abandon the *Ruala* in the hour of their greatest danger?" Akbar gazed in Travis's direction. "Well, I suppose it is understandable. He has avenged his servant's death, gained many horses and camels—as well as goats— and now thou hast given him Najila. I have no objections, either to his departure or to the gift of the mare. He fought well and bravely; he deserves all he has received."

"Father, I do not think he desires the horses and camels we won from Gamalat, and I am certain he does not want the goats."

"But they are his, not mine. It was for him I took them. What need have I for the beasts of my enemies? My herds are plentiful, while he has suffered and lost everything. Is he a fool then?"

Sadira swallowed against the sudden lump in her throat. "He is no fool, but he takes no pride in what he helped to do today—he disapproved of killing the survivors and the goat herder."

"Then he does not realize what is at stake here. Didst thou not explain?"

"I tried, Father. But . . . but . . ."

"He is a *frangi*," her father snorted, as if that explained everything, as indeed, it did. "After we return to the main encampment, I will arrange for a guide as he has requested. If he is going to go, he should leave immediately—before the war begins. Once Hajem Pasha hears about his son, I cannot guarantee the *frangi*'s safety. 'Tis a long way to Aleppo. Every step he takes will be dangerous. The *Shammar* will attack everything that moves; they will be searching the desert for victims to satisfy their thirst for vengeance."

"I know, Father. I told him that, but he did not believe me. He thinks there must be some gentler way to deal with the *Shammar.*"

"There is no gentler way, or I would have considered it. What do men do in *his* country, I wonder?"

"In his country, 'tis all different, Father. The government enforces the laws. Thou hast heard him speak if it, the same as I. They do not even have camels in America."

"Men will still be men—and the *frangi* fought like a man today. It grieves me to learn he feels as he does. I had thought to make him my blood brother. He is the first *frangi* I would have been proud to claim as brother. Ah, well. . . . See if thou canst persuade him to at least accept Gamalat's horses and camels. If there are no camels in his country, he can introduce them and become a rich man—assuming he is not rich already. If he is, he will increase his wealth. Once his people discover camels, everyone will want one."

Sadira had her doubts about this but did not express them. She only knew that Kentucky and America were nothing at all like the lands belonging to the heirs of Ishmael. Arabia, Syria, Turkey, the Empty Quarter—these were all occupied by Muslims, men who lived by the *Koran* and the call of the *muezzin,* who cherished the same things and did not need to explain their customs to one another. Vast differences separated the men of the desert from the men of the cities, but even greater differences separated men like her father and men like Travis. Their cultures were nothing alike.

She had been briefly and intensely drawn to Travis—she feared to call it love!—but she could never say she had truly known or understood him, not as she knew and understood her father, Hamid, or even Hajem Pasha, whom she had only seen from a distance. She would soon forget Travis; she *must* forget him. It was over between them. Thank Allah it had not gone beyond a few stolen kisses and heated caresses! And for these she would beg Allah to forgive her, and she would make atonement for the rest of her life.

They traveled all night without stopping and part of the next day, rejoining Alima and falling down to sleep like dead men immediately thereafter. Sadira welcomed the exhaustion that blotted out dreams and kept her from grieving, thinking about Travis, or worrying about Hajem Pasha. Only after she had slept a whole night through, awakened, eaten, and washed did all these things come crowding into her mind again, filling her with dread, fear, and sorrow.

Anxiety weighed heavy as a stone in her breast as she watched her father's men sitting in small groups—not sleeping, talking, or taking their ease—but cleaning their weapons. Preparing for war. Only Travis still slept; she did not see him among the men, which meant that he must still be resting inside his own tent. Avoiding conversation with everyone, even Alima who was supervising Samir in the milking of a goat, Sadira finally slipped inside her father's shelter and found him there alone, lounging on his pillows and gazing into space. He glanced up when she entered, then patted the pillow beside him.

"Come, Sadira, sit. 'Tis well thou hast come, for I was about to send for thee."

He had called her Sadira, not "Daughter," as he usually did. Sadira did not know whether this boded well or ill; it certainly meant something. Even her father's manner toward her seemed changed—almost wary. He did not look at her directly, as he normally did, but idly picked at the tassel of a pillow. As she took the place he had indicated and waited for him to continue, she felt like a child again, in awe of her father and fearful, wanting his notice but dreading it, too. She could not guess what he was thinking. When he did glance her way, his eyes were hooded.

"I have thought, and I have prayed, Sadira. And I now know what I must do to keep my people safe and stop the war before it begins."

She drew a deep breath of relief. Allah be praised! Some solution had occurred to Akbar. "I am pleased, Father. Whatever it is, thou must do it and be at peace with thyself. Nothing can be worse than to have all of the *Shammar* and all of the *Anazah* at war with one another. No one would be safe. The loss of life and the suffering would be unbearable."

He raised his eyes to meet hers, and she almost gasped at the change in his manner. Gone was the fierce hawk who intimidated men and took pleasure in it. Her father suddenly looked old, tired, and sad. There were lines about his mouth and eyes that she had never seen before—nor had she witnessed such agony in his expression.

"Sadira . . . Daughter. . . ." He paused, and she was amazed to see the glint of tears in his eyes—and a tenderness she had thought reserved only for Alima.

"What is it, Father? Tell me. It cannot be as bad as all that, not if thou hast thought of a way to avert this war. I will support thee in whatever thou hast decided, and so will everyone else."

Her father drew a deep breath. "We will go to Hajem Pasha and offer retribution for the death of his son. We will give him our swiftest horses, our finest camels, our best sheep and goats . . ."

"Oh, yes, Father! A splendid idea."

"But not fair recompense for the loss of a son, is it, Sadira? Not unless we also give him . . ." he hesitated, then blurted, ". . . thee."

"Me?" Sadira did not understand—did not *want* to understand, though her suspicions were growing.

"Thee and Sherifa. Thou art our ceremonial virgin, our precious Keeper of the Mares, and Sherifa is the finest of all the horses we own. The two of thee have brought us luck and good fortune. Thou hast protected us and increased our prosperity. The *Ruala* and the *Anazah* possess nothing more valuable. . . . Both of thee together are the heart and soul of our people. 'Tis a great blow we will suffer—a monstrous loss, but I fear we must hand thee over to our enemies."

Sadira could say nothing for a moment. She felt robbed of breath—could no longer sense her heart beating. "But . . . what will they do with me, Father? Sherifa, yes, I can see they would want her. . . . She would please anyone. But me? Father, any power I possess, any good fortune

I have brought to our people has come from Allah, not from me. I cannot so easily transfer my loyalty, my affections, my allegiance to . . . to the *Shammar,* people I have always regarded as . . . as . . ."

"Daughter, thou *must.* I can see no other way. If they are wise, and I do not count them stupid, they will accept thee as the ceremonial virgin for *their* people. Thou wilt do as thou hast always done, only thou wilt be doing it for the *Shammar,* instead of the *Anazah.*"

"And if . . . if they are *not* wise?"

Akbar gave a slight but noticeable shrug. "Who can say? Thou art a beautiful woman, Sadira. As beautiful as thy mother—nay, thou art *more* beautiful. Hajem Pasha may install thee in his harem and use thee to get another son. He has bred a tentful of daughters, but only one son . . . Gamalat. Perhaps thou wilt bring him luck and give him a new heir. He is no older than I am; 'tis still possible."

An image of herself living in a tent filled with hostile women flashed through Sadira's mind. It would be exactly as it had been when she was a child—only this time there would be no Alima to comfort and mother her. This time there would only be an angry old husband, resentful of who she was and what had been taken from him. Never again would she ride free on the desert; Hajem Pasha would not allow it.

"It would be better if he simply took my life," she murmured.

"That, too, is a possibility, Daughter. I would be lying to thee if I said it was not. Indeed, the *Shammar* may demand it. In any case, the choice of what will become of thee will belong to Hajem Pasha and the *Shammar.* In place of his son, I will give him my beloved daughter. He cannot refuse; he will not refuse. He will see immediately that the trade is a fair one. More than fair, for I am also delivering my best horses and camels, my finest breeding stock, the true wealth of my people . . . the very means of our survival. Yet that is why I will do it—in order that we might survive."

Sadira raised a trembling hand to her mouth. "Oh, Father!"

She hiccupped on a sob. She wanted to run from the tent, summon Sherifa, leap upon her back, and gallop away across the desert. But she knew she would never do it. Her people needed her now as never before. This then was her fate, her destiny. . . . Perhaps it was her punishment for allowing herself to yearn for a *frangi,* for permitting him to kiss her, for deceiving her people into thinking she was pure and holy, when actually she was as weak and human as the lowliest slave, as weak and human as her own mother had been.

This was one last chance to redeem her bloodline, to remove the taint of wickedness that had destroyed her mother—and threatened to destroy her as well. She grew conscious of her father's eyes upon her, seeking her approval . . . and her forgiveness.

"When shall we leave, Father?" she managed to get out. Her voice was quivering and barely audible, but she forced herself to make it strong. "Had it better not be soon?"

He nodded. "I will send a messenger at once to Hajem Pasha to tell him we are coming in peace to make restitution for a great wrong we have done him. He will delay making war against us until he hears what we have to say. His honor will demand it. I believe it will also demand that he accept my offer. If he does not, we will have lost nothing, for war will be inevitable then. He may reject us and attack us where we stand, but . . ."

"But thou dost not think he will because he is a man of honor," Sadira finished for him.

Honor. *Honor!* She thought she might be justified in hating the word. She could never explain *this* to Travis. Nor would she make the attempt. Travis must leave immediately. Tomorrow, at the latest. He must never know what was going to happen.

"I have selected a guide to take the *frangi* to Aleppo," her father said, changing the subject now that he knew he had her cooperation. Not that she had ever given him reason to doubt he would always have it. "Hamid would be best, but I cannot spare him. Therefore, I have chosen Haaris."

"Yes, Haaris will be excellent," she agreed. Haaris was no stranger to desert travel, and his name meant vigilant, a quality Travis would need on his long journey.

"Haaris will be ready early in the morning."

"I will tell the *frangi,*" she said, rising to depart the tent before her control completely shattered.

"Sadira!" Akbar reached for her hand and clasped it between his strong brown fingers. Once more, his dark eyes swam with tears. "Daughter, forgive me. As Allah is my witness, I swear to thee that I have long since forgiven thee for the sins of thy mother. Thou art truly my daughter, the child of my heart, the pride of my old age. I would not do this were it not necessary. I had almost rather sacrifice Nuri, but he is not here, and if he were, the *Shammar* would kill him of a certainty. I do not believe they will slay thee. Thy beauty will move them to mercy . . . and if Allah wills it, thou wilt find happiness among the *Shammar.*"

Sadira drew her father's head to her breast and hugged him. She had waited all these years to hear words of forgiveness and declarations of love. She had waited her entire lifetime. She could not hate him for what he demanded of her, yet she could not help noting that he had said he would *almost* rather sacrifice Nuri. Nuri was still his flesh and blood, his heart's treasure, though Nuri had fought with him at every turn, while she had surrendered all he had ever demanded. It was so unfair, so hurtful. Her father's tears were hot on the bare flesh of her arm, as at last she released him.

"Fear not, Father. I will do my duty and not hate thee for it. How could I hate thee when I have loved thee all the days of my life?"

She left the tent to the sound of Akbar's sobs as he lay back on the pillows and wept.

Sadira needed some time alone before she confronted Travis, and she swiftly returned to her own tiny quarters and there dried her eyes, washed her face, and composed herself as best she could. A curious numbness had taken hold of her, blunting her emotions so that she felt no pain, no fear . . . nothing. It was probably Allah's way of giving her strength to endure her parting from Travis and her coming ordeal—the parting from her own people. Whatever it was, she welcomed it.

After several moments, she felt prepared to meet him and stepped outside. Hamid awaited her there, but he did not speak nor try to stop her. He simply stood and stared at her, his heart in his eyes, and she wondered if he had already heard of her father's plan. She could spare him little sympathy when her own world was falling apart.

"Where is the *frangi*, Hamid? Thou art busy spying on him day and night, so thou must know. Is he within his tent?"

He recoiled as if she had struck him. "He left his tent not long ago. I saw him and Alima over near the goats with Samir."

"I thank thee for that information, Hamid. Now I know where to go." She moved to step around him, but he blocked her path. She lifted her eyes to his attractive brown face, now dark with anger or some other turbulent emotion.

"Sadira . . ." he murmured. "Sadira, *Habiba,* I would speak with thee. Have pity on my torment, and do not turn away from me!"

Habiba. Beloved. His plea was quiet, meant for her ears alone, but still, Sadira worried that someone might hear. From Hamid's expression alone, she could tell he meant to say things he should never utter—not to her, the Keeper of the Mares and ceremonial virgin.

"This is neither the time nor place, Hamid. And if 'tis love thou wish to speak of, there will never be a proper time or place. Do not make a spectacle of thyself."

"Sadira, I cannot help it! Too long have I been silent . . ."

"Maintain thy silence!" she snapped. "My father will slit thy throat if thou cannot restrain thyself."

"But I am in agony, *Habiba,* watching thee day after day—witnessing that *frangi* daring to gaze at thee with lust and longing. . . ."

"Enough, or I shall go to my father! Remember thy wives and thy children, Hamid. To them, thou must give thy love and loyalty. They are thine. I am not and never will be. Now, step aside. My father bids me bear a message to the *frangi,* and I must go and deliver it now."

"If Akbar knew what I know, he would slit the throat of the *frangi,* not the throat of his friend, Hamid. He would not send thee to the *frangi* bearing messages."

Could Hamid be aware that she and Travis had spent a

night together in her tent—that night of the storm? No, he would have said something sooner; he would have gone straight to Akbar then.

"Thou knowest nothing, Hamid. Thou only hast suspicions, nurtured and cherished because of thine own wrongful thoughts. Step aside. Thou hast delayed me too long already. I must go."

Hamid reluctantly stepped aside, his black eyes smoldering. Sadira dared not attempt to soothe him, though she felt sorry for his plight. Poor Hamid! He had committed no sin but loving her, and once, she had thought herself in love with him—had dreamed of becoming his wife. He was a good man, loyal and trustworthy, a devout Muslim, generous and kind to all he called friend . . . an excellent horseman. He was the sort she ought to have married, had marriage been permitted to her.

But he did not stir her deepest emotions, did not make her heart leap, or her blood race. He did not make her tremble with longing and desire. Only one man did that . . . and soon he would be leaving. She would never see him again.

Travis! she cried out silently. *Oh, Travis, thou art my* habib, *and I will love thee forever, until the day I die!*

Twelve

"Goat," Alima said proudly. "Goat milk. Good. *Frangi* like, yes?"

"It's not bad." Travis handed back the small brass cup into which Samir had gathered a small quantity of precious goat milk that Alima had insisted Travis try. He decided he liked it better than camel's milk, but could not claim to have a fondness for either.

Samir was now milking another goat, directing the stream of thin liquid into a large brass pail. He would probably have to milk half the herd to fill the pail completely— which was what Alima obviously intended. Interspersing Arabic with English, Alima kept up a steady stream of instructions and explanations. Her growing facility with English amazed Travis; she seemed to have a true gift for languages. Were he staying much longer, she would soon be speaking and translating as well as Sadira. . . . Too bad he wasn't staying, he thought gloomily.

Alima's optimism and cheerfulness were equally amazing. By now, she surely knew that the desert would soon be plunged into war—everyone else knew it—but with typical Bedouin resignation to fate, Alima was calmly continuing her normal activities. The arrival of the goat herd had delighted her; no sooner had Travis set foot outside his tent when she eagerly called him over to partake of the first reluctant offerings of a protesting she-goat.

"Aren't you going to have some?" Travis pointed to the goat, then to her, and made drinking motions.

Alima shook her head, her veil swirling about her frail shoulders. "No, *Frangi*. I save for Akbar. Goat milk give . . . give . . ." She frowned and flexed the muscles of one arm. "I do not know how to say."

"Strength? Vigor?"

She nodded happily. "Yes. Strength. Vigor. Make strong. Akbar grow old—like me. Need goat milk to feel young again."

Travis could not help liking and admiring this small, homely woman who doted so much on her fierce husband. Despite her wrinkled unremarkable face and fragile, slightly misshapen body, Alima had a beauty all her own. Travis had enjoyed the evenings he spent with her and Akbar—and Sadira. He would miss the *Ruala* when he left them. Despite what had happened at the well and his own bad experiences, they were a fascinating people and the desert an incredible place.

Earlier that morning, just before sunrise, he had walked out onto the hard, flat, stony ground of the surrounding plain and there stirred up a flock of birds—clumsy, desert bustards mixed with some sort of grouse or partridge. They had been feeding on bright red caterpillars. A patch of the furry insects dotted nearly every blade of grass and stalk of herbiage. The air had smelled unusually sweet and fresh, and the ever-present wind had carried enticing, earthy odors he could not identify. That air of elusive fecundity was one of the desert's greatest surprises. Just when he thought it barren and ugly, its beauty suddenly shattered his senses.

In the purity of the new-washed morning, the ugliness

of the recent violence had also faded, and he could think more clearly. Could take time to consider that he might be judging Akbar—and Sadira—too harshly, according to Western standards, not taking into account the mysterious ways of the East. He conceded he had a far greater horror of death than they did, and his views of morality differed. Though not ready to admit he was wrong, he did wonder if he had the right to condemn and criticize as freely as he had.

During the war, his own superiors and he himself had done regrettable things, but he had always given them the benefit of the doubt and withheld his criticism. Once, his commanding officer had ordered him to attack a school-house supposedly harboring the enemy. He and his men—a crack cavalry unit—had done so, and when the smoke cleared, they discovered they had killed a bunch of harmless Negro slaves hiding from their masters.

For weeks afterward, he had suffered nightmares about the incident, yet had continued following orders that could possibly result in other such tragic "mistakes." After all, it was war, and sometimes the innocent minority had to suffer in order to accomplish some greater good for the majority. Akbar undoubtedly excused his actions at the well in the same way. Travis could not explain to himself why he expected Sadira to condemn her own father; he just did . . . and he knew he was being unfair, particularly since Sadira *had* expressed regret and sorrow over her father's actions. And he himself could claim no exemption from sin when it came to the matter of violence.

He lingered awhile with Alima and Samir among the goats, laughing when one of the nimble little beasts kicked over the brass bucket and bolted, leaving a red-faced Samir shouting insults. Alima scolded the servant for frightening the animal, and in the middle of her tirade, Travis glanced up to see Sadira threading her way through the goats to get to him. As always, the sight of her lifted his spirits and made his heart pound erratically. He met her halfway, and they stood amidst the playful, curious goats and self-consciously greeted each other. At the same time, they carefully avoided meeting each other's eyes.

Sadira quickly announced the reason why she had come looking for him. *"Frangi,* I came to tell you that my father has chosen a man named Haaris to guide you back to Aleppo. He wishes you to know that the camels, horses, and these goats we brought back from the well are all yours to take. If you need herders, you can arrange a trade with a few of our men; they will gladly accompany you in exchange for a camel or a horse or a few goats."

"Sadira . . ." Travis used his knee to block a kid intent upon butting him in the thigh. "Let's get away from here and go someplace we can talk."

He took her elbow and steered her toward the open desert, but as they left the goats and approached the plain, she hung back. "There is nothing to discuss, *Frangi.* I have said what I came to say."

"Ah, but I haven't finished speaking with *you."*

As they reached a comparatively quiet area, Travis gave Sadira his undivided attention and noticed that she was deathly pale. All the color had drained from her face; even her eyes were a dull shade of green, not the usual vivid sparkling color that took away his breath whenever he gazed into them. "I have reconsidered," he informed her. "And I no longer wish to leave yet, Sadira."

She stopped in her tracks and stared at him. "You no longer wish to leave?"

Shock and dismay were not the emotions he had hoped

to arouse, yet her face revealed both, to his great disappointment. He could hardly blame her for wanting to see him gone; she had saved his life, but he had done little to express his gratitude and indeed had only criticized her and made her unhappy.

"I . . . I want to apologize for the things I said to you out there at the well, Sadira. I had no right to say them—or even think them. I'm as bloodthirsty as the next man, and what little I know of desert life does not entitle me to sit in judgment on either you or your father. Whether I agree or disagree with what you do, I should tend to my own business and let you tend yours. You both know what you're doing better than I do."

Her eyes widened. Her face brightened. "Thank you, Travis. Your apology means much to me. . . . However"—a shadow crossed her lovely features—". . . my father and I think it best you depart from here immediately. We can no longer ensure your safety."

"I don't hold you responsible for my safety. I will stay and fight beside you, if I must. I swore never to lift a gun again, but I find I can't just walk away from this. The whole mess is as much my fault as anyone's. I *wanted* your father's help to find Gamalat and punish him. When we did find him, I did my damnedest to kill him and everyone who was with him. As for the animals, I won't consider claiming them. I'll take Najila, but the rest belong to your father. If he doesn't want them, maybe he ought to give them back to the *Shammar,* as a kind of peace offering. Has he thought of going to Gamalat's father and apologizing? Well, maybe not apologizing but at least explaining *why* we attacked and killed his son and his friends?"

Sadira glanced away evasively. "We have thought of that."

"And what did you decide?"

She shifted from one foot to the other. Travis realized she did not want to tell him. "Trust me, Sadira," he begged softly. "I promise I won't be so quick to criticize this time. I'll try to be more tolerant and attempt to see things from *your* point of view."

"You will not like what we have decided, Travis. Therefore, I will not tell you. The best thing would be for you to go—to leave the *Ruala* and return to safety in Aleppo. You are neither *Shammar* nor *Anazah;* this is not your problem. It does not concern you. 'Tis a matter between the desert peoples only."

"Don't shut me out, Sadira! Considering what I feel for you *and* your people, you can't expect me to walk away from here and simply leave you to your fate. I'm an American, and when I break something, I try to fix it. When I see wrongs, I attempt to right them. If I can change something and make it better, I will. I don't believe in fate; I make my own fate. That's why I came here. Tell me no, and I'll get up and shout *yes!* That's the way Americans are. It's the way *I* am. I may not always be right, but I fight for what I believe, and I don't take no for an answer!"

"Not ever?" A tiny smile quirked the corners of her mouth. "Were it possible, I would like to see your country, Travis, and meet more of your brash, bold Americans. If they are like you, it would be a most interesting and enlightening journey."

"It's possible, Sadira. I know you would enjoy my countrymen, and in time, understand them, too. They are not nearly so complicated as the Bedouin."

"No." She sadly shook her head. "No, it can never be. But if it will ease your mind so you can leave us without guilt or anxiety, I will tell you this: My father has thought of a way to avoid bloodshed. As you yourself suggested, it involves making offerings of peace to Gamalat's father, Hajem Pasha."

"You will give him your best horses."

Sadira's expressive eyes told Travis he had guessed correctly.

"And camels. You will offer your best camels."

She nodded.

"Horses and camels—wonderful gifts. But will they be enough to console the sheik for the loss of his only son and heir?"

Sadira did not answer but began walking away from him, and Travis sensed there was more to it than she was willing to admit.

"What *else* will your father do, Sadira? What more can he possibly give the *Shammar?*"

No sooner had Travis voiced the question when an ugly suspicion formed in his mind. "He doesn't intend to give them Sherifa, does he? Not Sherifa. That would be a tragedy. She's yours!"

Sadira walked faster. Drawing the corner of her *keffiya* across her face, she deliberately hid her features from him. With long strides, Travis caught up with her.

"By God, he does! He intends to give them Sherifa, Lulu, and . . . and . . ." It came to him in a blinding flash. But no . . . no, it couldn't be! Akbar would never . . . Sadira would never. . . . *Oh, yes, she would.* To save her beloved *Ruala,* Sadira would agree to anything.

"Sadira, damn it, stop!"

She was running now, fleeing from him—dashing toward the distant horses grazing on the plain. He ran after her, seized her by the shoulder, and spun her around to face him. "You're going with Sherifa, aren't you? You're part of the bargain. Your father means to hand you over to his enemies along with his best horses and camels."

"Yes!" she spat. "And I will go, Travis! I will willingly accept whatever Allah decrees for me—becoming the Keeper of the Mares for the *Shammar,* marrying Hajem Pasha and living the rest of my days in his harem, or . . . or . . ."

"Torture and death," Travis finished for her. "You'll accept your own destruction if that's what they want to satisfy their desire for revenge."

"Yes, I will accept it and count myself fortunate to be able to save so many others from dying!"

"Sadira—no! You can't do it! You mustn't let your father and your people use you like that. They have no right to demand this of you. Haven't you already done enough? You've sacrificed everything in life that's worthwhile—you can't give them your life, too."

"I can, and I will, Travis. How many times must I say it? *You do not understand.* You are not one of us."

"I understand plenty." His fingers dug into her arms. A look of pain crossed her delicate features, and he forced himself to loosen his grip, though he was so angry he wanted to hurt her if that was what he must do to make her see sense. "Something else besides mere dedication is making you do this, Sadira. Tell me what it is. You're hardly more than a child. Nothing you could have done is so terrible that it justifies sacrificing your life in atonement."

" 'Twas not I!" she cried, her reserve suddenly shattering. " 'Twas my mother. Akbar is not my true father. I am the bastard daughter of a *frangi* who tempted my mother to break her marriage vows. . . . Now, do you see, Travis? My blood is tainted, and I have spent my whole lifetime trying to make it pure again. Trying to wipe away the stain of my mother's betrayal—to atone for her sin against my

father and our whole people. She behaved dishonorably!
She shamed Akbar! What she did was unforgivable, and
many still have not forgiven her. To this very day, they
remember and despise her for it!"

"That was *her* sin—not yours! You aren't responsible for
what your mother did."

"I am the same as she is. I am weak, Travis. Weak and
foolish. I, too, desire what I cannot have. Since you arrived
here, I have been in torment . . . I almost gave myself to
you in the tent that day of the storm. . . ."

"Nonsense! You've done nothing wrong. *Nothing,* do you
hear me? And you don't owe anybody anything because of
what your mother did."

He sought to gather her into his arms, but she broke free
and ran, fleeing like a frantic deer across the plain. She
didn't want his sympathy or his comfort. She would never
listen to his arguments. He had suspected her true heritage,
but never guessed she was so ashamed of it. Now at last,
he understood her determination to honor her vows. She
did not want to *be* like her mother—a symbol of shame,
deceit, and betrayal. Her mother had been a married woman
caught in adultery. Sadira's situation was far different, but
between her twisted sense of honor and her belief that Allah
controlled everything anyway, she was willing to seal her
own doom.

The injustice of it made Travis's blood boil. He wanted
to tear Akbar apart for playing upon Sadira's guilt, for ma-
nipulating and controlling her all these years . . . and for
sending her off to buy peace with the sacrifice of her freedom and possibly her life. Incredible as it seemed, Akbar
and Sadira both thought they were doing the right thing.
In their world, it made perfect sense. . . . So how in hell
was he going to stop it? What could he do?

He had no idea, but the one thing he would *not* do was leave the *Ruala* and abandon Sadira to her fate. If nothing else, he would stay and keep arguing. He would batter away at the wall of her defenses. He had to make her see reason, had to convince her she was not responsible for her mother's sins and that her own desires were not wrong and sinful. She may not be the right woman for him nor he the right man for her, but she deserved a chance to live life on her own terms, not her father's or anyone else's.

If it came down to it, he might have to kidnap her, steal her away before the *Ruala* handed her over to the *Shammar.* It was barbaric—sending a young woman to her enemies to submit to slavery, a marriage without love or caring, or a horrible, painful death! If the *Shammar* were anything like the *Ruala,* they would probably demand that she die. *An eye for an eye, a tooth for a tooth.* . . . He must not forget that these hot, arid lands had produced the harsh tenets of the Old Testament, and people had lived by them for centuries. Instead of embracing the gentle teachings of the New Testament, the Bedouin followed Muhammad who had once decreed that paradise belonged to those who made war on infidels. They would meet violence with violence and claim Sadira's life in exchange for Gamalat's; he was certain of it.

Travis watched as Sadira found Sherifa, leapt upon her back, and galloped toward the distant horizon. If by some miracle the *Shammar* did let her live, they would never grant her the freedom she enjoyed among her own tribesmen. Confined to a tent, swathed in a *burqa,* she would be miserable. He thought of her in the arms of a man who hated her for being *Ruala,* and he could scarcely endure the jealousy and pain provoked by the image. Gamalat's father would find it difficult indeed not to punish her for the loss of his son. Were she allowed to live, she would not be treated with respect or courtesy, either by him or by his other wives. He would use her body for his pleasure, but trample callously upon her heart.

I can't let this happen, Travis thought. I've got to save her somehow—but how? I'll find a way. No matter what Sadira says, I'm going to save her from herself, he vowed.

"No, Father, thou must not let the *frangi* stay! He said he wanted to go, now thou must make him go!"

Sadira stood in her father's tent, facing Akbar and Alima as they sat quietly on their pillows, weighing her arguments against Travis's. Travis stood behind her, having just informed Akbar that he wanted to accompany the *Ruala* when they took her and Sherifa to meet the *Shammar.*

"Tell him it's a matter of honor," Travis growled. "Go on, translate what I said. Or if you refuse, I can probably make myself understood without your help."

In halting Arabic, Travis repeated his claim, that it was a matter of honor that he accompany the tribe to settle the matter of Gamalat's death. "I shot Gamalat. I did it—no one else. And I know I killed many of the others. The *Ruala* would not be in this position were it not for me. Therefore, I should be permitted to explain what happened and why. Maybe my explanation will save Sadira, and she will not have to stay with the *Shammar.* At least, I demand the right to try. You must let me ride with you."

As he faltered once or twice and lapsed into English, Sadira unthinkingly repeated his words in her own language, then added her own opinion. "He is doing this only out of stubbornness and pride, Father. Do thou send him away. Do not let him stay. He is a *frangi* and should not be witness to a matter involving only our own people and the *Shammar.* Gamalat is dead, and all the explanations in the world will not bring him back. Thou knowst Hajem Pasha better than anyone. Tell the *frangi* that he is wrong, and we are right in what we are doing. *Tell him, Father.*"

"Enough, Daughter. I have a mind of my own. I can form my own opinions. Ask the *frangi* if he intends to interfere in any way if I let him accompany us."

"He *will* interfere. I know he will!"

"Ask him, Sadira. I trust him to speak the truth. He has done nothing to earn my distrust thus far—and he fought bravely at the well. Thou wilt remember I was most disappointed to hear that he wished to leave us."

Sadira stiffened her spine and repeated her father's words to Travis. But she would not look at him. She had not imagined he would do this; *why* was he doing it? She had told him the ugly truth about herself, and still, he would not give up. He had not turned away in disgust as she had expected him to do. Nor had he accepted her reasoning. He was stubborn and arrogant. The more she tried to explain things, the less likely he was to accept them!

She did not understand him, no more than he understood her. . . . And she did *not* want him to stay! To see him everyday, to feel his eyes upon her, to remember his kisses and know she could never have more of them would be an agony she could not endure! Not on top of everything else.

"My father wishes to know if you intend to interfere if he allows thee to accompany us," she muttered, forcing out each word between gritted teeth, mixing thee and you, scarcely caring about proper English at a time like this.

"Remind him that like him, I am a man of honor, and I will do whatever my honor demands of me."

"That is not a clear answer to the question!"

"Sorry if it displeases you, but it's the only answer I can give. It's the answer *he* would give if he were standing in my boots."

She translated this, trusting that Akbar would be offended, but her father only grinned at the *frangi*'s infuriating arrogance. "I begin to like thee more and more, *Frangi*," he said. "Thou possess the courage of a sheik. Being unafraid to think and act for thyself, thou wouldst make a good sheik, I think. Thou fight when thou must, but thou art not cruel; thou disapprove of cruelty. Yes, thou may ride with us, but thou wilt not change our minds about what must be done. We must surrender Sadira to our enemies, trusting all the while that Allah will watch over her."

"If Allah doesn't, I will," Travis snapped when Sadira finished translating.

"I cannot tell him that," Sadira flat-out refused. "He will misinterpret your concern and think you have some personal interest in my welfare. You must never let him think that, Travis, or he will kill you—and me—on the spot."

"If you don't tell him, Alima will. She understands English, and she also understands that my interest in you is purely protective and . . . paternal. I want no harm to come to you because of me—and what I did to Gamalat. I'll offer myself in place of you, Sadira. I'll tell them I'm the one who killed Gamalat, and I had damn good reason."

Alima stirred among her pillows, sighing with unhappiness or some hidden discomfort. "Thou art not worth much, *Frangi*. *Shammar* will want Sadira, not thee. Speak no more of . . . interests. Sadira is right; take care what thou sayest in front of Akbar."

"All right," Travis agreed, nodding in her direction. "But I'm still going to try and talk the *Shammar* out of accepting Sadira. I can do that, at least."

"Thou canst, *try, Frangi*," Alima assented. "But not succeed. Will they accept a piece of flint when they can claim a pearl? All desert tribes covet Sadira. Her fame is wide." She held out her hands as if to indicate how wide. "She brings great prosperity to her people. To lose her will be like hawk losing its wings."

"What are they saying, Daughter?" Akbar leaned forward and stroked his chin with a gleam of irritation in his eye. "I do not like it when all around me people are conversing, and I cannot understand. Must I, too, learn English? 'Tis an inferior language, not proper for a sheik to speak, but I will learn it if I must."

Sadira gave her father a diminished version of their discussion, leaving out anything that might arouse his wrath or suspicions. When she had finished, Akbar motioned for Travis to sit down beside him.

"Eat with me, *Frangi*. Take coffee. Rest. I will explain the perils of the journey to thee. First, we must return to the main encampment of the *Ruala*. Then we must prepare to travel a long distance, across a part of the desert where there is no water and little rainfall. It will not be easy—either for humans or animals. Tell him, Sadira. We will ride camels to spare the horses, and we will ration our water. Our food will be plain and simple. At times, there may be no food at all."

Sadira wanted to flee the tent and Travis's disturbing company. She had hoped he would soon be gone, and she would never have to see him again. Never have to look at his strong but gentle hands and imagine them caressing her naked flesh, never have to watch his mouth forming words and remember the warmth of his lips pressed to hers, never have to witness the ease and grace of his big body as he mounted a horse, and she pictured him mounting *her*. . . .

It would be so much easier if he went away now, and she did not have to endure another moment in his presence!

Just this once, at least, she would like to disobey her father and depart before he gave her permission. But as always, she quelled her own desires and did as her father requested; she knelt and began translating. Travis settled himself beside her, and the thought came to her that her own private torture was just beginning. Surrendering herself to the *Shammar* could be no worse than being forced to endure the close company of a man she wanted and could never have.

Thirteen

The journey back to the main encampment of the *Ruala* seemed to take no time at all, and as soon as they arrived, Akbar had the tribe begin preparing for the long, difficult trip to the main encampment of the *Shammar.* Hamid was assigned the job of teaching Travis how to ride a camel, and he spent several mornings attempting to acclimate himself to the peculiar—and uncomfortable—gait of a fawn-colored female of the Oman strain, whose name was Tarfa.

Since Sadira was occupied with her own preparations and avoiding him in the process, Travis received no explanation of the camel's name. But he would not have been surprised to learn that it meant "bag of rocks," for that's what she felt like the first time he climbed aboard her. Hamid referred to her as a *'dhalul* and treated her as if she were a queen and far too good for the likes of a *frangi.* He pointed out that she had an ideal racing build—possessing a long back and a high-swung belly-line that ran from her breastbone to her hind thighs.

Travis still could not understand Arabic perfectly, but Hamid made it clear that Tarfa had wonderful paces and was very speedy and comfortable to ride at the trot and gallop. Travis worried that his weight might overtax her, for she was fine-boned and smaller than Lulu—but she did have an attractive lionine head and great gazelle eyes. She

also had a sweeter temper than Lulu and did not seem to
mind his clumsy shifting and turning as he tried to find a
comfortable way of sitting in the saddle.

The saddle, called a *shedad,* was made of acacia wood
and encrusted with silver. It had leather cushions and three
sheepskins, along with other trappings—huge goat-hair
saddlebags and long rows of knotted tassels and braided
fringes that reached below Tarfa's belly and swung in
rhythm with her strides. Her *rashma* or halter was fashioned of wool in brilliant colors of red, blue, and green on
an ebony background.

Hamid made her kneel so that Travis could mount her,
which Travis already knew was called "couching," but
Hamid himself mounted his own camel by pulling down
its head, placing a foot on its neck, and letting it lift him
up to the saddle. Once in the saddle, Hamid showed Travis
how to sit on his calves and the soles of his feet, in a
kneeling position that required good balance and felt enormously stressful to muscles unaccustomed to it. When he
saw that Travis would soon tire, he then demonstrated a
sitting position, with a leg on either side of the camel's
hump. Travis much preferred the sitting to the kneeling
position, though his pride demanded that he master both.

Tarfa's walk reminded Travis of the motion of a ship's
deck rising and falling in heavy seas. Her trot proved far
more comfortable, and her gallop was downright exhilarating. Travis learned to direct her by means of a long stick
and taps on the shoulder, but Hamid used a kind of singsong chant or camel-song, which she seemed to prefer. The
camels were not, however, as responsive as horses—stopping whenever they pleased to snatch a mouthful of greenery and being far more difficult to guide in anything
resembling a straight line.

Three days of camel-riding toughened Travis's muscles, but he ached from head to foot at night, an almost welcome distraction that kept him from brooding over Sadira and her painstaking avoidance of his company. By the fourth night after their return to the main encampment, Akbar was nearly ready to depart for the journey to the *Shammar* Messengers had already gone ahead to locate the *Shammars'* main encampment and tell Hajem Pasha that the *Ruala* were coming. Stacks of supplies and mounds of water skins stood everywhere, and a great quantity of bread was being baked in the traditional manner even now, after dark. By the light of camel-dung fires, women and servants were mixing together flour and cold water, shaping it into balls of dough, and then fashioning small thin loaves to be nestled in the glowing ashes until they baked nearly as hard as bricks—and would last nearly as long.

On this last night before the tribe's departure, Akbar had ordered a feast of tender young camel, along with lamb prepared in the traditional dish of rice and lamb, with lamb's grease poured over all. Several young camels had been killed earlier in the day, and their blood caught in bowls. Each animal who would be given to Hajem Pasha had then been marked with blood. Horses and camels alike now bore the tribal emblem painted on their necks with brushes made from sprigs of herbs.

It was a wonder Sadira herself had not been marked with blood, Travis thought grimly, as he sat on a rug outside Akbar's tent and tried to eat roast lamb and boiled camel's meat in the company of his hosts and Sadira herself. She ate very little, he noticed, and would not meet his eyes.

"Sadira," he whispered when no one was looking. " want to talk to you, and you've been avoiding me. Is there somewhere we can meet?"

Her eyes widened in alarm. "No! No, we cannot. Please, Travis. Do not speak to me like this again. 'Tis over between us. You must accept it and do nothing to arouse suspicions regarding us. You will only harm me if you continue."

"I would never harm you, and you know it. Listen to me, Sadira, I want to help . . ." He paused as Akbar suddenly held out a piece of tender young lamb and urged him to take it.

"Eat, *Frangi*. Thou must eat to gain strength for the long journey. That is why we feast this night—to make ourselves strong for the ordeal that lies ahead."

Travis accepted the morsel and ate it, but the meat stuck in his throat. Sadira ignored him after that, and as soon as he could, he excused himself and retired to his tent—there to listen to the chants, songs, and stories with which the Bedouin amused themselves during feasts. His brief exchange with Sadira had plunged him into deep depression. When would he have another opportunity to try and talk her out of offering herself as a sacrificial lamb to her enemies?

The entire tribe knew what was happening, all had helped prepare for the journey, and to his knowledge, not a single person had protested Akbar's plans or suggested that Sadira should *not* be handed over to the *Shammar*. The normally cheerful *Ruala* had been uncharacteristically gloomy lately, but no one had come forward to insist that she be spared. It was as if they had already relinquished their Keeper of the Mares and had resigned themselves to managing without her. If anything, her people had ignored her the past few days as they baked their bread and filled their water skins and gathered the bounty of the desert.

On Sadira's behalf, Travis felt outraged. It shocked him that the *Ruala* could be so cruel. Perhaps it really was as

Sadira believed: Many still remembered her mother and thought it fitting that a daughter should pay the price of her mother's sins.

Travis longed to take Sadira in his arms and comfort her. Even more, he yearned to change her mind—to convince her to run away with him and leave the *Ruala* to solve this problem on their own. He doubted she would ever do it, but he wished he could convince her to take Sherifa and Tahani and flee under cover of darkness. The two mares were the swiftest and finest of all the horses; mounted upon them, they would stand a good chance of escape. He could arrange it—but without Sadira's cooperation, the undertaking would be difficult, if not impossible.

He needed more time to convince her that she was making a mistake—and that it was primitive, barbaric, and downright malicious of her father and her people to expect her to sacrifice her life on their behalf . . . yet how was he to convince her of anything when he had no time alone with her? Once they began the march, his opportunities would be even more limited. Between Hamid and Akbar, he had an audience for nearly every breath, and so did Sadira. With the whole tribe making the journey, Travis suspected that Sadira would seek the comfort of Alima's company or that of the other women. He couldn't count on a convenient sandstorm to come along and provide cover for a secret tryst in her tent.

Her tent. Tonight would be the last night their tents would be pitched amidst the sprawl and confusion of great numbers of people and animals strung out upon the plain. Tomorrow night, they would pitch their dwellings closer together, with Hamid's and Akbar's almost certainly separating his and Sadira's. Tomorrow night, watchmen would probably be posted to guard the tribe as it moved closer to their enemies. No longer would the *Ruala* depend solely upon their dogs and their horses to alert them to a stranger's approach.

At the moment, Sadira's tent still stood some distance alone out on the plain in the midst of the mares; why not pay her a secret visit in the dead of night, after everyone had fallen asleep?

Travis was sure he could avoid being seen making his way to Sadira's tent, and once inside it, he should be safe. No one would likely disturb them. It was worth a try. Akbar would kill them if someone found them together, but considering the danger Sadira already faced, such a risk was more than justified. Better he take it now, while he stood the best chance of success.

Having made up his mind, Travis spent several hours planning what he would say to Sadira—what arguments he would present. When at last the encampment settled down for the night, he silently threaded his way through the endless maze of black tents to the edge of the plain where the horses were grazing. Heads lifted and several horses snorted as he moved from one dark shape to another, concealing himself among them. It was a measure of their trust in humans that none of the horses galloped away or whinnied in alarm, as Travis's own animals back home would probably have done.

Sherifa stood near Sadira's tent. Travis approached the mare silently and scratched along her withers in greeting. She nosed his hand and finding no sweets there, calmly resumed nibbling the salt grass that rippled soundlessly in the night wind. Travis studied the surrounding landscape but spotted no guards; it was just as he had suspected. Here in the tribe's own grasslands, Akbar had not taken the precaution of posting watchmen at intervals around the camp's perimeter.

Travis considered whether or not he ought to enter the tent by the normal entrance, then decided against it. It was darker at the back, and he was less likely to be spotted there if someone did leave his tent tonight.

Going around to the back, he dropped to his knees and crawled toward a peg holding a section of Sadira's tent in place. Lifting the taut goat-hair covering, he slithered beneath it. Inside, it was black as pitch. He could see nothing, but he could hear Sadira's soft, rhythmical breathing. Beneath his outstretched hands, a rug felt soft and comforting. His questing fingers found a pillow and then the warmth of a hand—Sadira's hand. Quickly, he moved closer and prepared to muffle any sound of startlement she might make.

Her scent filled his nostrils—the enticing odor of lavender and womanhood intertwined. She stirred as he placed a hand over her mouth.

"Sadira! Don't be frightened. It's me—Travis."

"Travis?" Sadira awoke in an instant, every nerve ending suddenly aquiver. She tried to rise but his body covered hers and held her pinioned against the pillows and the thick, plush rug upon which she usually slept.

Her heart pounded so loudly in her ears that it drowned out all other sounds; Travis—here! In her tent. Once again, she was completely alone with him.

"Don't be afraid." His voice was low and reassuring as his lips brushed her ear. "I came because I had to talk with you alone. You owe me this, Sadira. You have been avoiding me too long."

"If anyone finds you here, my father will kill you, Travis. And me as well. There is no excuse for us to be together this time—no sandstorm or heavy winds."

"I know that, but I'm willing to take the chance. I had to see you alone again. I have to talk some sense into you."

She knew she had to stop him before he went any further. "Travis, do not do this! Do not make it harder for me than it is already. I am at peace with what I must do; do not raise doubts and make me question things."

"If you are at peace, why is it so hard? You already have doubts, Sadira, and I mean to raise more doubts. To make you question every aspect of your life up until now. This is not how the rest of the world solves its problems—by forcing a young woman to offer her flesh and blood to her enemies."

"It is how *we* can solve *this* problem, Travis. I do not mind; truly I do not. My life has not been so wonderful that I cannot bear to lose it! I have always been an outcast. Even as the Keeper of the Mares, I was never really accepted. Revered, yes . . . and held in awe, but all I ever really wanted was to be normal and ordinary, like everyone else—and this has always been denied me."

Travis's breath was hot on her forehead. His lips burned her skin as he nuzzled the hair framing her face. "Your life *could* be wonderful, Sadira. That's what I've been trying to tell you. It could be sweet, rich, and full beyond your wildest imaginings. Don't you want to know what it's like to be loved and cherished for your own self—not merely as a symbol? Wouldn't you like to experience the love of a man—if not me, then someone else—and the joy of a babe nursing at your breast? Wouldn't you relish having the freedom to ride and breed horses, to train them, to live among them forever, with no fear that they can be taken from you and your life be endangered? Sadira, there's a whole other world out there waiting for you to explore and conquer . . ."

"This is my world, Travis. This and no other. I am what I was born to be; I must live the life Allah has given to me."

"But what if *I* have been sent by Allah?" Travis's hands cupped her head, and his thumbs stroked along her cheekbones. "What if Allah meant for me to be here, to tell you these things, to arouse your doubts . . . and finally, to take you away somewhere where you can be safe and live a new life? Maybe *I* am your destiny."

"Allah would never send a *frangi,* an infidel and unbeliever, to carry out his wishes. What draws us together is wickedness and evil. 'Tis what my mother was not strong enough to resist, what made her betray her husband and bring shame upon herself and her people."

"No, Sadira . . ." Travis whispered. "What exists between us isn't the same thing at all. Your mother was already married. You are not. Therefore, you are free to fall in love and marry."

"But I am the Keeper of the Mares—the ceremonial virgin!"

"Someone else can be that now. They can take over your responsibilities. You've given your people enough of your life. They have no right to demand it all. A week or a month or a year after you've made this sacrifice, the *Shammar* and the *Ruala* will find something new to fight about, and your sacrifice will have been in vain. Sadira, you must think of yourself now and what *you* want. You've only been given one life, sweetheart, and you have to live it the best you know how—not according to everyone else's needs and desires, but according to your own."

"But Travis, I love my people!"

"Yes, damn it, but do they love *you?* You want what's best for them, but I don't see them considering what's best for you. Isn't that what love is—seeking what's best for the loved one? God knows I'm no expert on the subject, but I can't believe your people really love you, or they wouldn't do this to you. They couldn't do it."

"Perhaps I am . . . unlovable, with my green eyes and my streak of blond hair, and my tainted blood."

"I find you lovable, Sadira. You are the most beautiful woman I've ever met—the most unselfish, the most loyal, the most tolerant and forgiving. . . ." Travis's mouth was very close to hers now—and saying wonderful, unbelievable things. His hands were smoothing her hair back from her forehead with a touch as gentle and soft as silk. "Sadira, I've never known anyone like you, and I've never felt like this about anyone else."

His lips covered hers, and she savored the taste of him and the sweet explosion of pure joy and happiness that rocked her from head to toe. She could not help herself— could not resist any longer. She wound her arms around him and kissed him with all the love and longing locked up inside her and clamoring to be set free.

For several long, wonderful moments, they clung together in the darkness, succumbing to forbidden impulses. Travis's kisses became more heated. His hands began to roam. Sadira gasped when he touched her breast. She felt her own flesh responding, becoming fuller and heavier, aching with the need to know more of his touch. His tongue sought hers, and the intimacy of the act splintered her heart into tiny pieces.

She moaned deep in her throat, and Travis swallowed the small sound and gave it back to her in a kiss so deep and drugging that he seemed to flow into her and she into him. They rolled together on the rug, desperate to get closer. . . . A madness came over her, and she knew then why her mother had been willing to risk everything. To feel like this! To want a man so badly . . . to desire his kisses, his caresses, his hands on her body. It was magic; it was torture . . . sweet, sweet torture. She had never felt so alive.

She had never hungered like this—or thirsted, even when the desert was dry as bone. Travis clasped her to him, his body fitting to hers as if the two had been made to go together. . . . Was it always so between a man and woman? Or was it only like this because the man was Travis, and *she* was the woman? His hand found the curve of her hip, and he pulled her to him—teaching her the amazing differences between his maleness and her femininity.

His body arched, and he thrust against her—once, twice, as if seeking permission to carry the madness to its final conclusion. Then he paused and drew back slightly, breathing hard, as if he had run a long distance. "Sadira . . . you strip me of all control, but by God, I'll not do this to you. I'll not use you as your people do—without a thought or care as to what *you* want."

The words trembled on her lips. *I want thee, Travis. I want to love thee and give myself to thee and learn all there is to know about what transpires between a man and a woman.*

But she did not say the words. The brief pause restored her sanity, and she remembered who she was and who he was and why they could never permit themselves to be swept away on a tide of passion—*or* of love.

"You should not have come here, Travis," she whispered. "This only makes it harder for me."

"Come away with me, Sadira!" he begged, fiercely grip-

ing her shoulders. "Come away and let me give you a
ew life! Let me show you the world! For once in your
ife, think of yourself. Don't let your father dictate to
ou. . . ."

"He is *not,* Travis. I have *chosen* to walk this path of
my own free will."

"Then you can choose to walk another. It's not wrong
o change your mind, Sadira. You never knew what you
were missing before; now you do, don't you?"

"Yes, now I know. . . . You have opened my eyes, Travis,
ut I wish you had not! To abandon my people when they
eed me the most would break my heart. It would crush
my spirit. I could not live with myself if I did that to them.
Have you never loved someone so much that you would
acrifice even life itself to spare them suffering?"

"No," Travis said. "I haven't. Not until now. I've been
a selfish son of a bitch all my life, Sadira. I've loved only
my horses—and my family, too, of course, before I lost
hem all. I can't remember feeling anything even remotely
imilar to the loyalty you feel for your people. They don't
leserve you. *I* don't deserve you, but at least I would never
urt you. Your people will. They don't love you back. Think
bout it. They're a bunch of cowards—only too eager to
oss you to the wolves if it will mean saving their own
recious skins."

"Akbar is not a coward."

"Isn't he? Maybe not, but he doesn't mind hiding behind
our skirts, does he? Hiding behind your robes, I mean."

"He is thinking only of our people."

"And *I* am thinking only of you. Don't let yourself be
sed as a pawn, Sadira, in a game played only by men."

"A pawn? What is a pawn, Travis?"

"It's . . . it's. . . . Oh, forget it. Just do me one favor,

will you? I probably won't have the chance to talk to yo
alone again during this trip to the *Shammar.* But I don
want you to forget everything I've told you. Think abou
every single word—every argument. Ask yourself if this i
really what you want. Look into your heart, Sadira. Yo
don't have to choose misery, enslavement, and possibl
death. You can choose me instead. You can choose lif
and . . . and love. I don't claim to be an expert on love—o
that I'll be able to make you happy. But I *can* promise yo
I'll damn well try. I'll get you away from here, take yo
home with me, and spend the rest of my life trying to mak
you happy. . . . It can be *good* between us, sweetheart! .
know it. I feel it—and I think you feel it, too."

"Travis! Oh, Travis, you must not say these things!" Sh
clapped her hand over his mouth to stop the flow of prom
ises . . . to stem the flood of temptation. He pried her fin
gers away and kissed them, then folded her hand back upo
her breast.

"Think, Sadira. On this journey, you'll have plenty o
time for it. I won't approach you like this again. After thi
I'll leave you alone to make your own decision. All I as
is that if you want me, you let me know before the journe
ends. Before we reach the *Shammar.* I'll need to mak
plans. Just bear in mind that the closer we get, the mor
difficult it will be to escape. Once we reach that part o
the desert your father told me about—the barren part, .
will get much harder. I'll have to worry about water an
grazing for the horses. . . . Don't *you* worry about it, .
will. All you have to do is make up your mind what yo
truly want."

"Travis, if I had a choice . . . if I were not bound b
my vows and my concern for my people . . ."

"You aren't bound by anything, Sadira, except your ow

misguided loyalties. You *do* have a choice. I've given you one . . . and now, I'm going to leave you to think about it."

He kissed her forehead and brushed a finger across her mouth. "Now I'm going to get the hell out of here before the *real* Travis Colin Keene shows up."

She wondered what he meant by that, but made no move to stop him as he withdrew from her. She did not trust herself to let him stay. Had he not stopped kissing her on his own, *she* would not have had the strength to stop him; she would have allowed the kissing to go on and on . . . to culminate in the final intimacy. She was truly her mother's daughter. Now she must decide if she could rise above her in-born weakness and merit the esteem of those who depended upon her.

Merciful Allah! How had she ever come to this terrible impasse—this test of honor and loyalty? It was every bit as bad—no, it was worse—than Muhammad's testing of the mares by depriving them of water.

Fourteen

The speed with which the *Ruala* broke camp the next morning astonished Travis. Within two hours after the sun came up, the entire city of black tents disappeared. The women rolled the goat-hair strips, which were about sixty feet long and three or four feet wide, into fat sausages that could be easily loaded into litter baskets on the pack camels. The pillows, rugs, cooking utensils, water skins, and food supplies were all stuffed into bags ready to join the dismantled tents. Until now, the women of the *Ruala* had always seemed to be shy, reclusive creatures; Travis had not seen much of them, but they now proved their worth and efficiency far beyond what he would have thought possible.

When all was loaded onto the *dhallas,* huge racklike affairs that towered precariously above the heads of the camels, the women went among the animals, releasing the ties that bound their forelegs and kept them kneeling while they were being loaded. Jabbing and shouting at the camels, the women urged the animals to their feet. The beasts rose protestingly, repeating the groans, roars, whines, and assorted odd noises they had made all the while goods were being piled upon their backs. The loads must have run well in excess of a hundred pounds, perhaps as much as two hundred, evenly distributed on either side of the single humps of the camels, so Travis could well understand their complaints.

Many of the women mounted riding camels and seated themselves in curtained *mohaffas,* while others began to lead their pack camels on foot. Men on camelback herded their horses in front of them, or else tied their best war mares to the girths or even the tails of their camels. Shepherds drove their flocks of sheep and goats before them. Moving so many people and animals at one time was a monstrous undertaking. Travis had to remind himself that the *Ruala* did this all the time—not perhaps for such great distances, but they traveled constantly, as circumstances dictated. They grazed their herds until the forage was gone, then gathered them together and moved onward in an endless migratory cycle of feast and famine.

It was a beautiful morning. In this part of the desert, the land was still green and fertile, a never-ending pasture stretching as far as the eye could see. A diaphanous haze hung over the plain, bathing it in silver and green. From high up on Tarfa's back, straddling her hump, Travis had a view of the marching *Ruala* that he doubted he would ever forget: Animals and humans formed a slowly undulating serpent slithering across the desert floor. She-camels called to their clumsy, comical, long-legged offspring, goats and sheep maaaa-ed their excitement, foals galloped in circles around their dams, children ran laughing between the camels and horses, and men chanted camel-songs to urge the lumbering beasts onward.

There was a general sense of festivity—yet a sadness, too. Just before Sadira mounted Lulu to ride in a beautifully festooned *mohaffa,* several old women approached her. Without saying a word, one after the other knelt before her, lifted the hem of her robe, and kissed it. Travis did not need to be told that this was a mark of respect and reverence; the old ones, at least, recognized that Sadira was making a great sacrifice on their behalf. Because of her, the lives of precious sons and husbands—perhaps even their own lives—might be spared. Doubts assailed Travis, and his heart twisted painfully in his chest, as he watched them bow to Sadira, then hurry away.

Finally, he understood what held her—what bound her to the *Anazah* and made her so determined to renounce her own needs in favor of the needs of her people. He did not know how to fight old women—and children. Several little girls then appeared with handfuls of dried blossoms, which they scattered beneath Lulu's plodding feet. The she-camel dropped her head and ate a few, before resuming her place in the caravan. Sadira called out her thanks to the youngsters, then glanced up to meet Travis's gaze.

In her eyes, he read her thoughts as surely as if she had spoken them aloud: How can you ask me to betray these innocents—to abandon them to the wrath of the *Shammar?*

One of the black-eyed children ran up to Travis and laughingly pointed to Tarfa's head. He had haltered her incorrectly and was about to lose his only means of controlling her. Before he could do anything, Hamid suddenly appeared on the scene, riding his own fine camel, and leaning over, made the necessary adjustments to Tarfa's headgear so it would not be lost before the journey had barely begun. By the time Travis looked back at Sadira, she had retreated behind the blue and white-beaded curtains of her litter.

Akbar set a slow, leisurely pace, as if he had all the time

in the world to find his enemies. Travis soon realized that the Bedouin on the march were not given to rushing their animals; instead, they let them meander off the track, dawdle along the way to eat, and stop whenever a particularly appealing patch of grass presented itself. There was much to see in the countryside—a distant herd of gazelle, a bird's nest in a bush, tiny seedlings pushing up through the rocky soil—but Travis soon grew bored with the swaying motion of his saddle and the monotony of a journey that might possibly take forever at the rate they were going.

He took to marking time by counting Tarfa's steps between one landmark and another—a twisted lone tree, the remnants of a crumbling stone wall, a pile of rocks and granite. One day merged into another, and he saw little of Sadira. Meals were simple affairs consisting of round hard balls of Bedouin cheese taken with bread, sometimes offered with a handful of dates, and either goat or camel's milk. The only culinary luxury the people permitted themselves was their coffee—usually three tiny cups at a time to a man. The hearty beverage was brewed whenever the tribe stopped for the night or for a long rest during the day.

The only other indulgence was tobacco. Neither Akbar nor any other man smoked without offering his pipe to his nearest companions. The men would squat in small circles, and eventually one would remove a small leather pouch of tobacco from inside his robes where he carried it next to his skin. Stuffing a few grains of the precious commodity into a tiny stemless pipe cut from soft stone, he would light it desert-fashion using flint and the blade of a dagger, then take two or three puffs and hand it around the circle.

Travis did not care for smoking, but he never refused,

for the ritual was one of friendship. Not to smoke or drink coffee would be an insult, and he had no wish to arouse the anger of the *Ruala* any sooner than he must. He longed to share the evening hours with Sadira, but she rarely appeared, even for the evening meal, and Travis had to manage as best he could using his limited Arabic.

He did not have much opportunity to converse with Alima either. The women were constantly busy with the raising and lowering of tents, the endless packing, and the general care of children and animals. Akbar's many wives frequently made their presence known—especially the one called Jaleel. Travis saw her several times without her veil, and he supposed she was beautiful with her kohl-lined black eyes and elegant features. However, like Elizabeth, her beauty was deceiving; she possessed a nasty temper and complained unceasingly of the hardships of the march. . . . No wonder Akbar preferred the homely but cheerful Alima!

In these wide open spaces, Travis suffered from a deep loneliness. He tried to keep track of where they were by studying the position of the sun, moon, and stars, but he still felt as if he were lost in the middle of nowhere and might never see civilization again. It would all be different if he could talk to Sadira; she had to be lonely, too, for she spent nearly every moment of her time either in her tent or her *mohaffa*. She had withdrawn from the *Ruala,* as well as from him—preparing herself for the final separation.

The farther they traveled, the more barren the land became. Pasture gave way to long stretches of rock, stone, and sand, unbroken by any vegetation except the occasional clump of salt grass or camel thorn. When greenery appeared, the animals always stopped to eat it. No one hurried them onward, for they knew there would be less and less as the days passed. At least, the land was no longer flat. There were gentle hills and valleys, and wide sandy depressions. The wind sang a mournful, haunting song as it blew across the increasingly barren landscape. It was a song Travis knew he would never forget, for it spoke to him of the desert, the *Ruala,* and their beautiful horses, and most of all . . . Sadira.

At long last, they reached an oasis—a place where date palms grew, and water bubbled out of a shelf of rock and flowed among stones and gravel for a short distance before disappearing entirely. Here, Akbar ordered another feast. Again, young nursing camels, lambs, and goat-kids were slain, which seemed a terrible waste to Travis who had expected older, less valuable animals to be taken, and the young ones spared.

Sadira and Alima joined Akbar and Travis to partake of the meal, but Travis was far more eager to be near Sadira again than to taste the freshly roasted meat whose mouthwatering odors permeated the dry evening air. Robed in white, except for a silver and blue border decorating sleeve and hem, Sadira wore a gauzy white veil this night. An air of mystery clung to her, and people fell silent whenever they looked upon her. She removed the veil from the lower half of her face when the food appeared, but she did not speak to anyone or raise her eyes.

Samir served the men first, as was customary, and then the women. Alima did not immediately eat but occupied herself with choosing choice tidbits to feed Akbar from her own fingers. Sadira merely toyed with her food, tasting this or that, but consuming little or nothing. The shell of the woman still lived, ate, and breathed, but the heart and soul of her no longer dwelt among the *Ruala.*

By way of hiding his feelings—gladness mixed with despair—Travis made conversation and asked idle questions. "Why do the *Ruala* kill the youngest animals, instead of the oldest, when they wish to have a feast?" he inquired of no one in particular.

Alima was not paying attention, and Akbar did not understand English, so it was Sadira who finally answered. "Because we have come to the place of the Sands, and from this point onward, there will be no forage and no water. When our water supplies are depleted, we will have only camel and goat milk to sustain us and the horses. If we spared the young, they would claim the milk before we could use it. This way, we are able to enjoy both milk and meat."

A practical solution, Travis thought, but still heartless. "What about the mothers? Aren't they distressed about losing their offspring?" He had seen at least one frantic she-camel charging about roaring for her slaughtered baby.

Sadira shrugged as if he had asked a ridiculously sentimental question, then lowered her eyes. "Do you hear them complaining? Already they have adjusted."

Travis did *not* hear any more roars or howls of grief, and he wondered about it. "If you had killed foals, the mares would still be distraught. They complain bitterly at weaning time, often for a number of days."

"We do not kill foals unless it is absolutely necessary to spare them from suffering. As for why the mother camels, sheep, and goats have fallen silent, it is because their owners have taken a piece of the baby's hide and sewn it to their own robes. The mothers then smell the familiar odors and are comforted."

"Amazing! I would never think of such a thing—but

then I would never think of killing the babies in the first place."

"That is because you do not live as we do among our animals, depending upon them totally for our very lives. We do not see it as cruel to kill a newborn camel in order to collect the milk from its mother. It is our way—a way that has served the Bedouin and enabled them to survive on the desert for years beyond counting."

"One must die, so many might live, is that it?" Travis could not keep the scorn from his voice. "If you don't mind, even after your sensible explanation, I still feel sorry for the baby camel who never had a chance at life or any say about its future."

"Sorry enough to refuse its meat?" Sadira asked as Samir offered Travis a tray heaped high with pieces of tender young camel swimming in its own juices.

After days of meager meals, Travis was hungry enough to devour the tray itself, along with the meat, but the question gave him pause. Was that why he found it so easy to criticize—because he himself would not benefit from Sadira's sacrifice? The meat in front of him suddenly looked much less appetizing than it smelled. Only hours ago, the little victim had been frolicking about on its spindly legs, enchanting him with its antics and its trusting, long-lashed eyes.

Quickly, he seized a piece of meat. Was he a hypocrite? Back home in Kentucky, he relished beef, turkey, chicken, the occasional rabbit on his dinner table . . . and what was cuter than a rabbit with a twitchy nose? Sadira had missed the point. *She* was no animal, and that made all the difference in the world. The baby camels had suffered little, either from anticipation or their actual deaths, but she had hours and hours to dwell on morbid possibili-

ties. . . . What besides thinking did she do all day riding
alone in her *mohaffa?*

He ate the meat and appreciatively licked his fingers,
finding it delicious. Then his stomach suddenly revolted,
and he felt sick. After she was gone, Sadira's people would
remember her with about as much concern as they felt for
the baby camels. They would invent all manner of excuses
to justify what they had done to their Keeper of the Mares.
Travis could take no pleasure in the meal after that; nor
could he continue the pretense of making polite conversation. He sat and brooded. Sadira did likewise—speaking
when spoken to, but otherwise saying nothing.

As the evening wore on, it became more and more difficult for Travis to endure Sadira's withdrawal. He watched
her slender fingers plucking with the tassel on a pillow,
noted that she had lost weight and appeared thinner, and
that bluish circles ringed her exquisite green eyes. He
counted each breath she took. She might have been a thousand miles away for all the notice she took of him. Their
conversation had done nothing to pierce her self-absorp-
tion. She had shut him out entirely.

He fantasized taking her hand, dragging her into Akbar's
tent, and kissing some sense into her, forcing her to ac-
knowledge him and to agree to escape with him. He could
never let her go to the *Shammar,* but she would never flee
with him willingly. He would have to break something over
her head and tie her body across Sherifa's back. How much
easier it would be if she would only cooperate! But he had
pressed her as far as he could; now she would have to
make up her own mind. Unfortunately, it appeared she already had.

At it grew darker and the dung fires burned low, Sadira
rose and simply walked away, never so much as looking at

him or saying good night. He ached with the hurt of her rejection. It was much worse than what he had experienced with Elizabeth. Elizabeth had only tossed his ring over the railing of the racetrack; Sadira was cutting out his heart. He had opened himself to her as he had never done with anyone, and she did not want him.

His brain told him she had not really rejected *him*—she was only doing what she thought she must—but it hurt like hell anyway. He retired to his own tent and lay sleepless for hours, wishing he dared pay her another secret visit . . . but what was the point? She wouldn't look at him, wouldn't talk to him; why endanger her for nothing?

He rose early the next morning, intent upon making certain that Tarfa and Najila each had a good long drink from the spring before they set out again. He stepped outside his tent and discovered he wasn't the only one with that brilliant idea. Horses, camels, sheep, goats, and people crowded the water source. He would have to wait and take his turn. He waited half the morning, impatiently pacing back and forth, before he finally noticed what the Bedouin were doing that was taking so long.

Horses, goats, and sheep were permitted to drink their fill and move off, but the camels were not. When they had drunk all they seemed to want, they were led off a short distance, couched, and leg-shackled so they could not rise. Fetching a pail of water, the handler would bring it near the camel but out of reaching distance, and proceed to slap the water with his or her palm, and sing songs, as if urging the camel to come and drink the water, which it could not do. Travis could not understand what was happening, but he spotted Sadira doing the same thing with Lulu and seized the opportunity to approach her on the pretext of gaining an explanation.

Up close, Sadira looked as weary as he felt. She could not be sleeping any better than he was at night. She did not greet him, but only continued slapping and sloshing the water in the pail, and singing the same singsong chant.

"What in God's name is everyone doing?" Travis demanded. "If you want the poor beast to drink, why don't you simply untie her and let her have the water?"

Sadira gave him one of her "looks" that said he did not understand. He didn't. " 'Tis necessary to provoke her thirst," she explained. "She has already drunk a great quantity of water and does not desire more, but I am tempting her, so that when she is released, she will run to the water and drink again. Like you and me, she wants most what is denied her. . . . Watch a moment, and you will see."

Fascinated despite Sadira's inappropriate analogies, Travis turned his attention to Lulu. The camel's liquid brown eyes kept watching Sadira and the water. Her ears pricked toward the splashing sound. Sadira invited her to come and drink; she described how sweet and delicious the water was, though Travis had thought it barely potable, due to its salinity. Lulu began to whine and attempted to rise.

"Yes, my pretty," Sadira crooned. "Thou hast a great need to drink water and store it all away for the long journey across the Sands. Thou art very thirsty. Thou must slake thy great thirst. Yes, my pretty, 'tis time to drink . . ." Sadira stood and draped her robe over the bucket, so the camel couldn't see it. "Now, untie her, Travis . . . and she will run to the stream and drink."

Travis approached Lulu with some trepidation, not trusting her, half expecting to get another wad of half-digested cud spewed down the front of him. Quickly, he bent down and freed Lulu's shackled leg. Immediately, the camel rose and almost knocked him down in her eagerness to get to the spring. She crowded in among the other beasts and slurped water as if she hadn't been offered any for a week.

"I suppose I should be doing that with Tarfa," he said, impressed by this demonstration of camel psychology.

"Yes, you should. I thought Hamid would have told you to do it. I will do it myself at least three more times, until I am certain she has drunk all she can hold. Her hump must be high and plump. After several days of poor forage—which means she will have no way to replenish her body liquids—her hump will begin to shrink. If it goes away entirely, she will not be able to carry a load or rise with me in the *mohaffa*. You can tell a camel's condition and how long it has been without grass or water, just by examining its hump."

"They are incredible creatures—truly adapted to desert life," Travis opined. "Hamid—or someone—should have told me these things and made certain I was taking good care of Tarfa. *You* should have told me, Sadira."

"You do not need me anymore, *Frangi*. You know enough Arabic to get along now without me."

"You *hope* that's the case. You *want* it to be so. Is that why you've been ignoring me—to prepare me for when you're gone?"

Sadira regarded him solemnly, her green eyes expressionless. "I am already gone, *Frangi*. My people have accepted it, and so have I. In my own heart and mind, I no longer exist. Do not plague me anymore with your arguments. My answer is no, Travis. I will not leave my people. I cannot. Stay away from me. . . . Let me go. If you care anything at all for me, I beg you to let me go."

"Sadira, this is foolishness! It's primitive and cruel. You think this is all there is to life—this desert, these people, this religion, this way of doing things. But I tell you there is more. You need not submit. If you refuse, you will force your father to find another way of pacifying the *Shammar.* There *are* other ways. In civilized countries, people sit down together and discuss their differences. They argue and negotiate before they reach for their weapons. They try to avoid bloodshed through diplomacy and compromise."

He stopped a moment to draw breath and because he suddenly realized that what he was telling her was not precisely true. Even in his own part of the world, men sometimes—often—rushed to war. They sacrificed their own lives and the lives of women and children on the altar of vengeance and retribution. The *Ruala* were sacrificing only *one*—Sadira. So who must be counted cruel, foolish, and primitive? God have mercy! It was beginning to make a twisted kind of sense even to him.

"Sadira . . ." he began again, but Hamid came up behind her and stood watching, his face pinched in a familiar scowl.

Sadira behaved as if she had not noticed Hamid and had not been listening to *him.* "I must call Lulu now, and you must encourage Tarfa to drink. Do as I just did. Worry not what words you use—just be sure that your tone is encouraging, and you tantalize her with the sound of the water. Camels cannot resist the sound of water splashing or gurgling. They will run to it and drink. They cannot help it. That is their nature."

As I cannot resist you, Travis thought. Like the camel, he was leg-shackled and forbidden to drink, which only increased his thirst all the more. . . . He would have to figure out a way to save Sadira without her cooperation.

He had no idea how he could accomplish such a feat, but he would do it, one way or another. He loved her, and despite what she said or wanted, he could not let her go.

Fifteen

The journey across the Sands was taking forever. At the same time, it passed with terrifying swiftness. Wrapped in a cloak of silence, struggling to control her thoughts, Sadira grimly prepared herself to say goodbye. Her people made it easier by pretending she was already gone. For the most part, they ignored her. Only occasionally did they show by word or gesture that they would miss her and mourn her loss; she suspected that they were mourning the loss of the Keeper of the Mares, rather than her personally. By next year at this time, some other young woman would assume the position, not for life as she had done, but it would be filled . . . and when the new one married, yet another would be selected. Most of the desert tribes did it this way; if she had not borne the mark of the star, her own tenure would have been temporary.

Swaying to the motion of the *mohaffa* as Lulu bore her across the wasteland, Sadira reflected that she knew her people well. Life would continue whether or not she was there to witness it. All too soon, she would be a memory— a distant one, at that. Of all the *Ruala,* only Alima, Akbar, and Hamid showed any true remorse at her departure. They gazed at her with pity and sorrow, but offered no alternatives, knowing there were none to be had. . . . And then, there was Travis.

Travis challenged her resolution and destroyed her serenity every time he glanced in her direction. Because of him, she could not sleep, could barely eat, and must constantly fight to clear her mind of disturbing, contradictory thoughts. Confusion and conflict now ruled her world, a world that once had been ordered and unruffled, with everything in its proper place. Travis was forcing her to examine the very bedrock of her beliefs. What if Allah *had* sent him to rescue her from this predicament . . . ? Perhaps Allah did not even exist, or the Allah she knew was actually quite different from what she had been taught.

Perhaps she was simply being used by her people, manipulated and controlled as Travis had suggested. She wondered how women were treated in other countries. Were they permitted to make their own decisions and live their own lives without the interference of fathers, sons, and husbands? Travis was so different from anyone she had ever known that Sadira could not decide what to believe. The ways in which he was different went far beyond mere religion and whether or not he prostrated himself toward Mecca and prayed the prescribed number of times per day.

He had argued with her as if he actually believed she had a choice! But no women of her acquaintance had choices. From the moment they first drew breath, desert women were subject to the whims of men. Every aspect of their lives was governed by others—*males,* not females. A woman had little say in anything. Sadira could not imagine a woman tossing aside a gift from her betrothed. Gifts were more likely to be given to her family than to her anyway. Yet Travis had told her that a woman named Elizabeth had done precisely that, and he had suffered greatly because of her rejection.

In America, women possessed far more freedom than

they did in the desert countries, she decided. Yet she had been born here and were it not for Travis, would have no idea of customs elsewhere. She would live her whole life assuming that the entire world was subject to the same rules she was. Just knowing that it wasn't so made her question . . . doubt . . . rebel. Why must *she* be sacrificed? She had done nothing wrong and killed no one—women did not make war, men did. And until men decided to stop attacking each other and settle their differences peacefully, there would be no peace . . . and women would find themselves plunged into mortal danger, their entire lives ruined, their futures dismal.

She did not want to resent it, but she did. She resented it with every fiber of her being and resented even more that she could not turn her back on the *Ruala* and run away with Travis. No matter how she felt, she must see this through to the bitter end . . . and it would definitely be bitter.

In the brief time she had known Travis, he had taught her to hope, awakened desire, and filled the emptiness inside her, so that she could never again be satisfied with the limitations of her life even if she could remain forever among the *Ruala,* as their revered Keeper of the Mares. Yes, she was very much her mother's daughter, her feelings for Travis precisely what her mother must have felt for that other *frangi* long ago, the nameless man who had actually fathered her. Why else would a woman risk as much as her mother had and betray a husband who loved her?

These days, Sadira thought often of her mother. All these years, she had been ashamed of her—had never bothered to learn more about her. Had never dared to ask Akbar or Alima if her mother had married Akbar out of love or been forced into the alliance. Her mother's history and background were a mystery; all she knew was what Akbar had told her. He had loved Bashiyra, and Bashiyra had betrayed him. That, apparently, was all she needed to know.

Now she wished she had bothered to learn more. She wished she had tried to understand. She *did* understand now. Loving Travis was not something she had chosen. She did not want to feel the way he made her feel, but she could no more control her feelings than she could will her eyes to be brown or black instead of green, or her hair to be all one color—minus the odd streak of gold in it.

So the days of the journey passed in lonely misery. Food and water supplies ran low. It became necessary for the men to kill more baby camels, more young sheep and goats. The humps of the camels began to shrink. Each morning when the beasts were loaded and forced to rise, their complaints rent the air. The coats of the horses grew dull. Their eyes lost their luster. When an animal could no longer keep up, it was left behind or slaughtered on the spot. The days grew hot. Faces and garments coated with grit, the people no longer chanted and sang as they traveled. Silence hung heavy over the entire caravan.

Travis watched her from afar, but said nothing. Aware that her own silence was deeply wounding him, Sadira tried not to watch him. She tried not to care so much or wish things could be different. . . . Then the water ran out entirely, the goats stopped giving milk, and there was only camels' milk to relieve parched throats. Sadira wondered if they would ever find the encampment of the *Shammar,* and if there would be any animals left to offer them when they did arrive. At long last, they reached another oasis, and Akbar informed her that they were within a day's ride of Hajem Pasha.

"Prepare thyself, Daughter. Thine hour is at hand," he

told her in the midst of the general rejoicing, as people and animals refreshed themselves with the life-giving water.

"I know, Father." Obediently bowing her head, Sadira swallowed the protests she wanted to make. She clung to her pride and her determination to meet her destiny with courage and to offer this one last act as atonement for her mother's sins. "Wilt thou hand me over to them tomorrow?"

"Not for a day or two. The animals need time to rest and recover, and so do we." Akbar briefly caressed her bent head. "Thou makest me proud, Daughter. Now no one can say thy blood was tainted by thy mother and diluted by the *frangi* who fathered thee. Thou art true *Ruala*. Thy name shall be praised and revered among thy people forever."

At that, she raised her eyes to meet his. "But I will not be there to hear it, will I, Father? So what use will be their praise?"

"Look to paradise, Daughter. Thou shalt gain thy reward in paradise."

Paradise seemed far away—a shimmering dream. An impossible illusion. In that moment, Sadira severely doubted its existence. She questioned the faith she had been taught. Religion should make life on earth sweeter and more bearable. It should not condone suffering and offer some doubtful eternal reward for cheerfully borne misery. What good were beliefs that did not change how people treated one another—did not make them kinder and more loving—did not stop them from *inflicting* misery upon each other?

Instead of being reassured, she was more resentful than ever.

Leaving Akbar, Sadira encountered Alima weeping silently near the entrance to her father's tent. Wordlessly, the two women embraced. There was nothing to be said. They both knew that separation was imminent. As soon as everyone had recovered from the long, hard march, Akbar and all the men of the tribe would gather together the chosen camels and horses and go forth to meet the sheik of the *Shammar.* Sadira would ride with them, and when they returned to the *Ruala,* she would not be among them.

What could two women do to fight culture and religion combined? *Allah's will be done.*

On the second evening after their arrival at the oasis, Travis realized that this would probably be the last night Sadira would have with her people. A new air of purpose had taken hold of the camp. Men were cleaning their weapons, grooming their horses, conversing in low eager tones—behaving in every way as if the exhaustion of their long trek was only a memory. They had recovered and were ready to face the *Shammar.*

Travis had been dreading this moment, and now it was here. He had to accept the fact that Sadira was not going to come to him and tell him she had changed her mind. She meant to go through with it. Nothing he had said had made a particle of difference to her. He had kept hoping, but his hopes were in vain. If he was going to save her, he would have to do so in spite of her. She would not assist him.

He had wracked his brain, but thus far had not conceived a plan. Over and over he asked himself how he could possibly manage to kidnap a reluctant woman and flee hundreds—perhaps thousands—of men on horseback across a barren wilderness. He had no idea where they were. He knew he had come down through the Syrian desert to find the *Ruala's* winter pasturelands, and that they had been

traveling east to get to the *Shammar*. The barren sands they
had just crossed had probably been part of El Hamad, the
great interior desert that somewhere blended into Arabia
and other countries. Aleppo lay far to the north.

If he traveled east, he might eventually run into the
Euphrates. The Blunts had set out to travel along the
Euphrates, but perhaps he was already too far south to easily reach it. If he went west, he could possibly encounter
the Mediterranean. Which was closer?

He had left Aleppo with maps and a compass and lost
them in his encounter with Gamalat. Following the ambush,
some personal items had been found and returned to him,
but not these, the most important of all. He needed a guide
to take him and Sadira back north—even to decide which
route was safest. He needed supplies to get them through
the areas of sparse game and limited water. The return journey would be doubly hard because they'd be traveling later
in the season—may even run into the furnace heat of summer. What had been green and blooming then would be
dried and shriveled by now.

Sick with worry and disappointment, Travis cleaned and
loaded his own guns. He took inventory of all he possessed
and realized it wasn't much. He doubted he and the horses
could survive without a milk-producing camel, and neither
Lulu nor Tarfa were milk-camels. Both were unbred—Tarfa
because she was still so young and Lulu because she belonged to Sadira. Yet Travis did not want to leave them
behind, for they both possessed superior speed and endurance. They were among the finest the *Ruala* had to offer.

Yet he might have to leave them and take only the horses.
The horses were his only hope of success. Sherifa and Tahani could outrun anything. Used only as a pack horse—
and packed lightly—Najila could probably keep up, but

Travis knew he would lose her, too, if the *Ruala* pursued them for any length of time. There were others as sure-footed as she, who possessed as much stamina. If it came down to a horse race, and it probably would, he would have to depend upon Sherifa and Tahani . . . and he wondered if Sherifa would still run like the wind without the urging of her mistress.

Travis's fears compounded by the minute. Restless and anxious, he donned a warm woolen robe over his loose-fitting Bedouin trousers and walked out on the plain long after most of the *Ruala* had sought the comfort of their pillows and sleeping rugs. There he strolled aimlessly among the horses who were too busy looking for something to eat to pay him much attention. This near the oasis, the desert had begun to turn green again. Camel thorn and salt grass—the two most hardy species of plant life on the plain—offered meager grazing.

Travis stopped to stroke Najila's neck and run his hands over her body. He could feel her ribs beneath his finger-tips—and see them, too, during the daytime. Tonight was blacker than usual; there was no moon, and the stars were a distant cold glitter. His fingers discovered a bit of puffi-ness about Najila's hocks, and a long scrape above a cannon bone. The journey had been hard on the horses, but with a few days of rest, they should make a rapid recovery. Al-ready, their eyes looked brighter, their coats glossier. Other breeds could never have crossed a barren wasteland with nothing but camel's milk and a bit of hard bread to sustain them at the end.

Travis had seen a number of Bedouin feeding their spe-cial war mares food that could have nourished their own children. . . . To him, that about summed up the Bedouin; they looked after their horses better than they did their own families—and much better than they did their Keeper of the Mares. Giving Sadira to the *Shammar* was just one more sacrifice to ensure that desert life would continue as it always had. . . . How harsh they were! How unfeeling! Yet also so practical.

Travis sighed and draped one arm companionably over Najila's neck. The mare's presence comforted him. Horses weren't much given to debating philosophy or religion; maybe that's why he liked them so much. Najila's desires were simple—eat and stay alive. Reproduce when and if she had the chance.

Bachir and several other stallions had been brought along on the journey and allowed to run free with selected mares. Poor Najila had spent several nights whinnying and trying to break free from the hobbles that kept her near the tent. Travis had been tempted to let her go, but all breeding decisions were up to Sadira and Akbar. When stallions were loose, no one turned out a mare in heat unless he first had permission. Bloodlines were too important to the Bedouin, and matings carefully supervised. Mares and stallions had to perfectly suit each other. Only when the frustrated mare lost interest in the stallion could she rejoin the herd.

Thinking back on the incident, Travis apologetically scratched Najila's neck. "I'm sorry, girl. I should have let you go. Then at least one of us might have enjoyed this journey."

A flash of white near the edge of the herd caught Travis's eye. Squinting, he recognized a slender, white-robed figure swinging a leg over a familiar horse. With ease and grace, Sadira mounted Sherifa bareback and urged her into a gallop. Out onto the plain they raced, Sherifa's churning hooves barely skimming the grass. In the space of several heartbeats, they had disappeared. . . . Where were they going?

Travis suddenly didn't care about Sadira's destination; the important thing was that nobody from camp had followed her. This was his chance—his last opportunity to persuade her to escape with him. It might be the perfect time *to* escape. Doing as Sadira had done, but with less grace, he grabbed Najila's long mane, swung a leg over her back, and hauled himself astride. She half bucked, then leapt away like a deer when he signaled her to pursue Sherifa and Sadira.

Sadira crouched low on Sherifa's neck, urging the mare to greater speed. She dug her fingers into the mare's silky mane and let her fly. It was a marvelous feeling—the wind blowing through her hair, drying the tears streaming down her cheeks. This would be her last gallop—her last ride of complete and total freedom. One last time, she would savor the scent of the night wind, the powerful sleek muscles straining between her thighs, and the perfect rhythm of Sherifa's long strides as the mare flattened her belly and thundered across the darkened plain.

All day long the walls of the tent had been closing in on Sadira; terror and temptation had stalked her. Tonight, sleep had been impossible. Finally, Sadira had been able to stand it no longer. The only way she could endure this last night was to spend it galloping her beloved mare until they were both ready to drop. Maybe then, limp with exhaustion, muscles throbbing, she could return to camp and calmly prepare to meet her enemies. . . . It was worth a try anyway.

Sadira rode far and fast, as fast as Sherifa could go. Concern for the horse finally made her lean back and shift her weight so that the mare knew she wanted to stop. Trembling and snorting, Sherifa slowed to a prancing walk. Her head drooped. Her sides heaved. Ashamed of herself for pushing the mare so hard, Sadira bent over, clasped her friend about the neck, and murmured apologies.

"Forgive me, dear one. In my misery, I have grown selfish and careless of thy comfort. Thou hast just endured a harsh journey; thou didst not need a hard gallop tonight."

Sherifa made a low whuffling sound and snatched a mouthful of grass. Resting on the mare's neck, Sadira heard the pounding of hoofbeats behind her. She straightened and glanced back over her shoulder. No one had seen her leave camp; if they had, they would trust she meant to return soon . . . wouldn't they? She had always returned in the past. Tomorrow's meeting with the *Shammar* would not take place until the hour of the sun's zenith in the sky overhead. There was plenty of time to prepare for it.

A pang of hurt and resentment shot through her; her people no longer trusted her. All these years of proving herself had been in vain.

She stared hard at the approaching figure, and her stomach muscles clenched in recognition. Her heart leapt. Travis had come after her. Bareheaded, wearing no headcloth, he rode up to her dressed only in a flowing robe, the loose trousers the men sometimes wore beneath their robes, and his customary tall black boots, which Akbar had found among the fallen after the attack on Gamalat and returned to him. Immediately, he slid down from Najila, walked up to her, and without speaking, reached for her.

She gave a little cry and fell into his outstretched arms. There was no sense resisting—not when she already knew she lacked the strength for it. That was why she had been avoiding him, because she feared what would happen if he took her in his arms again. His embrace squeezed the air from her lungs. She managed to gulp another breath before his mouth captured hers. Then they were kissing, pressing close to each other, running their hands through each other's hair . . . writhing and twisting in a desperate attempt to get closer still.

As they hugged and kissed, her tears started to flow again, cascading down her cheeks in scalding rivulets. This was the last time she would ever see him—hold him—kiss him.

"Don't cry, sweetheart," he murmured between kisses. "Don't cry . . ."

"But this is goodbye, Travis!" she sobbed. "Tomorrow I go to the *Shammar.* Whether they decree that I may live or die, I will never see thee again."

He cupped her face in his hands. "Don't go, Sadira. Come with me tonight. We'll steal back to camp, take what we need to survive on the desert, get Tahani, Lulu, and Tarfa. . . . When morning comes, you'll be long gone from here."

"No, Travis, no! I cannot go. You *know* this. Tonight is all we shall ever have together."

He wrapped his arms around her, lifted her off her feet, and embraced her as if he would never let go. "How can I change your mind? How can I convince you? Has nothing I've said made any sense? Sweetheart, I love you. I want to marry you, take you home to Kentucky. . . . We'll build a new life together. We'll have children—raise horses— even goats if you want. Just come away with me. Don't *do* this to yourself, sweetheart. Don't do it to me."

As he set her down again, she covered his mouth with the palm of her hand. "Travis . . . my one true love, my life . . . my heart. Please try to understand and forgive me for hurting you, but I cannot go away with you. I *have* considered all your arguments, and I know you are right, but I cannot go. I can't abandon my people. . . . Travis, do not make me keep saying it. Let us not waste our last moments together arguing."

Travis's hands tightened on her shoulders. His body stiffened. He seemed about to say something, but before he could, a faint sound reached their ears. Near them, Sherifa and Najila were suddenly alert, the grass at their feet forgotten. Heads lifted, ears pricked, they stared out across the plain. Travis half turned to see what had caught their attention.

"What is it?" he whispered. "I don't see anything."

The wind carried the sound of a distant snort, then a shrill whinny of invitation. Sadira detected movement far out on the plain. " 'Tis only Bachir," she told him. "Sherifa . . . Najila . . . *stay.*"

She motioned for the two mares to remain where they were. Both animals were trembling—eager to join the herd of mares running with Bachir. Sadira grabbed Sherifa's mane and gave it a firm tug to remind the mare to obey. With her other hand, she encircled Najila's nose. "No. You may not go to him. You must stay with us."

Travis took her hand and removed it from Najila's nose. His eyes held a glint of starlight—and entreaty. "Let her go," he said. "Let Najila join him if she wishes. Let Sherifa go, too."

She could not stop Najila. As soon as the mare realized that no one held her, she bolted. Sherifa gave a cry of distress and anxiously pawed the ground, but true to her training, awaited Sadira's permission. "Sherifa, *stay,*" Sadira repeated.

The mare obeyed, but her muscles tensed. Her neck

arched. She raised her tail and gazed longingly after Najila. She nickered in appeal.

"Sadira," Travis said urgently. "Only duty holds her here. Only duty, love, and loyalty. . . . She is staying because of you. But are you being fair to her? I don't think so—no more than the *Ruala* are being fair to you. If you truly loved her, you would let her go."

This was the test he had once proposed—duty versus need and desire. Like her, Sherifa was torn between conflicting loyalties. The mare trembled with eagerness to join Bachir, but would not leave without Sadira's permission. Her blood ran true. Sherifa would have passed Muhammad's test with pride and honor. How could she herself be less worthy, less honorable than her own mare? . . . But how could she deny the mare one night of fulfillment, one night to remember and hold close all the rest of the lonely nights of her life?

She removed her hand from Sherifa's neck and spoke to her softly in Arabic. "All right, my friend . . . go. Be happy. This one night I give thee. This one night, thou shalt be free to follow thine own heart."

The mare reared and pawed the air in her excitement, then galloped across the plain, mane and tail flying. Sadira could just make out Bachir's silhouette as he rushed forward to greet her. The two touched noses, then turned and leaped away together.

Sadira then turned to Travis. "Oh, Travis! I cannot go away with you, but I, too, must have a memory of love to sustain me when all the world is dark and menacing." She moved into his arms. "Love me, Travis! Please love me."

He stood very still, his face and body rigid. "You are giving me your virginity? You—the Keeper of the Mares? The ceremonial virgin?"

She nodded and pressed closer to him. "Why should I give it to the *Shammar*? If I am no longer a virgin, perhaps my luck and power will leave me. The *Shammar* will be cheated, but they will never know it. In a way, I will be helping the *Anazah*."

"And is that the only reason you would give yourself to me now—to cheat your enemies?"

She tilted his head down and kissed his unyielding lips. "No, Travis. You know 'tis not the only reason. I am giving myself to thee because I love thee. . . . Whatever awaits me among the *Shammar,* I want to remember this one night when I listened to my heart and not my conscience. For as long as I live, I shall love no other but thee. Please, please love me! Give thyself to me. Oh, Travis, I need thee so much!"

Sixteen

Travis hesitated, torn between indignation at Sadira's continued stubbornness and gratitude that she was willing to give this much. Only one thing was certain: One night with her would never be enough—not when he wanted a lifetime of nights with her in his arms.

They needed this precious time to prepare for their escape, but what good was all the time in the world if she flatly refused to go away with him? First, he had to change her mind, and he could think of no better way to do it than to love her with such tenderness and passion that she would be convinced they belonged together forever.

"Travis?" She drew back slightly, searching his face, and her whispered plea shattered his sanity along with his resistance. When she looked at him like that, he could deny her nothing. If she asked him to walk through fire, he would cheerfully do it. Making love to her would be the easiest thing he had ever done in his life.

Quickly, he pulled off his robe, brushed aside the rocks and pebbles underfoot, and spread the garment on the sandy ground. He took her hand and together they knelt on the robe and embraced.

"This isn't good enough for you," he murmured into her hair. "You should have a bed of silk and satin, strewn with rose petals."

She laughed softly, her breath tickling his ear. "Have you forgotten, *Frangi?* I am desert-bred. The sand is my natural element; I was born on it, and I will die on it. Where else but on the sand should I give myself to you?"

"We should at least have a tent over our heads."

"I prefer a canopy of stars—and the wind blowing across our bodies. Look up, my love. Look up and see the sky. For us, the stars shine bright this night. For us, the wind sings a song of love and happiness."

Travis tilted back his head and studied the stars. Brighter now than before, they resembled a million sparkling jewels flung across a sweep of black velvet. The desert wind caressed his face and ruffled his hair, and it did seem as if the wind were singing, sighing a sweet love song, whispering of joy and pleasure. He filled his hands with the silky wealth of Sadira's hair and marveled at its texture. He stroked the soft skin of her cheek, the softest thing he had ever touched. He trembled to think of touching more of her and feared he would lose control before he had even begun to make love to her.

She rested her head on his shoulder and leaned into him. "There is no one else in the world this night but us. We are the only ones who exist, Travis."

This was her way of shutting out ugly reality and banishing fear and guilt. He could play the game, too, he decided, at least for a little while—and maybe, just maybe, she would reconsider her decision to go to the *Shammar.* Gently, he resumed kissing her. . . . Gently, he caressed her through her clothing. Her breasts were soft and full in his hands. The shape of her hips entranced him. Her responses were sweet, trusting, and totally feminine, exciting him beyond anything he had ever experienced.

She helped him remove her garments, then insisted that

he remove his. He marveled at her pure perfection—firm young flesh, tender round breasts, slender long limbs, rosy nipples, a thatch of soft-as-down curls nestled at the juncture of her thighs. He had never seen or touched anything more perfect. Awestricken, he paid homage to her beauty with hands and lips. Naked beneath the stars, they rolled together on his robe, and he forgot that he intended to control everything, to deny his own needs in favor of making it as wonderful as possible for her. It was too wonderful for him. He lost himself to passion and surrendered to raw instinct—touching, tasting, caressing, stroking Sadira—and exulting in all she did to him in return.

"Frangi, thou art so strong, so fine," she murmured in Arabic, all her English forgotten in the throes of her desire. "How I love thee! How I want thee and need thee!"

Her caresses were tentative at first, but as she grew more confident, she became bolder in her explorations. Her slender hands searched and discovered him, becoming instruments of the sweetest torture. He could scarcely bear the feel of her hands on his body, yet could find no words to tell her to stop. He reveled in her touch, delighted in it, and belatedly fought to restrain himself, to keep the pace slow and languorous. He tried to think of snow and ice—anything to cool him!—but their love play enflamed him to the point of no return. All too soon, he had to sheath himself within her heated flesh or explode.

He dreaded causing her pain, but knew there was no way to avoid it. She was slick and ready, writhing beneath him and half moaning with desire. His own need was an acute discomfort. He ached for her. Body and soul cried out for the ultimate joining. Rising over her, he parted her thighs with a trembling hand, positioned himself, and eased into her. She arched beneath him and uttered a whimpering cry. He forced himself to remain motionless above her, waiting for her body to adjust to his entry, wishing he could have taken her without hurting her.

She lay still a moment, then surged upward and wrapped her arms and legs around him. "Travis, I did not know it would be like this! I never dreamed I would feel this way."

He thought she was talking about the pain and kissed her in apology. "I'm so sorry," he muttered. His passion abruptly ebbed, and he nearly withdrew from her body.

"Sorry? Sorry for what, Travis? Why should you be sorry? I had no idea men and women could create such joy and pleasure between them. 'Tis magnificent, is it not?"

"But . . . didn't I just hurt you? I've heard that the first time is always uncomfortable for virgins."

She laughed huskily and bit his earlobe. "Not for me, Travis. When I was a small child, I fell from a horse and hurt myself down there. *That* was pain. *This* is . . . this is ecstasy, a rapture I never imagined." She moved beneath him, lifting her hips to clasp him ever more tightly, take him ever more deeply. "Oh, Travis! Lovemaking is truly wondrous!"

It was his turn to laugh—and to burn with desire. "I will teach you more about pleasure, Sadira. Hang on, little one, and I will ride you as Bachir is probably riding Sherifa about now."

"And are you like Bachir, lusting after as many mares as he can persuade to join his harem?"

"No, Sadira, I need only you—just you for as long as I live. I am not like Bachir nor your own father who has filled his tent with many wives. *You* are the only woman

I want, the only one I will ever desire. You are mine, Sadira—all mine. And I am yours forever. . . ."

Travis began to move within her. Wanting to see her face as he took her, he raised himself as he thrust inside her. She rose to meet him, and they found an ancient and altogether satisfying rhythm. Sadira's eyes lit the darkness. Wide and wondering, they reflected back the starshine and gleamed with love. Gazing down at her, he rode her gently at first, but then a wildness swept over him, the primeval need to conquer and possess his woman. He drove into her with a fury borne of lust and love combined. In his final possession, when he gained all he sought, he also relinquished all that he was . . . all he would ever be. At the very moment he poured his seed into her, a terrible—and wonderful—thought struck him: What if they had created a child tonight?

He would remind her that she might very well become pregnant as a consequence of their lovemaking. It was one more reason why she ought to flee with him. If she went to the *Shammar* posing as a virgin, and her womb then swelled with child, the *Shammar* would be outraged. They would kill her and the unborn child along with her. She could not take such a risk. She belonged to him now—could not possibly deny their right to be together. Not even the *Ruala* knew her as he now knew her. She belonged to him body and soul, and before dawn, he must get her away from here.

Sadira could not move a muscle nor even lift an eyelid for several moments after the culmination of their lovemaking. She felt drained of all strength and vigor, yet more stunningly alive than she had ever thought possible. Peace and satiation filled her; she felt bathed in a golden glow, as if the sun itself shone down upon her. But it was still night, and before the sun rose, she must return to camp and prepare to face her enemies.

Much too quickly, the lovely feelings faded . . . the glow subsided. Above her, Travis stirred and raised himself on his elbows. "Sweetheart, listen to me," he said urgently. "There's not much time, and we have to hurry. You've got to come with me now. What we just did may result in a child. If you are pregnant, the *Shammar* will not want you for their Keeper of the Mares. Nor will Hajem Pasha desire you for a wife. He will cast you out. The *Shammar* will kill you. As a virgin no longer, you can't risk going to them. Come away with me, Sadira. You're mine now. As soon as possible, we'll marry."

His twisted—and very masculine—logic jolted Sadira out of her daze; he considered their lovemaking as the final inducement to gain her consent to leave! It upset her that he would attempt to manipulate her in such a shameless, cold-hearted fashion.

"Do you think you own me now, Travis, because I have lain with you and loved you? If you do, you are mistaken. If I am with child, I can find herbs in the desert to solve that particular problem. I have heard women speak of such things."

"You would do that to our little son or daughter?" There was deep hurt in Travis's voice—and though it was too dark to see for certain, she knew there was agony in his eyes. "You would kill it with no more thought than your people give to slaughtering lambs and baby camels?"

No, her heart answered. *I would never do that to our child, Travis. Never. Never. I do not even know if I could find such herbs or if they would work. I knew what I was risking when I lay down with thee; I have taken my chances, and now I will accept the consequences—whatever they may be.*

To Travis, she said, "There is no child, Travis. Therefore, there is no need to worry about it."

"You can't be sure of that!"

" 'Tis not the right time for me," she argued, having heard the women discuss this also. Some believed a woman's fertility was ruled by the cycle of the moon and the configuration of the stars. Others thought it was strictly controlled by Allah or even by the will of one's husband.

"You don't know that either. You can't think only of your people now, Sadira. You have to consider the possible fate of our child."

"Our *possible* child," she reminded him, brushing his hair back from his temples with her fingertips. "It may not exist, Travis. It probably does not . . . but my people do. Therefore, I must do what is necessary to protect *their* children and babies."

He lowered his body to hers and rubbed seductively against her. "And this, Sadira . . . this means nothing? You've had your one night of pleasure, and it's got to last the rest of your life—is that it? You'll have your memories if nothing else."

She willed herself to lie still and quiet, not to respond, not to reach for him and surrender to the magic of his loving once again. "It means everything, Travis . . . and it means nothing. When I call Sherifa and Najila, they will come running back to me, eager to obey and do their duty now that they have had their time beneath the stars. So must I go running back to my people. I told you it would be like this before we lay down together."

Travis went rigid. "You are not a horse! You're not mere property, but a human being! You can make choices and direct your own destiny. For us, there's more to lovemaking than mere physical satisfaction. I didn't used to think that, but now I do. What we just did is sacred and binding, Sadira. It has joined us in more ways than one."

Yes. Oh, yes, I know, Travis! Especially now, after I have loved thee.

"In this I have no choice!" she blurted out, deeply distressed. "Why can you not understand? Oh, cease this endless argument, and let me up, Travis. Be happy for what we have had, and do not mourn for what is denied us."

"Is there nothing I can say—nothing I can do—to get through to you, Sadira?"

She shook her head and blinked back tears. "Nothing. There is nothing."

He groaned as if she had slid a knife into his heart and twisted it. Neither of them spoke, but after a moment, he lowered his body onto hers and nuzzled her hair. "Sweetheart, I can't let you go with anger simmering between us. I love you too much for that."

Only too happy to capitulate, she wound her arms around his neck. "And I love you! Travis, we still have a little time together. Let us not spoil it by arguing. We have time for more of this . . ."

She took his face between her hands and kissed him, employing all her newfound knowledge to please and arouse him. He did not require much encouragement. With another small groan, he clasped her tightly and returned her kisses. For the second time that night, they began climbing the peaks of passion, seeking to cram a lifetime of loving into the brief space of a few hours. Each kiss, each trembling caress seemed all the more sweet because they knew it would be their last, and fulfillment came in an explosive cataclysm that rocked them as if the earth had quaked.

Afterward, they lay entwined in each other's arms until the brightness of a particular star on the horizon alerted Sadira to the passage of time. The star was the one after which she had been named, and it always burned the brightest just before dawn. Already along the eastern horizon, a faint splash of gray heralded the morning.

Reluctantly, she withdrew from him and sat up. "Travis, we must go now. I will leave first. You must ride to the south and return to camp from that direction. Do not let anyone see thee."

"No one will see me," he assured her as they hurriedly donned their clothing, and she called Najila and Sherifa.

Sherifa came first, her pounding hooves creating a swirl of dust on the plain. Najila reluctantly followed, trailed by several curious mares from Bachir's little band. Bachir himself galloped up and down, neighing his distress at the loss of his two new conquests, but he seemed to know better than to approach too closely and risk being caught and hobbled. Past experience had made him wary.

Before mounting her mare, Sadira flew into Travis's arms and shared one last heady kiss with him. When it ended, she tugged free as he sought to hold her. "Goodbye, my dearest love!" she choked through her tears.

Allowing him no further chance to change her mind, she leapt onto Sherifa's back. To stay even a moment longer would cruelly test her resolution.

"Sadira, wait!" he called, but she would not listen. The time for listening—and loving—was past. Now was the time for sacrifice. She could spare him no more kisses and no more tears.

* * *

Clenching and unclenching his fists, Travis watched Sadira go. Then he quickly caught Najila before the mare decided she would rather rejoin Bachir than stay with him. He could not afford to lose his only means of transportation and be stranded out here on the plain; he had to get back to camp. An idea had been forming in his mind as to how he might kidnap Sadira. . . . Yes, that was what he was going to have to do: kidnap her. The question now was how best to go about it? How to gather together what he needed, have the horses waiting at a safe place, find a guide. . . .

He thought about it as he rode east, circling the camp and approaching from a different direction, as Sadira had suggested. He needed help, and he could think of only one person who might possibly assist him . . . and if she refused, he had no hope of succeeding. Alima loved Sadira; their mutual affection was obvious to anyone who saw them together. She also spoke English. To her, Travis must make his plea for help, trusting that she would not go to Akbar even if she did not approve of his plan.

Alima loved Akbar, but she also regarded Sadira as a daughter. She could not be happy about Sadira's fate; would she agree to help Travis save her? Travis would not know the answer to that question until he asked the woman. So intent was he on making his plans that he rode much closer to the camp than he realized before he remembered to take precautions against being seen. Luckily, no one was yet stirring as he slid off Najila's back, turned her loose, then quickly and quietly made his way toward his own tent.

He was almost there when a figure suddenly emerged from the dark shadows between the tents, and an angry voice muttered in Arabic. *"Frangi!* Where goest thou at this hour?"

Travis peered into the darkness, trying to identify the man coming toward him. His voice was hoarse and unfamiliar, but the stiff, indignant way he held himself struck a chord of recognition—Hamid. Only Hamid bristled with such dislike and jealousy. Only Hamid would be waiting to spy on him, eager to catch him doing something wrong. Thank God Sadira was nowhere in sight.

Travis carelessly straightened his robe as if he had merely gone out onto the plain to attend to personal needs. Whenever the Bedouin felt nature's call, they sought a spot off to one side of a busy area, away from people, and simply squatted. Their robes offered ample concealment and privacy, and no one thought a thing about it. Travis decided to offer no complicated excuses to further arouse Hamid's suspicions; he would stick to simple explanations.

"Too much water. I drank too much water," he explained in his halting Arabic. "Had to relieve myself, and now I'm returning to my tent."

"Hah!" Hamid snorted. "That is not where thou went!"

Travis brushed past him, refusing to argue, but his heart hammered loudly in his chest. Had Hamid seen him and Sadira? No, he couldn't have. If he had, he would have aroused the entire encampment by now.

"I shall inform Akbar," Hamid snarled. "I will go to him and tell him my suspicions. Thou must have been meeting with the Keeper of the Mares, for she, too, has been gone from her tent and has only just returned."

"Perhaps she, too, drank too much water," Travis shot back over his shoulder. He continued walking, making straight for his tent and entering it without a backward glance.

Once there, he began to toss his belongings together in a pile so that all would be ready for a quick escape. He could do nothing, unfortunately, until Alima left Akbar's tent at first light, which was not far off, and he had a chance to speak with her. He just hoped Hamid would wait until then to go running to Akbar. If all went as Travis hoped, he would be able to leave camp shortly thereafter. No one would ever suspect that Sadira was with him, hidden inside one of the huge baskets used to carry goods on the pack camels. In his robes and *keffiya,* with one end tied across his lower face, he would look like any other Bedouin riding out on his camel to check on his herds.

He had come up with the perfect plan. But he needed Alima to convince Akbar that Sadira had taken ill and should be delivered to the *Shammar* in her curtained *mohaffa* . . . except she wouldn't be in it. She would be with him, tied up or unconscious from a blow on the head. He would do whatever worked best. He also needed Alima to gather supplies and to bribe someone to act as a guide—someone who would meet him later out on the desert with the horses. There must be a man in camp willing to earn a small fortune by taking him and Sadira safely to Aleppo. He had left enough money with the British Consul to tempt the right person, and Alima would know who that person might be.

But before he could arrange for any of this, Travis had to see Alima and convince her to help.

After she left Travis, Sadira rode quickly back to camp and boldly returned to her tent as if she had nothing to hide. She met no one and thought her absence had gone unnoticed until she entered her tent and encountered a shadowy figure calmly seated upon her pillows awaiting her.

"Where hast thou been, Sadira?" came the soft inquiry. Sadira was glad for the darkness that hid her surprise—and gave her time to fashion a proper response.

"Alima! What is it? Is something wrong?" Sadira knelt at the old woman's side and reached for her hand. "What art thou doing here?"

"I came to pass this last night with thee, child, to soothe and comfort thee. But I found thy tent empty and thy pillows undisturbed."

"I could not sleep, so I went out and rode Sherifa. Thou knowest that I have always been able to find peace on the desert alone with my favorite mare."

"And is that all thou found on the desert—peace and serenity?"

It was difficult for Sadira to lie to someone she loved, someone who knew her so well. "I . . . I found all I needed there, Alima, as I always do," she responded evasively.

Alima sighed. "Thou art not telling me everything, child. I had hoped thou hadst more trust in me. I have been as thy mother, have I not? Nay, I have been closer to thee than thine own mother, caring for thee since infancy."

"Aye, that is true," Sadira responded. She was ashamed of her deceitfulness, but still unwilling to tell Alima the truth. She knelt down beside her old friend, but volunteered nothing further, and Alima reached over and took her hand.

"Dost thou still intend to go to the *Shammar* this day, my child?"

Sadira nearly jerked away in startlement. "Of course, I do! Why dost thou ask that, Alima? Have I ever given thee reason to think I might betray my people? Thou knowest me better than anyone, and I am *not* like my mother!"

"Hush, hush, child." Alima squeezed her hand reassuringly. "Thou takest offense too quickly . . . and while we are discussing thy mother, I think thou shouldst learn the truth about her at long last."

"What truth? What art thou talking about, and why dost thou bring it up today of all days?"

"Because today will decide thy future, child. Today will see thee handed over to thine enemies, and I cannot let thee go to them without telling thee these things. I have thought long and hard on this; I have prayed ceaselessly to Allah. And I find I cannot stand idly by and let thee make this sacrifice—let thee go willingly to thine own death, believing it is the right thing to do."

"It *is* the right thing! And death is only one of many possibilities."

" 'Tis the most likely one, I think, Sadira. And even if they do not kill thee, they will find a thousand ways to make thee miserable. Trust me, Sadira. I have lived long and earned my wisdom. I know what dwells in the hearts of men."

"But what is this truth about my mother, and how can it change anything?"

"Listen to me, dearest child. For the sake of the love thou hast for me, be silent and open thy mind to my words. Wilt thou humor an old woman who loves thee? Wilt thou listen and not take issue with every word I say?"

Sadira did not want to listen—did not want to be told truths that might shake her world any more than Travis had already shaken it. But she could not say no to Alima. Before Travis, Alima was the only person on earth who had ever truly loved her, accepted her as she was, and not demanded that she conform to some impossible ideal. Like Travis, Alima did not blame her or hold her responsible for what had happened long ago in the past. Alima had been her one true friend all her life.

"I am listening, Alima . . . go on, speak."

Seventeen

Alima settled herself more comfortably on the pillows. Still holding Sadira's hand, she began to speak softly, but with quiet determination. "Thy mother—thy poor, poor mother—came unwillingly to thy father. She was but a child, and she feared him, but feared even more to defy her family. Thus, she married Akbar and tried to be a good wife to him. She was to give him the children that Jaleel and I had thus far been unable to provide. . . ."

She paused and affectionately stroked Sadira's fingers. "Thy father hast told thee that he loved Bashiyra the best of all his wives. But in those days, he loved no one—not even me. What he loved was increasing his herds, making war on his enemies, and striking awe and terror into the hearts of all who heard his name.

"Poor Bashiyra dreaded every moment she spent in thy father's company. At night, after Akbar fell asleep, I could hear her sobbing quietly into her pillows. Though she was very beautiful—more beautiful than Jaleel—she could not please him. He found fault with everything she did. He needed a woman, and she was still a child, a frightened child who flinched when he came near and wept when he took her to his bed. This hurt Akbar's pride, and he treated her harshly and ridiculed her. In truth, I think he doubted his virility and blamed each of us for never having conceived a child—

Bashiyra most of all, for she was his newest wife, the one on whom he had fastened all his hopes. . . . Then Jaleel became pregnant, Akbar rejoiced, and in his happiness, life improved for everyone—until thy father, the green-eyed, golden-haired *frangi,* arrived among us."

"My father," Sadira repeated, thinking how strange it sounded to say that word and mean some other man besides Akbar. She had thought of Akbar as her father for so long that it was almost impossible to replace his image in her mind with that of a blond-haired stranger.

"Yes, thy father. He was good to look upon, and from the moment he arrived in camp, thy mother's eyes followed him everywhere. Akbar permitted us to appear before the yellow-haired *frangi* without our veils . . . and from the moment, thy father spotted thy mother, he was unable to resist her beauty. We all saw what was happening—all of us but Akbar. Thy mother and the *frangi* could no more remain apart than a stallion and a mare in season. Bashiyra blossomed and remembered how to smile. The *frangi* made excuses for remaining in camp, even after Akbar consented to sell him not one but two good horses. Perhaps Akbar *did* sense the danger, for he confided to me that he distrusted the *frangi* and thought he should be sent away. I could do no less than agree with him, and he ordered the *frangi* to take his horses and leave . . . but it was already too late.

"The damage had been done, only we did not know it for certain until we saw you. Bashiyra had a difficult pregnancy—which thy father barely noticed in his elation that *two* of his wives would soon give birth. Jaleel's pregnancy was far easier, but she complained day and night, so it was no wonder thy boastful father came to favor the company of gentle, kind, and beautiful Bashiyra. When thou appeared with thy strange-colored eyes and hair, he flew into a jealous rage. He had forgotten how cruelly he had treated thy mother when first she arrived among the *Ruala;* he felt betrayed."

"It makes little difference *how* he treated her," Sadira murmured. "She *did* betray him."

"Yes, yes . . ." Alima nodded. "That is all true. However, she was very young and in love for the first time in her life—and she had been married against her will. That makes it easier to understand, does it not? And to forgive."

"To understand, perhaps, but not to forgive," Sadira insisted. "She brought shame upon my father and upon the *Ruala.*"

"Thou art very harsh in thy judgments, child. Thy mother was not even as old as thou art now when all this happened. And she never left thy father, never ran away with her lover, though she could have."

"What do you mean—she could have? How do you know that?"

"One night after all had gone to bed, I overheard the *frangi* and thy mother speaking in low tones outside the tent. He begged her to go away with him, but she refused, weeping while she did it. She said it was her destiny to live among the *Ruala* forever. Allah had given her Akbar as a husband, and she would not shame him by running away with a *frangi*. He begged and pleaded, but still, she refused, saying: 'Though I can never love him as I love thee, 'tis my duty to uphold my husband's honor' . . . I remember it word for word."

"Thou didst not tell my father what thou overheard? Nor mention it to anyone else?"

Alima sadly shook her head and sighed. "Nay, child, I did not. But then I did not know Bashiyra was with child, nor was she aware of it. Nor was the *frangi*. She chose duty over love, honor over happiness. And she paid for that error with her life. . . . Child, I do not want thee to make the same mistake thy mother did."

Sadira took Alima's hand and clasped it tightly. "Why art thou telling me these things, Alima? For the love of Allah, speak plainly, I entreat thee!"

It was light enough now to see Alima's plain round face and sad, haunted eyes. "Thy gaze follows the *frangi,* Travis, and he gazes at thee the same way that thy mother and *her frangi* looked at each other—the same way Akbar and I regard each other. Child, I am not blind. Thou hast given thy heart to him and he to thee. Has he not begged thee to go away with him? Has he not entreated thee to become his wife?"

Sadira did not answer; she had thought her secret safe, yet Alima had known all along! How many others also knew? She released Alima's hand and nervously twisted a fold of her robe.

"Thou art feeling torn between thine own desires and the needs of thy people," Alima continued. "Thou hast been taught to put thy people first, but I say to thee that there comes a time to think of thine own needs and to decide for thyself what is right and wrong. That time is now, Sadira. 'Tis a great wrong that Akbar and our people should demand so much of thee, that they should send thee away as if thou wert a horse or a camel, with no feelings and fears at all. Thou art not a slave nor an animal, but a human being."

"Then should I let there be war?" Sadira cried. "Should I refuse to go to the *Shammar* and run away with Travis instead? I *have* asked myself these questions, Alima, and there is only one answer: if I do not stay, if I follow my heart, many will suffer and die. War may be inevitable, and the *Shammar* may not accept me as a fair exchange for Gamalat, but at least I will have done all I could to avert it. Thou claimest to love Akbar, yet by speaking to me like this, art thou not betraying thy husband?"

Alima appeared unruffled by the accusation. "Just because I love him does not mean I do not see his faults. He is only a man, child, and men are not all-wise. Akbar rules well, but he still makes mistakes. Many times I have held my tongue when I should have spoken. Now that I am old and my time is running out, I am resolved to keep silent no longer. Though I am a mere female, I, too, can think and reason. . . . Thus have I conceived a plan whereby thou canst follow thy heart and thy people will *still* be saved."

Sadira sat back on her heels in astonishment. "What plan? I am beginning to think thou hast taken leave of thy senses, Alima. In thine old age, thou hast grown reckless; Akbar would kill us both if he could hear us. It would be his right."

"And that is the injustice and tragedy of our lives, is it not?" Alima inquired with some asperity. "Men can say whether we women live or die. They can choose whether to murder us or to love us—and that is because we *let* them, Sadira! We meekly bow our heads and permit ourselves to be manipulated and controlled for the whole of our entire lives! Do not wait until thou art old to finally see the truth and decide to fight injustice. Learn to think for thyself. Trust thine own instincts. Dost thou wish to hear this plan—or wilt thou simply do as thou art told simply because a man has told thee to do it?"

Sadira had never heard Alima speak like this; no woman of her acquaintance dared to say such things. Yet Alima's opinions echoed her own innermost thoughts, and they echoed Travis's. First, Travis and now Alima were challenging the rules by which she had lived. She leaned forward. "Tell me thy plan, Alima, for if I could do both—save my people *and* gain Travis—I would do it."

Alima gave her a sorrowful, weary smile. " 'Tis this, child. Thou wilt go to the *Shammar* wearing a *burqa,* covered entirely, hidden from the eyes of all who look upon thee. Is that not so?"

"Yes, yes, I will," Sadira agreed, still not understanding.

"The *Shammar* have never seen thee, so they do not know thy face, or how old thou art."

"That is true."

"Thou might be of any age, perhaps even old and ugly like me."

" 'Tis possible, yes, though not likely. And I do not regard thee as old and ugly." Sadira was beginning to suspect where this might be leading. "But I would never let anyone go in my place, Alima. Not even thou—*especially* not thou, whom I love as my own mother in place of the one I never knew."

"But what if I was dying, Sadira? What if I had not long to live anyway?"

"Alima, no!"

"Yes, my child, yes. I *am* dying." Alima again reached for Sadira's hand and placed it upon her lower abdomen. "Feel this . . . right here. No, a little higher. There, dost thou feel it?"

Sadira groped along Alima's waist until she came to a firm, alien mound—oval in circumference and surprisingly large. It was almost where a woman would carry a child, only this was odd-shaped and off to one side. "Oh, Alima, what is it?"

Alima shrugged her frail, thin shoulders. "A growth,

child, a tumor. A foreign thing that is slowly sapping my life and soon will claim it altogether." She removed Sadira's hand and gently replaced it in her lap.

"But how long has it been there? Does it pain thee?"

"It has been growing for . . . oh, well past a year now. Maybe longer. I cannot remember. As thou hast already noted, I am often ill, and I have little appetite. . . ."

"Merciful Allah! I *have* noticed, but thou kept insisting 'twas not serious! . . . Does Akbar know?"

"Yes, he knows—though he thinks it is yet a small growth, not nearly as large as it has recently become. Surely thou hast also noticed how reluctant he is to leave me—why he insists that I accompany him wherever he goes. He suspects I have not much time left, and he is right. I can feel death approaching. There are moments when the pain grows severe, and I can scarcely bear it, yet most of the time I am comfortable. I have begged him to take his carbine and shoot me when the day comes that the pain grips me and will not leave, but thus far, he has refused."

"Dear Alima!" Sadira flung her arms around the old woman and embraced her. "I am so sorry! Forgive me for not realizing before this that something was dreadfully wrong with thee."

"Do not fret, child." Alima patted her shoulder, then drew back. "I see now that this all has a purpose. Allah has planned it down to the tiniest detail. 'Tis I who will go to the *Shammar,* and *they* who will perform the final kindness that Akbar cannot bring himself to do. They will end my life as soon as they look upon me and realize that I am too old and sick to provide another heir for Hajem Pasha. That is what I hope and pray they will do. I had

rather die now than grow weaker each day and be forced
to endure the suffering that awaits me at the end."

"No! No, Alima, I cannot let thee do this! Oh, 'tis too
much!" Sadira sobbed, lowering her face to her hands.
"Thou art too young to die! Thou art too wise! My father
and our people need thy counsel. I will tell Akbar what
thou art planning, and he will stop thee!"

"Nay, Sadira. If thou carest for me at all, thou wilt leave
here with thy *frangi* and pursue happiness in a new life
with him. Thou art half-*frangi,* do not forget. The first portion of thy life thou hast already given to the *Ruala.* Now,
give the rest of it to that part of thyself that is not *Anazah,
Ruala, Shammar,* or any other desert tribe."

Alima gently smoothed back Sadira's hair. "Forgive thy
mother her weakness, and do not scorn thine own weakness
nor find shame in it. 'Tis right thou shouldst love a man
and seek happiness with him. 'Tis unnatural that thou
should have stayed a virgin and the Keeper of the Mares
for this long, much less for life. Thou only agreed to it
because of thy mother, but I do not think that what she
did was so wrong. She was young and foolish, and she
made a mistake, but she tried to behave honorably. She
remained with her husband and sought to spare him sorrow.
Thou wert very young when that vow was made—as young
as thy mother. 'Tis not right for a woman to be bound by
a promise she made as a child. . . . Wilt thou grant an old
woman's dying wish and let her take thy place and go to
the *Shammar?"*

"Alima! I . . . I know not what to say. I am filled with
confusion. I am wracked by doubts and beset by grief and
guilt! I know not what to think, much less say."

"Say yes, Sadira. 'Tis the will of Allah. Choose love, not
death. Go with thy *frangi* and enjoy the special bond that is

remarkably similar to what I have been blessed to share with Akbar. There is no other experience to compare with it—not even motherhood. A mother knows she must one day relinquish her son or daughter, but when love blossoms between a man and a woman, 'tis so rare and fine a thing that naught else can overshadow it. Guard and nurture it, child. Fight for it with thine every breath. Cast it not callously aside as a thing of no value, for it is the rarest jewel on all the earth, worthy of any sacrifice. . . . Wherever thy beloved goes, Sadira, thou must go . . . go and be happy."

"Oh, my dearest Alima, thou hast nearly convinced me . . . but am I truly convinced or do I only selfishly desire to have my own way, and thou hast given it to me?"

"I hope I have given it to thee, child, for that was my intention. Offer me your hand now, that I may rise and go and tell the *frangi*. If thou art to escape with him, there is much to be done and not much time in which to do it. After I have spoken with him, I will return and tell thee what thou must do next."

Sadira offered Alima her hand and helped the old woman to rise. Even then, in the midst of a budding joy that she might yet be able to flee with Travis, doubts and worries assailed her. "How can I thank thee, and how can I say goodbye, Alima—true mother of my heart? I am bereft to think of losing thee. Were thou not dying, I should never consider this."

"Thou art going to lose me no matter what thou dost, child. But it will make my passing happier if I can go knowing thou art happy. . . . Cherish thy *frangi*, Sadira. Cherish and love him above all others; that is all I ask of thee, as mother to daughter."

"I will try!" Fresh tears sprang anew, as Sadira again embraced her old friend. She could not believe she was actually going to run away with Travis, but in the face of Alima's determination, all her objections disappeared like smoke. She could not refuse—not when Alima's desires echoed her own.

Alima turned to depart the tent, and it was then they both heard the summons. "Sadira! Keeper of the Mares! Come forth. The Great and Generous One, Emir Akbar el-Karim, thy father, has called thee to his tent."

"That is Hamid; I recognize his voice." Sadira clutched Alima's shoulders. "What does Akbar want, I wonder?"

It had been years since her father had sent for her so formally. Only a matter of great importance would have induced him to remind her of his rank and power.

"Courage, child," Alima whispered. "I will accompany thee, and we shall go together to see what Akbar wants."

"Allah watch over us," Sadira murmured, her heart suddenly racing.

When Travis left his tent to look for Alima, he found three men awaiting him—three men with grim faces and carbines leveled at his midsection. They motioned with their guns that he was to go ahead of them, following a fourth man he had not at first noticed. All were men he recognized as being Akbar's most trusted associates; they rode fine horses and camels, and they ate often in Akbar's tent. It did not bode well that these four had come for him; apparently Hamid's suspicions had convinced the sheik that something was amiss, and he ought to investigate.

Travis cursed his lost opportunities as he warily took his place among the men and walked with them to Akbar's tent. Instead of making love to Sadira during the night, he ought to have tied a sack over her head and escaped with

her. Now, if Akbar suspected something, he would not have
the chance. For both of them, it would all be over.

When they arrived at Akbar's tent, the men gestured for
him to enter ahead of them. He passed through the outer
chamber to the inner one and there encountered Akbar
seated solemnly on his richly colored pillows. Off to one
side stood Hamid, his familiar scowl deeply etched onto
his sullen features, as if he'd been born scowling. Akbar
motioned for him to be seated, but did not offer the customary cup of coffee. Indeed, Samir was nowhere in sight.

Then Akbar spoke. "Thou dost understand Arabic now,
dost thou not, *Frangi?*"

"Aye," Travis answered. "Though if I am to be accused
of something, I would prefer to have an interpreter, just so
there are no misunderstandings."

He hoped that Akbar would send for Sadira—or Alima—
but the sheik merely gazed at him with an expression of
deep distrust and disappointment in his snapping black
eyes. "I have already sent for my daughter, and she and
my first wife are here, awaiting my pleasure in the harem."
He jerked his head in the direction of the women's quarters.
"I prefer to speak to thee alone first. I had thought us
friends, *Frangi*. I had considered thee my brother. Yet
Hamid claims thou art a traitor and a thief—seeking to
steal what I hold most dear—my beloved daughter."

Travis kept his face as devoid of expression as possible,
except for a slight, scornful lift of his brows. "Say no more,
Akbar. I deny everything Hamid might have told you. He
cannot be trusted to speak the truth, for I have seen with
my own eyes that he lusts after your daughter, your precious Keeper of the Mares."

" 'Tis a lie!" Hamid burst out. "Thou speakest with the

tongue of a serpent. I have never laid a hand on Akbar's daughter."

"I do not accuse you of doing so, but I have noticed that no matter where I am, if Sadira is near, you are also. You follow us everywhere. You watch Sadira constantly. . . . I cannot be the only man in camp who has noticed this." Travis turned back to Akbar whose attention had shifted. He was now watching Hamid with narrowed eyes, his face as fierce and hawklike as Travis had ever seen it.

"Yes," Akbar said slowly. "I, too, have seen thee watching her, Hamid, and thou hast a guilty look about thee now."

" 'Twas not I who stole out upon the plain and followed Sadira last night. 'Twas he!" Hamid pointed to Travis. "And I believe he met her there and took her virginity. A *frangi* once compromised Sadira's mother, and now this one has done the same with Sadira."

"Silence!" Akbar exploded, his face reddening. "Sadira bears the mark of the star. Thou shalt not say otherwise, Hamid, nor imply that any man except me fathered her. *She is my daughter;* dost thou understand?"

"Aye, lord," Hamid answered, bowing slightly and looking greatly chagrined. "Forgive me for repeating gossip. There can be no doubt that Sadira possesses special powers conferred by a star. But this *frangi* met her last night, and I accuse him of taking what belongs only to Allah."

Akbar's black eyes sought Travis. "Is this true, *Frangi?* Hast thou compromised my daughter and robbed her of the most precious treasure she possesses?"

"I took nothing that belongs to Allah," Travis maintained, then added silently, *for it belongs to me, the man who loves her.* "As for the most precious treasure she possesses, I wonder that you do not count other things of far more importance than her virginity, her kindness and loyalty, for instance."

"A cultural difference between us. Dost thou hear, Hamid? He denies it! Hast thou proof of what thou hast claimed? Didst thou or anyone else witness them behaving improperly?"

"If thou dost not believe me, have the Keeper of the Mares examined. That alone will prove or disprove my accusation," Hamid responded in a bitter tone.

"And I suppose *you* wish to examine her," Travis blurted. "I would expect that of you."

"Infidel!" Hamid reached for the curved scimitar that hung at his waist. "Unbeliever! Thou shalt die for having said that!"

"Nay!" Akbar held up his hand. "Stay thy sword, Hamid. I shall do as thou hast suggested. I will have Sadira examined. If indeed she has lost her virginity, do what thou will with it, and I will applaud thee. But until I determine the *frangi*'s guilt or innocence, leave thy sword in thy scabbard or feel the bite of *my* sword."

"So be it, mighty Akbar," Hamid agreed, resting his hand on the ornately carved hilt of the weapon.

"Alima! Sadira!" Akbar clapped his hands together. A moment later, Alima came through the doorway to the women's quarters, accompanied by Sadira. Sadira wore a veil drawn across her face, and her green eyes were downcast. Only once did they flicker upward to meet Travis's gaze. She gave him a single beseeching look he could not interpret. She seemed to be trying to tell him something, but what it was, he had no idea.

Alima bowed low before Akbar, then knelt beside him. "Thou hast summoned us, my husband? To what purpose? If Sadira is to go to the *Shammar* soon, she must prepare herself. I went to her tent early this day to help her, then Hamid arrived and tore us away from the task at hand. We must hurry if she is to be ready on time."

The old woman looked very pale, and her mouth was quivering. She is not well, Travis thought, or else she is afraid, as I am afraid. An examination will reveal everything.

"Beloved," Akbar said gently, his face softening as he gazed upon Alima's homely face. "Thou art tired. Perhaps thou shouldst rest now, and let one of my other wives see to Sadira's needs. I will summon Jaleel, or little Jahara, my youngest wife. Either of them can assist Sadira. I have another task that must be performed before she can return to her preparations."

"What is that, Akbar?" Alima touched Akbar's chin, then ran her fingers along the line of his jaw. "What worries thee so, *Habib?* Fear and sorrow fill thine eyes. Hast thou changed thy mind about sending Sadira to thine enemies? I know how much it pains thee to see her go."

"Thou knowest I have no choice, *Habiba,*" Akbar responded. "But I do have a problem that plagues me greatly. Hamid has accused Sadira of giving her virginity to the *frangi.* He has denied taking it. But before I can send her to the *Shammar,* I must know if she is indeed still a virgin."

"How dare thee, Hamid!" Sadira burst out, her green eyes flashing. "Thou hast no right to accuse me of such shame and dishonor!"

"I have the right," Hamid petulantly insisted. " 'Tis the right of any man to voice his suspicions, especially when the ceremonial virgin, the Keeper of the Mares, is involved. The honor of the *Ruala* is at stake in this matter; the honor of all the *Anazah* is threatened."

"Of course, she must be examined," Alima said calmly, and Travis's heart jumped wildly in his chest. "I myself shall examine her. Sadira, return to the harem. This cannot be done before the eyes of men."

"Stay here, *Habiba,*" Akbar admonished Alima. "Stay here and rest. I will call Jaleel and have her do it."

"No!" Alima said quickly. "Not Jaleel. She has always hated Sadira. She cannot be counted upon to speak the truth. I and I alone will do it."

"She has always hated her?" Akbar's brows rose. "I never knew that. I thought Jaleel bore everyone an equal dislike. Perhaps Jahara . . ."

"Jahara is too young to be assigned such an important task. I trust only myself to do this, Akbar." Alima rose to her feet with difficulty, half stumbling as she did so, so that Akbar had to assist her.

"Art thou strong enough to do this, my precious dove?" Akbar kept a firm hold on her arm.

"Do not give *her* the task!" Hamid suddenly interrupted. "She has always protected and favored Sadira. She will do so now. She cannot be trusted to be impartial any more than Jaleel."

Alima drew herself up to her full height and leveled a look at Hamid that could wither stone. Made of a much weaker substance, Hamid sheepishly dropped his gaze.

"If my husband cannot trust me, he dare not trust anyone. I am not long for this world, Hamid, and I have loved Akbar for nearly all of my life. My husband *knows* he can trust me; is that not so, *Habib?*"

Alima again raised her hand to the sheik's fierce face. Between them passed such a look of love and tenderness that Travis's insides twisted in jealous longing. One day, he wanted Sadira to look at him like that—with a knowledge and communion only years of loving could produce. Akbar and Alima were two made one; in that moment, they even resembled each other, though Travis had never noticed much similarity between them before this. Yet it was there; they shared a radiance that almost blinded him.

Waiting for Akbar's answer, he drew a deep breath and prayed that Akbar would agree to let Alima conduct the examination. If Alima did it, there was a slim chance she would proclaim Sadira a virgin in order to protect her from Akbar's wrath. But if it were anyone else—the haughty, querulous Jaleel, for instance—Travis could easily predict the outcome: he and Sadira would be dead within the hour.

Eighteen

"All right, *Habiba*. Go thou and do it quickly," Akbar finally said. "Then return and tell us what thou hast found. *Frangi,* take thine ease. Hamid, thou also should sit while we wait."

As Sadira and Alima departed the chamber the same way they had entered, Hamid took a position near the doorway leading out of the tent. "Thine invitation is most kind, my lord, but I prefer to stand. I shall guard the doorway, for I do not trust this *frangi.*"

"Do as thou wilt," Akbar responded. *"Frangi,* regardless of what Alima discovers, thou shalt not directly approach the *Shammar* or offer any excuses for Gamalat's death. I give thee leave to watch from a distance, but not to speak. I shall do all the speaking, for this matter does not—in the end—concern thee."

"I disagree," Travis protested. "Hajem Pasha must understand *why* we ambushed Gamalat and his friends, and I killed Gamalat. If Hajem Pasha doesn't understand, he will not be inclined to show mercy toward Sadira."

"The life of thy servant can in no way compare in importance to the life of his son—nor will he consider any animals or goods as fair exchange. Sadira is another matter; he knows how much we value her and the good fortune she has brought our people. This matter has gone far be-

yond where it started, *Frangi*. Today, we shall either forge
a lasting peace between our tribes or commit ourselves to
endless war. I intend to encourage Hajem Pasha to take
Sadira to wife, assuming, of course, that she is still a virgin.
What we shall do if she is not, I do not know—but if she
is not, thou wilt not be here to witness it. Thy bones will
lie bleaching in the desert sun—no, not thy bones, thy skull
only, for I shall bury thee in the sand to thy neck and let
thee die a long, lonely, and miserable death."

"I shall dig the hole," Hamid offered. "With my own
two hands. And I shall gouge out his eyes before we leave
him to die."

Travis willed his face to show no emotion. "If you give
Sadira to the *Shammar,* you will be doing exactly that to
her. Her life will be long, lonely, and miserable; among her
enemies, she can never be happy."

"Ah, *Frangi*." Akbar sighed. "Thou hast learnt our language and how to ride a camel. Except for thine eyes,
thou hast the look of a Bedouin and thou dresses like
one. Thou canst sit a horse as well as any of us. Thou
hast developed a taste for desert food and goat milk, but
thou art *not* as we are. Thou dost not think like us, even
after all this time. . . . How are women treated in thy
country? Were they not created to serve the needs of men,
even as horses, camels, goats, and sheep are meant to
serve them?"

"No," Travis said. "They are not our servants and
slaves. We may not always treat them fairly, but they are
not regarded as animals either. I know of many men who
cherish and love their wives as well as they love themselves, and I would hope to do the same with *my* wife
when I marry."

Akbar flashed a white-toothed grin. "If all men's wives

turned out to be like my Alima, 'twould not be difficult to cherish them and treat them as equals, but if they are like Jaleel . . ."

"We do not take more than one wife at a time. We take only one and vow to be faithful to her until death do us part." Travis thought of marrying Sadira, and a chill ran through him. He wondered if he would ever get the chance. The way things were going, it did not seem likely.

"Strange customs, eh, Hamid?" Akbar winked at the younger man, but Hamid was taking his duties as guard too seriously to be distracted. He stared silently into space, and after a moment, Akbar reclined against his cushions and fell silent also.

Travis wished that Sadira and Alima would hurry. The wait was growing unbearable. Until he knew what Alima would say, he found it difficult to even think about escape. Escape would be next to impossible no matter what she said. From now on, both he and Sadira would be closely watched. Without Sadira's cooperation—and Alima's—his choices were severely limited. Unfortunately, he had not yet had time to gain Alima's consent to help. Time had run out on him. Alima's report could possibly spare his life, but this was undoubtedly the end for him and Sadira.

Travis sat brooding and thinking, but no easy way out of the dilemma occurred to him. If Alima verified Hamid's suspicions, he would have to overpower Hamid, seize his weapons, and turn them on Akbar. He might have to take Akbar hostage in order to gain safe passage back across the desert. It did not seem possible *he* could make it in one piece—let alone get Sadira there unharmed. The entire situation was hopeless.

Alima padded silently into the chamber. "Akbar," she

said softly, going to her husband's side. "Have no fear thy daughter hast betrayed thee. I have examined her, and I can assure thee that no man has touched her."

"Allah be praised!" Akbar lifted his hands in an attitude of elation and gratitude that echoed Travis's feelings. "Oh, Lord, I thank thee," Akbar continued. "Not that I doubted my daughter, but I am relieved to know she has remained true to her people."

"Her love and loyalty has never wavered, *Habib*."

Alima's all-knowing eyes met Travis's. He had no secrets from her now; she was aware of everything but had lied to protect Sadira. He had not been wrong about her. The old woman loved Sadira like a daughter. Was there still a chance she might help them escape? he wondered.

"Sadira and I must return to her tent now," Alima said. "Time is growing short. We must prepare her to meet the *Shammar*. She will wear the finest of *Ruala* robes and a *burqa* to conceal her face, so that none but Hajem Pasha shall be permitted to gaze upon her beauty."

"No!" Akbar sat up straighter and made a cutting motion with one hand. "No *burqa*, veils, or headcloth. All the *Shammar* shall bear witness to her beauty and note the mark of the star she bears. I want them to see for themselves that I am giving them a pearl of great price, the most beautiful woman we possess, our own ceremonial virgin and Keeper of the Mares. If they are still not satisfied, I shall invite the wives of Hajem Pasha to examine her, as thou hast done—so that the *Shammar* may be further assured that we bring our best—a virgin as pure as the driving rain that brings life back to the desert. . . . Yes, Sadira shall make the desert bloom with peace and harmony. She shall go forth dressed all in white, her hair flowing like a waterfall down her back. She will ride Sherifa, so that all may admire her horsemanship, another of her special gifts. . . . Ah, *Habiba!* There will be peace at last on the desert. From this day forward, the *Anazah* and the *Shammar* will be as brothers, united by marriage and sworn to respect one another's lands and herds. Never again will we bear weapons against one another."

Travis read the shock on Alima's face and knew his own features must reveal his feelings, but neither Akbar, Hamid, nor Alima were looking at him; they had turned to watch Sadira enter the chamber. "No *burqa,* Father?" she questioned, her face almost as pale as Alima's. "Will that not be a breach of custom—a shameful thing for thy daughter to go forth bareheaded to meet strangers?"

It was not the thought of going without a *burqa* that disturbed her, Travis knew, but the thought that her father might invite Hajem Pasha's wives to examine her. If this occurred, it would be Sadira's last and final humiliation before her enemies killed her.

"Nay, Sadira! 'Twill be no shame," Akbar chortled, clapping his hands together. "Rather, 'twill be the perfect message to send to Hajem Pasha: This is my beloved daughter, and thou art my friend, or else I would never send her to thee unveiled. . . . Dost thou not see, Sadira? He cannot refuse thee; I am according him the highest honor, the greatest trust, if I send thee to him bareheaded."

"But Akbar!" Alima protested. "What if thou art wrong? What if he takes it as insult? Perhaps he will think thou hast sent him a woman already shamed and unworthy. 'Tis too great a risk. And to invite his wives to touch her, to probe and defile her, why that is . . ."

"Perfect!" Akbar crowed. " 'Tis perfect! If his wives accept my invitation to examine her, they will find her worthy. Trust me, Alima. 'Tis the best approach. I will hear no criticism or arguments against it. Come now and rest. . . ." He beckoned to Alima and patted the cushions beside him. "Jaleel and the others can help Sadira now. I will send for her robes. She can prepare herself here, so I may be certain nothing will happen to her in the little time remaining. *Frangi,* go with Hamid. As I said, thou canst watch from a distance, but not interfere. Hamid, do thou make certain our guest does not embarrass us."

Hamid fingered his scimitar. "He will not embarrass thee, Akbar. I can promise thee that."

Travis had no choice but to precede Hamid out of the tent. He glanced over his shoulder at Sadira, but she did not look at him. Her face was as distant and unreadable as a statue's. Only Alima showed signs of acute distress. Her skin had gone gray, and a pinched look hovered about her mouth and nose. Travis guessed that this was probably the first time she had ever lied to Akbar, and the lie did not sit well on her conscience. To make matters worse, Akbar might very well discover her treachery. If the *Shammar* were not indignant that Sadira came to them bareheaded, they would certainly be outraged to discover that she was no longer a virgin—and if Hajem Pasha's wives examined her. . . .

God in heaven! Travis shuddered to think of the consequences. His only consolation about his own part in causing this tragedy was that Sadira had told him she had hurt herself as a child "down there," and that was why she had felt no pain when he broke her maidenhead. It had already been broken. . . . But who would believe it? Not the *Shammar,* Hajem Pasha, or his wives, and not Akbar and the *Ruala* either.

* * *

Sadira stood stone still as Jaleel lined her eyes with kohl. "There. That is much better," the older woman muttered. " 'Tis too bad I can do nothing to hide the color of thine eyes or to cover that ugly streak of yellow in thy hair. Akbar is mistaken if he thinks the *Shammar* wilt find thee beautiful. I see nothing in thy face or form to inspire the admiration of any man."

Except for Jahara, Sadira was alone in the women's quarters with Jaleel. It was the perfect opportunity to tell the vile-tempered female what she thought of her, but Sadira could summon no enthusiasm for the task, not with disaster hanging over her head. For a few brief moments, she had thought she might be spared—but then Akbar had removed her only chance of escape by forbidding her to wear the *burqa*. He had further sealed her fate by suggesting that she be examined by Hajem Pasha's wives.

How could her father do this to her and still claim he loved her? He treated her as if she were less than human and had no feelings, as if all that mattered now was to impress the *Shammar* with her worth as a sacrificial offering. She was a symbol, nothing more. As long as she did what she was told, she had value, but beyond that, she might as well be an animal, not a person. He did not trust her, love her, or seek to protect her; he only wanted to use her. He had been using her all these years, and she had cheerfully, willingly permitted it—even reveled in it. . . . Now, when it was too late, she could see it all so clearly. She had given up everything to gain love and acceptance, and all she had really won was the near certainty of dying young, scorned, humiliated, and reviled . . . just like her mother.

Cease thinking about it, she ordered herself. It will go easier if thou dost not think so much. Concentrate instead on Jaleel. She, at least, has never lied to thee or misled thee. There is no false pretense about her; she has always hated thee and always will.

Sadira studied her old enemy as Jaleel fussed over her hair. This close to the legendary beauty, Sadira could see that Jaleel's comeliness had long since faded. Her skin was lined and pitted. Sadira had heard that she bathed it regularly in goat's milk, but the remedy must not be working. There were pouches beneath her eyes, and her chin was sagging. Streaks of gray marred Jaleel's black tresses. Her hair was no longer healthy and shiny, as it had been in her youth. In a dim light, some might still find her attractive, but not many. Her worst fault was still the sour expression she always wore, as if she had been eating bitter fruit. Frown lines had etched deep grooves in her forehead and on both sides of her mouth.

"Jahara, fetch me a vial of sandalwood perfume," Jaleel ordered the pretty young woman whom Akbar had taken pity on and married when she was but a child and both her parents had died, leaving her an orphan. "Hurry up, girl, or I will beat thee for thy laziness! I may beat thee anyway; Allah knows thou art a constant trial to me."

As Jahara scurried away, Sadira stepped back from Jaleel. "Why dost thou treat little Jahara so cruelly, Jaleel? She has done thee no harm, nor will she. Jahara is a lamb, while thou art a scorpion. Dost thou do it to prove the differences between thee?"

"Who art thou to talk, Sadira? A scorpion I may be, but none can say that my blood is tainted. They cannot whisper behind my back that I am a curse and a blight upon the *Ruala*. Think not that anyone shall miss thee when thou depart for the *Shammar;* in truth, we shall all be glad to bid thee good riddance. Now our herds will truly prosper, while those of our enemies will decline beneath thy influence. Akbar is ever the wise ruler—to rid us of thy presence before my Nuri comes to power and is forced to send thee away."

Sadira realized that Jaleel was being spiteful; nevertheless, her words cut deeply, for they touched upon her deepest fears. "Thou art voicing *thy* sentiments, not those of our people, nor even of thy son. When Nuri was with us, he never said a word against me nor treated me with the contempt thou art showing now, Jaleel. Nuri was young and impetuous, but never cruel like thee."

Jaleel curled her upper lip and sneered. "He is my son, Sadira, and I alone know his innermost thoughts and opinions. I assure thee he shares my views. 'Twas because of thee that he left on his pilgrimage to Mecca."

"Because of me! How can that be? I did not encourage him to leave."

"No, but thou knowest that Nuri and Akbar often disagreed. 'Twas because of thee they fought. Nuri did not believe that a female of impure blood should be permitted to make decisions regarding the mares, the wealth of our people. The bloodlines of our horses must *never* be mixed and tainted, and neither should our own bloodlines. Thou— the bastard child of a *frangi*—should not have been appointed Keeper of the Mares, entrusted with so sacred a duty . . . and Nuri is not the only one who feels this way. Thy detractors are many, Sadira, and they are glad thou art leaving the *Ruala*. If the *Shammar* kill thee, 'twill be a just punishment for the wrongs thy mother committed . . . and it will leave us free to choose a new Keeper of the Mares, this time someone more worthy—a maiden who is at least pure *Ruala*. Hast thou never wondered why Akbar gave thee the position for life? It was to prevent thee from breeding inferior creatures and passing on thy defects and weaknesses to another generation. . . . Aye, the people fear to show their happiness before Akbar, but they are secretly overjoyed to be rid of thee."

"I do not believe it! Thou art jealous, wicked, and evil to say these hurtful things, Jaleel!"

"I only say them because they are true. 'Twas not a star that marked thee, Sadira. Alima created and spread that ridiculous tale, and everyone knows she is a foolish old woman who stooped to love thee only because she could bear no children of her own. Akbar himself promoted the rumor because his pride was sorely battered, and he disliked being thought a cuckold. In his heart, he despises thee and wishes thou hadst never been born. He will not grieve to see thee gone."

"Oh, thou art malicious! Until this day, I never knew how much. Akbar loves me," Sadira insisted, though she had been doubting it only a moment previously. "And so do my people. Never have I harmed a single one of them. I have given my whole life in service to the *Ruala,* setting aside my own desires in order to do what is best for them."

"Then thou art a fool, Sadira, and blind on top of it! If they love thee so much, why do they not fight to keep thee? Where are they when thou hast the most need of them? I see no one coming to thine aid, no one cleaning his gun to go out and defend thee. Thou wilt be handed over to our enemies and quickly forgotten. That will be the end of thee, and I rejoice that I need never see thee again. It offends my eyes to have to look upon thee and be civil to thee. Thou hast never deserved the honors that have been showered upon thee, for thou art not but an ugly, half-caste creature who should have been set out on the desert to die at birth."

By the time Jaleel had finished her diatribe, Sadira was shaking—from a combination of hurt, disbelief, and fury. Yet the more she thought about it, the more her heart ached with the realization that Jaleel was right. Her people did not really care, no more than Akbar cared. Many had demonstrated their grief at losing her and their gratitude that by going to the *Shammar* she would spare them suffering, but no one had offered to fight for her or die for her or rescue her. No one, that is, except Travis and Alima. Travis wanted to escape with her. Alima wanted to take her place. They were the only two people on earth who really loved her. Unfortunately, she had said no to Travis, and though she had consented to allow Alima to help her, it was too late now for either of them to rescue her from her fate. Only Allah could save her now, and Allah was far, far away—a masculine deity not known for his kindness toward women. She could not depend upon Allah to save her.

Jaleel remained standing, watching Sadira and smirking. She seemed to be waiting for some response, and after a moment, Sadira thought of one. "I pray that Allah will take pity on thee and forgive thee, Jaleel, for thou art a bitter, pitiful, and loveless woman. Jealousy has ruled thee always—a jealousy so deep that it never mattered that thou wert beautiful or had borne a son, the heir to the sheikdom. . . . Hast thou never been happy, Jaleel? I think not. Yet I—the bastard child with the impure blood—I have known happiness. And I have known love."

"Thou? But thou art a virgin. What could thou possibly know of love?" Jaleel demanded. "Unless thou, too, hast betrayed us, as did thy mother."

Sadira did not even bother to defend herself. She merely smiled as Travis's words came back to her. "There is more to love than physical satisfaction, Jaleel. There is far, far more. How I have discovered this—and with whom—I shall not tell thee, but if I must die, I will do so with a smile on my face. I shall die glad that I have loved and was loved. Thou canst not take that knowledge or joy away from me. What will thou be thinking when death comes to claim thee? Wilt thou be able to smile, I wonder?"

"Thou art a fool twice over!" Jaleel spat. "Thou makest no sense whatever!"

"Alima would understand," Sadira disputed. "She knows whereof I speak. Thou art the fool, Jaleel, for thou hast had many treasures in thy lifetime and tossed them all away . . . beauty, admiration, the purest of bloodlines. . . . Thou has tossed thy treasures on the dung heap formed from thy discontent."

"I have tossed away nothing! I have everything I want. Slaves do my bidding, and my husband and my people honor me as the mother of the next sheik. What more do I need? What more can I possibly desire?"

"Thou needs and wants what all the world is desperate to possess—true and everlasting love. And thou shalt never have it, for thou knowest not how to be lovable, to give love nor to receive it. Thy heart is cut from marble; thou art cold, hard, and beautiful. Or perhaps I should say thou art like granite, not marble, for these days, thou art no longer even beautiful."

"Bah! Thou speakest in silly riddles. Go quickly to the *Shammar,* Sadira; the *Ruala* and the *Anazah* do not want thee!"

"Jaleel! Jaleel!" a young voice cut in. It was Jahara— sweet, young Jahara—who had quietly slipped into the chambers and now stood watching them with wide, troubled eyes. "I have brought the perfume, as thou bade me.

Here 'tis, Jaleel." In both hands, she cradled the vial of precious perfume Jaleel had sent her to get.

"Take it back!" Jaleel snapped. "Never mind, I shall take it back myself. We shall not waste it on a woman who is not one of us and never was."

In this, thou art right, Jaleel, Sadira thought, as Jaleel stalked away from her. *I was never one of thee, and now I never shall be. . . . Oh, why did I not flee with Travis while I had the chance? Now, I have surely lost him, and soon, I will lose Alima. Then, I will have no one. I am a fool twice over—nay, a thousand times over—and the worst of it is, I can think of nothing to do to change my fate. 'Tis far too late.*

Jahara's wounded gaze followed Jaleel, then came back to Sadira. The girl seemed about to say something—to apologize or perhaps to wish her well—but years of training in subservience and docility prevented her.

"Jahara!" Jaleel shrieked from somewhere deeper inside the tent.

Jahara jumped and scurried after the elder woman, leaving Sadira alone with her fear and her gloomy thoughts.

Nineteen

Hamid dogged Travis's footsteps as he returned to his tent. Once there, the surly-faced Bedouin planted himself at the entranceway and glowered at Travis. "Thou might as well accustom thyself to my presence, *Frangi,* for I shall not leave thee until the Keeper of the Mares is safely handed over to the *Shammar.*"

"I didn't expect you would," Travis dryly responded. "But answer me one question, Hamid. Why are you so set on protecting Sadira from me, but only too willing to give her up to her enemies? If you truly cared for her, you would want to save her from the *Shammar,* who are very likely going to kill her."

Hamid regarded him silently for a moment, his black brows beetled together in a frown. "I . . . I am a man with several wives," he finally managed. "I have no personal interest in Sadira."

"You have never wanted to marry her?" Travis challenged. "You act like you have some claim on her. I know jealousy when I see it, and you've been jealous of every moment she's spent in my company."

"I . . . I am not jealous!" Hamid denied. "She is the Keeper of the Mares and far above me. I have no right to be jealous. 'Tis only that . . . we knew each other as children. We played together among the horses and camels.

She was always kind to me, and I . . . I came to regard her as one would a sister."

"A sister? Come now, Hamid, you don't have to lie to me. I'm leaving here soon. You care about her—and *not* as a sister. That's why I don't understand how you can send her off to her death—or at the very least, condemn her to a miserable existence. . . . Oh, come inside my tent if you're going to stand around spying on me. Just what do you expect me to do? Kidnap Sadira right from under your nose? Not that I wouldn't like to, you understand, but . . ."

Hamid's hand flew to the hilt of his scimitar. "I *knew* thou lusted after her! If thou touches even a hair on her head . . ."

"Relax," Travis sighed. "Any man would lust after her. You want her yourself. She's an extraordinary woman, the kind men can't help desiring. . . . The thing is, Hamid, we both know we can never have her. But are we willing to let her die?" Travis stopped talking long enough to hold open the flap of his tent. "Get in here, will you? We shouldn't be talking about this outside where the whole camp can hear us."

Hamid stood looking at him, indecision written all over his swarthy features. Travis could imagine his inner conflict; cultural values and religious beliefs demanded one thing, but personal interests demanded another. Glancing hesitantly in both directions, waiting until several curious children passed by with a half-dozen goats, Hamid condescended to enter Travis's tent.

"Since I must keep watch over thee and guard thee, *Frangi,* I might as well do it inside. Thou might attempt to escape by crawling out under the back of the tent."

"I might, but I wouldn't get far, Hamid. Not without a really fast horse and someone to guide me through the desert. Oh, and supplies, too. I'd need supplies and a camel or two. Some especially swift and hardy specimens."

Hamid squinted at him suspiciously, and Travis motioned for him to take a seat on the cushions. He had to shove aside a pile of his things—which he had been gathering to take with him—before he could sit beside the short, but uncharacteristically stocky and powerfully built Bedouin. "Now then, Hamid, you and I had better talk."

"What could thee and I possibly have to talk about, *Frangi?*"

Travis took a deep breath and slowly exhaled. It was now or never. "Saving Sadira's life?" he tossed out, watching Hamid closely.

Hamid straightened, frowning intently. "The fate of our beloved Keeper of the Mares is in the hands of Allah," he piously intoned.

"And in the hands of the *Shammar,*" Travis added. "The *Shammar* most of all."

This wasn't going to be easy, he realized. Still, it was a slender chance where before there had been none. "How about some coffee? I've never made it myself, but I'm sure we could find Samir or another servant and have him prepare it for us. I could use a cup of coffee about now, couldn't you?"

Since the sharing of coffee was an act of friendship, Travis's invitation required a softening of Hamid's hostile attitude, but Hamid's glance remained wary and stubborn. "I do not share coffee with infidels."

"Why not? Akbar does, and he's your sheik."

" 'Tis his duty to entertain all those who come to buy horses or cross our lands. 'Tis not *my* duty. I may choose my friends and companions, and I would never choose thee for either, *Frangi.*"

This was going to be damn hard, Travis decided, and noon was fast approaching. Still, he would be patient and try. This was his last chance; he had no other choice. "We're not so different, Hamid. When I prick my finger and bleed, my blood is red just like yours."

"Thou dost not worship Allah."

"That's not altogether true; I simply call him by another name."

"Hah! I do not believe thee."

For the better portion of an hour, Travis sparred with Hamid, pitting his accented and sometimes incorrect Arabic against the other man's prejudices. With typical flowery diplomacy, Hamid tiptoed all around the issue of whether or not he might be willing to help Sadira escape. Travis could not risk suggesting an actual plan, but he did manage to convey his intentions without clearly stating them. Hamid did the same, never admitting he would help, but strongly implying it. The entire conversation became an elaborate game, the kind the desert people relished. Travis might have enjoyed it, except that he knew if he made a mistake, Hamid was entirely capable of whipping out his pistol or scimitar and abruptly ending it.

Bedouin men—of whom Hamid and Akbar were good examples—were a dangerous, volatile mixture of exaggerated politeness and good manners combined with explosive, barely controlled violence. One moment, they seemed the friendliest and most reasonable of men, but in the next, they were as fierce and bloodthirsty as tigers.

The sudden loud blast of a ram's horn brought Hamid to his feet before anything had been resolved. Travis had heard such blasts before; when the *Ruala* were traveling, it meant the tribe would soon move out.

"Is that the signal for everyone to gather?" he asked.

WINDSONG   301

Hamid nodded. "Akbar is summoning us for the march to the *Shammar.*"

A second and third blast sounded, then a short series of mournful toots. Travis could make no sense of them, but to Hamid, they conveyed a great deal of information, or else he had received it earlier from Akbar.

" 'Tis time to assemble our weapons and dress in our finest robes," he explained. "We will go to the *Shammar* as if we are a wedding party accompanying the bride. Therefore, we must don our best attire and ride our best horses. However, beneath our robes we will carry our pistols and carbines in case there is treachery, and the *Shammar* attack."

"In case? I would think we ought to expect it. Do they know we're coming?"

Hamid grunted impatiently. "Art thou aware of so little, *Frangi?* Of course, they know. Our messengers arranged for this meeting some time ago. Not only are we expected, but Hajem Pasha has agreed to listen to all we have to say. 'Tis time now to leave." Hamid pointed to Travis's rifle propped in a corner of the tent. "Take that with thee but hide it. As I told thee, the *Shammar* must not see it, or *they* will suspect treachery. . . . But wait, *Frangi!* One more thing I wish to tell thee."

Travis paused in the act of grabbing the rifle. "Yes?" He lifted the gun and waited, debating whether or not he should turn it on Hamid here and now. But what would be the purpose if he could not get to Sadira?

Hamid seemed to be having difficulty swallowing. *"Frangi,* I am . . . I am sympathetic to thy cause, but thou must restrain thyself and do nothing that might start a war. A war will destroy all of us, not only Sadira. And she herself does not desire a war."

"I've no wish to endanger anyone, Hamid. I only wish to save a woman who does not deserve to die or suffer."

"I agree with thee. She does not deserve it. But . . . neither do others deserve to die and suffer. Akbar does this only because there is no other way. I dislike it as much as thee, but this is *our* concern, not thine, and thou shouldst not interfere. Were circumstances otherwise, I, too, should be eager to rescue Sadira, my childhood friend and the woman I might have taken to wife had she not been the ceremonial virgin and the Keeper of the Mares."

Having said this much, Hamid retreated once more into frustrating ambiguity. "Still, Allah watches over us all and sometimes directs men to feel—and act—in certain ways. Trust in the Almighty One to protect Sadira."

Travis lost his temper. "Hamid, we're wasting time! We could have used *this* time to form some kind of plan. Now, we're leaving and we still don't have one, and I don't know if you're with me or not. Are you or aren't you?"

Hamid lifted his hands in a helpless gesture. "Merciful Allah! How can I trust a *frangi?* I will be betraying my people if I agree to assist thee. Yet, I assure thee I do care for Sadira."

"Oh, forget it!" Travis snapped. He waved his gun at the indecisive Bedouin. "Tell me how to hide this so I can get to it quickly, but the *Shammar* can't see it."

"Here, I will help thee with this at least," Hamid said, surprising Travis with his first and only straight answer. "With this I have no inner conflicts."

"Wonderful. Let's get to it."

By the time Sadira departed her father's tent, walked calmly to Sherifa, and mounted for the short journey to

the *Shammar* encampment, all of the *Ruala* were waiting
to say goodbye. Mothers held up their children for a last
look at her, old women waved and dabbed at tear-filled
eyes, young boys raised their hands in salute. The men of
the tribe were already astride their war mares, and Akbar
sat straight and tall on Tahani who was prancing and snorting with excitement.

The ram's horn sounded again, and Akbar leaned down
and took Sherifa's reins to lead her away. Sadira twisted
around to steal one last look at Alima. The old woman
lifted her hand in a trembling gesture of farewell. Sorrow
clouded her eyes, but she appeared composed, having resigned herself to the inevitable.

"Allah go with thee, child. Never forget that I love thee."

"I could not forget, Alima. Thou wilt live forever in my
heart, for as long as I live and beyond. Never fear; we shall
meet in paradise."

"Allah grant thee long life and happiness." Alima's voice
broke, and she raised the hem of her veil to dab at her
eyes and turned away.

"Come, Daughter." Akbar tugged on Sherifa's reins. "No
more farewells. 'Tis time to ride."

"I am ready," Sadira answered, though her readiness consisted only of her outward appearance. Her robe was blinding white in the sunlight, her hair flowed down her back
as Akbar had ordered, and her face was uncovered. Sherifa
was groomed to shining perfection and fitted with silver-
encrusted trappings. Sadira knew she made an impressive
picture mounted upon her flame-colored mare—but a great
vise had closed around her heart, and she found it difficult
to breathe. Her pain was acute.

She would never see her people again; they were sending
her away. Alima, Akbar, Hamid, Jaleel, and little Jahara . . .

all would soon be naught but a memory. Worst of all, she was leaving Travis. . . . She twisted around in the saddle to search the surrounding crowd. Where *was* Travis? And Hamid, who had been set to guard him? Sadira scanned the onlookers for the two men, as Akbar led her through the throngs of people gathered to witness her departure. She finally spotted Najila next to Hamid's little bay war mare. Hamid and Travis himself resembled every other Bedouin riding out to escort her, except that Travis's height and distinctive carriage gave him away, making him easy to pick out for anyone who looked closely. The two men had wound the ends of their headcloths around the lower part of their faces and blended in so well with the rest of the men that she had scarcely recognized them. The fact that they rode on the fringes of the band convinced her that Travis had given up all hope of trying to rescue her . . . but then why should he not abandon the idea? She had refused to flee with him when she could have, and now escape was impossible.

She and Akbar rode all the way to the *Shammar* encampment in silence. The ground was flat and level, the sky an intense fiery blue, the afternoon hot. In the distance lay a range of low hills and a scattering of trees; it would make a good place to camp, and she suspected that the main body of the *Shammar* tribe could be found there. Several distinct clouds of dust indicated the placement of the *Shammar* herds. Another cloud of dust was moving toward them as the men of the *Shammar* rode out to meet the men of the *Anazah*. She was the only woman among the mounted figures gathering on the plain.

The closer the enemy came, the more Sadira's heart began to pound with dread. Akbar signaled for a gallop, and as one, her tribesmen surged forward, their pennants robes, and *keffiyas* flapping in the wind. It was so like her father to insist upon arriving in a show of splendor, his magnificent horses proving their superiority to all who watched.

Sherifa's ground-eating strides carried Sadira too quickly toward her enemies. In no time at all, the two huge groups of men met in a swirl of dust and neighing horses as everyone reined in and halted their overeager mounts. A silence fell as the dust settled. Two distinct lines formed and faced each other—*Ruala* and *Shammar* alike warily watching and judging one another.

The first thing Sadira noticed about the *Shammar* was that they were all armed to the teeth. They bristled with weapons. Most carried firearms, and belts of ammunition crisscrossed their chests. Others had brought swords, scimitars, and Bedouin lances. Though the sun was beating down mercilessly on the dry and arid plain, Sadira could not help shivering.

The second thing she noticed was that the *Shammar* very much resembled her own people. They were dark-eyed, often hawk-featured, with serious, weathered-brown faces. They wore the same robes, headcloths, and turbans, some striped and colorful, some plain. The men were all ages, some bearded, some old, others young and proud, most in-between.

Their horses were plainly or richly decorated, according to the whim and wealth of their masters. The same pride and ferocity emanated from the *Shammar* as did from the *Anazah,* surprising Sadira, who had grown up believing that the *Shammar* were all a cowardly, shifty-eyed lot. These men did not look cowardly—quite the contrary. They looked ready to fight, even eager for it. Sadira sensed the vulnerability of her own people. At the same time, she admired Akbar's courage at riding unarmed into the midst of his tribal enemies.

One of the figures facing them on horseback detached himself from his fellows and rode forward to greet them. Sadira had never seen Hajem Pasha up close, only from a distance, but she knew it was he. He rode a magnificent mare, every bit the equal of Tahani, perhaps even of Sherifa. Silver-bearded like Akbar, he held himself as arrogantly as her father, and no one watching the two men could doubt that they were young enough and strong enough to meet this challenge.

"Come, Sadira." Akbar's voice was that of a much younger man. It was the voice she remembered from her youth—a voice of power and challenge, daring anyone to disobey.

She had not the strength to resist. Her future had passed out of her hands now. It rested on the man riding toward her, and he did not appear the least bit inclined toward mercy or gentleness. Sadira guided her mare with her knees, having no need of the reins that Akbar still held. She urged Sherifa to go forward willingly, rather than waiting for the tug on her halter. Akbar came to a halt a camel's length away from the *Shammar* leader and greeted him.

"As salám al aikum!" The ancient admonition to peace and friendship echoed across the plain but sounded more like an invitation to battle than to peace.

"Alaikum as salám!" came back again, another obvious challenge.

The two leaders sat and glowered at each other for a moment, then Hajem Pasha lifted his hand, and several servants scurried out from between the mounted figures behind him and began preparations for the ritual of welcome,

the sharing of coffee. No one spoke, nor would they until
the coffee had been poured and drunk at least three times.
Sadira sat motionless astride Sherifa and looked straight
ahead. She willed her face to show no emotion, especially
no fear, and she prayed that no one could hear the wild
thundering of her heart inside her rib cage.

Hundreds of eyes ruthlessly examined her, and a few
grunts of approval—or scorn—reached her ears. The
Shammar men were studying her, amazed that she appeared before them unveiled. Perhaps Akbar had been
right after all; she hoped so. Without saying a single
word, he had said much. The fact that she was mounted
on a splendid animal did not escape the notice of the
Shammar either. Hajem Pasha's eyes caressed Sherifa and
lit with greedy possessiveness. When he gazed directly at
her, however, he displayed no such eager enthusiasm. His
eyes were cold and unforgiving. His harem undoubtedly
held a number of beautiful women; one more would not
impress him—and her odd coloring might already have
put him off.

In a short time, the coffee was ready. Like the *Ruala,*
the *Shammar* knew the trick of keeping an ember alive in
a small, fireproof container, and using it to quickly start a
fire to heat the brass pot. The rich scent of the brew wafted
beneath Sadira's nose, but no one offered her any, nor did
she expect them to do so. This was a masculine ritual.
Akbar waited to dismount until Hajem Pasha had done so,
and he waited for the *Shammar* sheik to lift the tiny brass
cup to his mouth before drinking. Then he drank the coffee
in a single gulp and held out his cup for more.

The servants, two wiry men who scuttled about like bee-
tles, ran back and forth between Akbar and Hajem Pasha
until the ritual three cups had been consumed. They then

spread a beautiful large rug upon the ground and heaped crimson and gold cushions on either side of it. Stepping back, they looked to Hajem Pasha for approval, but the *Shammar* sheik never once glanced at them. With a flick of his hand, he sent them scurrying back to the line of mounted horsemen.

Each movement thereafter was studied and elaborate, as if Hajem Pasha had carefully planned each gesture. He motioned for Akbar to join him in reclining on the rug and cushions. Surprisingly, Akbar shook his head and refused.

"There will be time later for visitation and polite discourse," said the *Anazah* leader. "Let us not pretend we do not know why we are here. We have traveled far and endured much, and I grow impatient to learn what recompense thou wilt demand for the life of thy son, whom we killed by mistake. Thou hast heard the story from our messengers, so I shall not repeat it. Merely tell us the penalty for our grave error, and if we can, we shall gladly pay it."

Hajem Pasha's brows lifted in surprise. Sadira herself was shocked. She had expected a long time to pass before either man mentioned the reason for this unusual and historic meeting. The joy of any Bedouin was to spend hours probing another man's mind before opening his own. Sometimes, passages from the *Koran* were recited—or bits of poetry. But Akbar had cut straight to the heart of the matter; he wanted to know whether to expect war or peace. And he wanted to know now.

"This is my beloved daughter, Sadira," Akbar continued, pointing to her. "She is our ceremonial virgin, our Keeper of the Mares. She is the source of our prosperity, the maiden who brings us success in battle. Thou wilt note that she is very beautiful and resembles no other woman in either of our tribes. There is no one like her, for she is marked by the star that shone brightly on the night she was born."

"I have heard of her," Hajem Pasha admitted. " 'Tis said she can make a barren mare fertile. 'Tis also claimed that she causes thine enemies to fall down in fear from their horses. Yet all of my men remain mounted. Are these rumors untrue then, and her powers exaggerated?"

"Weak and superstitious minds will always invent tales and believe the impossible." Akbar shrugged dismissively. "Thou art a man of the world, Hajem Pasha. I did not expect thee to believe such nonsense. However, she has given us good fortune, and there is no one on earth dearer to my heart than she is. Thou knowest why I have brought her—as a peace offering to express my sorrow over the death of thy son, which was a tragedy we sincerely regret. Had we known who he was, we never would have slain him. We would have come to thee instead and requested that justice be done."

At the mention of his son's demise, Hajem Pasha's face hardened. "Nothing can compensate me for the loss of Gamalat, my Beautiful One. He was my only son and heir. Where is thy Nuri? Why didst thou not bring him as a peace offering? He would be a more fitting exchange for my son than a mere daughter."

"Come now, friend. What wouldst thou do with Nuri? Thou canst not breed more sons on him. He possesses no special powers, and anyway, he has gone on pilgrimage. I had expected him to return by now, but he has not. He may well be dead. Therefore, I understand thy distress over losing Gamalat. What more can I offer thee than my dearest daughter? Take her to wife, Hajem Pasha. She is young

and strong and will give thee another son. Nay, she will
give thee many sons. . . . Or else let her serve thee as she
has served us. Make her thy Keeper of the Mares and ceremonial virgin. Either way, she will bring thee good fortune,
and we may live in peace, thy tribe and mine. . . . Doubt
not that she is all I say she is. She is pure and holy; no
man has touched her. If thou wilt not take my word on it,
have thy wives examine her first. I invite them to examine
her. Put up a tent, and I will permit *thee* to examine her,
to discover with thine own fingers whether or not I speak
the truth."

Sadira swayed in the saddle. . . . What would her father not do to protect his people from the wrath of the
Shammar? She understood his motives, but could not help
hating him for submitting her to this outrage and humiliation. He would be amply punished for his cruelty should
Hajem Pasha decide to accept his offer and discover the
truth. . . . *Oh, Akbar! Thou goest too far!* she cried out
silently.

Hajem Pasha walked slowly toward her. When he had
reached Sherifa's side, he reached up and fingered a strand
of her hair. His eyes were like those of a serpent before it
strikes. His fingertips grazed her cheek, and his flesh was
cold as ice. She gazed down into his face, noted the downward slant of his mouth, and knew before he spoke what
his answer would be.

His hand fell away, and he turned back to confront her
father. " 'Tis a shame to waste such beauty, Akbar, but I
have always embraced the wisdom of 'an eye for an eye,
a tooth for a tooth.' I am too old to change my philosophy
now; therefore, I demand the life of thy precious daughter,
even as thou took the life of my son. Give me her blood,
and there shall be peace between our people from this day

forward. Refuse, and there shall be no peace anywhere. The *Shammar* will hunt the *Anazah* to the very ends of the earth and slay them wherever we find them."

Twenty

From where Travis and Hamid sat on their horses, near the fringe of the band of riders, Travis could not hear what was being said. But he knew that something momentous had just occurred. Akbar's face was ashen; a circle of white rimmed his mouth. He did not say a word, but only nodded, and Hajem Pasha then picked up Sherifa's reins, which had been lying on the ground where Akbar had dropped them. Walking to his own horse, the *Shammar* sheik mounted, and leading Sherifa, turned and began trotting back toward his men.

"Damn it, what's happening?" Travis leaned over and prodded Hamid's thigh. "Have they accepted her?"

"I do not know, *Frangi*. I cannot hear. Let us watch and see." Grim-faced, Hamid urged his horse closer to the one next to it.

Too worried and impatient to wait, Travis trotted Najila around to the back of the line, all the while keeping an eye on Sadira. Her spine was stiff and straight as a war lance. He could not see her face, but as he drew closer he hoped he could hear something.

Hajem Pasha led Sherifa almost all the way back to his men. Four of them rode out to meet him, and when they reached Sadira, one leaned over and calmly and efficiently shoved her off the mare. Sadira did not attempt to catch herself. She simply toppled to the ground and lay there, stunned or unconscious. The mare screamed, reared, and pawed the air over her mistress.

The man who had knocked Sadira down tried to grab the horse's halter, but Sherifa eluded him and pranced around Sadira, whinnying and snorting, letting no one come near her or her mistress. In the midst of the commotion, several more men rode out from the *Shammar* line. Hajem Pasha resolutely waited off to one side until the newcomers had subdued the mare and led her off, leaving Sadira where she had fallen, a crumpled white heap upon the stony ground.

Gritting his teeth in fury, Travis resisted the impulse to rush to Sadira's aid. He forced himself to remain rational and furtively pulled up his robes to retrieve both his rifle and pistol from where he had hidden them by tying them at his waist with strips of cloth as Hamid had shown him. In his haste and anxiety, he fumbled and dropped the rifle. It clattered to the ground near Najila's feet, but he managed to hang on to the pistol. Jamming it out of sight inside his sleeve, he edged Najila closer, reined back, and again attempted to discover precisely what Hajem Pasha had decided. The sheik's actions thus far did not bode well for Sadira's future, but there was still a chance he might be testing the intentions of the *Anazah* by treating Sadira roughly in front of them.

"What do they mean to do with her?" he asked the men nearest him. "Did any of you hear what was said?"

This time, he got an answer. "Go back to thy place, *Frangi*. Do not interfere. They mean to execute her here and now. As part of the punishment, we will be forced to watch and do nothing."

The man who spoke appeared angry, and so did his companions, but not one of them moved. They sat still as statues on their horses, their eyes fastened on the scene before them. In disbelieving horror, Travis watched as the *Shammar* hauled Sadira to her knees, so that she was now kneeling before Akbar. A man stood behind her, holding her hands behind her back, while another seized her long hair and held it aside, baring her neck. Sadira did nothing to resist them; she seemed totally oblivious to what was happening.

Hajem Pasha then withdrew a long, curved scimitar from a scabbard at his waist. The lethal blade flashed in the sunlight. "You're going to sit here and let them do it?" Travis demanded, abruptly finding his voice. "You're too damn cowardly to defend your own Keeper of the Mares?"

Several of the men shifted uneasily in their saddles, but others just shrugged and leveled hostile glances at him. " 'Tis the will of Allah that she be sacrificed," someone said, and the others grunted in assent.

"Better she dies than we do," another man defended. "A life for a life. 'Tis more than fair."

"Not when she's innocent, you sniveling cowards!" Travis pulled out his pistol and dug his heels into Najila's sides. The mare leapt into a gallop just as Hajem Pasha raised the scimitar over Sadira's head.

Travis had no time to think; he acted purely on instinct. As the mare extended herself, he stood in the stirrups, raised the pistol, and sighted carefully between the mare's ears, aiming for Hajem Pasha's hand—the one holding the scimitar. At the same moment the blade fell, Travis fired. True to her training, Najila did not swerve or flinch, but Travis's ears rang, and his nose stung from the acrid smoke the pistol emitted. Through the smoke, he saw Hajem Pasha drop the scimitar. His white robes were splattered with blood. Sadira still knelt before him in an attitude of dazed submission.

A great roar of outrage rose from the *Shammar*. A series of *pop-pop-pops!* signaled the firing of rifles. Whether they were *Shammar* or *Anazah* rifles, Travis could not tell. A second roar sounded behind him as Akbar and the *Ruala* surged to life. The world exploded into gunfire, smoke, and shouting. Horses neighed, and hoofbeats drummed against the sand. Screaming at the tops of their lungs, the two lines of Bedouin charged each other across the plain.

Crouching low on Najila's neck, Travis concentrated on reaching Sadira. In the confusion, she rose to her feet, her hair flying wildly about her face and shoulders. No longer was she a lifeless doll, seemingly unaware of her surroundings. She was shouting something. As Travis bore down upon her, he could hear her impassioned plea, "No! No! No! Do not fight. Stop this at once! I will gladly give my life to avoid this. . . . Oh, do not fight one another! Please do not fight!"

Travis leaned over Najila's shoulder and reached for her. When he caught her, the force of impact made him lose his balance so that he fell, carrying Sadira down to the ground with him. Hitting the sandy earth, they rolled together; he had just enough presence of mind to make certain he wound up on top. All around them, men were fighting, horses rearing. Hajem Pasha had picked up his scimitar with his remaining good hand and was slashing at the men on horseback riding down upon him.

Travis scrambled to his feet and grabbed the reins of the first free horse he saw—the magnificent mare belonging to the *Shammar* sheik. The animal was white with a silvery mane and tail. Her eyes rolled with fright, and her flared nostrils showed red, but as brave as Najila, she stood her ground amidst the confusion and refused to abandon her master.

Keeping hold of the mare with one hand, Travis helped Sadira to her feet. "Here, get on!" he cried, handing her the animal's reins.

"I cannot!" Sadira responded, her eyes determined. "I must stay and try to stop this madness."

"The hell you will!" Travis roared. "Get on the damn horse!"

"No! I will not abandon my people!"

Exasperated, Travis picked her up, tossed her bodily into the saddle, then swung up behind her. At first, Sadira fought him, trying to signal the mare to go in one direction while he directed it to go in another. Then Travis clamped his arm around Sadira's waist and shouted in her ear. "You can't stop them now! They're going to fight no matter what. They abandoned *you,* Sadira! Do you hear me? They were all going to sit there and watch Hajem Pasha cut off your head."

"No, no, no . . ." Sadira sobbed, collapsing against him, her resistance suddenly draining away like water running through a sieve.

Travis urged the mare to a gallop, and she took off— dodging horses and men with the speed and agility of a jackrabbit. Now that Sadira no longer fought him, Travis could turn his attention to where they were going. He had no sense of direction; the important thing now was to escape the scene of battle and flee both the *Shammar* and the *Ruala*. To his intense relief, neither side paid him the slightest heed. Either they did not see him or did not realize that he carried Sadira.

The men from both sides had but a single thought: to destroy one another. In their bloodlust, they forgot about

the Keeper of the Mares. Travis doubted they even knew
why they were fighting. Like two lions suddenly unchained,
they lunged for one another's throats, eager to fight to the
death. All Travis had to do to escape with Sadira was ride
around them.

Pinioned in Travis's arms, Sadira wept against his shoulder. She wept because she had come so close to death, and
because she had not died, after all, and exactly what she
had feared had come to pass. The *Shammar* and the *Anazah*
were killing one another. She had been spared, but too
many others would die this day and in the days and weeks
to come. She wanted to clench her fists and pound on
Travis for saving her; at the same time, she wanted to hug
him and never let go. Relief warred with anger. Tenderness
vied with indignation. She loved him, and she hated him,
which was very much the way she felt about her own people—except her own people had abandoned her at the end,
and Travis had not. He had risked his life to rescue her,
coming to her aid when no one else would.

They rode far out onto the plain, until they could no
longer see or hear the *Shammar* and the *Anazah* fighting.
Only then did Travis slow the mare to a walk. The poor
animal was heaving and blowing. Her head drooped. She
had given her best, and Sadira felt sorry for her.

"Let her go where she will," she said to Travis, the first
words either of them had spoken. When he raised his brows
in question, she explained. "If we give her the choice, she
will lead us to water."

"What if she leads us back to Hajem Pasha instead?"
Travis grunted.

"She will not. No one has called her, and we are out of

hearing distance now. Perhaps Hajem Pasha is dead. Perhaps they are all dead—my father, Hamid, and all the rest of the *Ruala*."

"If Hajem Pasha is dead, I didn't kill him. I only shot him in the hand. It was messy but not fatal."

Sadira turned sideways on the saddle and laid her palm across his mouth to silence him. "Hush, *Frangi*, hush. Let us not speak of it just yet. I thank you for what you did, but . . . but I am not happy about it. I think I shall never know happiness again. When the men of the *Ruala* and the *Shammar* have finished turning their anger on one another, those who are left will carry the battle to the two encampments. They will rape and pillage and plunder; no one will be safe. Women and children will die before this day is finished."

"Don't blame that on me!" Travis's arm tightened around her waist. "And don't blame it on yourself. As I believe I've told you before, we're not responsible for the misdeeds of others. We're only responsible for our own sins, whatever they may be."

"But my death would have satisfied Hajem Pasha! It would have put a stop to . . ."

She got no further. Travis suddenly slid down from the horse, pulled her down after him, took her in his arms, and stopped her arguments with a hot, demanding kiss, a kiss that took as well as gave, that obliterated all thought and feeling except the desire to be close to him. All at once, she wanted desperately to lose herself in passion, to shut out all the world's ugliness in sweet surrender to Travis's kisses.

He broke away, but still held her close. "Your death would have devastated me," he growled. "It would have destroyed me. I could not let it happen. We deserve a chance—you and I. And I intend to see that we get it. Somehow I'll get us back to Aleppo, and from there we'll go to the coast and secure passage on a ship. . . . I won't permit any objections, Sadira. You're free now, and you'll stay free. You don't belong to the *Anazah,* the *Ruala* or the *Shammar* any longer. You belong to me. I saved your life, and now it's mine, and I fight for what's mine. I'll do whatever I must to keep you safe, and that includes tying you up and stuffing a headcloth in your mouth to keep you quiet, if I have to. Do you understand?"

"Travis . . ." She gazed into his implacable blue eyes and recognized the truth of his threat. He would do exactly what he said. The burden of decision had been removed from her and now rested with him. He would force her to his will—no, not force, for how could it be force if she wanted him to take her away to a safe place where no man had the right to raise a scimitar over her head again?

"Travis!" His name came out in an agonized sob. She could say no more. Words, thoughts, and feelings jumbled up to form a huge knot in her throat. She swayed and caught hold of Travis's arm for support.

"Sweetheart . . ." He wrapped her in his arms and pressed her against him so that she could feel his heart beating steadily and strongly against her breast. "I'll never let anyone hurt you or use you like that again. As God is my witness, I'll protect you forever!"

Swept with a sudden heady sense of desire, she clung to him and bathed his face with her kisses. She combed her fingers through his hair and shamelessly rubbed her aching breasts against his chest. Her need for him overwhelmed her, ripping through her like a violent wind sweeping the desert clean and destroying everything in its path. She could not breathe or think. Their mouths met in a searing kiss, and they sank to their knees together. He stroked and caressed her, and her need was so great that it made no difference that they were both fully clothed. She hardly noticed these minor impediments to their love-making.

They separated just long enough to lift robes and remove the barriers to final union, then Travis bent her backward and fell on top of her. He entered her in one swift, sure thrust. He thrust again and again, branding her with his ownership. It was what she needed—to be taken fast and hard, at a furious pace, to ride the crest of physical pleasure into a land of magical enchantment where no one could hurt her, and she felt no guilt. She arched beneath Travis, straining upward, clawing at his back and calling his name.

Fulfillment came in an explosion of rapture. Wrenched physically and emotionally, she balanced precariously at the very peak of sensation, then slid downward in a long, slow, glorious descent into oblivion. Moments later—or was it hours?—Travis stirred and nibbled her ear. "Sweetheart, I hate to call you back to reality so soon, but our horse has wandered off, and we're going to need her."

Her eyes flew open. Half naked in the late afternoon sunshine, they were lying in a tangle of robes and his *keffiya*. It had all happened so fast she was uncertain how they had gotten there. She did not remember lying down; all she could recall was how much she had needed Travis, and how he had sensed that need and filled the hollow core of her with light, heat, and intense, shimmering pleasure. For a brief time, she had been able to forget the turmoil, sadness, and violence of the day. . . . Now, she remembered, and the hollowness returned, though not as strongly as before.

"We must track and find her then," she whispered, tracing Travis's mouth with her fingertips. "We can go nowhere without horses . . . a horse, I mean."

But she had really meant *"horses,"* in the plural, and they needed camels, too. They were out on the desert alone with nothing but the clothes on their backs and Travis's pistol. They had no food or water—no water skins even. And at the moment, they had no horse.

Pushing him away, she sat up. "We must find her. She's a beautiful animal, not as good as Sherifa, but far better than nothing."

"She is the equal of Tahani, and we'll find her, and she'll get us back to Aleppo," Travis stated, sounding calm and positive.

Sadira smoothed down her rumpled robe and shook the sand from her hair. "I pray Allah you are right, Travis."

New worries assaulted her, as the full implication of their escape dawned on her. It was not enough that they had gotten this far; they had a lot further to go, and if they were caught, she and Travis both would be slain. Travis offered her a hand to help her get up, but when she had gained her feet, he did not release her. Instead, he pulled her close, tilted up her chin, and gazed directly into her eyes. "Whatever happens, I'm not sorry, Sadira. I would rescue you again in a minute. And then I would make love to you again on the floor of the desert. Do you understand? *I'm not sorry,* and nothing you or anyone says will convince me that we did the wrong thing today."

Sadira thought of Alima, her father, and the women and children of the *Ruala* who might, at this very moment, be bleeding and dying. And then she thought of the scimitar poised to fall on her neck and end her life. She was unworthy to be Keeper of the Mares and the ceremonial virgin, for she prized her own survival so much that she could not help being glad to be alive, even though others might be dying because she had escaped. "I am not sorry either, *Frangi*. Allah forgive me, but I cannot find it in my heart to be sorry!"

Jerking away from Travis, she set off tromping across the desert in the direction of the hoof tracks plainly imprinted in the sand.

They found the *Shammar* sheik's mare at a well located near the remnants of an old stone wall. The mare was nosing a dry wooden bucket and neighing her disappointment at finding no readily available refreshment. She could smell the water and knew it was there somewhere, but she could not reach it. Sadira quickly attached the bucket to the rope hanging from the wooden winch and let it down into the stone cairn that protected the well. Travis helped her raise the brimming container and give it to the thirsty horse. When the mare was satisfied, they refilled the bucket and they themselves drank, then searched the nearby area for the well's guardian. They found a hut not far away, but it did not look recently occupied, and no one appeared on the scene to lay claim to the well.

"There is no one here," Sadira finally decided, turning to Travis. "We should collect camel dung and light a fire to warm us during the night."

It was evening and still quite warm, but Sadira knew that the night air would feel chilly without tent or shelter.

"No fire. We can't risk it. They may come looking for us, you know—your people, the *Shammar,* or both of them together. We'll have to take turns standing guard tonight, and if we spot anyone coming this way, we'll take the mare and run."

"Run where, Travis? Where will we go without food, water, and supplies? As you say, they may be looking for us. If they find us, they will kill us in retaliation for what happened today. I wish I knew everything that *did* happen."

"Don't think about it. Don't worry. That part of your life is over, Sadira. If you want to worry, worry about our survival and how we can make it back across the Sands alive."

"We cannot do it without another horse, some milk camels, food, and a tent for shelter. I think I could find the way, for it is due north, but we will have to steal what we need."

"Steal?" Travis looked surprised, then thoughtful. "That'll be a dangerous undertaking, but I suppose you're right. We can't go anywhere without provisions, and stealing them is the only way to get them."

"Stealing from one's enemies is a time-honored Bedouin tradition." Sadira managed a small smile. "You may yet become a Bedouin, *Frangi,* with a little more time and effort."

She was gratified to see a slow grin spread across his handsome dark features. "I'm already more of a Bedouin than I ever thought I would be. If it takes theft to complete the transformation, then I'm prepared to become a thief. How soon do you think we can pull it off?"

"Let us rest for tonight and make our plans tomorrow," Sadira suggested. She was suddenly very weary and did not feel equal to the task of formulating a plan. The mare was also tired from the long, fast ride carrying two people; she needed rest to restore her strength. If her legs gave out, they would be left with nothing.

"Good idea." Travis started to yawn, then suppressed it. He took her arm and steered her toward the shelter of the wall. "You take a nap, and I'll stand guard."

Sadira sat down and started to get settled, then stopped. "You will wake me, won't you, Travis? You need sleep as much as I do."

"Don't worry. I'll wake you. I'm a hero with very unheroic needs. Sleep is definitely one of them, and I could name one or two others that might or might not surprise you."

"Just do not forget that you are *my* hero, Travis," she whispered, leaning back against the wall and closing her eyes. "You saved my life today, when no one else would help me."

"That's because I love you. Now go to sleep."

She smiled into the gathering darkness, warmed and comforted by his nearness. Tomorrow, they would think of some way to steal what they needed without getting caught. Tonight, she was simply too tired to concentrate. That was her last thought before the anxious neighing of a horse jolted her awake. She bolted upright and peered into the heavy blackness pressing close on every side. All was silent, and she wondered if she might have dreamed the sound. Overhead, the brightness and the position of the stars told her that the night was more than half over. Dawn would soon be here.

"Travis?" she said softly.

There was no answer, but she detected a steady, rhythmic sound that must have been Travis breathing—or snoring. The sound came from the top of the low wall. Carefully, she groped among the rocks and discovered that Travis was indeed asleep upon the wall. He must have been sitting there keeping watch, but had lain down and dozed off. A movement out on the plain caught her eye, and she was startled to recognize a familiar silhouette. Ears pricked, nostrils flaring, Sherifa stood gazing in her direction. Sadira would have recognized that proudly arched neck anywhere.

With a little cry of gladness, she hurried around the wall and ran out to greet her old friend. "Sherifa! Dear one, you found me—but how? How did you manage to break free of your captors?"

Sherifa nickered in answer. A moment later, a voice came to her from farther out on the plain. "I knew she would come to thee if I let her loose and then followed her."

"Hamid!" Sadira recognized the voice immediately.

Behind her, the hammer of a pistol clicked—absurdly loud in the night silence. "Don't move, Hamid, or I'll shoot," Travis said with deadly calm. "What are you doing here? Why have you come?"

Twenty-one

Travis was wide awake as he climbed down from the wall, being careful to keep his pistol leveled on Hamid's chest. Hamid and his horse made a large target, easily seen in the starlight, and Travis had no qualms about killing the man. If Hamid had brought the *Ruala* or the *Shammar* out to get them, he *would* kill him and not think twice about it. He meant to protect Sadira at all costs.

To his surprise, Hamid casually dismounted and approached with his hands held high, so Travis could see he held no weapons. "Do not shoot, *Frangi*. I am alone. I only came to speak to Sadira. I knew no other way of finding her than letting Sherifa lead the way."

Sadira ran to Hamid, Sherifa trotting happily at her heels. The mare of the *Shammar* sheik lifted her head and gazed at them with a benevolent expression; she had been grazing on the sparse greenery nearby. "Hamid, thank thee for bringing Sherifa to me! That is why thou art here, is it not? Thou knew how much we needed her."

"That is not the only reason," Hamid replied evasively.

Travis kept his pistol leveled at the stocky Bedouin. "Then what is the reason? We aren't going back, Hamid. We prefer to die out here than to go back and let Hajem Pasha or the *Shammar* kill us."

Hamid shook his head, his face unreadable in the dark

shadow of his *keffiya.* "Hajem Pasha will not harm thee. He lies dying inside his tent."

"I only shot him in the hand; how can he be dying?" Travis demanded.

"The fighting this day was terrible," Hamid explained. "On both sides, many have died, and many more are wounded. After we battled one another on the plain, we rode to one another's camps and spread death and havoc. We scattered one another's herds—even killed one another's war mares. I never knew so much hatred existed in the world as I saw today."

"And you took part in it," Travis accused. "You added to it."

Hamid nodded. "Yes. Allah knows I did. 'Tis a wonder I myself was not killed. Eventually we all came to our senses. The ram's horn reassembled the *Ruala,* and the *Shammar* gathered when Hajem Pasha fell, mortally wounded. By now, he may be dead. . . . Yet to bring that news is not why I came."

"Why didst thou come?" Sadira asked before Travis could get out the words.

"Because thy father also lies dying. He was wounded in three places, and only a man as strong and stubborn as he would still be alive. He claims he must live until he has the chance to talk with thee once more, Sadira. He sent me to find thee and bring thee back."

"It's a lie—a trick!" Travis stalked up to Sadira and stationed himself between her and Hamid. "You want her to go back so you can kill her and get it over with. She's still the sacrifice that Hajem Pasha and his people demand before they will settle for peace, isn't she? That's why Akbar wants her to return—so he can die knowing that peace is assured and his precious *Ruala* will now be safe."

"No, *Frangi*. That is not true, and if it were, I would not have come. I am ashamed that it took a *frangi* to awaken the pride of the *Ruala* and inspire them to fight. We behaved like yellow dogs today, like cringing whining cowards, showing no bravery whatsoever. 'Twas thy courage that ignited *our* courage and gave us the will to fight."

"Yes, and see what has happened because of it!" Sadira cried. "Two great men are dying, and many, many more have already died!"

" 'Tis better a man dies behaving as a man than that he live with the shame of knowing he is a coward," Hamid stonily replied. "The Prophet Muhammad approved of *jihad,* holy war. Protecting thee, Sadira, would count as such, yet none of us wished to fight for thee. 'Tis only just that we suffer, and the *Shammar* along with us. We were both wrong in what we did, and I am sick with shame. The *frangi* was the only one among us who showed true courage."

"Well, it's too late now. I have slept with your Keeper of the Mares," Travis blurted, desperate to prevent Sadira's return. "She is no longer a virgin. Therefore, she can serve your people no longer. She's going away with me now, back to Aleppo and then to my country. She has consented to become my wife."

"Travis!" Sadira gasped. "What good can be served by telling Hamid all of these things?"

"Maybe now he'll understand why you can't go back. Maybe now he'll return to your father and tell him he couldn't find you, that you've disappeared."

"My father knows that Sherifa can always find me," Sadira disputed. "Besides, I *must* go back. If Akbar is truly dying, I must see him once more."

"No!" Travis seized Sadira's arm. "I didn't save your life for you to throw it away all over again. . . . Trust me in this, Sadira. The danger is too great, and I won't risk losing you again. She's not going with you, Hamid, so you might as well get out of here."

"Travis, please . . ." Sadira touched his face. "We can trust Hamid. And we can trust my father. If he has said no harm will come to me, none shall."

"No harm shall come to thee, Sadira. I swear before Allah," Hamid reiterated. "Yesterday, I would have killed thee both if I had known what thou hast done. But tonight, everything has changed, and I find I have not the stomach for it. There has been enough killing. I can justify such violence no longer. I am done with it. From this day forward, may Allah strike me dead if I take the life of any other living creature. I shall kill no more. My hands are already stained with too much blood."

"A noble speech," Travis scoffed. "But does Akbar feel the same?"

" 'Twas Akbar who opened my eyes to my own wickedness. 'Twas Akbar who sent me to find Sadira. 'I must beg her forgiveness,' he said. 'I have shamefully wronged my daughter, and I cannot die in peace until I have set things right between us.' "

"I will come with thee, Hamid," Sadira told him. "We can leave now, immediately. I am ready."

"Sadira! Don't go! Don't believe him. You can't take the chance that he might be lying."

Sadira flung her arms about Travis and embraced him. Switching to English, she whispered urgently in his ear. "Travis, please let me go. I cannot marry you until I settle this. Let me see my father one last time, and then I shall be ready. Then nothing will stop me from accompanying you back to your homeland."

Travis knew when he was licked. There was no way to

argue with her once her mind was made up. No matter what he said, what arguments he offered, she was determined to return to the den of lions. "All right," he finally agreed. "But I'm coming with you. And my pistol will be aimed at Hamid. If anybody so much as looks at you the wrong way, Hamid dies. . . . Understand that, Hamid?"

"Allah's will be done, *Frangi.*" With typical Bedouin resignation, Hamid shrugged his shoulders and remounted his horse.

The new day was more than half over by the time they reached the *Ruala* encampment where Akbar lay dying in his tent. All around them were signs of the devastation Sadira had so dreaded. Tents had been burned or pulled down, bodies of animals and humans lay where they had fallen, and a pall of smoke and death hung over what remained. Sadira had expected some reaction to her return, people creeping out of their tents and pointing fingers, children running to get their parents, dogs barking, and goats bleating. . . . Instead, there was a horrible silence, broken only by the sound of weeping and groans of misery. No one paid her the slightest attention. They were too involved in their own anguish.

The entire encampment had been trampled and left in chaos. Camels, horses, sheep, and goats wandered aimlessly, poking their noses where they did not belong. Here and there, small burial parties were trying to remove the carnage before the jackals grew too bold. Sadira rode past a dead and bloated camel covered by a flock of vultures tearing at its flesh. The stench was awful, and she abruptly wished for a veil to cover her nose and mouth—perhaps even her eyes.

She did not want to see this—the consequences of her survival. Yet she could not stop looking. As if he knew what she was thinking, Travis rode closer to her and muttered, "Those who did this are the only ones responsible, Sadira. I refuse to accept any blame for it, and you had better not blame yourself either. We didn't do this; *they* did."

They. He meant the *Shammar*, but Sadira suspected that the *Ruala* had left the *Shammar* camp in much the same situation—devastated. Both sides had dealt the other a terrible blow and for now had retreated to lick their wounds. When they had recovered their strength, they would probably rise and fight again. The two tribes had fought one another for centuries, for as long as memory existed, and they would continue fighting long after she was gone from the earth. Her death might have bought peace for a time, but sooner or later, the old hatreds would flare up again, and the raids begin anew. Travis had been right when he pointed this out to her.

Hamid led them straight to her father's tent, half of which had been burned. The burnt part still smoldered. Someone—Alima?—had managed to cut or tear the tent into separate sections so that the whole thing would not be lost. As Sadira drew rein and dismounted, a woman in a *burqa* staggered up to her. For one sickening moment, Sadira thought it might be Alima, until the woman spoke in a voice she did not recognize.

"So the unworthy one returns! See what thou hast done? This is all thy fault." The woman gestured to the devastation surrounding them.

"Get away from her." Travis stepped between Sadira and the heavily veiled figure. "Whoever you are, you'd better leave her alone or you'll answer to me."

"Oh, thou art brave to come among us, *Frangi!* Now, when we are bowed and beaten, thou darest to show thy face—the very man who has brought us all to ruin."

"Why don't you show *your* face?" Travis challenged. "Sadira is not afraid to show hers, nor am I afraid to show mine. We didn't do this. All I did was save Sadira's life, which her own people—including you—had sacrificed. You've only gotten what you deserve."

"Travis, stop." Sadira touched his arm. "This poor soul has suffered enough. Do not add to her burdens. . . . Where is thy husband, woman? If he still lives, we will take thee to him. If not, we will at least find shelter for thee."

"Dost thou not recognize me, Sadira?" The voice scornfully inquired. It was deep and hoarse, as if the woman had lost the power of speech for a time and was only just now recovering it.

"No, I do not. Not with that *burqa*. Forgive me, but thy voice eludes me, too."

" 'Tis because I lost it screaming, when they did this to me." The woman's hand came up and tore away the veil.

Sadira gasped at what was revealed—Jaleel. Jaleel with puffy black eyes, a smashed nose, and a bruised, swollen face. "Oh, Jaleel! I am so sorry!"

"What they did to my face was the least of it," Jaleel snapped, her eyes burning. "There are bruises over the rest of me, too, in places no man but Akbar had ever seen before yesterday. I am fortunate to still be alive. Half a dozen men knelt between my thighs, and they only spared my life because I begged and pleaded and groveled at their feet."

Sadira's heart filled with pity—and fear for the other women she cared about. "What of Alima and Jahara?"

"Jahara is dead. When they did the same to her, she fainted and never awakened. Alima they did not touch; she is too old and ugly. She escaped everything."

"Then where is she?"

"Inside what is left of thy father's tent. She sits with Akbar while he is dying. . . . I have not the stomach for it. I never loved him anyway. I shall rejoice when he is gone, for he did not protect me from this ordeal. He was not even here when it happened. The *Shammar* rode through the camp like demons, shrieking for vengeance. They were enraged that thou escaped, Sadira. Had they succeeded in killing thee, we would have been spared. 'Tis all *thy* fault this happened."

"That's enough! Step aside now," Travis ordered, moving closer. "Sadira has come at her father's request."

"I pray he curses thee with his dying breath," Jaleel spat. "Thou art welcome here no longer, Sadira. Neither thee nor thy *frangi*. Do not stay, or thou wilt regret it. . . . I will turn the entire tribe against thee. I will not rest until thou hast suffered as I have suffered."

"We're leaving as soon as possible," Travis told her, taking Sadira's arm and steering her clear of the embittered woman.

They entered the tent and passed through the outer chamber to the entranceway of Akbar's private quarters. There they paused, giving Sadira the chance to assess the situation. Inside the second chamber, Akbar lay on his back, his head and body cushioned with plump pillows. Alima bent over him, holding his hand. Looking up and seeing them, she laboriously rose to her feet and came to greet them. "Sadira! Oh, Sadira, how glad I am to see thee once more! I had feared thou were dead, and I would never see thee again this side of paradise."

Sadira embraced her old friend, then gently drew back. "Akbar. . . . Is he sleeping? Will he recover? Tell me how bad his injuries are, Alima, for I have been greatly worried. I came as soon as I heard."

Alima gave her a sad look and gently patted her hand. "He is dying, Sadira. His wounds are hideous, and he suffers greatly. I know not what to do for him. Occasionally, he slips into unconsciousness, but then the pain awakens him."

"Is there nothing anyone can do?" Sadira whispered. "Nothing we can give him to ease his suffering?"

"We have tried various remedies, but none work. His injuries are too severe. Come, and I will wake him, for he has been asking for thee." Alima led her further into the chamber, and Travis followed a step or two behind.

On a tray next to Akbar was a plate of dates, a cup of water, and a loaf of flat bread. Next to that, on a pillow by itself, lay a pistol. Travis started to reach for it, but Alima grabbed his wrist and doggedly clung to it, preventing him from touching it.

"Why is that gun here?" Travis whispered, watching Alima closely.

"Because Akbar wants it," Alima began, but before she could explain why, Akbar himself answered.

"Never fear, *Frangi*. 'Tis not so I can shoot thee or Sadira. 'Tis for protection only, should we need it."

Sadira interpreted that to mean that he wanted the weapon nearby in case the *Shammar* returned to finish what they had started. She quickly dropped to her knees beside her father and took his hand. "Father, thou art awake! But thou lookest so pale. So weary. I had rather thou still slept and guarded thy strength."

He looked terrible, she thought. Already he resembled

the dead man he would soon become. His lips were blood-less, his skin like clay. But a spark of life and determination still lit his dark eyes. "I have been waiting for thee, Sadira. I knew thou wouldst return if Hamid begged thee, even though thy people—and I myself—have done thee great wrongs. Great . . . great wrongs."

He coughed then, and a bubble of blood appeared on his lips. Sadira wiped it away with a cloth that lay nearby and already bore bloody stains. Noting them, she glanced up at Alima. The old woman simply shook her head, her eyes brimming with tears. Sadira scanned her father's body, but he was covered chin to toe with a fresh clean robe, and she could not discern his injuries. Gently, she squeezed Akbar's bloodless fingers. "Do not talk if it hurts thee, Father. I understand why thou sent me to the *Shammar;* thou did it only to protect thy people."

"But I should have protected *thee,* Sadira. . . . Thou hast never done anything wrong, yet I blamed thee for so much—not least of all, possessing thy mother's rare beauty. Whenever I looked upon thee, I was reminded . . . of her and of what I did to her in a fit of jealous rage. . . . I should never have sent thee to the *Shammar.* I should have looked for another way to avert Hajem Pasha's wrath over the death of Gamalat. . . . Well . . . I am suffering now for my many sins. A tiger gnaws at my vitals, Daughter. . . . Soon he will devour me entirely."

Akbar's hand moved to his stomach, and he held it there a moment. When he removed it, blood seeped through the white robe and slowly blossomed into a spreading stain as she watched in pity and horror. "Oh, Father, I am so sorry it has come to this!"

Sadira bent down and pressed her lips to her father's

forehead. His skin felt cold to her touch—and clammy, the way she imagined the flesh of a dead man would feel.

"Forgive . . ." Akbar begged in a strangled voice. "Forgive me, Daughter . . . for not having loved and cherished thee better . . . for sending thee away to die. 'Tis the one thing in my life I cannot excuse myself for doing. . . . All else was minor compared to that. I can find reason for everything, but not for what I did . . . to thee. Please, Sadira . . . forgive me."

"I forgive thee, Father. Thou art judging thyself too harshly, for never did a leader love his people better. That must count for something on the scale of good and bad, right and wrong."

"Nay, the scale is tipped heavily against me, Daughter. But if thou dost not hold it against me, can Allah do so? Can thy goodness . . . and love be greater than his? I think . . . not."

"I am not so perfect, Father. Do not make me more than I am. I . . . I, too, have my weaknesses." Sadira was about to confess all when she felt Travis's hand on her shoulder and glanced up to see his blue eyes warning her to keep silent.

Akbar caught the look, however. He gazed first at her and then at Travis and—amazingly!—he smiled. "So thou hast found love . . . is that it, Daughter? Thou hast joined thyself to the *frangi*."

"Aye, Father. I am my mother's daughter, after all."

"Nay, thou art only a woman in need of a man to love thee. . . . Give me thy hand, *Frangi*." Akbar's voice was barely a whisper. When Travis had given Akbar his hand, Akbar shakily placed Sadira's hand in Travis's. "She is thine, *Frangi*. Thou art deserving of her, for thou hast fought for her, and I did not. I give thee both my blessing . . . and gifts. I give thee gifts—Tahani, Lulu, and Sherifa . . . plus thy choice of whatever other mares or stallions thou desire . . . and whatever other camels. Take Tarfa, and. . . . Aaaah!"

"Father, what is it?" Sadira clutched his arm, devastated to see him suffering so. His body had gone rigid, and his teeth were clenched. Beads of moisture popped out on his brow. He shuddered and shook in the grip of terrible torment.

"Aaaaah!" he cried again, the sound wrenched from his very soul.

Then Alima was there, pulling Sadira away from her father's side. Travis and Alima together drew her back toward the entranceway. "Let me stay!" she pleaded. "Do not send me away! I want to be with him at the end—and 'tis surely not far off! Please. . . . Oh, Akbar!"

But Alima pushed her out of the chamber and let the flap fall behind her. "There is naught thou canst do, child. Akbar is dying, and when the pain claws at him like that, he cannot keep from crying out. Thou knowest how brave he is, how courageous—therefore, it shames him that any should see him lose control. Dost thou not remember when he was wounded the last time?"

Sadira nodded, blinking back tears. Akbar had taken a ball in the shoulder, and Alima had dug it out with a dagger, then cauterized the wound with a burning knife. Akbar had jerked and shuddered, but never made a sound. How much worse he must be suffering now to have cried out in her presence!

"Alima's right, sweetheart," Travis agreed, and behind him, Hamid nodded. "He would not want you to witness him groaning and thrashing about in his last torment. I'm sure he doesn't want you to remember him like this."

"But . . . but . . ." Sobs welled in Sadira's throat.

Alima gathered her into her arms and held her a moment, then whispered in her ear. "Go now, child. Fear not, for he shall not suffer long. I will not allow it. The sooner thou goest, the sooner I can . . . help him."

Sadira drew back and searched Alima's face. "But . . . how?"

Alima touched a wrinkled, gnarled hand to Sadira's cheek. "Trust me, child. Allah watches over us all. . . . May he go with thee to thy new life in a new land. Hamid wilt help thee gather what thou needs for thy journey. Go quickly now, and do not look back."

"But how can I leave thee? What will happen between the *Ruala* and the *Shammar* if I go?"

"They will survive as they have always survived. The *Shammar* sheik is also dying, is he not, Hamid?" Alima looked to Hamid for confirmation of that fact.

Hamid nodded. "I myself saw him fall and his men carry him away. Later, when we attacked the *Shammar* camp, we scattered the mourners who were weeping, wailing, and praying around his tent."

"Then if he dies, and Akbar also dies, the tribes will retreat to a safe place to pick a new sheik. With Gamalat dead and Nuri gone, who knows who will be chosen? There will be no more war for a time, not until each side once again gathers strength, and perhaps not then, if the new leaders are wise. Thou art needed no longer, child. Thy time among the *Ruala* has ended. 'Tis the hour for thee to depart."

"Goodbye, Alima!" Sadira flung her arms around the old woman and hugged her, then swiftly stepped away.

She knew that Alima was anxious to return to Akbar . . . and indeed, the old woman wasted no more time on fare-wells, but simply nodded, then turned and hurried back to her husband. Wrestling with her grief, Sadira walked out on the plain with Hamid and Travis to choose the horses and camels they would take with them on their journey to Aleppo. Moments later, they heard the gunshot. A single loud *pop!* came from the direction of Akbar's tent.

"What is that—another attack?" Hamid cried, ready to run back.

"No, wait a moment." Sadira stayed him with her hand.

She knew what was coming, and a moment later, they all heard it. A second gunshot came from the same place.

"If it's not an attack, what is it?" Hamid persisted.

Sadira's eyes met Travis's in complete understanding; they both knew exactly what had happened.

"Art thou going to tell me or not?" Hamid demanded, unwilling to accept the obvious.

"Alima and Akbar have gone to paradise," Sadira whispered. "They have gone together. May Allah have mercy on them, and may they rest in peace."

Twenty-two

Sadira and Travis prepared to leave that very day for Aleppo. They gathered flour, dates, coffee, butter, and other staples for the journey and loaded them on Lulu. Travis did not want to leave Tarfa behind, but since she was not a milk camel, they chose two other animals instead, a large, sturdy, fawn-colored beast named Aza and a shorter white one called Rahil. Aza's name meant "comfort" and Rahil's "traveler." In view of their auspicious names, Travis hoped they had two good animals who could stand up to the rigors of recrossing the Sands.

He knew they could not select many horses. Despite Akbar's invitation to take what they wanted, it would be too difficult to find grazing to risk moving more than a few all that distance. Sherifa, Tahani, Najila, and the mare of the *Shammar* sheik were the most important ones, and he and Sadira agonized over two others and finally settled on one more mare—a young bay filly with the promise of great speed. Bachir had impressed Travis as a worthy stallion, and Hamid rode out to get him, while Travis and Sadira completed their preparations a short distance away from camp.

As they loaded Aza's *dhalla,* they could hear the wails and lamentations of the *Ruala* mourning Akbar's passing. Tears glistened in Sadira's eyes, but she never said a word or succumbed to weeping as she efficiently packed a tent and several water skins onto the *dhalla.* All was ready for the departure by the time Hamid returned with Bachir. The young stallion whinnied a joyous greeting to the little band of mares, his new harem, but when he took an avid interest in Sherifa, the flame-colored beauty kicked him in the nose for his trouble.

At any other time, Travis would have broken out laughing, but today, he could not muster a smile. This was a sad, momentous occasion for Sadira. Her sorrow was plainly evident. He ached for her and could only imagine how she must feel after all that had taken place and all that she was now losing forever. Not only was she leaving the *Ruala,* she was leaving the desert and journeying to a far place where the climate, food, clothing, language, religion, and nearly everything else would be different from anything she had known.

They intended to sell the camels in Aleppo, so her only reminders of her homeland would be the horses. But despite the sadness of the occasion, only once did Sadira stop working and gaze over at the camp, where her people were carrying the bodies of Akbar and Alima on a single large bier borne on the shoulders of six men. Travis immediately went to her and slid his arms around her waist. Wordlessly, she turned to him and buried her face in his shoulder. He stroked her hair and back, and she clung to him, but after a few moments, resolutely pushed away and went back to her packing.

Travis wished he knew how to comfort her; he was thrilled she was going home with him, but he could not promise that she would never miss her people or the life she had led up until now. He resolved to make her so happy and keep her so busy that she would have no time to dwell on the past. He reminded himself that Greenbriar was a beautiful place; surely she would grow to love it as much as he did.

It was nearly sunset by the time they were ready to depart. They were impatient to leave but did not want to do so without bidding farewell to Hamid who had left them to witness Akbar's and Alima's burial. They had thought it best not to attend it themselves because the remaining *Ruala* might resent their presence. Now, as they mounted their horses to await his return and be ready to move out as soon as possible, they spotted him coming toward them on horseback in company with a man riding a camel.

"Who is that with him?" Travis shaded his eyes against the long golden rays of the setting sun. Most of the *Ruala* men were familiar to him, but he did not recognize this fellow, who was swathed in a *keffiya* that covered everything but his eyes.

"I do not know." Sadira sat waiting on Sherifa until the two men reached them. Then she said, "Oh, 'tis Mijem. One of our renowned guides."

Hamid came up to them and lifted his hand in a brief salute. *"Frangi,* I bring thee a man who can take thee safely back to Aleppo, for which service he requests the choice of only one of thy fine horses."

"No horses," Travis quickly objected. "But he may have our camels, as we intend to sell them there anyway."

To Travis's surprise, Sadira objected. "No camels either. Art thou trying to cheat us, Mijem? I already know the way back to Aleppo, so we do not need thy services. But thou art welcome to accompany us on our journey if thou wishest."

Mijem did not look pleased by the offer. He was a scrawny, wizened man—seemingly ageless in the way of many desert dwellers. With elaborate care, he unwrapped his *keffiya* to reveal a large hooked nose above a wispy, gray-streaked beard and thin mouth. "Anyone can find their way back across the Sands, 'tis true," he observed. "One only needs to go north, and if one lives long enough, one will get there. But from there to Aleppo, the way is not nearly so easy. Thou wilt need me then, and three camels is not a high price to pay for such guidance."

" 'Tis much too high, considering that when we cross the Sands, we will already be more than halfway to Aleppo. Therefore, we will need thee for only one third or less of the journey."

Mijem sat on his camel and considered that information. Travis was tempted to make a different offer, but sensed that Sadira had the matter well in hand and would not welcome his interference.

"Two camels?" Mijem inquired, his eyes narrowing. "Two camels and I will serve not only as thy guide, but as thy servant."

"One camel," Sadira answered, ". . . and thou wilt serve as servant as well as guide."

"Robbery!" Mijem scoffed. "What thou art suggesting is robbery."

"Nay, Mijem," Sadira corrected. " 'Tis a fair bargain, for we shall give thee the biggest milk camel, and she will make an excellent addition to thy herds."

"Lulu . . ." Mijem insisted. "I will take Lulu."

"Not Lulu, for she is going with us to the land of my husband, the *frangi*."

Travis almost fell off the mare of the *Shammar* sheik, the lovely animal they had named Shammar because of her origins. It shocked Travis to hear Sadira call him husband and astounded him to learn that she intended to take Lulu back to Kentucky. Then he realized that when Akbar placed her hand in his, the act was as binding as any wedding ceremony; in Sadira's mind, they were married. He had intended to do it properly in a grand ceremony at Greenbriar, attended by all his friends and acquaintances, but now he realized that such a ritual would only be superfluous. Perhaps he would change the wedding to a party instead, where he could introduce his new wife to everyone he knew. As for taking a camel back to Kentucky, it was out of the question.

"Done!" Mijem exclaimed. "Thou art taking advantage of a poor Bedouin, but I will guide and serve thee for the price of one camel—the largest milk camel."

"Aza," Sadira said. "Get us safely to Aleppo, and Aza is thine."

Looking pleased and happy for the first time in days, Sadira beamed at Travis. Travis had not the heart to begin an argument over Lulu, but there was no way he would take a camel aboard a ship back to America—especially not a bad-tempered, unpredictable beast like Lulu. While they were loading her, she had swung her head around and nearly bit him!

He had one other reservation about the bargain Sadira had just made: He had eagerly anticipated that he and Sadira would finally be alone together for the days—and nights—of this long journey. Now they were going to have company, a prospect he found less than appealing. Of course, it was always better to have an escort when crossing the desert, as he had learned from experience, but after the trouble with Gamalat, he had concluded they would probably be safer on their own. They possessed fast horses and camels, and Hamid had furnished him with additional firearms and bullets. Now that he had a chance to think about

it, he wasn't certain he wanted Mijem along to usurp their
privacy!

But everyone else—Hamid, Sadira, and Mijem himself—
seemed delighted, so Travis bit his tongue and said nothing.
There would be time enough later to take a stand against
Lulu, and since he himself could never find the way back
to Aleppo, he could hardly refuse to accept a guide.

Sadira rode Sherifa closer to Hamid and smiled at him.
"Thank thee, Hamid, for all thou hast done for us. Farewell
to thee and thine. May Allah watch over thee."

Hamid's face reflected an array of emotions, but he
quickly subdued his feelings and gazed steadily back at
Sadira. "Farewell to thee, Sadira. And to thee, *Frangi.*"
Hamid nodded to Travis. "Should thou return one day to
visit the *Ruala,* I will welcome thee into my tent. Akbar
himself welcomed thee—and in the end, gave thee his
daughter. I can do no less than call thee brother. I trust
thou wilt keep my sister safe."

Travis leaned over Shammar's satiny white neck and extended his hand to Hamid. Hamid was still in love with
Sadira, but honor forbade him from doing or saying anything to express it. In this instance, at least, honor had its
place. "I will cherish her all the days of my life," he promised the younger man.

They shook hands, Western-fashion, and then Travis motioned to Sadira and Mijem. "If we are going to leave tonight, we'd better hurry, before it gets dark."

"We can travel at night," Mijem said. "At night, we have
the stars to light our way. 'Tis best to travel when it is
bright enough to see our tracks, but not so bright that robbers can spot us. Therefore, we shall not travel when the
moon is completely full, nor when it is gone altogether—
but only on the nights in between. From the eighth to the

eighteenth day of the moon's cycle is best; on such nights one can see farther than a rifle can shoot. They are called the white nights and are the safest for crossing the desert."

"We'll travel when I say so and *only* when I say so. Got that, Mijem?" Having asserted his authority at the onset, Travis rode ahead, leaving his new servant and his wife to make certain all the other beasts were following.

The journey back across the Sands seemed both longer and shorter than the first time they had crossed it. The heat was worse and the days more miserable—but the nights! This time, the nights were magnificent, because Travis was sharing them with Sadira. Mijem endeared himself to Travis the very first night by pitching his tent a discreet distance away from their tent. Before retiring, he made the fire, baked bread, melted butter for dipping the dates, boiled coffee, tended the horses and camels, and performed whatever other tasks were necessary—and then he disappeared inside his tent, not to be seen again until morning.

In Travis's view, this made him the perfect servant, even without the added bonus that he knew the desert well, could almost always find patches of salt grass or camel thorn for the animals to graze on at night, and was an interesting, voluble companion, full of information, superstitions, and opinions on every subject. If there was water anywhere about, he could locate it. If a barely discernible dust cloud appeared in the distance, he would notice it first and lead them away from it. And he adored the horses and camels—lavishing special attention on Aza, whom he dubbed his "precious jewel," his "heart's desire," his "beloved turtle dove."

But best of all, in Travis's opinion, Mijem knew how to

disappear. With uncanny accuracy, he made himself scarce
when Travis wanted to be alone with his new bride. Sometimes, Travis and Sadira walked alone away from camp and
embraced beneath a vault of stars that made them feel as
if they were the only two people in the universe. Sometimes, they retreated immediately into their tent and tore
off their clothing like two shameless, ravenous creatures
starved for the sight and feel of each other. Sometimes,
they did not make love at all but only held each other and
whispered far into the night, laughing and giggling at their
own small jokes, sharing reminiscences of their childhoods,
and exploring each other's thoughts on a variety of subjects.

It was a time for tenderness, sensuality, and wondrous
discovery. Travis had to know where Sadira was and what
she was thinking every minute of every day. When she
smiled, he wanted to know the cause of her amusement.
When she frowned, he wondered what displeased her. When
she laughed, he could not help but laugh with her. He had
desired her from the moment he first saw her, but had
never really known her until now. Before, she had been a
desirable female whose beauty aroused him to a peak of
uncontrollable passion; now she was his woman, his lover,
his closest friend and confidante, his heart and soul . . .
his beloved wife.

He gloried in his possession of her and imagined that it
would be like this for them always. . . . He could endure
the tedium and hardship of the days, because Sadira was
with him, and eventually, the night would come, and he
would have her all to himself. One evening, he retired early
to the tent ahead of Sadira. Mijem was off with the camels
and horses, checking them for scratches, swellings, or injuries. By the time Sadira entered the tent, Travis lay
stretched out, naked and grinning, upon their sleeping rug.

It was not yet dark, and when Sadira came in and saw him lying there waiting for her, her green eyes lit up, and she smiled the special smile reserved only for him. *"Frangi,"* she whispered in Arabic. "Hast thou no shame?"

"None, where thou art concerned," he answered, using the same flowery Arabic and enjoying the biblical richness of the language. "Thou art more beautiful than the sun or moon, my beloved, and I cannot wait to love thee this night."

Eyes shining, Sadira removed her veil and then her garments, one by one, making a gift of the act of undressing. Then she knelt beside him, took his hand, and placed it on her full, soft breast. "Dost thou feel my heart leaping, *Frangi?* Will it always be like this for us?"

"Always," he promised, leaning forward to kiss her. Savoring the sweetness of her lips and mouth, he drew her down to lie beside him. Tonight, he intended to go slowly and prolong their lovemaking for hours and hours, but she suddenly turned to him and gazed earnestly into his eyes.

"Travis, when we go to your country, will I still be me? Or will I change and become someone else?"

A shadow of worry darkened her beautiful green eyes, and her voice held a trace of fear. Feeling the first stirrings of disquiet, Travis raised himself on one elbow and smoothed the dark hair back from her brow before answering. He recognized the importance of the question; they had talked much about their past, a lot about the present, but only a little concerning the future. In the desert, time hung suspended, and he himself found it difficult to conjure up the image of home. He tried to picture Sadira in Kentucky, standing beside him at the races, sitting at the long polished table in his dining room, or pouring tea in the front parlor. She would be wearing a gown, her hair done up in ringlets or however women wore their hair these days. . . . A chill closed around his heart. He could not quite imagine it. Could not see her as he had once been able to see Elizabeth, presiding over his home, his social affairs, doing what a wife always did to ease a man's life.

"We all change," he began. "But we're still ourselves, aren't we? We can adapt to different cultures and new ways of doing things. I've almost become a Bedouin, haven't I? I've learned your ways and figured out how to survive here. You will have to do the same, sweetheart. And I'll be right at your side to help you."

"But Travis . . ." She touched a finger to his mouth. "Could *you* live here forever—forsaking everything you believe, all you are, to become a Bedouin following his herds across the desert until the day you die?"

He paused, doubting he *could* become a Muslim like Mijem, saying his devotions everyday at the precise same times, erecting his tent in the prescribed manner, spending his entire life wandering in the wilderness. He could never learn to think like a Bedouin, yet he was expecting Sadira to somehow learn to think like a Kentucky housewife.

"No, I . . . I guess I couldn't. But you see I always planned on returning to Greenbriar one day."

"I *never* planned on going to America," she whispered. "Not until . . . until Akbar died. Rather, until he gave me to you. And even then, I . . . I . . ."

"You what?"

"I did not actually consider it. Not really. I did not think of how it would be. . . . What if I cannot fit in, Travis? What if people find me too odd and different?"

"Sweetheart, I don't care what people think. I never have. And I've already told you that I don't have any close family to worry about pleasing or upsetting. You know horses. You love horses. That won't change. We'll be breeding them, raising them, and training them—activities that are similar to what you've done here. We'll have the same decisions to make regarding the horses."

"But will I still be Bedouin? I am *Ruala* to the bone, Travis, and I do not know how to be anything else." She sat up and faced him, her long dark hair spilling down over one shoulder. In the dimness of the waning light, the gold streak in the black tresses glistened and shimmered. "I am suddenly afraid, Travis. Indeed, when I let myself dwell on it, I am weak with terror."

"You, terrified? How can that be? You're the woman who faced her enemies alone, who never flinched when a scimitar was poised to cut off her head. I can't believe you're afraid to have adventures in a new land. It will be exciting, sweetheart. I know you'll love it."

He managed to put more enthusiasm into the statement than he suddenly felt . . . for he realized for the first time just how difficult it might actually be. He would have to teach her everything, from how to dress and arrange her hair, to how to pour tea and make small talk at parties. Not that he cared much for entertaining. He had told Elizabeth he didn't want to decorate her tea parties or be a social success at the cost of his privacy and freedom. Yet he had never imagined doing no socializing at all and living like a recluse. A small amount was necessary for survival and success in the horse breeding business; parties were where people bought and sold horses, revealed the strengths and weaknesses of their breeding experiments, and made the first tentative moves toward business deals.

One of the reasons he had been attracted to Elizabeth in the first place was because she did excel at socializing, made guests feel at ease, and knew how to smooth the way for further productive dealings. He had never been very good at those things, and while he didn't want his life to be dominated by such events, overseeing them was certainly a proper role for the wife of someone in his position. Sadira did not possess such skills, and she would be as awkward and uncomfortable at it as he was, if not more so . . . but surely they could work it out!

The most important thing was that he truly loved Sadira, and she loved him. . . . So what could possibly go wrong? The first few weeks would be the worst—a challenging adjustment period—but after that, as she learned and adapted, her fears would evaporate, and they would be deliriously happy. He couldn't wait to show her off to all of Lexington, but he would happily postpone any large gatherings until she was comfortable in her new home.

"You'll *love* it," he repeated with more certainty. "You love me, don't you? Therefore, you'll learn to love the life I live. We can make it work, sweetheart. I promise you this."

Her fingers stroked the hair at his temples, and her eyes grew soft and dreamy. "Wither thou goest, my love, I shall go, and thy people shall be my people."

"Now where did you learn that? I can't believe it's written in the *Koran*."

" 'Tis written in the Holy Book of your people, is it not?"

"Yes, but how would you have read it?"

"I told you I learned English from others who came before you to purchase horses from my people. One of them had your Holy Book, and we read from it together. Each time I read from it, I had to translate the passages for my father. Religion was always of great interest to him. He always wanted to know whether his guests worshipped

Allah or some other God, and in what manner they paid homage to their God, and how He differed from ours."

"I do recall several interesting conversations we had together," Travis reminisced. "I was amazed by how much he knew of other customs and beliefs. Even when I was arguing with him about religion, however, I could not help wondering what you would look like without your clothes."

"Travis! Thou art wicked."

"I fear thou art right," he teased. "Yet look at how much restraint I have exercised lying beside thee in thy nakedness and not yet falling upon thee."

"And hast thou reached the end of thy restraint?" Sadira purred, rolling over on top of Travis.

"What dost thou think, temptress?" He lifted his head to claim her lips, and she laughed softly and bit at his nose, then deliberately enflamed him by rubbing her breasts against his chest.

It was too much. With a low growl, he rolled over on top of her and began kissing her in earnest, beginning first with her luscious, saucy mouth and then proceeding to the round globes of her breasts. She was infinitely soft and yielding, her hands seeking and finding his most sensitive spots, her lips following the path of her hands, until his breathing grew ragged, and his heart threatened to jump out of his chest.

When he could take no more of her gentle torture, he held her down and buried his nose in the feminine mystery of her and kissed her gently between her thighs, then with growing urgency. Spasms of desire wracked him. She clutched his hair and drew him upward, kissed him deeply, and at the same time lifted her hips to take his thrust. He drove into her, marveling at her heat and tightness, reveling in her strength as she squeezed and held him in the most feminine of all embraces.

How he loved her! He would never let her go. They had come too far together to ever go back; they were man and wife now. Wherever he went, she would go . . . and she would stay. She would be happy. He had to believe it. He *did* believe it. But as they lay together afterward, drifting on a sea of contentment, he felt a little twinge of doubt. He had had everything in common with Elizabeth—or thought he had—and it had not worked out. He had almost nothing in common with Sadira, except their mutual love of horses. And their love of each other. Would it be enough? Only time would reveal the answer to that question . . . and if it *wasn't* enough, what would they each do then?

Twenty-three

With a swiftness that terrified Sadira, they reached Aleppo, and before she knew it, she found herself entering a world she had only heard about and then only superficially. It was like plunging into a sandstorm and suddenly realizing that all the familiar landmarks were gone. Everything was new and strange. Everything was different, and she could not retreat or return to what she had known previously.

"Welcome to Aleppo, Mrs. Keene. I am delighted to meet you." The serious, sober-faced *frangi* clasped Sadira's hand and bowed low over it, and she could not decide whether to snatch it back in horror at such brazen familiarity, shake hands as Travis had just done with the man, or simply stand there, feeling foolish.

She wound up doing the latter. Fortunately, Travis quickly rescued her from the embarrassing situation, at the same time bombarding her with more information than she could readily assimilate.

"This is Mr. Skene, the consul general, Sadira. I first met him when I arrived in Aleppo. We'll be staying here at the consulate until I can make arrangements for us to travel to the coast with the horses and book passage on a ship there. Thanks for your invitation, Mr. Skene. My wife and I are pleased to accept."

Relinquishing Sadira's hand, Mr. Skene smiled. "My pleasure, Mr. Keene. I must say I never dreamed you would return with so many remarkable horses and a wife in the bargain. Do sit down, and I'll send for coffee. I am most anxious to hear about what must have been a fascinating and highly successful journey."

Sadira panicked when both men turned to look at her, as if waiting for her to do something. Mr. Skene had said to sit down, but Sadira eyed the room's furnishings with misgivings. Where was she to sit? On the floor, the cushions, or on the long narrow thing whose purpose might not be for seating? Seeing her expression, Travis took her hand and sat down with her on the . . . the . . . she didn't know *what* to call it, and a wave of heat flooded her cheeks.

"This is a sofa, sweetheart. And those are chairs. You sit on them. The room's a bit different from the inside of a Bedouin tent, but you'll soon get used to it." Travis grinned at Mr. Skene. "She finds Aleppo amazing—been asking questions about everything. You see, she grew up on the desert and has never been to a large city before. Only to the small towns, and then she stayed outside of them with the rest of the women. This is her first time inside an actual building, other than a simple *khan* perhaps."

Sadira felt her cheeks flame even more as Mr. Skene's eyes flicked over her. His expression was kind but guarded. She could not tell if he approved of her or not. Perhaps he could not decide. "Oh, I knew she was Bedouin the moment I saw her. Her garments, of course. We shall have to see about locating suitable clothing for her—something more in keeping for the wife of an American. With her unusual hair and eyes, she'll soon look the part; the right clothes will do wonders in that regard, I'm sure."

"We would appreciate any help you could give us there." Travis smoothed down his travel-stained robe. "Can't wait to get into my own Western clothes, though I think I'll miss the freedom of desert garb."

Sadira swallowed hard, but the huge lump in her throat refused to go away. She wanted to run from this strange room with its unfamiliar furnishings and from this strange man whose title—consul general?—meant nothing to her. She wanted to run and find Sherifa, mount her, and go galloping back to the desert. There, she felt at home, knew what was expected of her, and how to act. Here, she knew nothing at all; the rules had all changed. Her English hardly seemed an advantage, because she had no idea what to say.

"Desert garb *is* comfortable," Mr. Skene agreed. "It always takes me a few days to adjust when I return from my own forays into the desert and once again encounter civilization. Well, it won't take long, I can tell you from experience. In no time at all, you'll wonder how you ever endured the harshness of nomadic existence. I've always found it to be greatly romanticized by those who have never traveled with the Bedouin. Much as I like horses and camels, a man can get his fill of them after living in such close proximity for a long period of time."

"Get his fill of them?" Sadira burst out, then bit her lip until she tasted blood. She sensed she had asked an inappropriate question. But how could a person tire of being around horses and camels? she wondered. They were essential to life as she knew it.

"Forgive me, I did not mean that there's anything wrong with horses and camels, Mrs. Keene. They're wonderful creatures, actually." Mr. Skene grinned apologetically, and Travis chuckled and patted her hand.

"My wife is quite partial to horses and camels. It's one of the things I love about her."

"Then you are indeed fortunate. Your English is excellent, Mrs. Keene. I never met a Bedouin female who could speak it. Your proficiency is most unusual."

"I learned from other foreigners who came to our tribe seeking horses." Sadira lifted her chin a bit and tried not to be intimidated. "I became a translator for my people. My father often had me join him and his guests to take part in the conversation."

"Remarkable! I am well traveled myself, but I regret to say I never visited your particular tribe, or I might have met you."

"Sadira is remarkable in every way." Travis squeezed her hand, and she drew comfort from his unspoken support. Suddenly, she was much less nervous and fearful of making a mistake or shaming him. With Travis beside her, she could get through this. She *would* get through it and make him proud of her.

"I can speak English fluently, but no one ever taught me *frangi* ways," she continued. "You must correct me when I do not behave as I ought. I have no wish to appear the fool or embarrass my husband."

"Embarrass me!" Travis frowned and shook his head. "That's one thing you'll never do, sweetheart. Don't worry about it for a single moment."

"No . . . no, you will not embarrass anyone, Mrs. Keene." The consul general's pale blue eyes seemed to soften as he gazed at her. "You are a lovely young woman with a great deal of charm and obvious intelligence. Any mistakes you do make will be quickly forgiven."

"Do you really think so?" Sadira leaned forward, anxious to win this man's complete and total approval, for Travis's sake, not necessarily her own. She was accustomed to being an outcast, but he was not. Marriages between *frangi* men and Bedouin women were all but unheard of, yet she desperately wanted her union with Travis to succeed. Each night she prayed that he would never come to regret marrying her!

"I know so." Mr. Skene's lips quirked upward in a genuine smile, the first Sadira had received from him. "Now then, let us discuss what you two intend to do with the wonderful horses and camels you brought back from the desert. They can remain below in our stables until such time as you choose to leave, but what will you do with them then?"

"Take them home with us—the horses, that is," Travis said. "We already gave our guide, Mijem, one of the camels, and the other two we wish to sell."

"Not Lulu," Sadira protested, hating to correct Travis in public but feeling that in this case, it was necessary. "Lulu belongs to me, and she must accompany us to America."

Travis's blue eyes darkened at her pronouncement. "Sweetheart, it's a long way to America, and when Lulu gets there, she won't have any other camels to keep her company. I think she'd be much happier staying here with her own kind, don't you?"

"She will have me," Sadira insisted. "I will be her family."

"Sadira, I really don't think. . . . Well, we can discuss this later in privacy. I'm sure Mr. Skene has no real interest in the subject."

"Ahem." Mr. Skene awkwardly cleared his throat. "Precisely how many horses will you be taking home with you, Mr. Keene?"

"Five mares and one stallion. The passage for them alone will cost a small fortune." Travis gave Sadira a meaningful glance, as if to imply that he could not afford to take a camel, too.

Here 'tis, she thought, our first argument. Yet she couldn't leave behind her dear friend, Lulu, who had depended upon her for years and years. Poor Lulu would never understand. Besides, it would be like severing her arm and leaving it behind.

"If we cannot afford to transport Lulu, we could always leave the little bay filly behind," she suggested on inspiration. "The filly would fetch a good price here in Aleppo. Perhaps you might like to buy her, Mr. Skene?"

"Dear me! I wouldn't dream of playing any part in this disagreement! I believe I'll see about that coffee I mentioned and leave you two to discuss this issue in the privacy you require."

"Yes, that would be kind of you," Sadira said.

"Entirely unnecessary," Travis scoffed, glowering. "There's nothing to discuss."

"Excuse me, please." Mr. Skene rose, quietly departed the room, and closed the door behind him, leaving Sadira to face her obviously angry husband alone.

"Sweetheart," he began on a conciliatory note at odds with his expression. "I'm sorry, but we cannot take Lulu. I know how you feel about her, but she'll be very unhappy in America all by herself."

"But Travis! Could we not take the other milk camel, too—so she will *not* be by herself?"

"Sadira, be reasonable. I can't afford to ship one camel, let alone two."

"Then we'll have to sell the bay mare for a very good price."

"The mare is too valuable to lose. She has a purpose.

She and the other horses are why I came to this country in the first place."

"But Lulu is valuable to *me*, Travis. She is my friend. I cannot bear to lose her." Sadira hated to beg, but for Lulu's sake, she would. "Please, Travis. I shall not ask you for anything more."

He sat staring at her for a long moment, then he sighed. "You won't, will you?" His tone had softened, reflecting an abrupt change of mood. "You'll never demand anything for yourself. That's not your nature. You gave your people everything and begged for nothing, not even your life. Even now, you're thinking of Lulu's benefit, not your own, aren't you?"

It was uncanny how he could read her. "She *needs* me, Travis. No one else will love or care for her as well as I can."

"I can understand why. She's too damn ornery."

"If I leave her behind, her new owner will grow impatient with her and treat her cruelly, perhaps even kill her."

Travis chuckled and threw up his hands in a gesture of surrender. "I suppose we can't let that happen, can we? Even though she deserves it."

"But she does *not* deserve it. She has faithfully served me for the past ten years. That loyalty must count for something."

Still grinning, Travis reached for her. "All right, Sadira . . . you win. We'll take her home with us somehow, though what we'll do with her when we get there, I have no idea."

"Oh, Travis, thank you!" Sadira flung her arms around her husband. Caught by surprise, he toppled sideways on the sofa. She followed him down, and in the midst of a wonderful embrace, realized that the sofa was marvelously soft and comfortable, a fine place to show her gratitude in a manner pleasing to them both. She kissed him deeply and touched her tongue to his in open invitation. He clasped her more tightly to him and nosed her hair.

"Sadira, you temptress, you vixen . . ." he muttered, nipping at her ear. "This is hardly the time or the place for what I'd really like to do to you. Anyway, you've already got what you want. When you give me that wide-eyed pleading look, I can't say no to you, and you damn well know it."

"You will not regret letting me take Lulu with us to America, Travis. She will be no trouble, I promise you. I will insist that she practice good manners."

"She better not be any trouble, or I'll make camel stew out of her. Now, sit up and behave yourself, before Mr. Skene returns with his coffee."

"Will there be sofas in our house in America?" The thought of sofas pleased Sadira. "Is your house large like this, or small and cozy like a tent?"

"It's large, and yes, there will be sofas. And soft, comfortable beds. If you think a sofa is great, just wait until you see—and try—a bed."

"I cannot wait. But oh, there is so much to learn!" Reluctantly, she sat up and straightened her garments. "I do not know how I can possibly learn it all."

"We have plenty of time, Sadira—a whole lifetime. You must learn to be patient. You can't learn everything in a single day."

"I know. But . . . but I just want to make you happy, Travis. We are so different, and I do not want our differences to one day tear us apart."

"Nothing can do that, little one. Not if we don't let it."

A discreet knock on the closed door alerted them to Mr.

Skene's return. They glanced up to see him entering, accompanied by a servant bearing coffee.

"Ah. . . . Have you resolved your differences of opinion?" He motioned for the servant to begin serving them.

"We're taking Lulu home with us," Travis announced. "I have changed my mind and decided that I can't live without a camel in my life. My beautiful wife has convinced me that dromedaries are essential to happiness."

Mr. Skene smiled broadly. "Splendid! I do hate to see my guests disagree. It's always best when a married couple, especially, can maintain harmony between them."

"Speaking of harmonious couples, what have you heard from the Blunts?" Travis accepted a cup of coffee from the tray held by the servant. "You remember them—Wilfred and Lady Anne?"

"Of course. They are still traveling along the Euphrates. According to the last correspondence I had from them, they were both well and had purchased several horses. They will be most unhappy to have missed you if you leave before they return."

"Too bad we can't wait for them. I would love to see the horses they've bought. I doubt they can compare with ours, but I would still like to see them. You must let them know of our success and assure them that I would be pleased to have them come visit us in America if they ever have the chance."

"I will do that," Mr. Skene said. "Coffee, Mrs. Keene?"

The servant—a youth with a wide, pleasant smile—was holding out a small brass cup to her. Steam curled up from its contents, and it smelled inviting, but old habits made her hesitate. No Bedouin woman would share coffee with a man who was still a stranger to her.

"Go on," Mr. Skene softly encouraged, as if he had

guessed her dilemma. "Take it. You aren't a Bedouin any longer. In England and America, men and women often take coffee or tea together. It's entirely proper. No one thinks a thing about it."

"Thank you." Sadira could hardly conceal her pleasure. All at once, she found herself looking forward to the great changes her new life would bring. Sofas, coffee, and . . . beds. She wanted to try a bed most of all. She hoped they might find one big enough for both her and Travis. If such a thing existed, she would put a rug on it and some large fat pillows and feel perfectly at home!

Mr. Skene raised his coffee cup and said, "Let us drink to America then. To America, to love, and to camels and horses, which apparently brought you two together."

Sadira raised the cup to her lips, and heedless of burning her tongue, drained it in a single swallow. It was delicious, and her spirits lifted as high as her hopes.

Six months to the day after they had arrived in Aleppo, Sadira got her first view of Greenbriar nestled in the gently rolling green hills of Kentucky near Lexington. It was early spring, and the flowers were just beginning to bloom, spreading a perfume over the land that rivaled lavender. It had been a long journey involving ships that made both her and Lulu seasick, trains that frightened the horses with their noise and smoke, and a long layover at a place called Saratoga Springs, which Travis had insisted was necessary to improve the health of the horses and camel before subjecting them to more travel.

He had finally managed to convince Sadira to leave the animals in the care of friends there, for he wanted to get home and check on his other horses, especially those who had foaled during his absence. Sadira had nearly refused to abandon Sherifa and Lulu, but she knew that they needed time to grow sleek and fat after the rigors of the journey. Then, too, Travis was most anxious to return to Greenbriar. The closer they had gotten, the more excited he had become. His enthusiasm helped to blunt the homesickness for the desert that sometimes swept over her.

Saratoga Springs had been a beautiful place where races were sometimes held. Travis had shown her the racetrack there, and the farm where they had briefly stayed had impressed her because all of the horses looked well groomed and well fed. She could not argue that their own animals would not be well taken care of when there was so much evidence to the contrary. Travis's friends loved their animals; even their dogs were fat and healthy, in sharp contrast to the painfully thin greyhounds usually seen in Bedouin tents.

The wife of Travis's friend, Carl, was a woman named Mildred, and Mildred had been of great help in teaching Sadira how to dress fashionably and arrange her hair so she would not feel so awkward and out of place in this strange new country. Mr. Skene's wife had started the process of her evolution into an American wife, and Mildred had completed it, not without Sadira experiencing some moments of real fear that she might have made a terrible mistake in leaving the desert. But she was here now, riding in a light, four-wheeled carriage pulled by two long-legged, shiny brown horses up a long, winding drive toward a house that looked far too grand to be her new home.

Trees with pink blossoms lined the brick-paved drive. The graceful trees scattered their fragile petals across an expanse of grass too lush to be believable. Stone fences divided the pastures or paddocks as Travis called them, of Greenbriar. Sadira had also seen white and black fences on the drive through the surrounding countryside. The paddocks held grazing mares, mares with glistening coats and dainty feet. At their sides gamboled spindly legged foals with fuzzy ears and curious eyes. Sadira was enchanted, so intent on the horses that she hardly noticed the house until the carriage rolled to a stop.

"Well, what do you think?" Travis nudged her with his elbow. "Does Greenbriar meet your expectations?"

Sadira was too overwhelmed to immediately answer. As the horses blew through their nostrils and stamped with impatience, she glanced up at the four white columns adorning the front of the building. The walls were red brick, the sparkling windows framed by black shutters, and the heavy wooden door held a great brass knocker in the shape of a horse's head. A wealth of greenery crawled across the whole of the house, partially obscuring the windows.

"I'll have to see about cutting back that ivy," Travis mused aloud, following her gaze with his own. "It's swallowing up the damn place. Jem's too busy to notice it, and my housekeeper, Cora Browne, doesn't consider outside work part of her responsibility."

"Please do not cut it back," Sadira murmured. "I think 'tis beautiful. I never realized that so much green could be found anywhere in the world."

Travis leaned over and kissed her forehead. "This isn't the desert, sweetheart, and you still haven't told me what you think of it."

" 'Tis . . . 'tis like paradise, Travis. The land is so gentle and tame, so . . . so very fertile and lovely."

"I *knew* you would like it!" Travis crowed. "And the horses will like it, too. This is perfect country for horses.

The grass is so rich it gives them all they need to grow up to be swift and strong."

"I can see that. . . . Oh, Travis! We will be happy here raising our horses! I know it now that I've seen it."

"I told you," he said smugly. "Come along now, Mrs. Keene. I'm anxious to show you the house and introduce the staff who keeps Greenbriar running while I'm off chasing around the world for horses and falling in love with pretty Bedouin girls."

The driver of the carriage, a grinning yellow-haired youth, opened the carriage door for them. "Good to have you home, Mr. Keene, sir."

"Glad to be here, Tommy." Travis stepped down, then turned to take Sadira's gloved hand. She still found it difficult to walk in the silly slippers Western women wore and to manage her voluminous skirts, which today were a deep russet color to match the feathers in her straw bonnet. She had flat-out refused to wear some of the ridiculous, confining undergarments she had been told she must endure, and in this, Travis had supported her.

"Never could understand why a woman wants to be laced into something that makes breathing so difficult," he had said, delighting her. "If you want to wear your robes and caftans when we're home alone, you can damn well do so. We'll both wear robes. After all, they're so much easier to get *under.*"

So they had easily solved the clothing problem, except that the new garments he had had made for her in Saratoga Springs continued to baffle her now and then, and she resented them when they got in her way, like now, stepping down from a carriage. Travis solved the problem by putting his hands around her waist and lifting her down, then surprised her further by suddenly picking her up again, one arm under her legs, one around her waist.

"Travis! What are you doing?" she shrieked. "Put me down."

"No, sweetheart. Here, we have the custom of carrying a bride across the threshold of her new home. So that's what I'm going to do—carry you across the threshold and right up the stairs to our bedroom."

"Grand idea, Mr. Keene, sir!" Tommy was grinning from ear to ear. "I'll just get the door for you, sir."

Sadira could feel her face reddening from embarrassment as Travis carried her up the steps to the front door, which Tommy opened with a flourish. A large, big-bosomed black woman immediately confronted them—the largest, blackest-skinned female Sadira had ever seen, a handsome woman with a cloth wound around her head, turban-style, and another cloth in her hand.

"Here now," the woman snapped. "What's goin' on here—why, it's Mr. Keene, you scoundrel! What do you mean not lettin' me know you was back in town, suh! I ought to box your ears for not sendin' me word."

"Now, Cora, don't go boxing my ears in front of my wife. She might not take kindly to it."

"Your wife! Oh, Mr. Keene, you done gone and married—at long last! Now we gonna get some babies around here. I always wanted a few to liven up this big quiet house. Oh, Missus Keene, welcome! Y'all don't know how pleased I am to meet you. We all done thought Mr. Keene was *never* gonna marry."

"I am pleased to meet you," Sadira managed to get out before Travis headed for a polished stairway with a huge glittering chandelier hanging over it.

"That's Cora Browne, my housekeeper," Travis told her

as he started up the stairway, taking them two at a time.
"You can get to know her better, after I've shown you the
master bedroom and my great big bed."

"Mr. Keene, you're a wicked, randy old stud, you are!"
Cora Browne called out to him from the foot of the stairs.
"Behavin' like a new bridegroom, an' right in front of
young Tom here."

She sounded enormously gratified, and looking past
Travis's shoulder, Sadira saw that her round black face was
shining and her eyes dancing.

"It's no worse than you do with Jem, and the two of
you have been together for years and years," Travis tossed
back to her.

"But Jem don't go pickin' me up and carryin' me up no
stairs like that. If he did, he'd break his back."

"See you later, Cora. Go tell Jem I've arrived, and I'll
be down to the barn shortly. I'll want a full report on each
and every horse and what's happened to them since I've
been gone."

"I'll tell 'im, Mr. Keene. Y'all take your time now,
y'hear?" The sound of Cora Browne's hearty laughter followed them down the hallway as Travis carried Sadira
across polished wood floors past several doors to the very
end of the hall, where he finally stopped to catch his
breath.

"Are you certain you do not want to show me the house
first, Travis? Or the horses?" Sadira asked. She gave him
a reproving look, which he ignored. "You have scandalized
and shocked your servants."

"No, I've delighted them . . . and I'm about to delight
you, dear wife."

He stepped inside a sun-splashed room, one wall of
which had tall windows overlooking the paddocks. Brass

and fine woods gleamed throughout, but what dominated the entire room was a great, huge bed with four polished wood posts set at each corner. By now, Sadira had seen beds—and slept in them—but she had never seen one like this. It was big enough for four people. Big fluffy pillows and a coverlet sewn with designs in brilliant colors lay on top of it.

Closing the door behind them with his foot, Travis carried her to the bed and gently deposited her in the very center. When she tried to sit up, he pushed her back down, so that her head sank in one of the pillows. Still not satisfied, he removed her hat and flung it across the room, then pulled out the pins in her hair, dismantling in less than a minute what had taken her half the morning to arrange.

"Don't move," he said in answer to her unasked question. "I've dreamed of you here in this bed, and now I'm finally going to get to see you here."

He combed his fingers through her hair, spreading it out on the pillow, then began to unbutton the bodice of her russet gown. She thought he must want her naked, and her fingers moved to help him. She smiled at his impatience as he spread the two halves of her bodice apart, baring her breasts, then giving a long low whistle of approval.

Next, his hands lifted her skirts to reveal her lower limbs. He stripped off her stockings and garters—foolish inventions!—and arranged her petticoats to suit him, which meant they were bunched up above her hips. He then insisted upon removing the last lace-trimmed bit of cloth concealing her femininity.

"Now, just lie back, sweetheart," he instructed. "And let me enjoy what a fetching picture you make. . . . Open your legs a bit, will you? There, that's it!"

"Travis!" she cried, simultaneously shocked and excited. "This is . . . this is . . ."

"Decadent? Arousing? Oh, yes . . . but not obscene." He worked on his own clothes while he talked. "I've tortured myself with visions of you lying just like that, waiting for me, unashamed of your beauty . . . looking like a ripe peach and eagerly anticipating our lovemaking."

"But this is the middle of the day, and we have only just arrived!"

He had half his garments off now—all the proper, stiff, ridiculous garments of a gentleman. He had discarded enough that she could plainly see the evidence of his arousal stretching the fabric of his trousers.

"I ache for you, Sadira. I ache for you right here." His hand brushed across his bulging groin. "Show me where you ache for me—if you do ache, that is."

She did, covering herself with her hand as he had done. "Here, Travis." Then she moved her hand to her heart. "And here also . . . both places."

"Then we had better soothe these aching parts before we do anything else, hadn't we? We need to make certain this bed suits us for our . . . ah, most intimate and strenuous activities."

She was sure it would. After making love on sand, stony ground, in narrow ship cabins, and on other beds that were small and lumpy, making love in this big bed would surely be wonderful.

"I know it will suit me, Travis. Greenbriar suits me. I haven't been here very long, but already it feels like home . . . well, almost anyway."

"Almost?" he queried, moving closer and unfastening his trousers.

She reached for him. "I need you, Travis. I need you now. Hurry and come into me."

He joined her on the wide bed, and very soon, the big bed in the big bedroom at Greenbriar did feel like home, the home she had never really had.

Twenty-four

Greenbriar, Kentucky, Three Months Later

It was early evening, and Sadira and Cora were standing on the front porch overlooking the vast lawn. "Does it look all right, Cora? Tell me what you think."

Sadira motioned to the results of weeks of effort in preparation for Travis's party to introduce both her and his newly arrived horses to Lexington society. She and Cora, along with everyone else at Greenbriar, had been working day and night to complete the arrangements that Sadira had planned down to the tiniest detail. Within the hour, the guests would be arriving, and suddenly, she wished she had not attempted to recreate a typical Arabian feast from the land of the Bedouin.

At first, it had seemed so perfect; she would set up tents on the lawn and furnish them with rugs and pillows, then provide traditional foods. Travis had added his own ideas—oil lamps and stone-ringed fires to light the night, servants preparing hot, sweet coffee and serving it in tiny cups, he and Sadira dressed in elegant versions of desert robes, he in a *keffiya,* she in a veil, the servants garbed like Bedouin tribesmen and their wives.

"What better way to introduce our beautiful horses than to give them the proper setting?" Travis had asked. "And in what better manner could I show off my wife's incredible beauty than to let my friends see her as I first saw her?"

Yes, it had seemed like such a good idea a month ago. Now, it seemed risky and foolish. What if everyone laughed at her and criticized her Bedouin ways? Sadira had never been so nervous, not even when she faced the *Shammar.* Then she had abandoned herself to fate and given up hope; now, she wanted more than anything to please Travis and not shame him in front of the people he had known all his life.

"Cora?" The woman's name came out sounding like a plea, which it was. Cora had not said anything, and Sadira feared it was because she, too, realized that they had made a mistake.

"Oh, Miz Keene! You done created a fairy tale! It takes mah breath away. In all my borned days I never seen the like of this." Cora picked up the hem of her caftan and walked over to the nearest tent. It was not made of goatskin like the real thing, nor was it black, but in size and shape, it resembled a Bedouin tent. This particular one had been fashioned out of a pink and green-striped fabric that Travis had assured Sadira would be charming. Cora stuck her head inside the tent and chuckled.

"Oh, my! Nothin' but big fat pillows to sit on. Evahbody gonna be talkin' 'bout this here party for years t' come. It's . . . it's like steppin' right into the desert, jus' the way you and Mr. Keene described it."

"Oh, but Kentucky is not at all like the desert. And these tents are not absolutely authentic. I am afraid they look . . . out of place. And so do we."

"Not t' me, they don't, and we don't either. I like this here gown." Cora swished her pretty lemon-colored caftan. "It's cool and comfortable. Can't wait to put on that veil

that covers my face. Ain't nobody gonna recognize me as
Mr. Keene's old housekeeper."

Sadira doubted that anyone could mistake Cora. She had
a presence that even a *burqa* could not hide. "You don't
think the guests will object to sitting on pillows, or eating
with their fingers from a common platter?"

"Well, now, Miz Keene, I do think you oughta let 'em
use forks and knives and little dishes to eat their lamb an'
rice, but it's *your* party, so whatever you decide is fine with
me. That's the way we'll serve it."

"Perhaps I should relent on the silverware and dishes.
Oh, I don't know! I'll have to ask Travis."

"Ask me what?" Travis came up behind her and slipped
his arms around her waist.

"Oh, Mr. Keene!" Cora exclaimed. "I almost didn't recognize you. Y'all looks like a handsome sheik in that getup.
That there robe and the cloth on your head is more be-
comin' than I would have thought possible if I hadn't seed
it with my own eyes."

Sadira turned around to get a better look at her husband.
She inhaled sharply. He *did* look handsome tonight and
exactly like a desert sheik, except for his blue eyes. A wave
of nostalgia swept her as she remembered Akbar's fierce
majesty; her father was the only other man who could compare to Travis in his desert robe and *keffiya*. For a moment,
she couldn't remember what she was going to ask him,
until he reminded her.

"You were saying . . ."

"Silverware! I was going to ask you if we should let
our guests use silverware and individual plates when they
eat."

"Absolutely not." Travis's blue eyes were grave, but
Sadira thought she detected a devilish twinkle in them. "I

was rather looking forward to watching everyone try to be polite about sucking lamb's grease from their fingers."

"They're supposed to use the unleavened bread Cora and I made to sop up the gravy. . . . Oh, Cora, we had better offer them the choice of using eating utensils, at least. If one of the ladies should drip lamb's grease down the front of her gown . . ."

"Stop worrying," Travis scolded. "Everything's going to be fine. There will be no disasters, I guarantee it. How can there be when you've worked so hard to make everything perfect? The only thing that needs to be done now is for you to change your clothes. It's getting late. You'd better hurry."

"Yes, suh, Miz Keene," Cora chimed in. "You go on upstairs and git ready. I'll take care of things down here, startin' with findin' Jem and makin' sure he's got hisself dressed and ready."

As Cora started off across the lawn, Travis bent closer. "I could come up with you. In case you need my help dressing—or undressing."

Sadira could just imagine what sort of help he would be. If he had his way, his guests would be arriving, and the two of them would still be up in bed *un*dressed. "No, no, Travis. You stay here. I will not be gone long."

He shook his head in disappointment, then gave her an indulgent smile. "All right. If you insist. . . . Oh, wait! I almost forgot." He reached inside his robe and extracted a folded sheet of paper. "Guess what this is?"

Sadira had no idea. "What?"

"It's a letter from the Blunts, the couple I told you about—the one I met when I first arrived at Aleppo."

"The couple who, like you, was looking for horses."

Travis nodded. "They found five good horses and are going to establish a stud in Egypt."

"In Egypt! Why there? I thought they had a breeding farm in England."

"Oh, they do, but the Egyptian operation will concentrate solely on breeding Arabian horses. They'll take the horses back to England eventually, but they intend to maintain two places, and they want us to come visit one or the other from time to time. Right now, they're searching for knowledgeable people to help staff and run the Egyptian operation, which will be a base from which they can continue their search for the best Arabian breeding stock."

"Oh, I should love to visit Egypt!"

Travis grinned. "I thought you might—particularly since it's in such a familiar part of the world. Lady Anne says they have many fine horses there. We might go with the idea of purchasing one or two to complement our own breeding program." He lightly caressed Sadira's cheek. "A trip like that might do wonders to cure your homesickness."

She blushed. "I am not homesick anymore. . . . Well, perhaps a little. Tonight, I may be. All of this . . ."—she waved a hand to encompass the tents—". . . reminds me of desert life and some of the things I miss about it."

"I miss a few things myself. I'm looking forward to seeing you in that embroidered silk robe and veil I had made for you. You'll be the most beautiful woman here tonight, sweetheart, and Lexington is known for its beautiful women, half of whom will be attending just to get a good look at you."

Sadira smiled ruefully. "I hope we have not made a mistake doing this, Travis. Perhaps I should dress like everyone else, so I will not seem so different."

"It's too late to back out now." Travis took her hands

and squeezed them. "A sheik needs his favorite wife, you know."

"His *only* wife," Sadira corrected. "I am glad American men do not have harems. I do not wish to share you, Travis Colin Keene. That is one Bedouin custom I do not miss."

He brushed a kiss across her lips. "Run along now, and take your time dressing. Don't worry if the guests start arriving, and you aren't ready. A late entrance will help build suspense—since you're the main attraction of this party."

"I thought the horses were the main attraction—not I!"

"Oh, they are, but so are you. I'll wait to start taking people on a tour of the stable and paddocks until you make your appearance; I only plan to do it in small groups. I don't want to upset the mares with a huge crowd traipsing through the barn all at once."

"Whatever you think best, Travis." She smiled with as much bravery as she could muster.

"And now, ladies and gentlemen, I should like to present my lovely wife who made possible everything you've been enjoying this evening." Travis held out his hand to Sadira who stood off to one side. She was a vision of shy loveliness and grace in her exquisite silk robe and veil. He had chosen the right color for her. The garments were the hue of eggshells and embroidered at sleeve and hem with gold threads, a perfect foil for *her* unique coloring.

Sadira walked toward him smiling, flushed but happy, and entwined her fingers in his. The evening had been a resounding success. Everyone had exclaimed over the beauty of the horses, the charm of the dinner arrangements, the deliciousness of the feast, and the marvel of Sadira herself. The men had been fawning over her and the women gushing; Travis had no doubt she was now accepted into the fold of Lexington's elite horse-breeding families. Even Elizabeth, who had had the audacity to show up uninvited, had gone out of her way to compliment him. Elizabeth had driven her own carriage but walked in with the Blairs, old friends of Travis's family, making it difficult for him to be anything but cordial to her.

After seeing the look of surprise on his face, Leticia Blair had apologized for the awkwardness of the moment. She had thought that he and Elizabeth had long since resumed speaking to each other; apparently Elizabeth had not told the Blairs that she hadn't seen Travis since the day she tossed his ring onto the racetrack. Still unmarried, Elizabeth was as stunning as Travis remembered, but seeing her again did not move him one way or the other. He felt neither anger nor pleasure. She might have been a potted plant for all she stirred his emotions.

Sadira, on the other hand, had only to glance his way, and he felt the impact in his very soul: He was so proud of her! No other woman at the party could compete with her for sheer poise and elegance. Her simple desert garb contrasted sharply with the ruffles, bows, and lace of the other women. She was beautiful in the same natural way as a flower, a cloud, or an Arabian horse. She needed no cosmetics, jewels, fancy undergarments, or hairstyle. Beneath her wispy veil, her hair flowed down her back without a single comb or pin to confine it; its only adornment was the shining gold streak down the center.

She had not lined her eyes with kohl, but they shone like emeralds. Her cheeks and lips glowed with healthy color, requiring no assistance from paint pots. Travis thought he must be the envy of every man at the party as he watched her nod in acknowledgment of the applause from the onlookers. They were applauding her outward beauty and accomplishments, but the inner woman was even more beautiful. In time, as they got to know her better, his friends would come to appreciate Sadira in her entirety; tonight was just the beginning.

"Sadira and I wish to thank you for coming tonight. We are delighted to have you here. The night is young yet, so please relax and continue to enjoy yourselves. Try the coffee if you haven't yet had some; if you prefer something stronger, you'll find it in the house in my study. There's also tea available in the parlor, and more of those delectable Eastern pastries. No one can have too many pastries."

"Hey, Travis!" a man called out. "Don't the men in those desert countries ever sneak a taste of good Kentucky bourbon when their wives aren't looking? Or is coffee all they ever drink?"

"Well, now . . ." Travis thought a moment. "There's camel's milk and *lebben*."

"What's *lebben?*"

"*Sour* camel's milk, I believe. Or maybe it's goat milk, I can't remember."

The gathering erupted into laughter. In the midst of the general hilarity, elderly Mrs. Agnes Worthington tottered over to Travis and wrapped her fingers around Sadira's arm. "Your cushions and rugs are an intriguing idea, young woman, but we old folks with our rheumatism would appreciate a good old American chair."

"Do forgive me!" Sadira looked stricken. "I should have thought of that myself. I'll have a servant fetch one for you."

"Don't bother. I'd prefer going up to the house. This night air is bad for my swollen joints. Hope you don't mind, but I think I'll join a few of the other ladies I saw heading toward the parlor."

"I'll take you there," Sadira offered. "Travis, please excuse us."

"Certainly, sweetheart. You and Mrs. Worthington go right ahead. I'm going down to the stables with a couple of the late arrivals who haven't had a chance to see the horses."

"I'll join you there in a bit. I want to check on Sherifa. I don't think she's forgiven me for leaving her so long at Saratoga Springs with your friends."

"Maybe not, but it did her good. She's looking better now than she did after that long sea voyage," Travis pointed out. "She's got some meat back on her bones."

He watched Sadira depart with the white-haired old lady. The Worthingtons were one of the most respected families in Lexington. If Mrs. Worthington took Sadira under her wing, his wife's acceptance in the highest level of bluegrass society would be assured—not that such acceptance mattered that much to him, but he suspected that Sadira would be devastated if his so-called friends and acquaintances rejected her.

"Now then, my dear," he heard the old woman say. "How and where exactly did you meet our dear Travis?"

"On the desert," Sadira answered. "I met him on the desert where he had come to buy horses. Unfortunately, when he first arrived, he was set upon by robbers."

"Robbers! Dear me. You must tell me all about it."

Travis debated whether or not he ought to rescue Sadira from the inquisitive Mrs. Worthington, instead of sending her off to the lion's den. He decided against it. Sadira could handle the old busybody's curiosity. They had already discussed what they would tell people about her past. They would reveal very little except the bare facts: They had met and married in the desert, where he had gone to purchase horses from Sadira's father, the sheik of the *Ruala*.

Sadira settled Mrs. Worthington in a chair in the parlor where a number of the ladies had already gathered.

"How many wives did you say your father had?" Mrs. Worthington inquired, and suddenly, the feminine chatter stopped, and it grew very quiet.

Sadira regretted that she had let slip more than she had planned, but on the way into the house, Mrs. Worthington had demonstrated an astonishing ability to obtain information Sadira had not intended to reveal.

"He had seven wives altogether, but only four at any one time," she answered. "His favorite was his first wife, Alima. When he died, he had only three—Alima, Jaleel, and Jahara."

"What happened to the others?" asked a lovely blond woman in a gown the color of the lilacs that had recently bloomed down near the stable.

"One died in childbirth, another of an ailment of the liver, and two he divorced."

"Divorced? They have divorce in that part of the world? Your people actually believe a married couple may end their marriage?" The blond woman's expression revealed an intensity of interest that surprised Sadira. She wished she could remember the woman's name and to whom she was married, *if* she was married.

Sadira nodded. "It is not common, but if a husband and wife can find no happiness together, a man may divorce his wife by repeating three times in succession, 'I divorce thee,' and the woman is then free to return to her family."

"That's it—just 'I divorce thee?' "

"Yes." Sadira sought to change the subject. "Is there anything else you ladies would like—more tea or coffee perhaps?"

"No, no . . . we've all had more than enough," the blond woman replied for everyone. "We'd much rather hear more about your fascinating customs. I had no idea divorce was so easy. If Travis wanted to be rid of you, is that all he would have to do—say 'I divorce thee' three times?"

"Elizabeth! What a question!" Mrs. Worthington scolded. "I'm sure Travis has no intention of divorcing Sadira. Anyone can see he dotes on her; they make a wonderful match."

The blond woman—Elizabeth—looked unrepentant. "I'm only curious, Agnes, that's all. I certainly meant no harm, nor do I have any personal interest in the matter. Why, what happened between Travis and me ended long ago!"

Something had happened between Travis and this woman? Sadira narrowed her eyes and closely examined Elizabeth. The blond was indeed a ravishing creature in her lilac-colored gown that revealed more of her voluptuous figure than seemed proper to Sadira. She would stand out anywhere with her creamy complexion and golden curls—not just a streak of color but a luxurious mass of silky-looking hair. However, the slant of her mouth suggested that she was given to pouting; here might be another Jaleel—a woman of great attractiveness but one who possessed a meanness of spirit.

Sadira decided it would be better to confront this potential enemy right away than to let her stir up trouble as Jaleel had always tried to do. "What *did* happen between you and my husband?" she bluntly inquired.

Every woman in the room—there were at least ten females—inhaled sharply. Eyes widened. Tongues moistened lips. Sadira realized she might have been wrong to challenge Elizabeth, but it was too late to back down now.

Elizabeth straightened; she was sitting in a chair near the open window, through which the sounds of the party still going on outside could be heard. Those sounds were magnified in the expectant hush following Sadira's question.

"I was his fiancée, the woman he intended to marry. We had a foolish argument—nothing serious, mind you—but he went off to Arabia to look for horses before we had resolved the matter. No one was more surprised than I to learn that he had brought back a wife, especially a foreigner. A man in Travis's position needs someone to help further his ambitions, not stand in the way of them."

"I do not intend to stand in the way of them." Sadira lifted her chin. "Travis and I share the same dream, the same ambitions. We both want Greenbriar horses to be the very best—successful on the racetrack and sought after by other breeders. If you have seen the horses we brought back with us, you cannot doubt they will improve the bloodlines of the horses Travis already possesses."

"I haven't seen them yet, but I've heard that they are small and fine-boned, with muzzles so tiny that one could easily fit inside a teacup. I can't imagine how such horses could do anything but weaken Travis's breeding program."

"Elizabeth!" Mrs. Worthington exclaimed, and a murmur of shock—or agreement?—ran through the gathering.

"Well, it's true." Elizabeth shrugged off the older woman's reprimand and glanced at the other ladies as if for support. "Poor Travis isn't thinking properly. No doubt he's been blinded by the demands of his . . . his lower appetites. I can tell you from experience that they are formidable. Once he gets over his infatuation with the unusual, he will realize he's made a terrible mistake—both in his choice for a wife and in his horses. While it's all very amusing to sit on the ground and eat with one's fingers, I suspect that doing it everyday will cease to charm after a time."

"We do not do this everyday," Sadira protested, stung because the comments echoed her own deepest fears, that Travis *would* realize his error in choosing to marry her. And he *did* have formidable lower appetites, as she well knew. . . . Just how much of Travis's appetites had this woman experienced?

"I find Bedouin customs *most* amusing." Mrs. Worthington was glaring at Elizabeth, but now turned to Sadira with a grim, determined smile. "And I should adore another one of your Eastern delicacies, my dear. Do you suppose you might fetch me another cup of coffee and one of those pastries?"

"Of course," Sadira agreed, glad of a chance to escape the measuring looks of the women seated in her parlor. Some were sympathetic, but most appeared to agree with the beautiful blond woman. Even the sympathetic ones appeared less critical of what had been said than the fact that Elizabeth had dared to say it. Obviously, they had all been thinking the same thing.

Her face flaming, Sadira kept her head held high as she exited the room. She walked partway down the hall, then stopped. Sure enough, as soon as the women thought she was out of earshot, they all began talking at once.

"Elizabeth! You should be ashamed . . . !"

"Why should I be? *She's* the interloper—the one who stole Travis right from under my nose. Everyone *knows* we were going to marry. All we had was a trifling argument, and she took advantage of it."

"You're right about one thing, Elizabeth. Travis will

wake up one of these days and realize he's made a fool of himself."

"I think she's very beautiful. *Any* man might have his head turned by her."

"But to go and *marry* her! Really, my dear, that's going a bit far, don't you think?"

"Did anyone hear the details? What sort of wedding did they have?"

"Maybe they didn't have an actual wedding—not as we know it. Maybe he traded something for her; isn't that how men obtain a woman's services in that part of the world? Gentleman that Travis is, he probably just brought her home with him."

"I bet he bought her for the price of a few camels. I seem to recall reading somewhere that that's how they do it over there—they pay for their wives with camels."

"Do you think they're even legally married? Just because a man marries a foreign woman in her own country doesn't mean it's considered binding over here."

"What do you think of that getup she's wearing? Pretty, I suppose, but very odd—like she is. Where do you suppose she got that streak of blond hair and those green eyes? . . . And how did she learn to speak English so well?"

"Oh, I imagine Travis taught her *that,* among other things. Too bad he didn't teach her American ways while he was at it. Aside from the meal itself, which was certainly passable, I find it rather scandalous to eat one's dinner while lounging about on pillows. It's a very suggestive situation, don't you think?"

"But that's how people actually live in that part of the world, in tents. And to think they drink camel's milk—ugh! How disgusting."

The comments went on and on, until Sadira could bear no more. Picking up the hem of her robe, she ran for the stairway and went racing up to her and Travis's bedroom and their wide, comforting bed. Maybe, instead of visiting the Blunts, she ought to join them. Travis had said they were looking for staff to care for and train their horses. Who could be better for the job than the former Keeper of the Mares of the *Ruala*? At least, she would be back where she belonged—or closer to it, anyway. And she could never be accused of ruining Travis's entire life.

Yes, she had better think seriously of returning to the East, to work for the Blunts or for whomever else would take an outcast Bedouin woman. She had been a fool to think she could ever fit into Travis's world. He would be much better off with the beautiful Elizabeth.

Twenty-five

Sadira lay on the bed fighting tears. She was hurt and angry—and not a little jealous of the blond woman and the relationship she had apparently had with Travis. Then she remembered that plain Alima had won and held Akbar's love, not the pretty peacock, Jaleel. She had no reason to fear Elizabeth; Travis had chosen *her* over everything Elizabeth represented. She was the one who would share this bed with Travis tonight and every night. Travis did not harbor any warm feelings for the woman he had almost married; if anything, that relationship had nearly soured him on *all* women.

Sadira sat up and determinedly wiped the dampness from her cheeks. She had been wrong to hope that winning Travis's friends might be easy; clearly, it would be difficult, but that did not mean she was doomed to failure. Most of the women's comments indicated ignorance, not malice. They were curious, and in the manner of women everywhere, *could* be malicious if given half a chance—only she would not give them any chance. She would answer all their questions honestly and without taking offense. She would smile and keep smiling, until the good-hearted among them accepted her as a friend. The rest she did not care about; they were unworthy of friendship, and she would not allow them to cause her a moment's suffering, no more than she had allowed Jaleel to destroy her serenity. If none of them wanted to be her friend, she could accept that, too. She had lived before on the fringes of society, on the outside looking in, and she could do so again. Only this time, she had Travis, and that was all that really counted.

Feeling much better, she rose from the bed, went to the large mirror that hung over the cherrywood dresser, and made some adjustments to her appearance. When she was satisfied that no trace of her distress showed upon her face, she left the room, descended the stairs, and fetched the pastries she had promised Mrs. Worthington. By the time she re-entered the parlor, several of the ladies had left— Elizabeth among them.

"Oh, they went down to the stable, I believe." Mrs. Worthington waved a hand as if to add that their presence would not be missed. "Set that down, my dear, and come sit beside me. Those of us still here would love to hear more about your Bedouin customs. You must not mind Elizabeth; she is still kicking herself in the behind for behaving like such a fool in regards to your husband. I'm sure Travis must have told you that he and Elizabeth were once engaged to be married."

"Yes, he told me, but . . . kicking herself in the behind? I have never heard such an expression."

"A figure of speech, my dear, meaning that she regrets she tossed away her one and only chance to become Mrs. Travis Colin Keene. She overplayed her hand, you see— grew too confident and attempted to reorder Travis's priorities. I think she's forgotten that she told me all about it once. She thought he actually preferred dancing attendance on her to mucking about with horses."

"Overplayed her hand? Dancing attendance? Forgive me,

but you must explain. I understand English perfectly well, but these phrases are new to me."

"Dear me! I can see we have much to teach you—as well as to learn from you. Now sit down and tell me about . . . camels. I have a great curiosity about camels, and I understand you brought one of the beasts back to Kentucky with you."

"Yes . . . Lulu. All right, I will tell you everything I know about camels."

Sadira spent a pleasant hour or more in the parlor with Agnes Worthington and the remaining ladies, and she discovered that she had been right about the majority of these women. They were not malicious, only uninformed. She told them not only about camels, but about desert life and how Bedouin women lived—constantly on the move, raising and lowering tents, having babies and running after children, baking bread, milking goats and doing all the work themselves if they were too poor to possess slaves or servants. The more the women learned, the more they wanted to hear, and the more they identified with certain aspects of Bedouin life.

"Gracious sakes, it sounds as if women everywhere have some of the same problems—how and what to feed their hungry families, keeping things clean—only Bedouin women have it worse than most," declared a plump, friendly-looking lady named Hortense.

"At least they do not have to wear garments that squeeze in their waists and push out their bosoms so they begin to look like odd-shaped gourds," Sadira responded.

Every woman in the room stared at her blankly, and finally, one of them said, "Do you mean corsets?"

"Yes, corsets. I do not understand how you can put up with them. They are instruments of torture."

"Do I look like an odd-shaped gourd? I suppose I do," said Hortense. "And so do you, Martha. You look exactly like a squash."

"Well, if I am a squash, you are a . . . a watermelon. *Two* watermelons, one on top and one on the bottom."

"Then I must be a cucumber! With only a small dent in the middle no matter how tightly I lace my corset," piped up a third, a tall thin woman.

As the women burst out laughing, it seemed as good a time as any for Sadira to excuse herself. "Forgive me, ladies, but I ought to go outside and check on my other guests."

"Of course, my dear." Agnes Worthington waved her off. "You are an excellent hostess, a fine asset to your husband. Do not let anyone tell you differently."

"Thank you, I will not." Sadira picked up the empty tray—all the pastries were now gone—and departed. Halfway down the hall, she again stopped to listen.

"She's not so bad, after all, even if she is a foreigner. Travis could have done far worse picking out his new bride."

"I agree. Why, listening to her is much more entertaining than listening to Elizabeth gossip about whichever of us isn't present to hear her. I'd say Travis made himself an excellent match."

"Tents and all, she served a fine feast. I can't wait to see what she comes up with next time she entertains. I am quite looking forward to it—assuming I am invited, that is."

"Me, too."

"Well, she's right about corsets anyway—mine is killing me."

Sadira had heard enough to know that the tide of battle

had turned in her direction. She hurried from the house feeling as if she could fly. Outside, the tents glowed softly, illuminating the darkness, and people lounged inside them, or strolled from one tent to another, laughing and talking. They seemed in no hurry to leave, and Sadira knew then that the party was a huge success. She searched for Travis, but did not spot his tall, unmistakable figure anywhere. However, she did see Cora and quickly waylaid her.

"Cora, do you know where my husband has gone?"

"Saw him headed toward the stable, Miz Keene. Might be good you went after him, 'cause he didn't look too happy. Miz Lizbeth Covington, a lady he used to know real well, was hangin' on his arm and givin' him an earful 'bout something. Here, give me dat tray. I'm goin' back in the kitchen anyway."

Sadira could just imagine what Elizabeth was saying to Travis. Handing Cora the tray, she picked up her skirts and hurried across the lawn toward the barn.

"Really, Travis, you call this horse a stallion? Why, he's barely big enough to mount a tall, leggy Thoroughbred. And those mares you brought back are pitiful things— pretty about their heads, but entirely unremarkable otherwise." Elizabeth moved on to the next stall down the aisle and peered inside it. "Take this one, for instance. Her color is nice, and her face is sweet, but I can't imagine she has much speed. Her legs are just too short; goodness, are her pasterns the right angle? I can't see very well in this poor light."

On a convenient hook overlooking the stall, Travis hung the lantern he had been carrying. He was making a great effort to restrain himself; all he really wanted to do was grab Elizabeth by the neck and throttle her for her stupidity and arrogance. He reminded himself that he would probably be seeing her at every race and breed sale. Not only that, but her family's opinion mattered a great deal to some people. Therefore, he should be glad of this chance to establish a new relationship with her—a polite business association that might relieve the unpleasant awkwardness between them and work to their mutual advantage. Somewhat belatedly, it occurred to him that perhaps he ought not to have agreed to come down to the stable alone with her. Because of their well-known past, people might gossip . . . but it was too late now to worry about gossip.

He sighed wearily as he turned to her. "Bachir, the stallion you were just maligning, is indeed big enough to mount anything that's put in front of him. He's fast and has plenty of stamina, which my much vaunted Thoroughbreds sadly lack. As for the mare you're looking at now, her name is Sherifa, and she's one of the finest you'll see anywhere in the world. She can go for miles on a mouthful of camel's milk and never get tired. I've seen her exist on nothing but thorns and salt grass for over a week and show no ill effects from the deprivation. When she moves, she's a piece of music written by the finest composer . . . and she can gallop over the worst sort of ground imaginable and never put a foot wrong."

"My, my. . . . What did you have to do to obtain this paragon of equine virtues—marry a Bedouin?" Elizabeth's eyes glinted with contempt. "It could not have been easy to persuade her owner to part with her. You must have had to offer *some*thing, Travis dear. Was Sadira the daughter some old sheik demanded that you marry in payment?"

Travis gritted his teeth. He probably should have refused to show Elizabeth the horses, but he had hoped to force her to admit she was wrong—and had been wrong all along about the Darley Arabian. The horses he and Sadira had brought home were magnificent examples of the best traits of the Darley strain; he had thought that once Elizabeth had seen them she was horsewoman enough to realize their value. But she wasn't horsewoman enough; she was nothing but a jealous harridan, and she could criticize his horses all she wanted from now on. In time, they would prove their worth to everyone.

"Sherifa belongs to Sadira, and I didn't have to offer anything to get either of them," he said evenly. "Let's go back to the party, Elizabeth. I'm sorry I agreed to bring you down to the stable. Obviously, you haven't the eye for fine horseflesh I always believed you did, even when I didn't agree with you on breeding matters."

"Oh no, Travis!" Elizabeth caught the sleeve of his robe. "We're not going anywhere until you tell me how you could possibly have married that . . . that little goat-herder when you could have had me."

"Maybe it's because I grew to love her and because she and I have more in common than you and I ever did."

"What do you mean by that?" Elizabeth's eyes flashed with fury. "I am everything she is not. I'm one of your own kind, Travis. I grew up here, and I know these people. I know this world. I wouldn't embarrass you by doing or saying foolish things . . . by arranging silly parties where the guests have to sit on the ground and eat strange foods with their fingers. I would have made the perfect wife for you—you can ask anyone."

"There's more to marriage than knowing how to entertain properly, Elizabeth. Besides, I thought our party went rather well tonight. It's still going well, as a matter-of-fact—and had you wanted silverware, we *did* provide it for the less adventuresome types like yourself."

"It's a disaster, and you know it! Why, the women are even speculating as to whether or not you're legitimately married. If you are, which I doubt, it would be easy to undo it. Since she's a Bedouin, all you have to do is say 'I divorce thee' three times, and she'll think it's over. In her country, it *would* be."

Travis was taken aback. "Did Sadira tell you that?"

"She must have or how else would I know it? You've made a mistake, Travis. Why won't you admit it? I made one, too, when I tossed your ring over that railing. Later, I felt so badly about it that I hired three little black boys to rake the track near there and see if they could find it."

"Did they?" Travis coldly inquired.

"No, they didn't, and I cried for a week after you left for Arabia. I knew I'd been foolish, you see, and I waited all this time for you to come home so I could apologize and tell you how wrong I was."

"You were wrong, Elizabeth, but so was I. I never should have asked you to marry me in the first place, because I really didn't love you, and you didn't love me. I *lusted* after you, but that isn't the same as love and certainly not a good enough reason for marriage."

"Oh, but lust must have played a big part in your marriage to Sadira!" Elizabeth shot back. "Why else would you have married her if it wasn't for lust or to get her horse? She's not the sort of woman you could love, Travis. She's just too different—too odd. You're a Kentuckian, born and bred, and Greenbriar means everything to you. It makes no sense that you would jeopardize your whole future by marrying outside your class!"

Tested past his endurance, Travis seized Elizabeth by the

shoulders. "Where do you get these ideas, Elizabeth? How do you come by your conceit and snobbery? I happen to think Sadira's done a wonderful job as my hostess tonight, and our party's a grand success. But even if it wasn't, even if she were a social outcast, I would still love her. We would still have a good, satisfying life together, which is more than I can say you and I would have had no matter how many great parties you managed to give."

"Then it must be lust that holds you to her. What can she do that I can't? If it's lust you want, I can give you *lust.*" Red-faced and wild-eyed, Elizabeth began to tear at her bodice.

Horrified, Travis let go of her shoulders and grabbed her hands, but only succeeded in tearing the delicate fabric. Her gown ripped straight down the front, and Elizabeth's large breasts protruded through the gaping hole. As she struggled, her situation worsened, until she was all but half naked, and her hair had tumbled down around her shoulders.

"Elizabeth!" Travis let go of her and took a step backward, but Elizabeth launched herself in his direction and flung her arms around his neck.

"Travis, please! I am begging you. Divorce her and give me a chance. She doesn't belong here at Greenbriar, and I do! We've known each other for years and years, since we were children. . . . Please, Travis!" She began to sob and clung to him so tightly he could not immediately free himself.

At last, he was able to set her away from him, but she was still sobbing, and he didn't know what to do. He couldn't very well go off and leave her in this state, but neither did he want to remain. If someone suddenly came into the barn and saw them like this, it would create a scandal and totally ruin everything he and Sadira had tried so hard to achieve tonight. Elizabeth was entirely capable of accusing him of having torn her gown; any woman who would toss an irreplaceable heirloom ring onto a racetrack was capable of anything.

"Elizabeth, stop sniveling and try to get control of yourself," he counseled. "Before someone comes into the barn and sees you like this."

"Someone has already come," a voice said from the far end of the stable aisle.

Travis turned to see Sadira standing in the wavering light of a second lantern hung farther down the aisle. Elizabeth saw Sadira at the same time and immediately stepped closer to Travis.

"So you caught us!" she muttered hoarsely. "Well, I don't care if you did. Travis did this to me, and I'm glad of it. If you hadn't come along just now, he would have done far more."

"That's a lie, Elizabeth. . . . Sadira, she did it to herself." Travis edged away from the distraught blond whose eyes were glittering exactly as they had when she tossed his ring over the railing.

"I know, Travis," Sadira said calmly, moving toward him. She gave him a smile that said everything was all right between them, and he wanted to shout with relief. He nearly did shout when she added, "I saw and heard everything."

"Liar!" Elizabeth spat behind him. "You're just saying that to protect him—and yourself. You didn't see anything. He was overcome with passion, and he was . . . he was going to *rape* me. He tore my gown. A woman certainly doesn't go around tearing her own gown."

"You did. I saw you," Sadira disputed in the same reasonable tone. "And if you say a word about this to anyone, I will tell them exactly what you were trying to do—seduce my husband. Win him away from me. Your reputation will be ruined, Elizabeth."

"You wouldn't do that!"

"Oh, yes, I would. Or else you could stay here a few moments while Travis and I go back to the house. I'm sure I have a wrap there you could borrow. You can wear it home tonight. It will adequately cover you; you can say you were feeling chilled, and I lent it to you for the journey home. You *are* going home in any case, Elizabeth."

Elizabeth lifted her head and gazed at them haughtily. "Bring the wrap then. I'll wait here for it."

Sadira took Travis's arm, and they left the barn together. Once outside, Travis pulled his wife into the shadows beneath the huge lilac bushes growing nearby. "Sweetheart, I'm sorry you had to see all that." He took her in his arms. "But I'm glad you did see it. If you had not, if you had come a little later, she might have convinced you I was trying to attack her—or that we were in the throes of mutual desire."

"You do not desire her, do you, Travis? She is very beautiful, and as she claims, she is one of your own kind." Sadira gazed up at him, asking for reassurance but also trusting him. Despite the darkness, he could see the love and trust shining in her eyes.

"I'm already holding the only woman I'll ever desire," he murmured. "And whatever kind *she* is, is the kind I want."

"Oh, Travis! I admit I have had my doubts." Sadira hugged him, her body sweet, warm, and supple in his arms, fitting perfectly, offering all he had ever wanted. "I have been afraid I might be too different to fit in here. I have worried you might come to regret marrying me."

"I *never* will, but what about you? Will you have regrets?" Travis stroked her back and hips. "Will you grow to miss your desert too much? I've worried about that."

"Home is where you are, Travis. I thought you knew that by now. If I do miss it too much, we can go and visit the Blunts, as you suggested. I do miss the lavender when it blooms, filling the air with fragrance and painting the land purple for as far as the eye can see."

"We'll witness the blooming of the lavender again, sweetheart. I promise you. We'll go all the way back to Syria to find it, if we have to."

"Travis!" Sadira's eyes widened as she gazed past his shoulder, and her voice held a note of panic.

He turned to see what had alarmed her, and a bolt of fear shafted his own heart: Through the wide open door of the stable aisle, he could see smoke and the glow of flames licking at hay and straw. He heard the anxious whinny of a horse and then Sadira's frantic cry.

"The horses! Travis, the horses!" She was off and running before he had barely had time to react.

He sprinted after her. "Sadira, ring the big bell on the post in front of the stable. I'll start getting the horses out. Ring the bell for all you're worth, because we're going to need help. Our guests are all experienced horse people, and they'll know what to do."

She veered off to do as he had told her, and Travis tore at the sleeve of his robe until it came off. On his way into the stable, he quickly dunked it in the water trough standing outside, then tied the strip of cloth over his mouth and nose. He knew the danger of fire; every horse breeder did. It was his worst fear, his greatest nightmare. Fortunately, most of his Thoroughbreds were turned out in the paddocks, but all of the Arabians were stalled in the barn—in the very section near the end of the aisle where the flames were the worst. It had to be one of the lanterns that had started it—and the only person who had been in there alone with the lanterns was Elizabeth.

Twenty-six

The ringing of the bell brought everyone racing to the barn to help put out the fire. As soon as Sadira saw that assistance was on its way, she wrapped her veil around her face and joined Travis inside the smoky barn. One wall was already ablaze, the heat intense as greedy flames consumed the straw stacked along that wall. On the other side of the aisle, the horses were neighing and stamping in their stalls.

"Elizabeth! Where is Elizabeth?" Sadira cried as Travis met her in the aisle. He had hold of Sherifa by the halter, but the mare was half rearing and snorting.

"She isn't here." Travis was grim-faced. "But then I didn't expect her to be. She's done her work, and she's gone."

"Travis, you cannot think . . . !"

"There isn't time to discuss it. We've got to get the horses out."

"I will take Sherifa." Sadira reached for the mare's lead rope. "You get another one."

Travis relinquished the rope, and Sadira spoke soothingly to the frightened animal. Listening to her voice, Sherifa quieted, then the crackling sound sent her off again, and she danced about almost out of control, terror making her wild and disobedient.

"Come, my love. Come, my beauty. Do not be afraid."

Sadira put her hand on Sherifa's neck. Murmuring comforting sounds, she managed to lead the mare past the leaping flames. Once outside, Sadira let the horse go free and instantly realized her mistake; of course, the mare would return to a place where she had eaten and known safety. Sherifa wheeled and bolted back through the doorway of the barn, almost knocking down Travis who was leading a wild-eyed Bachir. The stallion uttered a piercing scream, broke away from Travis, and likewise charged back into his stall.

Sadira had no experience putting out barn fires—or indeed of keeping horses in a barn. Their behavior in the face of this danger baffled her. She had taught Sherifa to withstand rifle fire, stampedes, sandstorms, and all kinds of hazards, except for this one, the worst of all. Now, it seemed her beloved mare might die because of her own ignorance. "Travis, what can we do? They will not come out."

"Take off your veil and blindfold them!" Travis was already on his way back into the barn. "Hurry! We haven't much time."

Suddenly, men were running into the barn beside Sadira— Jem and the guests from the party. Tearing off pieces of their garments, they wound strips of cloth around their faces and prepared others to cover the eyes of the horses. Others attempted to beat out the flames with their coats and jackets. A line of people formed outside and passed water buckets from hand to hand to the last person in line who then tossed the contents on the blaze.

Sadira blindfolded Sherifa and found it much easier to lead her outside to safety. Eager hands took the lead rope from her, freeing Sadira to return for another animal. Tahani was rearing in her stall, refusing to let anyone near her. Despite everyone's efforts, the wisps of hay and straw littering the aisle had ignited. Soon, they would have to abandon the horses still inside the barn; it would be too dangerous to try to get them out.

"Tahani!" Sadira shouted, and her father's mare stood quivering, ears cocked in her direction, as if she sensed this was a familiar voice. "Let me get her. She knows me."

Sadira pushed her way through the small group of men gathered in the front of Tahani's stall and stepped inside. Soothing and patting the mare, she deftly fastened the blindfold across her eyes, and Tahani finally surrendered. Prancing through the smoldering bits of chaff, she allowed Sadira to lead her out. No sooner had Sadira reached the safety of the yard when she heard a loud crash behind her. One end of a burning beam had fallen, partially blocking the aisle and preventing any further exits.

Travis! Where was Travis? Sadira thrust the end of Tahani's lead into a strange man's hands and dashed back into the barn, which was now so smoke-filled she could scarcely breathe.

On the other side of the fallen beam, Travis had hold of Najila. "Get out of here, Sadira!" He began to cough and choke.

"No! I am not leaving here without you." She whirled back toward the entranceway. "Someone come and help me move this beam."

She ran to the fallen end, but it was red and smoldering, too hot to handle, and she had to grasp it at a spot higher up. The beam was too heavy to lift—until several people joined her. Together, they managed to raise the heavy obstacle, though everyone was coughing by then, and tears streamed down their cheeks. Carrying it to one side, they cleared a path for Travis and Najila. "Everybody out!" Travis croaked as he led the mare out of the barn. "We've got them all, I think."

It wasn't necessary for him to repeat the order. People stumbled about the yard gasping for fresh air.

"What about Lulu?" Sadira asked before she remembered that the camel was too tall to fit inside the low-ceilinged stable. Travis had put her in a distant paddock until a larger enclosure could be constructed.

"Is there another horse in there?" one of the male guests inquired. "If there is, I'm afraid you've lost it. We can't risk going back in now. The smoke is too bad."

"No, no. My husband's right. They are all safe."

A second crash indicated the fall of another beam. Sparks spiraled upward into the black night sky, followed by more crashes. "The ceiling is collapsing!" someone cried. "It's burnt clear through."

"Faster!" another voice shouted. "Keep those water buckets coming."

Sadira had no time to spare for the spectacle or to continue fighting the fire. She was too busy checking on Travis. Filthy and coughing, he stood in the yard trying to catch his breath. His face was ashen, and his hair had been singed. Cora shoved a cup of water into his hand. After he had drunk it, he looked much better.

"Thank God—or Allah—we got the horses out, and no one was hurt while we were doing it." He sighed in a gravelly voice. He reached for Sadira, and they held each other a long moment, saying nothing, simply savoring the fact they were still alive and had managed to save the horses. Nothing else mattered; the barn could burn to the ground, and Sadira would not care. She shivered to think of one of those heavy beams falling on top of Travis, trapping him in the burning building.

Reluctantly, he pushed her away. "It's too late to save the stable; let's make certain the animals are all right. I think Bachir cut himself coming out of his stall."

How like Travis to be thinking first of the horses instead of his own near brush with death or the loss of his stable! Sadira joined him in examining each of the horses, one by one. Aside from a singed tail or two, a few insignificant scrapes and scratches, and some labored breathing, they appeared in good shape. The guests had removed them from the immediate area of the barn, taken off their blindfolds, and were letting them graze among the tents. They had all settled down and like Travis, eagerly drank water when it was offered. Sadira's own throat felt raw and swollen, and she welcomed the cup of water that Cora insisted she take time to drink.

Satisfied that the horses had survived with minimal harm, Sadira and Travis joined the water line still attempting to get control of the fire. Men and women passed bucket after bucket from well and water trough to burning barn. No matter how fast they worked, it was not enough. They could not put out the fire. It had spread too rapidly, and the entire stable and attached shed were now engulfed. As Travis had pointed out, it was too late to save anything; even the nearby lilac bushes shriveled and crackled, succumbing to the heat.

At last, Travis waved everyone away. "This is useless. Let it burn," he growled in a smoke-hoarsened voice. "We saved the most important thing—the horses, and for that, I thank you. Fortunately, my Thoroughbreds are all out in their paddocks, and the horses you rode or drove here are up near the house. Only our new Arabians were endangered. Unless they've suffered some lung damage we can't see, we shouldn't lose any of them. All we've lost is the stable and its contents, which can all be replaced."

As somber-faced figures backed off to silently watch the inferno lighting the night, Sadira hooked an arm around her husband's waist and leaned against him to offer comfort and support. She was trembling from weariness and an excess of emotion. Her beautiful caftan was torn and soot-stained, her hair tangled and reeking of smoke. She noted that their guests did not look much better. The women were all disheveled and dirty, the men as filthy and soot-blackened as Travis. In a silence borne of exhaustion and disappointment that they could not have done more, everyone stood and quietly witnessed the collapse of the entire structure.

It was dawn before the fire completely died down from lack of fuel; by then, there was nothing left but a smoking pile of refuse. Still, the guests had not gone home—not even the elderly ones, such as Agnes Worthington. They stayed to help clean up the remnants of the feast, pull down tents, care for horses, and offer whatever other help was needed. The willingness of Travis's friends to stand by him and give him aid in his time of travail deeply touched Sadira.

The men stood or sat on the lawn in small groups, discussing the rebuilding of Travis's stable and how they might best provide hay, feed, tack, and equipment until he could replace what had been lost. Interspersed among them, the Arabians placidly grazed, while the women congregated in the house, assisting Cora and the servants in preparing breakfast, for everyone was hungry again. Only one of the guests was conspicuously absent—Elizabeth—and Sadira

could not help wondering what had happened to her and
if, indeed, she had been responsible for the fire. She had
been the only one there, so she must have been, incredible
as such treachery seemed. Travis had told the woman to
wait there until Sadira returned with a wrap, and the next
thing they knew, the barn was on fire. Where had Elizabeth
gone after setting it? Perhaps she had run away, fearing the
consequences. If she had, Travis would find her. He would
not rest until he discovered the truth about the destructive
blaze.

Sadira sat down beneath a tree on the lawn and leaned
back against its trunk. She was too tired to eat or even to
think. Sherifa came over and nuzzled her shoulder, and she
reached up and idly stroked the mare's sooty neck. A little
ways off, Travis stood talking with several men. Snatches
of the conversation drifted over to her, but fatigue blunted
her attention, and she closed her eyes and listened only
halfheartedly.

"I'll have to prepare a materials list before I can gauge
how much rebuilding will cost," Travis was saying.

"You'll need to make a list of everything you lost, too.
It will take months before you remember all that's missing. . . . Why, when lightning struck my barn . . ."

The clop-clop of horses' hooves coming up the drive
distracted Sadira, and she listened more intently. The rum-
ble of a wagon accompanied the clop-clopping sound;
someone was coming. She sat up and rubbed her stinging
eyes. The rosy glow of morning outlined a heavy-laden
vehicle pulled by a team of two spanking white horses. In
the driver's seat sat a blond woman in an immaculate pink
and white gown and wide-brimmed straw bonnet trimmed
with flowers. Sadira could not believe what she was see-

ing—Elizabeth, looking fresh as the dew and waving gaily to everyone.

Sherifa whinnied a greeting to the equine newcomers just as Elizabeth stopped the wagon and announced, "Breakfast, my dears! I've brought breakfast. Come and get it. . . . Ivy, get out the china and silverware, and let's start serving."

A tall black woman got down from the back of the wagon and began rummaging through the baskets and chests loaded in the wagon bed. Sadira scrambled to her feet and hurried toward Elizabeth who smiled benignly down at her from her high perch and calmly began peeling off her white gloves.

"Oh, there you are, Sadira. I almost didn't recognize you underneath all that soot. So sorry I couldn't stay last night to help fight the fire, but as you know, I was feeling quite ill—in no shape to be of any use to anyone. After you left me to go get a wrap, I went looking for a servant to fetch my carriage and horse. Shortly thereafter, I drove straight home. I fear I'm not much good at fighting fires anyway, but I knew you'd all be needing breakfast by this morning, so here I am!"

Sadira was dumbfounded. Elizabeth was behaving as if she had had nothing to do with the fire! As if the ugly scene in the barn just before the fire had never happened.

"Travis, dear!" Elizabeth called out. "You poor, poor man. I do hope none of your new horses was injured. I see them grazing so you must have gotten them out. Truly, I was most upset to witness flames shooting out of your barn so suddenly, and if I hadn't been so wretchedly ill, I would have been more than happy to help fight the fire. Can you ever forgive me, Travis dear?"

Travis was glowering like a thundercloud. "Ill?" he

grated, coming up to Elizabeth on the same side of the wagon as Sadira. "Is that what you were—ill?"

Elizabeth fluttered her long blond lashes. "You would not believe how ill. It must have been all that strange foreign food I consumed last night. It did not agree with me. And I had the chills. You remember—you and Sadira went to get a wrap or a cloak to warm me."

"Stop it!" Travis snapped. "You were the last one in the stable last night, Elizabeth. We left you there and less than a half hour later, the whole building was ablaze, and you were nowhere to be found."

Elizabeth's eyes widened in a very good imitation of shock. "Oh, surely you do not think I had anything to do with *starting* that fire! As I said, I became ill. The chills were just the beginning. After you left me, I left the barn to look for a servant. Why, I got sick in the bushes and almost fainted before I found one. Seeing how sick I was, he went immediately to fetch my horse and carriage."

A white line rimmed Travis's mouth; he looked as furious and incredulous as Sadira felt. "Who was the servant, Elizabeth? Tell me his name."

"It was Harry, my own groom who came with me to look after Buttercup, my hack. He drove me home. You can ask him, if you like. Or ask Ivy. Ivy, didn't I come home ill last night—and terribly disturbed that I had to leave everyone here fighting the fire without me, and I didn't know how it was all going to come out?"

Ivy looked up from her baskets and hampers. "Yes, Miz Elizabeth. You surely did. Harry said you was cryin' and sobbin' all the way home."

"There! You see?" Elizabeth turned triumphantly to Travis and Sadira. "Really, Travis. It was your own care-

lessness that started that fire. You set down a lantern on a
bale of straw, a most dangerous place to leave a lit lantern."

"No, Elizabeth. I hung that lantern on a hook—the same
hook where I always hang it when I'm in the barn at night."

Elizabeth slowly shook her head. "Oh, no, Travis, dear!
You may not remember, you may have shut it out of your
mind, but you set the lantern on a bale of straw. I was
going to say something about it, but in my illness, I forgot.
By the time I *did* remember, it was too late. The barn was
on fire."

Sadira wracked her brain to think of where the lantern
had been—on the hook or sitting on a bale of straw—when
she herself arrived at the barn. She could not remember;
she had been too upset by the scene she had witnessed, a
scene Elizabeth would undoubtedly deny ever took place.
Her so-called illness and chills were pure invention to conceal the ugly truth: She had needed a wrap to cover her
nakedness after attempting to seduce Travis.

A muscle worked in Travis's jaw as he stepped closer to
the wagon and glared up at Elizabeth. "That lantern was
on a hook, Elizabeth, and you and I both know what happened in that barn last night. What you're claiming now is
a pack of lies."

Elizabeth leaned down and without a trace of falsehood,
gave Travis a sympathetic pat on the cheek. "Dear Travis,
you are overwrought. I would never do anything to harm
you. I'm the best friend you ever had. Who else do you
know would come to your party and wish you well with
your new wife, when her own heart is breaking? You were
mine before *she* got her claws into you; none of this would
have happened if we had married as we ought to have done.
I'm the wife you should have had, darling, and everyone
knows it."

It was more than Sadira could bear. She almost lapsed into Arabic she was so angry. Reaching up, she grabbed Elizabeth's hand. "Do not touch my husband. Cease pretending to be his friend. Thou art his enemy, and thou hast caused us enough trouble. We want thee to leave Greenbriar and never return—and take thy breakfast with thee. We never wish to see thee again."

"You!" Elizabeth snatched back her hand and straightened. "The beautiful little goat-herder. The barefoot Bedouin. Why, you can't even speak proper English. This is all your fault. If it weren't for you, I never would have lost my temper and . . ."

"And *what,* Elizabeth?" Travis's tone was deadly calm. "You never would have what?"

"Nothing!"

Sadira gripped the side of the wagon. "We know what you did. And if you ever dare return here, we will see that you are punished."

"Don't touch my wagon!" Elizabeth seized the buggy whip lying on the bench beside her, lifted it, and struck at Sadira.

The whip cracked in the air, but Travis caught it on the downward stroke and gave a sharp tug to pull it out of Elizabeth's hand. Refusing to let go, Elizabeth tumbled out of the wagon on top of Sadira. Before Sadira could react, Elizabeth was upon her, shrieking and screaming, beating on her with clenched fists, trying to gouge out her eyes. It all happened too quickly to predict or prevent what would happen next.

There was a snort of equine outrage. From the corner of her eye as she squirmed beneath Elizabeth, Sadira caught a glimpse of a shiny red coat. Then Elizabeth was scream-

ing in agony and rolling away from her. "She bit me! That
horse bit me on the shoulder."

Elizabeth's bonnet had come off, and her yellow hair
flew wildly about as she cowered on the ground to avoid
Sherifa's pawing hooves. The mare reared over her head,
intent on trampling her.

"Sherifa, no!" Sadira cried.

The mare came down, missing Elizabeth's head by a
mere whisper. Travis grabbed Sherifa's halter and held onto
it. "No, girl. Easy, now," he soothed her. "Easy now. It's
all right."

He had his hands full trying to restrain her. The mare
was trembling but watching Sadira for new instructions.
Scrambling to her feet, Sadira motioned for her to be still
while Elizabeth rolled over on her stomach and sobbed into
the grass.

"How can you treat me like this, Travis, when all I ever
wanted was to be your wife?"

Sadira observed the sympathetic glances some of the onlookers exchanged and knew she had to force Elizabeth's
confession or lose all the ground she had gained tonight.

"My war mare does not appreciate lies, Elizabeth. She
will stamp out falsehoods wherever she senses them. Shall
I put that statement to a test—or will you admit that you
set the fire?"

Elizabeth raised her head, and her eyes went to Sherifa,
still prancing and blowing through her nostrils as Travis
fought to keep hold of her. Something shifted in her expression, and her face crumpled.

"All right, I did it! I tossed the lantern into the straw. I
wanted to hurt you, Travis Colin Keene—hurt you the way
you've hurt me! *I* should have been the one giving your
party last night, and it would have been done *properly*. We

would have eaten off the finest china, drunk from the best crystal. . . . We'd have had baked ham and breast of pheasant. Young spring vegetables, perhaps. Imported French wines to accompany the meal. . . . I know how to *do* these things. They're a part of my *breeding* for pity's sake. How could you choose *her* over me, Travis? How could you? I thought you'd come back on your knees to me. Instead, you went and married that . . . that . . ."

"That lovely, talented young horsewoman," Agnes Worthington announced, pushing through the crowd. "The perfect match for our dear Travis." Reaching Elizabeth, she gazed down at her contemptuously. "Seems to me we need to send for the authorities. If I'm not mistaken, burning down a man's barn is a serious crime."

Elizabeth sat up, sniffling and wiping away her tears. "I'm glad I did it. *Glad,* do you hear? Travis deserved it. I'd do it again if I had the chance."

Sherifa whinnied and stamped, upset by Elizabeth's tone of voice.

"Mercy me!" Mrs. Worthington exclaimed. "If I didn't know differently, I'd think this mare *does* understand every word you're saying."

"Jem, come here and hold . . ." Travis started to say, but just then, there came a mighty bellow, and the ground seemed to shake underfoot. "What the devil?"

Men and women scattered and jumped aside as Lulu suddenly came barreling through the crowd at a furious pace.

"A dromedary!" someone gasped. "An outraged dromedary."

"You mean a camel! Travis, you said you'd brought back a camel, but it was in a field far away from the house."

"This is the one," Travis said. "Somehow she got out."

"Lulu, behave yourself!" Sadira commanded.

But Lulu wasn't listening. She lumbered to a stop in front of Elizabeth who stared up at her disbelievingly. Camel and woman regarded each other hostilely, then Lulu made a gurgling sound deep in her throat, opened her mouth, and spewed out a stream of slimy, half-chewed cud.

"Oh! Oh! Oh!" Elizabeth shrieked as the mess splattered across her pink and white gown, utterly ruining it.

Lulu gave a deep, contented sigh and laid her big brown head on Sadira's shoulder. There was a moment of stunned silence, then a loud guffaw. Suddenly, everyone was laughing—chortling, snickering, and pounding each other on the back in their hilarity. Travis laughed so hard that tears ran down his cheeks. Sadira could barely contain her own mirth. The only person who didn't join in the laughter was Elizabeth, who sat frozen in the grass, staring at everyone as if they had all lost their senses.

"Well, I *never!*" she huffed, folding her arms across her green-splattered bosom. "I've just never seen the like!"

Convulsed with laughter, Travis made his way to Sadira and slid one arm around her waist. "I knew," he gasped. "I knew there had to be a reason why we brought back Lulu—and this is it! *This* is the reason. It was fate . . . destiny . . . the will of Allah."

Sadira wiped the tears from her eyes and looked at him more closely to see if he was serious. He was. "I'll never doubt your beliefs again, sweetheart. Tonight—this morning—you've made a believer of me."

Then he went off into fresh gales of laughter, and she knew without any doubt that from that moment on, everything was going to be all right. More than all right. Despite all the differences between them, it was going to be perfect.

When everyone had recovered and Elizabeth had been helped to her feet and led to the house to await the arrival of the authorities, Travis urged Sadira to demonstrate more of Sherifa's and Lulu's amazing capabilities, achieved after years of patient and meticulous training. The shared laughter had banished everyone's exhaustion, and Sadira herself felt as if she could do anything. She had the strength and energy of ten women and eagerly accepted the challenge of dazzling their guests with feats of horsemanship and the Bedouin methods of handling camels.

She made both Lulu and Sherifa lie down and rise on command, bow, kneel, and perform other tricks. To the sweet sound of enthusiastic applause, Sadira gathered up her sooty skirts, leapt upon Sherifa's bare back, and galloped across the lawn, jumping whatever obstacles she met. Her newfound friends cheered, hooted, and hollered their approval, and flushed with joy, Sadira returned to claim a hug and a kiss from her beaming husband. As she slid down from her mare and fell into Travis's outstretched arms, he gathered her close and whispered in Arabic, "I love thee, Mrs. Travis Colin Keene, and I pray Allah grants us many long years together."

"So do I love thee, my husband," she whispered in return. Then she added in English, "Now, let us go and serve our good friends some breakfast."

Epilogue

Louisville, Kentucky, Three Years Later

Travis and Sadira stood at the railing overlooking the Louisville racetrack, Churchill Downs, where the Kentucky Derby was about to begin. Sadira was so excited she could hardly remain still, for she *knew* they were going to win this race. Sherifa's son, Sandstorm, a tall, flame-colored colt, was about to make his name in history and prove the value of Travis's breeding program, thereby establishing Greenbriar as one of the top breeding and racing farms in all of Kentucky and perhaps even the world.

Travis's English stallion was Sandstorm's sire, and from him, the colt had inherited his height, much of his speed, and his Thoroughbred appearance. But from his dam, Sherifa, he had received his stamina, his will to win, his shiny red coat, and his eagerness to please his human handlers. Few besides Travis and Sadira believed that the combination could triumph over the toughest competition in the country, but today should convince the worst cynics. Sandstorm would win the run for the roses; Sadira had no doubt of it.

Unfortunately, Travis seemed to have lost his optimism. Now when all his dreams had finally reached fruition, and he was about to gain all he had ever wanted, he looked like a man awaiting his own execution. His blue eyes were bleak and shadowed with doubt. His mouth was a grim slash. Worry lines creased his forehead. Sadira reached for his hand, entwined her fingers in his, and whispered, "Do not worry so, my love. Have faith. Sandstorm will be true to his heritage."

Travis barely managed a smile. "I don't know what's wrong with me," he admitted. "We've got the best horse in the field, he's in peak condition, and we've done everything possible to ensure his success. I should be elated, but suddenly, I feel sick. I wish I could pull Sandy out of this race, go home, and never set foot on a racetrack again. I wish . . ."

Travis's wish was drowned out by the explosion of noise and the sudden roar of the crowd as the horses broke free of the starting gate. Sadira leaned over the railing to catch a glimpse of Sandstorm who was already out in front of the field. Then she realized that Travis wasn't even watching, but had turned away. His face was pale as milk, his brow sheened with sweat, his wide shoulders shaking.

"Travis, what is it? Are you ill?"

"No, I . . . I just can't watch. This is it, Sadira, all we've worked for these last few years. All we've sacrificed, fought for, and promoted. What if he doesn't even place? What if he gets hurt? What if . . . ?"

The thunder of hooves as the horses passed the grandstand and the shrill clamor of thousands of voices exhorting their favorites onward again drowned out Travis's question. Someone jostled Sadira, and she lost her place at the rail. She did not attempt to regain it; at the moment, she was more concerned about Travis than she was about Sandstorm or the race. The big colt and his competent jockey could take care of themselves, while Travis appeared ready to faint. Her strong stalwart husband could work eighteen hours a day and never tire, infect everyone around him with the fire of his enthusiasm, labor all day and still make love all night. . . . Her wonderful friend, partner, lover, and companion could do anything and everything, except watch his horse run its most important race. Travis now looked as sick and anxious as a small lost boy. He could hardly stand on his own two feet.

If she were not witnessing it with her own eyes, she would never have believed it. "Travis! Do you want to sit down? Lean on me if you must."

"I need some air," he grumbled. "I just need to get the hell out of here and get a breath of fresh air. There's too damn many people."

He tugged at the collar of his shirt, and she sought to open the fastenings with fumbling fingers. "Is that better? Can you breathe now?"

"Hell, I'm suffocating!" He tore at the constriction, and scraps of cloth went flying. He drew a deep breath and sought to calm himself. "Where's Sandstorm? What's happening in the race?"

"I . . . I don't know." Sadira listened more intently to the constant roar of the crowd and the voice of an announcer calling the race up in one of the boxes. She could not decipher what anyone was saying and could not reclaim her place on the rail. There were too many people.

The shouts and screams grew louder, swelling in volume. Out of all the hundreds of voices, Sadira finally untangled bits of information from the people closest to them.

"Who in tarnation is that big red colt who's got the lead and won't get over?"

"Sandstorm! It's Sandstorm, a long shot nobody thought could maintain the pace."

"Well, he's damn well maintaining it! He's so far out in front nobody can catch him."

"Travis, he's winning!" Sadira gloated to her stricken husband.

Travis's haggard face brightened. "Damn! He is, isn't he?"

Thousands of voices began to shout. "Sandstorm! Sandstorm! Sandstorm!"

The chant rose and grew more rhythmic until it seemed that every person in attendance at the Derby was shouting Sandstorm's name.

"Everyone will remember his name from now on!" Sadira began to cry. Tears streamed down her cheeks, blurring her vision. Even if she had kept her place on the rail, she could not have seen a thing through the waterfall.

Head cocked as he listened, Travis seized both her hands and held them in an iron-hard grip. "Come on, Sandstorm! Show them what you're made of!"

"Look!" someone cried. "The favorite's gaining on him."

"Don't quit now, Sandstorm!" Travis muttered, closing his eyes and squeezing her fingers until she thought her bones might snap. "Keep going, boy. Keep going. You can do it."

Travis and Sadira held each other's hands and listened to the roar of the crowd telling them what was happening. Travis opened his eyes, and they gazed intently at each other, and Sadira knew she would remember this moment for the rest of her life. Sight and sound merged, and the only reality was Travis holding tightly to her hands, sharing each second while Sandstorm strained for the finish line and his place in history.

They knew the exact moment when their horse won the race. The crowd drew in its breath, a single moment of silence ensued, and then everyone went wild, cheering, screaming, stamping their feet, and shouting Sandstorm's name.

Sadira smiled tremulously. "Do you feel better now?"

Travis nodded, too elated to speak. He pulled her into his arms and hugged her, squeezing the breath from her lungs. She hugged him back with all the strength she possessed. He stopped hugging her long enough to give her a victory kiss that was hard and wonderful, then the outside world intruded. People shook their hands, pummeled them on the back, and shouted in their faces. A sea of congratulations engulfed them, sweeping them toward the winner's circle, where Sandstorm awaited them, looking very pleased with himself and surprised by all the commotion.

More kisses and hugs—with Sandstorm getting his share and prancing and blowing in excitement and astonishment. There were questions to answer, more people to greet, the governor to meet, a bubbly liquid called champagne to drink, and roses . . . a blanket of roses for Sandstorm and an armful for Sadira. She grew dizzy from the scent of them. Finally, the roses were passed to a beaming Cora, Sandstorm was led back to the barn, and the crowds began to disperse.

Travis steered her toward the shade of a huge old tree on the racecourse grounds and there pulled her into his arms again. "What a day!" He sighed. "What an incredible, magnificent day."

"It was, was it not? And I am now so tired that I am the one who feels sick."

Instantly, his smile vanished, and he studied her in concern. "You do look pale. Are you all right? Sadira, you should have said something. I would have found a place for you to sit or lie down. The excitement—it must have been too much for you."

"No, no, Travis. I am fine. Truly. And I would not have missed one moment of the celebration. Everyone wants to know how long we intend to race Sandstorm and how soon we might retire him to stud. Dozens of people said they had mares they wanted to breed to him. They could not believe he possessed so much stamina and speed, and that his dam is a desert horse."

"I know. Now everyone will recognize what a contribution the Arabian horse has made to Thoroughbred breeding and racing."

"I do not know about that, Travis. Some will still debate the point. I have lived long enough in this country to know that people will always argue over bloodlines and what produces a great race horse."

Travis laughed. "You're right. We've proved something to ourselves today, but the rest of the world may not be ready to believe it. I don't care what anyone thinks. I'll conduct my breeding program in my own way in my own good time and produce great racehorses *and* beautiful Arabians."

He held her close and nosed her hair. "I think it's about time we made that long delayed trip to visit the Blunts, don't you? I promised you we would go, and we've been too busy to actually do it. We both need a rest, and that trip would be just the thing for us."

"I would love to return to the East, Travis, but we will have to plan the journey around . . . around . . ." This wasn't how she had intended to tell him. Such momentous news deserved its own special celebration. After all, she had begun to despair that it would ever happen—had feared something might be wrong with her. But nothing was wrong, and now she was certain, and she couldn't keep it secret any longer.

"We'll have to plan the journey around our own private breeding program," she blurted. "I will soon be producing an heir to all we have built at Greenbriar."

"An heir!" He drew back to look at her, his blue eyes filled with a joyous light. "Do you mean . . . ?"

"Yes!" she nodded happily. "I was waiting until after today to tell you."

"This . . . this is even better than winning the Derby!" he crowed. "A baby! We're going to have a baby!"

She could see that he meant it, and her heart overflowed with love for him. As much as he craved winning and producing excellence in his horses, even more did he cherish their love and the treasures *it* could produce. She leaned against him, sighing with happiness.

"Wait a minute. I almost forgot," he said, pushing her away. "I was saving something for after today, too."

He rummaged around inside his jacket and withdrew a long, slim, velvet case. "Here," he whispered. "This is for you—to match your green eyes."

"For me? You did not have to do this, Travis. I already know how much you love me."

"Open it," he urged. "Whether we won or lost today, I wanted to give you something to mark the occasion—and to let you know how much you mean to me."

She took the case in trembling fingers and carefully opened it. Inside on cream-colored satin lay an exquisite necklace of emeralds interspersed with diamonds. At the very center of the necklace was a beautifully carved and detailed horse's head of gold in Sherifa's exact image.

"It's magnificent!" she breathed, overcome with awe. "Oh, Travis, you should not have done it."

"Here. . . . Turn around and let me put it on."

He picked up the necklace, and she obediently presented her back to him. She did not have to lift up her hair because it was already piled on top of her head beneath a stylish hat. She was wearing an equally stylish green and white gown with a neckline that could not have been more perfect for the necklace, which felt warm against her bare skin as Travis handled it and fastened it in place.

"There," he said, kissing the crook of her neck and shoulder. "Now you mustn't take it off until tonight, *after* you've taken off all your frills and lace. As a matter of fact, you can leave it on. I want to make love to you while you're wearing only my necklace. The piece will be a family heirloom we can pass down from generation to generation—beginning with our first daughter or granddaughter."

"Oh, Travis!" was all she could say.

She turned around to embrace him, and a sudden gust of wind ruffled her skirts and tugged at her hat.

"Where did this wind come from?" Laughing, Travis helped her hold down her petticoats as the breeze blew more strongly, bringing with it the scent of roses and other springtime flowers. "I haven't felt a breeze like that since we left the desert."

She sniffed the air, and that was when she smelled it— the faint, elusive scent of lavender. She lifted her head and sniffed again. Was she only imagining it? No, she couldn't be. She *did* smell lavender, borne on the soft breath of the wind, a wind like that which blew constantly across her desert homeland. She listened a moment and fancied she could hear the wind singing, as it did in the desert . . . only this song was a happy one, telling of love, joy, and belonging. It spoke of home and family, and held not a trace of sorrow.

"What is it?" Travis asked. "What do you hear?"

"Oh, 'tis only . . ." She hesitated, not sure if he would understand, but hoping he would. "I hear only windsong."

He grinned. "Of course. Windsong. I know exactly what you mean."

Afterword From the Author

Two very special Arabian horses, El Synraff and Mirzon, inspired me to research the origins of the Arabian horse and ultimately to write this book. Syn Syn, as we called El Synraff, became the first horse I ever owned, fulfilling a lifelong dream that began in childhood with Walter Farley's *Black Stallion* series. I and my three daughters and two nieces learned to ride on him, and he was always the perfect gentleman, sweet, good-natured, and patient. He did love to run, however, especially when the wind blew hard, and some ancient memory reminded him of long gallops across the desert sands.

Advanced in years, he is now teaching another family of young children how to ride, and they love him every bit as much as we did. Once you get to know an Arabian horse, it's easy to fall in love with it, for it is a creature of grace, beauty, and spirit who loves people in return and wants to please them. Some say that the Arabian horse's empathy with humans derives from the unique relationship its forerunners enjoyed with their Bedouin masters, a relationship I hope I have accurately portrayed in this story. Today, the Arabian can be found in every riding discipline, successfully competing in them all but particularly excelling in endurance trials, where its unique stamina and sure-footedness set it apart in fifty- and one-hundred-mile races across some of the roughest terrain in the world.

It has contributed much to other breeds, such as the Thoroughbred, and is cherished by many and rightly so. I hope you have enjoyed Travis's and Sadira's tale. Writing this book has opened my eyes to the fascinating possibilities for romantic stories to be found in the history of other breeds of horses. If you would enjoy reading about a particular breed or have any questions or comments, please write to me in c/o Zebra Books, 850 Third Avenue, New York, NY 10022.

Katharine Kincaid

LIST OF FOREIGN WORDS AND PHRASES IN ORDER OF APPEARANCE

Sadira—female name
Anazah—tribal name
Emir Akbar el-Karim—male name
Alima—female name
Bashiyra—female name
atiya—gift
Sherifa—female name
adra—virgin
Hamid—male name
Fadoul—male name
Jaleel—female name
aba—cloak
keffiya—headcloth
Frangi—foreigner or stranger
Muhammad—male name
jihad—holy war
Halim—male name
Ruala—tribal name
bashi—caravan leader
beshliks—Syrian coins
mohaffa—sedan chair for a camel
khan—rooms where caravans stay
Gamalat—male name
burqa—face veil
Nuri—male name
Rashid—male name

Sherif Awad—male name
Farasat—female name
as salám alaikum—"peace be with you, my friend"
alaikum as salám—"the same to you"
Samir—male name
Najila—female name
Kehilan, Seglawi, Abeyan, Hamdani, Hadban (strains of
    Arabian horses)
Tahani—female name
Bachir—male name
wadi—river bed
Hajem Pasha—male name
muezzin—one who calls men to prayer
Haaris—male name
habiba—beloved female
habib—beloved male
Tarfa—female name
dhalla—camel carrier
Oman—strain of camels
Aza—female name
Rahil—female name
Mijem—male name
Jahara—female name

WHAT'S LOVE GOT TO DO WITH IT?

Everything . . . Just ask Kathleen Drymon . . . and Zebra Books

CASTAWAY ANGEL	*(3569-1, $4.50/$5.50)*
GENTLE SAVAGE	*(3888-7, $4.50/$5.50)*
MIDNIGHT BRIDE	*(3265-X, $4.50/$5.50)*
VELVET SAVAGE	*(3886-0, $4.50/$5.50)*
TEXAS BLOSSOM	*(3887-9, $4.50/$5.50)*
WARRIOR OF THE SUN	*(3924-7, $4.99/$5.99)*